THE *Victoria* IN MY HEAD

THE

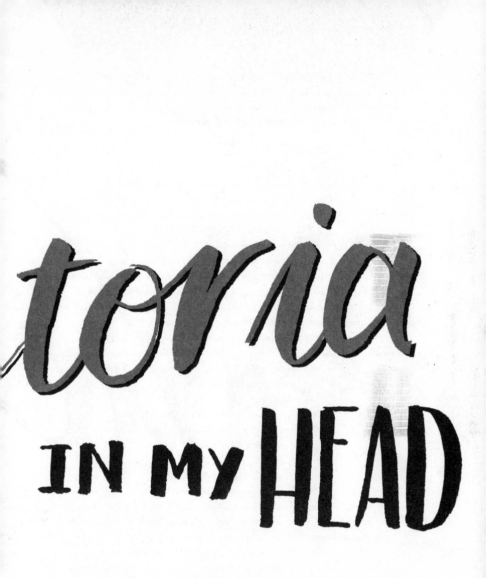

toria IN MY HEAD

JANELLE MILANES

SIMON PULSE

NEW YORK   LONDON   TORONTO   SYDNEY   NEW DELHI

SIMON PULSE

An imprint of Simon & Schuster Children's Publishing Division
1230 Avenue of the Americas, New York, New York 10020
First Simon Pulse hardcover edition September 2017
Text copyright © 2017 by Janelle Milanes
Front jacket photograph copyright © 2017 by Gallery Stock
Jacket and case photographs of records copyright © 2017 by Thinkstock
All rights reserved, including the right of reproduction in whole or in part in any form.
SIMON PULSE and colophon are registered trademarks of Simon & Schuster, Inc.
For information about special discounts for bulk purchases, please contact Simon & Schuster
Special Sales at 1-866-506-1949 or business@simonandschuster.com.
The Simon & Schuster Speakers Bureau can bring authors to your live event.
For more information or to book an event contact the Simon & Schuster Speakers Bureau
at 1-866-248-3049 or visit our website at www.simonspeakers.com.
Jacket designed by Sarah Creech
Interior designed by Tom Daly
The text of this book was set in Adobe Caslon Pro
Manufactured in the United States of America
2 4 6 8 10 9 7 5 3 1
Library of Congress Cataloging-in-Publication Data
Names: Milanes, Janelle, author.
Title: The Victoria in my head / Janelle Milanes.
Description: First Simon Pulse hardcover edition. | New York : Simon Pulse, 2017. |
Summary: Shy fifteen-year-old Cuban American Victoria Cruz feels trapped by the
monotony of running on the cross country team and keeping up with her studies to
maintain her scholarship to her prestigious college prep school, but the chance to join a
rock band in need of a lead singer gives her the opportunity to confront her anxieties,
find love and disappointment, and create a new playlist for her life.
Identifiers: LCCN 2016048819 |
ISBN 9781481480895 (hardcover) | ISBN 9781481480918 (eBook)
Subjects: | CYAC: Rock groups—Fiction. | Musicians—Fiction. | Bands (Music)—Fiction. |
Dating (Social customs)—Fiction. | Preparatory schools—Fiction. |
Schools—Fiction. | Cuban Americans—Fiction. | New York (N.Y.)—Fiction.
Classification: LCC PZ7.1.M556 Vic 2017 |
DDC [Fic]—dc23
LC record available at https://lccn.loc.gov/2016048819

TO MY ENTIRE FAMILY, BECAUSE IT WAS
IMPOSSIBLE TO CHOOSE JUST ONE OF YOU

THE *Victoria* IN MY HEAD

—— *Chapter One* ——

"YOUR BEST
AMERICAN GIRL"
—MITSKI

I can predict my life with scary accuracy. I know my morning will start with a piece of toast for breakfast, slathered in peanut butter and topped with sliced banana. After breakfast I'll get on the downtown A train and put on a perfectly timed playlist for my twenty-three minute commute to school. I'll meet my best friend, Annie Lin, at my locker, and we'll go to first period with Mr. Davis and stare at his mustard-yellow pit stains for forty-five minutes. I'll have cross-country practice after school, where Coach B will make us run six miles along the murky Hudson River. At home, Mom will make spaghetti for dinner, and my bratty little brother, Matty, will complain that the tomato sauce is too chunky.

I'm not psychic. My life is just *that* boring. Every day moves like a treadmill, a straight line without fluctuation.

I shouldn't complain. I know it could be much worse. But when I really think about it, I realize that every day of my life is exactly the same, and it'll continue to be the same as it was yesterday, and the day before that, until the end of high school.

Until, suddenly, it isn't.

Across a sea of plaid uniforms on the opposite side of the sophomore hall, I see him, and the treadmill that is my life comes to a grinding halt.

"Hello?" Annie snaps her fingers at me. Her black hair is swept off her forehead by a satin headband that perfectly matches her pleated skirt. "What's with the face?"

"What face?" I reply. I have no awareness of what my face is doing. You know how in movies, when a girl sees a halfway-decent-looking guy and all of time stops and this wah wah indie song plays and it's so dumb because she doesn't even know the guy and that never happens in real life?

"You're blushing," Annie says with a frown, following my gaze.

It happens to me when I see this boy. Cue the soft, strumming guitar, the thumping drums, an airy falsetto in the background.

He's stapling a flyer onto the bulletin board, and when he lifts his arms to push into the stapler, I catch a glimpse of what I imagine to be soft cotton boxer-briefs peeking out from his pants. With his slouchy posture and tangled hair, he looks nothing like the preppy breed usually found at this school. He's . . . messier. Different. And yes, indisputably gorgeous, but that's not the point.

Annie thrusts her watch into my field of vision, effectively blocking my view of the pretty boy. "Helloooo. We're going to be late."

This is Annie's mantra. She's punctual to a fault, while I'm in no rush to snag a front row seat for Mr. Davis's underarm sweat.

"I'll meet you there," I say, blinking myself awake. "I forgot something in my locker."

"What did you forget?"

"My, um . . . snargenblag," I mumble.

"Your what?"

The warning bell shrieks overhead, which sends Annie into a panic. "Come on, Vi!"

"Go ahead. I'll meet you there," I assure her, and she gives me a final disapproving scowl before hurrying to math.

All at once the hallway drains as students swarm to their first period classes, but the boy doesn't rush. As he steps back to admire his handiwork, I inch toward him. I'm not entirely sure what my master plan is, but I have to know what's on this flyer. I have to know more about him.

He turns his head and looks right at me as soon as I reach him, like I tripped a sensor.

Holy sweet Jesus, his eyes. Those were unexpected. His eyes are the stuff of those Harlequin romances Mom reads, the kind of eyes that are always compared to something cheesy, like a midwinter sky. Annie and I used to sneak the books into my room and pore over passages about tight breeches and ripping bodices.

The thing about this boy's eyes, though? They *are* the color of a midwinter sky, which I didn't think was possible in reality.

3

"Do you sing?" His voice echoes through the empty hallway.

I stare at him, my brain officially a useless lump. "Huh?"

Ugh. Get a freaking grip, Victoria. I'm not one to turn into a puddle of idiocy when I see a cute guy. I'm better than that. Usually.

He nods toward the flyer he's posted. It's simple—black Sharpie against stark white computer paper. In large block print it says:

LEAD VOCALIST WANTED.
MUST HAVE A DECENT VOICE AND
GENERALLY NOT SUCK AS A HUMAN
BEING. BAND WILL PERFORM AT THE
BATTLE OF THE BOROUGHS IN THE
SPRING. MUSIC TASTE SHOULD
BE ECLECTIC.
PLEASE E-MAIL LEVI.SCHUSTER@EA.ORG
FOR AUDITION INFORMATION.

"Oh," I manage, brilliantly. I can't process the fact that a school like Evanston has other people like him, people who do things besides study and play lacrosse and run for student council. "Um . . . no."

"Maybe you should try." He twirls his stapler around and snaps it shut with one hand like some pistol-packing cowboy. It's weirdly hot.

The final bell rings. He and I are officially late for class, but neither one of us moves.

I should fess up at this point. I should let him know that I am way too boring to be a lead singer. I should let him know that I can barely speak, let alone sing, in front of people. I should also let him know that there is no way, under any circumstances, my overprotective Cuban parents would let me join a band.

"Okay," I blurt out instead of these important things he should know. Then, without another word, I bolt.

Mom studies me as we sit around the dinner table that night. "You okay? You look pale."

"I'm fine." I twirl some overcooked spaghetti noodles around my fork and silently refuse to go into any more detail. It's helpful to remember my Miranda rights when it comes to dinner with my family. Anything I say can and will be used against me.

"Are you sick?" Matty asks me, his eyes lighting up with interest. "Are you gonna puke?"

"Eat your food," Dad tells him.

Matty pokes at his pile of noodles. "I think I'm sick too."

We all ignore him. Matty will do anything to get out of eating dinner, unless it's one of the three meals that he tolerates: mac and cheese, pizza, or peanut butter sandwiches (no crust, hold the jelly). Sameness doesn't seem to affect him yet. Actually, he thrives on it.

"Maybe I'll make you a doctor's appointment," Mom says to me.

"I'm fine, Mom. Really."

"You don't look fine."

"I just have a lot on my mind."

"Are you depressed?" Mom asks, her voice rising. She eyes me with intensity. Ever since I bought a vintage Nirvana T-shirt last week, Mom has been on teen suicide watch. It's ridiculous.

"Of course she's not depressed," Dad says, speaking right through me. "What does she have to be depressed about?"

"Can I have a sandwich?" Matty asks. He pushes his plate away in disgust.

"You can eat spaghetti like the rest of us," Mom informs him.

"But I don't like spaghetti."

Dad points his fork at me. "Did you eat any dairy today?"

"Dairy?" I echo. I'm not fully here at the dinner table. I've been replaying the scene with the blue-eyed boy all day, wishing I had said something smarter, or funnier, or *anything at all*. I should have at least asked him his name.

"Yes. Dairy," Dad says. "Maybe at breakfast?"

Since he found out he was lactose intolerant, Dad believes dairy to be the root of all evil. In his opinion, it's the underlying cause of every malady known to man. He can't even look at a cow without a vein popping out of his neck.

"I had toast for breakfast," I reply absentmindedly.

He scratches the stubble on his chin. "What about lunch? You're always eating pizza for lunch."

"I'm making an appointment with Dr. Ferber," Mom decides.

"Fine," I concede, hoping it will shut them both up.

Of course it doesn't. Nothing does.

"I know you all insist on eating dairy," Dad continues, "but it's been linked to heart disease, diabetes—"

"Mrs. Soldera told us that milk is good for your bones," Matty pipes up.

"Mrs. Soldera is an idiot."

"Jorge . . . ," Mom cautions, pouring herself a glass of wine.

"Whatever." Matty's ten-year-old body heaves a weary sigh. "Can I have dessert now?"

We go through this every night. Practically word for word.

Mom closes her eyes and massages her forehead. "Matty, you didn't even *touch* your dinner. Jorge?"

"Eat your dinner, Matty," Dad says automatically. He's already wolfed down his entire plate of spaghetti, sopping up every drop of sauce with a bread roll.

"At least ten more bites," Mom adds.

"But the sauce is too chunky!" Matty slams his fist against the table, and my parents go bug-eyed.

"Ten cuidado," Dad warns. "Listen to your mother or you'll go to bed hungry."

They continue to argue back and forth, Matty trying to haggle his way out of dinner and Mom and Dad crushing each attempt. In about ten minutes one of them will cave and fix him a sandwich. This is the Cruz family dinner experience, every night at seven.

I stare down at my fork and contemplate sticking it through my eye.

Chapter Two

"AMERIGO"
—PATTI SMITH

I arrive at school five minutes later than usual, and the sophomore hallway buzzes with activity—lockers slamming shut, shoes squeaking against the tile floor. Life is back to moving at normal speed. Annie, I know, is already waiting for me at my locker, checking her watch and muttering to herself about my tardiness.

At the end of the hall a cluster of admirers surround the two best-looking girls in the grade, Sophia Lowell and Olivia Bennett. Together, they're a shampoo commercial, with silky curtains of hair spilling down their backs. Hair that grows vertically, not horizontally like mine. Both bask in the attention, wearing their usual shiny smiles.

They have plenty to smile about. They're tall, they have boobs, and they're perfectly groomed from head to toe. Because they're rich, they can afford to have our boxy Evanston uniforms tailored. Their collared shirts are taken in at the waist to accentuate their hourglass figures, and their hemlines graze the tops of their thighs for maximum leggy effect.

Mom scoffed when I asked if I could have my uniform tailored, and Dad flat-out refused, saying my school was costing him enough as it is. I'm forced to roll up my skirt so I don't look like a Puritan.

When I first interviewed at Evanston, I expected to become a member of the elite. I thought going to a school like this would finally help me become someone. Someone who had a life, a purpose. I could go to Harvard like my parents always dreamed, because Evanston placed that goal within reach.

I got my acceptance letter to Evanston on Friday the thirteenth. I should have taken it as a sign.

My parents hovered over my shoulders as I opened the letter, and before I could finish reading out "Congratulations," they enveloped me in a suffocating hug. In their arms I remember thinking that I should feel excited, or nervous. Scared, even. Something other than empty. I stretched my lips into a straight line, the best I could do at a smile, before pulling away from their grip.

As one of the top twenty-five high schools in the country, Evanston oozes exclusivity. It's a gated oasis amidst the mass of dour buildings comprising Manhattan's Upper West Side. The campus's ivy-laden buildings are arranged in a square with a manicured lawn in its center—Evanston's own mini Central Park. Inside Evanston, everything seems serious and scholarly. Students walk around in crisp buttoned uniforms, and teachers have essays published in renowned academic journals.

From the beginning it was clear that I wasn't one of them. My family doesn't own a summer home in the Hamptons, and we don't take luxurious trips to Turks and Caicos over winter break. We're not destitute, but we're strictly middle class. My parents came to the US from Cuba when they were young, and they act like they're playing a game of catch-up with the rest of the country. They don't just work to make money; they work like they have something to prove. Mom teaches Spanish at St. Mary's, the middle school where Annie and I went. Dad dropped out of high school to work at a company involved in refrigerators. I'm not sure what exactly he does with refrigerators, because I've never cared enough to find out. I think he either manufactures, repairs, or sells them. Maybe all of the above.

The only reason I'm here is because of my scholarship. Evanston pays half of my tuition (already enough to drown my parents in debt), as long as I keep my GPA above a 3.0. Being a scholarship kid adds one more layer of stress to the load I already carry. Most Evanston students can coast through their classes, knowing Mommy and Daddy will buy their admission to a top college, but I'll lose my scholarship, and my entire future, with the slightest dip of my GPA.

Sometimes I wonder whether getting kicked out of Evanston would really be so bad. What would happen if I just stopped?

Life would be easier. I could breathe again. But then I picture the disappointment on my parents' faces as I shatter their American Dream, as all their sacrifices are flushed down the drain, so I continue playing the dutiful daughter.

Students in tucked collared shirts swirl around me, and my mind flits back to the blue-eyed boy yesterday. To the midwinter sky and the small patch of skin exposed by his loose shirttail. There's no sign of him in the hall today. I doubt he's a sophomore, because I've never had a class with him. Is he the Levi Schuster from the flyer? Or is he a bandmate of Levi's? Maybe he's not even in the band. Maybe he just really enjoys stapling flyers.

If he appeared here and now, I could have a do-over. Force myself to speak like a normal human being. I envision him approaching me, and my brain flips through a slide show of our day off, Ferris Bueller–style.

You wanna get out of here? he might say, and I'd toss my stick-straight hair around (if I'm fantasizing, I might as well give myself manageable hair). I'd take his hand, and we'd skip school to spend the day holding hands and walking the Bow Bridge in Central Park.

He would save me from another day of my treadmill life.

My eye catches on the giant bulletin board where we met yesterday. It's plastered with flyers advertising everything from school clubs to student gov elections to puppies for adoption. Today I'm pulled to his flyer, tacked onto the board's top right corner.

Maybe you should try, he said, in a tone like it was no big deal.

I can't decipher any of my actions that follow. Momentary

demonic possession maybe, or a blip in my brain chemistry. The idea of me joining a band is laughable. There are glaring reasons why I shouldn't, like keeping my scholarship, the fact that I've never sung in front of anyone but Annie, and the teeny issue of my all-consuming stage fright, the kind that paralyzes me when I'm called on in class.

Yet inexplicably, despite all these reasons, I tear the flyer off the board and stick it in my blazer pocket.

Chapter Three

"CAROUSEL RIDE"
—RUBBLEBUCKET

Remember the music video we made in fifth grade?" I ask Annie at lunch. We're eating on the grassy knoll beside the patio area. Annie's having her usual Cobb salad and I'm on my third slice of pizza.

I use the phrase "music video" loosely. Really, it was the two of us sitting in Annie's living room with her parents' laptop propped up on the coffee table. I sang to "Edge of Glory" by Lady Gaga, and Annie accompanied me on the violin.

Annie's taken violin lessons since she could wrap her fingers around a bow. She's the only sophomore enrolled in AP Music and has made it to the All-State Orchestra for the past three years. Last year, at Principal Tishman's request, she composed the orchestral arrangement for our school song. In short, Annie's a prodigy destined for the philharmonic while I'm destined to sing exclusively for my shower tiles.

Annie pierces a lettuce leaf with her fork. "What music video?"

"To Lady Gaga? Remember?"

"Oh right." She smiles slightly.

"I think we were pretty good," I say, picking at a string of cheese hanging off my pizza.

"We were decent. For eleven-year-olds."

Sometimes she acts as though we're geriatrics instead of high school sophomores. She wasn't always like this. The intensity was there, of course, since we were young, but she used to channel it into fun. Like when she volunteered at summer day camp and taught sixty kids how to play Iron Maiden on their recorders.

I blame this school for squashing her spirit. Going to an intense college prep school like Evanston is like stepping into a human pressure cooker. There's no more time to sing Lady Gaga or conduct a heavy metal orchestra, because you can't put those activities on a college application.

"What's with the trip down memory lane, Vi?"

I avoid her eyes, fiddling with the flyer lodged inside my blazer's front pocket. If I look at her, I'll realize what a completely stupid idea it is and I won't say it.

"I'm thinking about doing something crazy."

"That extra credit project for Ms. Hammond?" she asks.

It saddens me that, in Annie's world, this is the definition of "crazy."

"No." I pull the flyer out of my pocket and toss it to her.

She unfolds it gingerly, scans it, and blinks at me. "Are you, like . . . having some kind of existential crisis?"

"No," I say again, a little huffily. My heart droops in response to her brush-off, which is dumb, because I wasn't *actually* going to audition. It was another one of my elaborate daydreams.

"I don't get it," she says with a shrug.

The thing is, fifth-grade Annie would have gotten it. The fifth-grade Annie who played Iron Maiden and hated salads and had stained red lips from overdosing on strawberry ice pops.

"I thought it could be interesting," I say, taking a giant bite of pizza. It's so stupid, but all of a sudden I feel seconds away from crying. I shake myself out of it. It's too early in the month for me to be getting so premenstrual.

"I didn't know you wanted to sing," Annie says.

"I don't. I mean, maybe."

"If you want to sing, you should totally join the choir. You get to sing *and* it'll look good on your college apps."

"Or, my life doesn't have to revolve around what a college admissions committee thinks."

"But it does, Vi. Do you know what Harvard applicants are like? They're superhuman. Not to mention you're going for a scholarship, which is like—"

"Okay, Annie," I cut her off. "You're right. It was a stupid idea."

Annie flicks a blade of grass off her skirt. "I didn't say stupid. I'm just saying you have a lot going on and I don't see the point of joining a band on top of it all."

"The point is to have fun. Remember fun?"

"There will be time for fun after Harvard," she replies, completing her transformation into my mother.

Right. Because life only gets more fun when you're an adult who's saddled with a spouse and kids and a mortgage and car payments.

I unbutton my shirt collar and take a gulp of air. It's gone from warm to suffocating out here.

"Vi?" Annie asks. "Are you okay?"

"I'm fine." This is *my* mantra. I'm fine, always. Not ecstatic, not depressed. Just fine.

Her voice softens. "Hey. I'm sorry. If you think it'd be fun to join the band, you should audition. I'll help you!"

"Nah . . . I don't think I will."

"I didn't mean to freak you out."

"It's not you, it's . . . I don't know. Things have been weird."

"They'll get back to normal."

Annie means to be reassuring, but she only seals my sense of doom. That's the point. I'm tired of normal. I want the ups and downs. Normal means not feeling anything. Normal is boring and claustrophobic.

Annie checks the time on her watch. "We're going to be late."

And life continues to be normal.

Coach Bridget is pure evil, but you wouldn't know it by looking at her, because she is the human incarnation of Barbie. Blond, with long, shapely legs and liquid blue eyes. There's a reason why our school has one of the largest male cross-country teams in New York.

Somehow I'm the fastest girl on the cross-country team, but Coach B named Rachel Levine captain because Rachel's a senior. I'm happy to let Rachel have the honor. I don't have the motivation or the pep to lead our team. I'm only here because Mr. Adams, my college counselor, told me to "Think GAAS" when I asked him what colleges wanted.

"Gas?" I repeated. I thought it was a joke, but his face was pinched tight.

"G-A-A-S. Colleges want a well-rounded applicant. Someone Giving, Artistic, Athletic, and Smart."

I told him sports aren't really my thing. In gym class I dodge every ball in the vicinity because I'm deathly afraid of one knocking out my teeth. I've had nightmares about it, actually. Annie says it represents a fear of growing up. I think it represents an entirely reasonable fear of objects hurtling toward my face.

"So play a sport without a ball," Mr. Adams suggested simply. "Cross-country in the fall, track and field in the spring."

"You want me to run?" I asked, raising my eyebrows sky high.

"It's putting one foot in front of the other, Victoria. That's all."

Like it's so simple. Like it's not misery incarnate.

Mr. Adams fed me a line about how running would give me a personal feeling of accomplishment, and begrudgingly I signed up for the team. I have yet to get that feeling of accomplishment, but from the first practice, Coach B wouldn't let up.

"You have the perfect runner's body," she gushed. Translation: I'm skinny and flat chested. No bouncing boobs to interfere with my momentum. "You won't believe your own potential."

She was right, in a way—I'm pretty good at running, which is annoying because it sucks to be good at something you hate. It's the constant monotony of it that gets to me. I have enough monotony in my life.

Now I'm puffing away on mile four, listening to the steady smack of my sneakers against the pavement. As usual, I play a song in my head to get my mind off the remaining miles to go. I picture myself auditioning for the band from the flyer, and my stomach somersaults at the thought.

Annie's right. It makes no sense to audition when I need to focus on getting into Harvard. So instead, I audition in my head, because in my head it's always the best possible outcome.

Sometimes it feels like I'm living an alternate life in there. I can do all of the things I want without any of the repercussions. In my head I'm performing live, effortlessly hitting high notes and thrashing around onstage. The Victoria in my head has purple streaks in her hair and a fearless attitude. She doesn't care about pleasing anyone.

Of course, the real me would probably have a coronary onstage. I would stand there, motionless, with the spotlight glowing on my frizzy mud-brown hair, because my parents would never let me dye it. (Mom: *What would your teachers think? They'd never recommend a girl with purple hair for Harvard.*)

The real Victoria remains a loser. Not lead singer material.

But if I *did* audition . . . which is totally out of the question and purely hypothetical . . . what's the worst that could happen? I'm not a terrible singer. At the very least, I'm on-key. My voice is deep with a hint of chain-smoker rasp even though I've never touched a cigarette.

I shake my head to clear my thoughts. I need to stop humoring myself. I'm not actually doing this.

"You're almost there!" Coach B chirps as she rolls up beside me. She's sitting primly on a red bicycle, her cheeks glowing. If I snapped a picture of her this second, she'd be model-ready for the cover of a fitness magazine. There isn't a drop of sweat on her, while my cotton T-shirt is soaked through. It's like she's *trying* to give me an inferiority complex.

"Open up your stride, Victoria! There, that's it!" She flashes a toothpaste-commercial smile at me as she pedals to join some of the boys running ahead.

"Why don't you get off your bike and try it yourself," I mutter when she's out of earshot, but it doesn't sound tough when I'm struggling to get the words out through panted breaths.

Behind me I hear my teammates talking and laughing, perfectly content to spend an hour of their lives running in circles. My irritation grows with every labored step. Isn't running supposed to make me feel at peace with the world? Where are those famous endorphins everyone raves about? I flip back to the movie in my mind, and for the last mile I imagine myself crowd surfing, weightless and euphoric, connected to everyone in the room.

Chapter Four

"BETRAYED BY BONES"
—HELLOGOODBYE

Hi Victoria,

We all loved your Lady Gaga video (lol) and want to invite you to our auditions next Saturday at the Jackson Tavern on Bleecker. Everyone auditioning is singing "Whole Lotta Love" by Led Zeppelin. You're slotted for 12 p.m. Let us know if you can make it!

Best,
Levi

I stare at my laptop screen until it goes black. My smudgy reflection looks back at me, petrified and confused. I tap my finger on the touchpad and reread Levi's e-mail for the sixth time, my eyes flitting through the words, searching for meaning. Lady Gaga. Auditions. Led Zeppelin. No matter how many times I try to decipher it, none of it makes sense.

How? How has Levi Schuster e-mailed me about a video I never sent him? I may actually be losing my mind. Yes, I have a tendency to sleepwalk through my life, but this? E-MAILING LEVI SCHUSTER, an event that has the potential to ruin my life? This I would remember.

Sure enough, when I check my sent e-mails folder, there's one from me to Levi. In it, I gush about my love of music, strong work ethic, and interpersonal skills. It doesn't even sound like me. It sounds like this shrill, uptight . . .

Wait.

I lunge toward my blazer and snatch my cell phone from its pocket, knocking against the leg of my desk in the process.

"Dammit!" I hiss, rubbing the blotchy red spot that begins to form on my knee. With my other hand, I call Annie.

She picks up on the first ring. "Hi, Vi."

"What did you do, Annie?"

"I'm fine, how are you?" I can picture her, sitting at her kitchen table, cradling her cell between her shoulder and her ear as she does her homework.

"Annie, I'm not joking. What did you do?"

"I did you a favor."

I sink into my bed, wishing it could devour me whole. I picture the band watching the video, seeing me at eleven years old. Laughing at me. I vaguely recall wearing my hair in a Princess Leia updo, and oh my God, it was definitely two days after I had gotten my Herbst appliance at the orthodontist, the one that gave me a speech impediment for weeks.

"Why?" I wrap my fingers tightly around the phone, wishing it were Annie's throat. "Why would you do this?"

"Because," she answers, "you were too scared to do it yourself."

I try to get my voice to work, but instead I sputter like a faulty car engine.

"It's not a big deal, Vi."

The more blasé she becomes, the more out of control I feel. That's how we work, a yin and yang friendship.

"How did you even get into my e-mail?" I ask.

"For starters, you haven't changed your e-mail password in five years. And I've been meaning to talk to you about that. Victoria123? You're pretty much begging to get hacked."

"You're kidding me, right? I mean, you have to be." The words sound ridiculous, even in my state of panic. Annie doesn't kid. "I know you're a control freak, but this is . . . this is a violation of privacy!"

"That's not true! Out of respect for your privacy, I didn't even read your e-mails."

Her logic is infuriating.

"I can't audition for a band, Annie!"

"Why not?"

"Which reason do you want first?"

"Look," she sighs. "I know I wasn't fully on board when you showed me the flyer, but the more I thought about it, the more I thought you could pull it off."

My rage subsides at her words. If there's anyone whose musical opinion I trust, it's Annie, with her perfect pitch and lifetime of orchestral experience. Besides, she wouldn't lie to me. She's told exactly one lie in the eight years I've known her, when she denied stealing my ice-cream-cone eraser in the third grade. It took her two minutes to break down in tears and confess to the crime.

As pissed as I am at Annie, there's a tug of hope in my chest that I can't ignore. The hope that maybe Levi Schuster or the blue-eyed boy or whoever watches the video will see something in me, beyond the Victoria that sleepwalks through her life.

And then it hits me: I actually want this. If I got into this band, it would prove that life doesn't have to be a series of ordinary events. It would mean that the Victoria in my head has the opportunity to exist in real life.

What if I'm not a completely terrible singer? What if there's a chance that Annie's annoying lack of boundaries can change everything?

"I gotta go, Vi." Annie interrupts my mental impasse. "I have violin practice."

I can't do it, though. When I think about auditioning, my stomach clenches like I'm staring down at the street from the height of a rooftop. My breath comes out in short, choppy gasps.

"Wait!" I screech into the phone. Panic floods my veins. "You have to e-mail Levi back and cancel the audition."

"If you really want to cancel the audition," Annie says, "why don't *you* e-mail Levi back yourself?"

I don't have an answer for her.

On Friday night we take my grandmother, Abi, to Malecon for dinner. I eat beans and rice with smashed plantains while Abi pinches my waist and tells me, in Spanish, that my vegetarianism will kill me.

Abi is not like the grandmothers I used to hear about growing up—these quiet, mysterious gray-haired women who sit in rocking chairs and knit scarves. Abi is a blaze of color and life. She wears shiny gold jewelry that jangles when she walks, as if to announce her presence, and she dances to Willy Chirino every morning while she cleans her apartment.

I can barely fight Abi off as she tries to force-feed me *croquetas* all night. I can only think of my audition next week. I grow more and more convinced that I'll bomb it. I'll bomb it so hard that music will forever be ruined for me.

I remember Mom once had this self-help book that talked about positive visualization. You have to picture what you want to happen and the universe will manifest it for you. So while I eat my food, I create a detailed movie in my head, imagining myself commanding the spotlight and wowing the band members. The blue-eyed boy, who may or may not be Levi Schuster, makes multiple appearances, and my mental movie ends with us shamelessly making out onstage.

"Ria?" Dad's voice interrupts my thoughts. I'm plucked offstage and back inside the restaurant.

"Uh-huh?" I notice my whole family is standing up, pushing away the empty plates and wads of paper napkins cluttering the table.

"You ready to go?"

"Um, yeah." I hastily rise and throw out my trash.

Abi asks me what I was thinking about, and I shrug.

"School?" I offer.

But she knows I'm lying. Abi doesn't speak English, and my Spanish is severely limited, but we somehow understand each other perfectly well.

She calls me *mijita* and tells me not to worry. Then she plants a giant kiss on my cheek, marking me with a bright red lip print. I fleetingly wish Abi could be the one judging me at the audition next week, because Abi thinks everything I do is praiseworthy. I could burp into the microphone and she'd give me a standing ovation.

I think about the audition the entire walk home, a tense feeling in the pit of my stomach growing so quickly it takes over my limbs, my blood, my bones. By the time I walk into our apartment, my body is hot and cold at the same time, and I'm worried that I'm going to see the remains of Malecon leaving my stomach through my mouth.

I don't know why I've gotten so worked up over this.

It's not too late to cancel. I'm not sure what would be worse, canceling the audition or going through with it and failing. But canceling it would mean more of the same. More cross-country practices, more of Mr. Davis's pit stains. It would mean being satisfied with normal.

Chapter Five

"THE SHADE"

—METRIC

I'm physically ill, trying to decide what to do in case I have to puke on the train. There's nowhere to go, no bathroom to duck into. I can move between the trains and throw up onto the tracks, or I can let it out all over the subway floor. As I contemplate worst-case scenarios, I clutch the railing by my seat. Better yet, I could get off at the next stop, head back north, and forget all about this audition.

Why am I putting myself through this? The sweaty palms, the shaky stomach . . . each side of my brain engaged in a battle with the other. I should be home in my pajamas, challenging Matty to a round of *Super Smash Bros*. My treadmill life is okay. All I need to do is keep walking in a straight line. Don't complicate things.

I wipe my hands on my miniskirt. It took me an hour to pick this outfit, and I'm still not happy with it. I am so obviously a girl posing as a rock star, wearing her mom's red lipstick and purposely ripping a hole in her stockings so they don't look brand-new (which they are, for two dollars at Rosa Discount Sales).

I swiped the tube of lipstick off Mom's dresser. The color is called Ravish Me Red, and she doesn't wear it for work, only for date nights with Dad. I tried not to think about Dad ravishing her in any way as I carefully spread the color over my lips. The lipstick contrasts sharply with my pale skin, giving me a slightly vampiric appearance. It's a dramatic departure from the ChapStick I wear on a daily basis. Sometimes when I'm feeling daring, I wear a pale-pink gloss that I bought three years ago for my cousin's confirmation. I never go for red. It's much too bold.

But today calls for bold.

My hair is twisted into a messy bun. There's no other way to tame it. I've tried gel, but my hair hangs in sticky curls all day. I've tried blow-drying it, but my arm aches ten minutes into the process. Since there's no helping it, I have to conceal as much as I can.

"This is not Caucasian hair," a stylist once murmured to me as she fried my waves into submission with a flat iron.

No shit.

The subway slows down at Fourteenth Street. I'm one stop away and twenty minutes early. And that's another thing I'm doing wrong. Shouldn't lead singers arrive fashionably late? I'm supposed to look like I stumbled out of bed and wandered into the bar as an afterthought. Damn my punctuality.

I chew on my left pinkie nail before remembering that Annie took a black marker to my nails last night so I'd look more alternative. I quickly check my reflection in the subway mirror to make sure I didn't stain my lips.

"This is West Fourth Street," the conductor announces as the train crawls to a halt.

This is my stop. The toast I ate for breakfast clogs my intestines as I get up and walk through the sliding doors. My feet slide around in my high-heeled boots and my head feels too light, like it could roll right off my body. One stumble and I'll topple into the tracks. I walk up the subway steps and the sky opens up to me, gray and drizzly.

Jackson Tavern sits a block from the subway stop. At the sight of it, my stomach lurches. I swallow, take a few shuddering breaths, and enter the bar.

It's a nondescript pub, not the ninth circle of hell I was expecting. Dim lighting, dark wooden tables, and a Guinness sign perched over the liquor shelf. My nostrils are greeted by the smell of fried food, which does nothing for my stomach's current state. At the corner of the bar is a small elevated stage, and I see a guy frowning over his bass guitar. His black hair is slicked and parted to the side and he wears thick-rimmed glasses, ones that might be for optometric purposes or a geek fashion statement. He looks nerdy, but nerdy by choice, which possibly makes him cool.

Behind him an Indian girl with a Mohawk, an actual Mohawk, is setting up her drums. I know who she is, but only by reputation. Krina Chaturvedi. When you see someone with a Mohawk clomping around a prep school like Evanston, you tend to know that person's name. Today Krina wears torn low-riding jeans and a cropped shirt revealing a pierced belly button. Unlike me, she probably didn't tear her clothes on purpose to look cool.

Krina is the type of person you hear things about, and you can't quite separate fact from fiction. She becomes more of a myth than an actual person. There was a rumor going around that she had sex with our gym teacher, Mr. Dobbs, on the wrestling mat in the gym. Someone else said Krina once got caught shoplifting a pregnancy test. The rumors spiraled from there. One student swore Krina got a zombie tattoo across her entire back, and Ned Rowley claimed she drank a cup of pig's blood on a dare. (I'm pretty sure that last one has to be fake.)

Krina terrifies me. Everything about this moment terrifies me.

I hesitate by the bar's entrance. I'm not sure I can handle fantasy and reality crashing together. This won't turn out to be the stunning, flawless performance the Victoria in my head always gives. I'm actually here. I'm going through with this. Maybe I should go. The band is still setting up, and no one's seen me come in. There's no sign of the beautiful boy who put up the flyer, so he would never know that I came, I saw, I chickened out.

As I turn to leave, I hear, "Victoria, right?"

Dammit. I've been spotted by the boy in glasses.

"Um, hi!" I call, my voice emerging too chipper. It's too late to leave now, so I trot over to the stage.

"I'm Levi," he says.

Levi Schuster is not the sex god who put up the flyer. He's much less intimidating, like his picture would accompany the definition of a nice guy. The glasses are a big help. His nonscariness makes up for

Krina, who is glowering at me from behind her drum set.

"Nice to meet you," I say.

Levi props his bass against the wall and nudges his glasses higher on his nose. "You're a little early—"

"I know. I'm sorry," I cut in. "I can be annoyingly punctual."

"No, I mean . . . I like it." Levi smiles at me, exposing a chipped front tooth. "It shows you're responsible, which is definitely a plus."

"Levi gets off on punctuality," Krina adds drily. She steps away from her drums and extends her hand. "Krina."

"Victoria," I reply as we shake hands. I hope Krina isn't grossed out by the film of sweat on my palms. If she is, she doesn't show it.

"Victoria, do you want a water or anything?" Levi offers.

"Oh no, I'm fine. . . ."

"You sure?"

"Yup."

Krina goes back to fiddling around with her drums, leaving Levi and I to make conversation on our own.

"So." A bead of sweat appears above Levi's upper lip. "I haven't really seen you around school."

"I'm kind of a loner." What sounded cool in my head sounds unbearably pathetic out of my mouth.

"Really? No . . . boyfriend or anything?"

I bite back a laugh. If only he knew how nonexistent my dating life was. "Nope. I'm a free agent."

"Oh yeah? That's cool. I'm a free agent myself."

It occurs to me that Levi Schuster is hitting on me. I'm making him *sweat*.

It puts me in an awkward predicament. If I'm too nice, he'll think I'm flirting with him. If I'm not nice enough, he won't want me in his band.

So, I make an unintelligible "hmph" sound to his revelation that he's single, and we stand there in silence.

"You sure you don't want anything?" he asks again. "Not even a water?"

"No, no," I say quickly. "Thank you, though."

Again, I regret showing up early. I've never been one for small talk, and I'm grateful when my painful attempt at conversation is interrupted by the swing of the front door.

"Our first audition," Levi tells me as a bearded man with a stringy blond ponytail enters the bar.

Beardy strolls over to us and I instinctively straighten up as if I'm meeting someone's dad. Up close, I can see that Beardy is well into his thirties. He introduces himself as "Greg" and he doesn't seem nervous at all. Where did they find this guy? He's obviously not an Evanston student, and I can tell that, unlike me, he's no virgin to the audition circuit. I try to imitate his loose stance so I don't seem so uptight standing next to him.

"This is Victoria," Levi says to Greg. "She's auditioning today too."

Greg glances over at me, obviously unimpressed. "Cool."

We don't shake hands. He's probably wondering why I'm here so early, imposing on his audition time.

"We're just waiting on Strand and then we'll get started," says Levi.

"A strand of what?" I blurt out, hoping it's not drug lingo. Last year one of the kids at Evanston was suspended for doing coke in the bathroom. When Mom and Dad found out, they sat me down and rattled off a bunch of scary drug statistics they printed off the Internet. Then Dad told me a totally made-up story about his friend who overdosed when he took some extra Tylenol.

Krina snorts. "Not 'a strand,' just Strand. Our guitarist. His dad owns the bar."

And then I realize who Strand must be. The blue-eyed boy has a name. A weird one.

"Victoria, you're totally welcome to stay put and watch," Levi says, motioning to the tables scattered in front of the stage, "if Greg doesn't mind . . ."

Greg shrugs. "Cool."

Greg doesn't seem fazed by much. Does that confidence come with age or experience? Whatever the case, I want to bottle it up and chug it down. I need it now.

"And look who deigned to show up," Levi announces, staring over my head at the door.

I turn and the blue-eyed boy, Strand, is there in reality. He *exists*. I haven't seen him since that day in the hallway, and I had almost chalked up our encounter to a fevered hallucination. But this time he isn't alone. He hauls a guitar case on one arm and a girl on the other. The girl is short and chesty, with wavy black hair cropped to her chin.

I feel my fantasies of Strand collapse around me. He has a girl-friend. Of course. He's too pretty to be single.

"You're late!" Levi calls.

Strand pries the girl off him and whispers something in her ear, then saunters over to us. His curly brown hair sticks up in multiple directions, and a confident smirk lingers on his face. All he's missing is a leather jacket and a cigarette lodged between his lips. I can already tell he's not the kind of guy who hurries, because he knows people will wait for him.

"Who's this one?" Krina asks Strand, her eyes darting to the chesty girl who has seated herself at the front table. "Five bucks if you get it in ten seconds."

"For your information . . . ," Strand stalls, glancing back at the girl, who waves at him eagerly. He snaps his fingers. "Her name is Jenna."

"Jenna," Krina repeats doubtfully.

Levi rolls his eyes. "Can we please get started?"

"Hey!" Krina calls to the girl. "What's your name?"

The girl blinks back at us. "Janine." Her voice is surprisingly chirpy, almost birdlike.

Strand groans under his breath. "Did I not say Janine?" he asks in feigned innocence, but he slips a bill out of his back pocket and slaps it on the snare drum in front of Krina.

"Janine . . . ," Krina muses as she pockets the money. "Pretty name . . ."

A sudden stab of disappointment infuses my already-nervous state. So it turns out that Strand is kind of a jackass.

Not that I thought anything would happen between us anyway. Guys like Strand don't notice girls like me. And honestly, I wouldn't be interested in someone who couldn't remember my name. No matter how pretty he is.

"No visitors allowed at practice, Strand," Levi says, his fingers twitching. "Krina, don't encourage him."

"Ah, but this isn't a practice," Strand replies with a crooked grin. "It's an audition."

Greg and I are still standing onstage, awkwardly taking in the exchange.

When Strand sees me, his grin grows wider.

"Glad you changed your mind," he says to me, and despite my newfound disgust for him, I'm the tiniest bit pleased that he remembers me.

"Their names are Victoria and Greg," Krina says to him. "Try not to forget."

Strand taps the side of his head. "It's locked in here forever."

"Let's get started," Levi cuts in. "Greg, you ready?"

"Yup," Greg answers. Being monosyllabic seems to be his thing.

As the band gets ready, I sit at the table with Janine. She doesn't speak to me. She doesn't even look at me. I must have uncoolness seeping out of my pores. Onstage, Krina adjusts her stool and taps the foot pedal, then pauses to readjust her seat again. Levi stretches his long fingers over the neck of the bass. He periodically stops and frowns as he plucks the strings. Strand is laughing and talking to Greg as he tunes his guitar.

My heart thuds against my chest. What am I doing here? They all look so cool and confident. What will they do when they find out that I'm the type of girl who practiced for this audition by serenading a lamp?

It's not too late to leave. Greg deserves this more than I do. From the look of him, he's been at it longer.

But I want this. I need this.

I hope that Greg sucks. I hope his voice gives out and he falls off the stage. Not so badly that he's terribly hurt, but enough that he'll be put off from performing in the near future. Maybe a twisted ankle or something.

"Are you with the band or what?"

I turn to find Janine staring at me icily.

"No," I answer quickly. "I mean, I hope to be *in* it . . . I'm auditioning."

Her face slackens as she determines I'm not a likely threat to her claim on Strand.

"He's hot, isn't he?" She juts her chin in Strand's direction.

I watch him, noting the way his thin T-shirt clings to his body and how his smile reveals a crescent-shaped dimple on his left cheek. Hot is an understatement.

"I guess," I agree. He is, but he knows it, which now makes him a little less hot in my eyes. Not so for Janine. Every time he looks at her, she visibly turns red. It's like sitting next to a fire hydrant about to explode with sexual longing.

"Test," Levi says into the microphone, and the word reverberates throughout the bar.

Levi nods at Greg to take his place behind the mic. Strand has his guitar plugged into an amp, and as his fingers strum the song's opening chord progression, I momentarily forget my jangling nerves. I'm excited for the music, which sounds like it will be harder and grittier than the version I'm used to.

Then Greg opens his mouth and reality smacks me in the face.

The man can sing. He can *really* sing. It sounds as though he's practiced for this moment his entire life, like his mom pressed a speaker onto her stomach while Greg was still in the womb. His voice soars and glides over the notes, hitting each one precisely on pitch. His face doesn't clench with effort when he sings like mine does. It's like he doesn't even have to try. Janine bobs her head in appreciation and I want to throttle her.

You don't need to do this, the little voice in my head murmurs in reminder. And I want to listen to it. I think about leaving right in the middle of the song, without an explanation. I think about the relief of not having to audition.

Then I see Levi and Strand exchange a look. Their faces are blank, expressionless. Strand's smirk has vanished. They seem . . . bored.

Even as the song gains momentum, Greg's voice is unaffected. He's almost *too* calm. Too easygoing.

"What do you think?" I whisper to Janine.

"He looks great," she sighs, without so much as a glance at me.

Oh geez. She's still focused on Strand, who is listlessly strumming his guitar. He and the rest of the band do look great. They sound great too. I would never guess I'm listening to a high school band. I realize that the reason I'm ignoring the little voice in my head is because I want to be near this greatness a little longer. Maybe it'll rub off on me.

The song winds down and ends on a final sustained note. I clap politely, while next to me Janine loses her mind, whistling and hooting like it's the height of Beatlemania. She reeks of desperation, and I see Krina clamp her lips shut to keep from laughing.

"Do you want to run it again?" Levi asks Greg.

Greg shakes his head slowly. "Nah . . ."

There's the look again. They're disappointed with Greg! I still have a chance. The four of them huddle together onstage, speaking in hushed tones. After a minute they each shake hands with Greg.

"We'll call you," Levi says as Greg turns to leave.

"Cool."

I wonder what Greg will do for the rest of the day. Practice some yoga, maybe. Pick up some hemp at the local farmer's market. Float through life without a care in the world.

And then there's me, the girl with tiny puddles of sweat gathering in her boots. The polar opposite of cool, composed Greg.

"You ready, Victoria?" comes Levi's voice through the mic, and my chest squeezes.

I get up and walk onto the stage, and it's a strange contradiction, because my heart is palpitating rapidly but my body moves like I'm walking in Jell-O. Even though I stare down at the floor while I walk, I feel the band's eyes on me. I am about to collapse into a sweaty heap on the stage. I can't breathe. I can't breathe normally, let alone through my diaphragm or whatever Annie was spouting off about when she helped me rehearse for this.

Levi adjusts the mic stand for me, and I stare out into the nearly empty bar. The band waits silently for me. I nod at them.

I'm ready.

Chapter Six

"SHOULD HAVE KNOWN BETTER"
—SUFJAN STEVENS

I wasn't ready. Not even close.

I wake up on Sunday morning hoping the entire fiasco was a nightmare that never actually happened. Flashes of it sneak up on me like a horror movie montage. The way Janine wrinkled her nose throughout the performance. The way Levi smiled when I looked over at him, the kind of smile that didn't reach his eyes. And the worst part?

The shaking. The way my body, from my toes to my vocal cords, wouldn't stop shaking. No matter how much I tried to cling to a note, it would slip away like a pool of water seeping through my fingers.

I stay in my room the rest of the weekend. Annie's left me nine hundred texts, but I can't talk to her. I can't stand the thought of her disappointment layered on top of mine. Not to mention the band's disappointment.

"We'll call you." Levi said it the same way he said it to Greg. Practiced, measured. We both knew it was a lie, but I kept up my part of the deal, smiling tightly, shaking everyone's hand.

My only plan now is to avoid the junior halls like the plague. I never want to see any of them again.

Chapter Seven

"BIRTH IN REVERSE"
—ST. VINCENT

Entering Evanston on Monday morning, it hits me that avoiding the band forever is an unrealistic goal. I'll probably spot them in the library or the quad at some point. Evanston is a big school, but it's not totally anonymous. So I need to act normal, in case I do run into anyone. Unfazed.

The unfazed version of me begins first thing in the morning. I put on my uniform. I eat peanut butter toast for breakfast. I take the train to school. La di da. Another insignificant day in the life of Victoria Cruz. Saturday was a weird anomaly, a bitter taste of another world to make me realize I belong back on Earth. I belong here, at Evanston, earning my future scholarship to Harvard.

Then I see Annie stationed by my locker, her lips as tight as her ponytail. She taps her nails against her crossed arms and narrows her eyes at me. "You couldn't spare five minutes to call me back?"

I open my locker and shove my books inside. "Hello to you, too."

"Victoria." She eyes her reflection in my locker mirror, zeroing in on a stray wisp of hair inching out of her headband before poking it back into place. "Explain yourself."

"I didn't know you cared about the stupid audition so much."

"Um . . . yeah? I helped you get it, didn't I? I'm emotionally invested in the outcome."

"You're right. I'm sorry for my lack of updates."

"Darn right you're sorry," she says, and I try to hide my smile. Annie never curses, so her intimidation tactics can fall short. Plus she's, like, four foot eleven.

"It's not funny, Victoria!" she admonishes as I close my locker and we walk in step toward Ms. Hammond's room.

"Did you get the bonus problem on the homework?" I ask her, hoping the tangent will throw her off.

"Of course I did. Stop trying to distract me."

"I'm not."

"What happened? You're being cagey. Did you warm up before the audition like I taught you?"

"I don't really want to talk about it." I hope for once Annie will stop being Annie and leave me alone.

She doesn't. "Give me something, Vi. A crumb of information. I deserve it, don't I?"

We walk into Ms. Hammond's room and Annie takes a seat

directly behind me. I pivot to face her. "It was . . . humiliating? The worst experience of my life?"

"Oh, come on."

"I couldn't stop shaking, I was pitchy . . ."

"That's just nerves. They'll look past it."

"I don't think so." I shake my head. "The guy who auditioned before me was perfect. Solid band material."

Annie flicks her hand. "Perfection is overrated."

I don't bother to point out the irony of Annie, perfection personified, uttering those words.

"Anyway . . ." I sigh. "I'd like to forget the whole thing ever happened, if that's okay with you."

"That is absolutely not okay with me. Why don't you ask Levi for a second chance?"

"Sure," I say. "Because one time wasn't enough trauma for me. I need to relive it."

"Victoria Cruz."

"It's over," I say, forcing a shrug. "And I'm fine with it."

Annie leans back in her seat and shakes her head at me. "You always do that."

I don't want to give her the satisfaction of asking, but I can't help myself. "Do what?"

"You clam up when you're upset."

"I don't 'clam up.' I just don't want to dwell on the negative. It's unhealthy."

"And stifling your emotions is healthy?"

"When did you become a shrink?" I don't point out that she

would make the worst shrink imaginable. She's a ticking time bomb of anxiety.

"We can figure this out," she urges. "We can look for Levi during lunch. We'll stake him out."

"No. No way."

"We can make it look like you ran into him by accident!"

"Annie. *No.*" I try to sound as firm as possible, like I'm disciplining a dog for chewing up a pair of shoes. Maybe Annie will respond to that since she won't listen to human logic. Besides, I can't imagine anything more embarrassing than stalking Levi and begging him for a second chance. It would be the most pathetic of pathetic moves.

"Why are you giving up on this?" she asks me. "I thought you wanted it."

"I did. I do. But it's not meant to be."

"You can't sit around and wait for things to happen. That's your problem. You complain about things, but you don't do anything to fix them."

"I auditioned, didn't I?" I retort. "I auditioned and I failed, end of story. Now drop it. Please."

Annie purses her lips and sticks her chin in the air, the way she always does when she gets huffy. "Whatever you say, Victoria."

We take our lunches outside today. Annie is momentarily distracted by the latest school gossip, so she drops the topic of my audition failure. I'm thankful to avoid another lecture on pursuing my dreams at all costs. Today Annie's on about how a teacher caught Ethan Ackerman passing Brittany Moore a dirty note during class.

"He's so skeevy," Annie says as she offers me a crouton.

"They are *dating*," I point out, popping it into my mouth.

"So? Can't they wait until after school to skank it up?"

"What did the note actually say?"

"Something about having sex in the bathroom." She shudders.

It's still hard for me to wrap my mind around anything sex related, considering I haven't even kissed anyone yet. Talk about sexually stunted. Annie shares my lack of sexual experience, but she knows more than I do. She's like a walking Wikipedia. Her brain stores all kinds of information, like how to waterproof your shoes and the names of every Barry Manilow album.

It's been exactly two minutes since I've thought about the audition, thanks to Brittany and Ethan. Everything is as it should be.

Then Krina shows up and the world is unpredictable again.

Annie is the first to look up, eyes bulging as she takes in Krina's Mohawk.

"Hey," Krina says, like her appearance at our lunch spot is a normal occurrence. She plops down on the grass in front of me and Annie without asking permission.

"Hey . . . ," I manage to reply, and Annie nudges me.

"Oh, right," I say. "Krina, this is Annie. Annie, Krina's the drummer in the band."

"Nice to meet you," Annie says formally.

Krina nods and pops the tab of her soda. The two couldn't look more different. Annie is polished and prim, while Krina is . . . Krina. Multiple body piercings, grungy appearance, devil-may-care attitude. It's like watching the sun meet the moon.

The three of us sit there in horrible silence. Inside, I'm screaming, begging Krina for answers. If she's here to tell me I didn't make the band, she should do it quickly. Dragging it out like this is just cruel.

Annie abandons her salad to gawk at Krina. "I helped Vi with her audition," she suddenly announces, and I literally feel like I want to die.

Now Krina will know that my audition wasn't a spur-of-the-moment mess, it was a rehearsed mess. That's even worse. It tells her that the kind of screwing up I do takes practice.

"Is that so?" Krina asks. She looks Annie up and down with amusement, the way you would look at a child who's got a finger up his nose.

"Yup," says Annie. "She's got an amazing voice. She'd be a great addition to your band. To any band, really. She's in high demand."

Shut up, Annie. Please shut up. I try to zoom the message to her telepathically, but she barges ahead. She's trying too hard, and I feel like a rundown house being pitched to a reluctant buyer.

"How did you feel about your audition?" Krina asks me.

Is that a trick question? Does what I feel matter? I want to pretend it never happened. I want to jump into a DeLorean and warn the past Victoria never to record the Lady Gaga song.

"I think it was . . . okay," I reply carefully.

"I'm sure it was way better than okay," Annie cuts in. She turns to Krina. "Victoria constantly underestimates herself."

"I do not," I argue. "I'm realistic." I wish Annie would stop playing therapist, especially in front of Krina.

"What did *you* guys think of Vi's audition?" Annie asks her. Just like that. So blatant, so to the point.

"You don't need to answer her," I tell Krina quickly. "I know it wasn't . . . my best."

Krina leans in, and I get a close-up view of the smoky black liner rimming her eyes.

"I probably shouldn't be telling you this," she says to me in a low voice, "but you're one of our top choices."

"What?" I grab her wrist to steady myself. "You're serious?" She eyes my hand warily until I yank it away.

"It's not a done deal," she warns.

"How do we make it one?" Annie asks.

Krina gives a throaty laugh. "Are you her agent or something?"

"Overbearing friend," I answer before Annie can open her mouth again.

Krina twirls a metal ring around her thumb, looking from me to Annie. "I'm going to be honest."

I nod, inwardly cringing. People only say that when bad news is coming.

"You're talented," she says. "That's not a question. But you're inexperienced. You need to work on your performance and managing your nerves."

What can I say to that? Krina's right. I'm a nervous wreck onstage.

"The voice is what matters," Krina says. "And you have that."

"So, what now?" I ask.

"We're still figuring things out. I shouldn't even be talking to you."

"Then why are you?" Annie asks.

Krina raises an eyebrow at her, which miraculously silences her. I've never seen anyone shut Annie down that easily. She turns back to me. "Because you can do better than what we saw."

I look at her doubtfully.

"Look," Krina continues, "if anyone asks, I didn't tell you this, but we're going to the Cave on Friday. I think you should be there."

"What's the Cave?" Annie asks.

"A bar. Downtown."

I wring my hands together. "But . . . I'm fifteen."

"Your point?" Krina asks.

"How do we get in?"

"You don't have a fake ID?"

"I, um . . . no."

She closes her eyes and I feel like a world-class loser. "I'll get you one. This guy I know charges fifty bucks."

I'm not this girl. I play by the rules. But Krina is acting like it's no big deal, and she's watching me with that expectant look on her face, and this will help me make the band.

"Okay . . . ," I say slowly, against all my better judgment. My mind is already running through the excuses I'll have to give my parents about where I am on Friday.

"Okay," Krina echoes. "What about you, Agent Annie? You in?"

Annie's eyes widen with fear or anxiety or both. "Me?"

"You don't have to," I reassure her.

Annie will not set foot in this bar. She's more of a goody-goody than I am, and even I'm not sure I can go through with all of this.

This is why I'm so shocked when she raises her hand to stop me and says to Krina, "Yeah. I'm in."

Chapter Eight

"CROOKED CROWN"
—THE ANNIVERSARY

K rina finds us again at lunch on Friday, but she doesn't stop to sit down. She drops an envelope onto the freshly manicured grass in front of us and walks off without a word. I grab it and slide it under my lunch tray.

"She's so cool," Annie says wistfully as she stares at Krina's retreating form. "Do you think we'll ever be that cool?"

I follow her gaze. "Definitely not."

We're so uncool that we don't open the envelope until after school at Annie's house. It's the fear of Principal Tishman materializing out of nowhere to catch us with the incriminating IDs.

I tell my parents I'm sleeping over at Annie's. Annie's parents go to sleep at nine o'clock every night without fail, and their room is on another floor in the house. Annie assures me that we'll be able to sneak out with no problem.

Annie lives up in Queens, in an older area dotted with picturesque brownstones and tree-lined streets. Her family is wealthy enough to afford the Evanston tuition, but not wealthy enough to live on the Upper West Side. Mom always says Annie's family *está forrado*, which means they have enough money to not worry about money.

We're holed up in Annie's immaculate room, double the size of mine. There aren't any posters tacked onto the walls, only framed pictures and shelves sagging under the weight of her trophy and plaque collection. Annie tears into the envelope and takes out the IDs, studying them with narrowed eyes.

"These are pretty good matches," she remarks.

"Do they look like us?"

She passes mine over to me. The woman in the picture has slightly fuller lips and tanner skin, but we share the same wavy dark hair and brown eyes. She stares confidently into the camera without smiling. Her name is Natasha. Natasha Benitez. Natasha looks like someone who, unlike me, doesn't give a damn. I wonder where Natasha is now, at this moment, and if she still doesn't give a damn. Or has she been beaten down by life? Fallen victim to the treadmill like everyone else?

"Can I see yours?" I ask Annie, and we switch cards.

Annie's ID belonged to a Mara Cheng, a pretty girl wearing heavy liquid eyeliner and a nose ring. Annie is not allowed to get any body part pierced until she's eighteen, so she MacGyvers her way around the situation by cutting up a paperclip and clamping it around her nostril.

"We need to memorize this information in case the bouncer asks us any questions," Annie instructs. "If we're doing this, we're going to do it right."

In ten minutes we embody Mara and Natasha. Natasha is from Miami, Florida, a Leo, born on August third. Mara is a Sagittarius from Boston.

"Look what I bought for you," says Annie, after she's quizzed me multiple times on Natasha's birthday. She pulls a pink box out from under her bed and tosses it to me. I open it and find a pair of what looks like chicken cutlets inside.

"They'll make your boobs look much bigger," she says.

I gape at her. "Have you lost it?"

"I'm trying to make you look twenty-one!"

"You realize there are twenty-one-year-olds with A cups, right?"

"Yes, but with some added cleavage the bouncer is less likely to stop you. You have a young face, you know."

The cutlets are cold and jiggly in my hands. "I think I'll pass."

"Fine," she replies. "Don't blame me if you get thrown out."

To argue is futile. I roll my eyes and stick the cutlets into my bra, actual boobs shivering on contact.

At a quarter to nine the Lins come to Annie's room to wish us good night, and I can't look into their faces. Annie and I have never done this before. We're not good at being regular teenagers who don't respect their parents. I actually like my parents a lot, even though they annoy the crap out of me. And I've known Mr. and Mrs. Lin for half my life, so I feel just as guilty lying to them, too.

When they finally leave Annie's room, I can feel the oxygen returning to my lungs. We wait until we can hear the Lins ascend the creaky carpeted stairs and shut their bedroom door. Then Annie and I change into our preplanned outfits of crop tops, skirts, and boots. We trace our eyes with heavy black liner and wear vampy lipstick. Annie even adds bronzer to my cheekbones to replicate Natasha's tan. When we examine ourselves in Annie's full-length mirror, she nods in approval.

"We look like Mara and Natasha," she declares.

I'm not so sure about that, but we definitely don't look like Annie and Victoria.

It's a liberating feeling, pretending to be someone else. It feels like anything is possible tonight, because it's not Victoria's night, it's Natasha's. In a strange way, I want to make her proud.

When we leave Annie's house, I tell her, "I'm surprised you're doing this."

"Me too." A nervous look flashes across her face, then quickly dissipates. We hold hands so we don't lose our balance descending her front stoop.

"I mean, I'm doing it to get into the band," I press, "but what's your excuse?"

Annie hikes her purse onto her shoulder, looks straight ahead, and says, "Maybe tonight I want to take a break from being Annie."

It never occurred to me that Annie might feel trapped sometimes too.

Chapter Nine

"LEFT HAND FREE"
—ALT-J

The Cave is loud, and I hear the thumping bass line and chatter of voices from blocks away. A long awning leads to a set of steps that descend into the underground bar. Sitting on a stool by the entrance is a surly-looking man with glazed, bloodshot eyes. I stop abruptly outside his range of vision.

"What's wrong?" Annie slows beside me.

"I changed my mind," I say. "Let's go back to your place."

"What?! Why?"

"Come on. We'll wipe this makeup off, get in our pj's, and watch crappy rom coms."

Annie plants a hand on her hip. "You're doing it again."

"What?"

"Clamming up. Besides, I paid for these IDs, and we're using them."

Everything is too foreign, too overwhelming. The dark street corner, the smell of booze, the noise. I'm so far outside of my comfort zone that I can't even see my comfort zone anymore. It's a distant speck on the horizon.

"I don't think I can pull this off," I confess. "Can't we get arrested for this? How the hell am I supposed to pass for twenty-one?"

"You have no reason to be nervous, okay? We studied. We're prepared. Now tell me. What's your name?"

"Natasha," I say in a small voice.

"Say it like you mean it."

I suck in my breath. "Natasha."

"Yes! You are Natasha Benitez! And do you know what Natasha Benitez would do right now?"

Natasha wouldn't run home and watch TV all night. Natasha isn't scared of anything. I pull my shoulders back and puff out my chicken cutlets. "Natasha would walk into the bar like a boss bitch."

"Exactly," Annie confirms, hiking up my skirt by the waistband. "Listen. When you pull out your ID, don't say anything. Keep a neutral face and act like you've done this a hundred times before. Follow my lead."

Annie marches down the steps and I trail behind her. She pulls the ID out of her purse and hands it to the bouncer, her eyes locking onto his face. The bouncer gives it a brief glance and waves her through without a word.

"Come on, Natasha," she calls to me over her shoulder.

I stop in front of the bouncer and grit my teeth into a smile. He opens his palm without smiling back. I fumble before giving him Natasha's card. My motions are jerky and awkward, my chicken cutlets slippery with sweat.

The bouncer doesn't wave me through right away like he did with Annie. He pauses—why is he pausing? He looks up at me, then down at the ID. I try to play the part of a calm twenty-one-year-old woman.

"You from Miami?" he asks me.

His tone is casual, but I know what this is. A test.

"Yes," I say. "Yes, I'm from Miami."

"Me too," he says, and my heart skitters. "Where in Miami?"

Fan-freaking-tastic. Of course the bouncer's from Miami. I swallow hard and pray my face isn't showing my insides self-destructing. This is what I know about Miami: Humidity. South Beach. The Dolphins. Do people in Miami live on the beach? Or is the beach more of a tourist destination, like Miami's equivalent to Times Square?

"Coral Gables," Annie says from the doorway.

The bouncer looks at us skeptically. I manage a weak smile.

"Coral Gables," I repeat. "What about you?"

"Kendall."

"Oh, Kendall . . ." I say it with what I hope sounds like a tone of recognition. I'm grateful when a couple of other people bump up behind me so this agonizing conversation can end.

The bouncer hands the ID back to me. "Enjoy your night."

And it's like heaven's gates open up to me—if heaven is a loud, dirty bar smelling of pee and vomit. When we're safely inside the bar, Annie and I squeal and jump up and down. This is officially the biggest act of rebellion in our entire lives.

"How did you come up with Coral Gables?" I ask over the pounding music.

"What?" she shouts back.

"How did you come up with Coral Gables?!"

"My aunt Deb lives there!"

We have to scream over the speakers blasting Katy Perry at top volume. The bar is packed and we squeeze into a corner to regroup.

"Can you see Krina?" I ask Annie.

She stands on her tiptoes and gazes over the sea of bar goers. "I think they're in the back!"

They might as well be in Guam. We move inch by inch, pressing through the wall of people surrounding us. I dodge a splash of beer that hits my boot. In the slivers of space between bodies, I spot the three of them—Krina, Levi, and Strand—sitting on a long built-in couch. The crowd parts for us, not much, but enough so that I notice the small stage at the back of the bar.

My legs almost give out at the sight of it. I realize it's not Katy Perry I hear through the speakers. It's the voice of a wobbly drunk girl onstage, wearing a glittery top that makes her look like a human disco ball. She's slurring her words into the mic so badly that the crowd starts to boo.

I yank on Annie's purse strap to stop her from moving forward.

"This is a karaoke bar?" I shriek into her ear.

"Ow!" She scowls at me. "And yeah, I don't think this girl is a professional."

"Nope." I turn to head back out the door. "I'm out of here."

Annie grabs me by the hair. "Stop, Vi! We've made it this far!"

"I am *not* singing in front of all these people!" I screech, my panic building.

"No one asked you to!" she retorts. "We're just hanging out. Come on, *Natasha*!"

She has a point. No one's asked me to sing, and even if they do, I'm a grown-ass twenty-one-year-old woman tonight. I won't be forced to do anything I don't want to.

As we approach, Strand sees us first. His face slips into a smile, like he's waiting for the punch line to a joke only he knows.

"Victoria," he says. That's it. No "hi" or "hey." I'm surprised, *shocked*, that he remembers my name. Then I'm disappointed in myself for caring.

"Strand," I reply in the same obtuse manner.

At the sound of my voice, Krina and Levi both look up. I'm relieved to see Levi smiling, like I'm not a completely unwelcome presence in his life.

"Fancy seeing you here," Krina says in her monotone.

"Sit down," Levi invites us, and the group smushes together so that Annie and I can fit. I'm wedged in between Annie and Levi. The small table in front of the couch is littered with napkins, beer bottles, and empty glasses.

They don't seem too drunk. They seem happy. Then again, I'm not around drunk people very often. Despite my Natasha clothing, I feel prudish. I tuck my hands under my legs and try to take up as little couch space as possible.

"Do you guys want something to drink?" Levi asks us.

I open my mouth to say no, but Annie speaks first. "Water for me, and Victoria will have a whiskey sour."

I stare at her. Did she and the real Mara pull a *Freaky Friday* and switch places?

"Actually, I think I'm okay," I tell Levi, but Annie nudges me in the ribs.

"Bring her one anyway," she says.

"Sure." Levi rises from his seat. "Be right back."

I elbow Annie back when he's gone. "What are you doing?"

"The band needs to see you loosen up," she hisses. "One drink isn't going to kill you."

Another performer is up onstage, a skinny pale guy who sings Ariana Grande in a high falsetto.

"That dude sings way higher than I ever could," Krina comments.

I want to respond and have a lighthearted conversation, but looking directly at the stage makes me break out in hives. It reminds me of the shaky mess I was last week. Luckily, I have Annie to maintain conversation while I battle my posttraumatic stress.

"Do you sing?" she asks Krina.

Krina shakes her head, but her Mohawk doesn't move. "There's a reason I stay behind the drum set."

"What about you?" Annie leans over to look at Strand.

"Only when I drink," Strand says, "but no one wants to hear it."

"Oh, shut up," Krina tells him. She turns to us. "Strand has the voice of a goddamn angel. He just prefers the guitar."

Strand grins at her and doesn't reply, just takes a swig of his beer.

"Will we see you up there tonight?" he asks me, nodding toward the stage.

I try to laugh, but my throat is tight. "Doubtful."

"Why not?"

I shift in my seat, suddenly uncomfortable. The couch is flat and cushionless against my rear. "Sore throat. I think I'm coming down with something."

"Shame." He studies me a little too intensely, and I look away. It's a habit of mine, to avoid eye contact when I lie. When I sneak a glance back at Strand, he's still watching me. I'm grateful when Levi returns with my whiskey sour.

"Maybe a few drinks will dull the pain," Krina suggests, raising her glass to mine.

Annie offers me an encouraging smile, but all I can think about are my parents' faces were they to witness this moment. I think about the D.A.R.E. representatives that come to our school every year to lecture us on the dangers of alcohol consumption. Then I push all of those things out of my mind and tilt the glass to my lips.

I'm not sure what I'm expecting sin to taste like, but when the drink floods my mouth, it's not bitter or harsh. It's like liquid candy. Tangy sugary sweetness. In five minutes I'm halfway through it. I feel warmer. Looser.

I'm bold enough to ask Levi, "So when will you guys decide on a singer?"

"Probably this weekend," he says.

I take a gulp of my drink. "I really screwed up the audition."

At this point I should probably stop talking, but I'm almost finished with my whiskey sour and my head is light, like my brain filter decided to go off duty.

"You didn't," says Levi. "You need more practice, that's all." He blinks at me from behind his glasses and looks so earnest, I start to feel better. Maybe all hope isn't lost.

"Oh, hey! I know you guys!" A girl with cherry-colored hair edges her way into the group. "Didn't you perform at Lauren's party last year?"

She wiggles in next to Strand and continues to talk animatedly. I feel unreasonably annoyed that this girl has invaded our area.

"You guys get groupies?" I ask Levi.

"Strand does," he says, watching the girl as she laughs and pets Strand's arm.

"What about you?"

"Eh . . ." Levi shrugs. "Not really."

"That's surprising," I say, with uncharacteristic boldness. "Some girls really like that Rivers Cuomo look."

"You think I look like him?"

"Yeah, circa *The Blue Album*? Totally. You're rocking the geek chic thing."

"It's the glasses." He pushes them up the bridge of his nose as he says it. I can see Levi having a few of his own groupies. He's not as obviously attractive as Strand, but with his button-down shirt and neatly parted hair, he has his own appeal.

As we speak, Annie is bent over a karaoke songbook, flipping through its pages.

"Don't even think about it," I warn her.

"Speaking of Rivers Cuomo, they happen to have some Weezer in here . . ."

I drain the rest of my glass and stand up. "Not happening." I'm a little dizzy, so I press my hand against the wall for balance.

"Where are you going?" Annie asks.

"I'm getting another drink. You want one?"

"I'm okay. . . ." She studies me. "Want me to come with you?"

"I'm good," I insist, turning to leave. I'm not drunk, but I do feel different. I feel loose, like I could do a little jig and not care if someone saw me. I push through the crowd until I reach the bar.

"Excuse me, sir?" I say to the bartender. "Can I get a whiskey sour please?"

I'm so grown-up right now, I can't even handle it. The bartender shakes a bunch of ingredients together and strains it into a glass, then garnishes it with a maraschino cherry and an orange slice. Moments later, the liquid candy is back in my hands. When I reach the group, Annie is now sitting next to Krina. They're pointing to entries in the karaoke book, so I scoot to sit in between Levi and Strand. The groupie is on Strand's other side.

"This," I announce to no one in particular, sloshing my drink around in the glass, "is delicious."

"It's a little too sweet for me," Levi says.

Strand looks amused. He inches away from his groupie. "You don't drink often, huh?"

"How can you tell?" I ask.

Gulp, gulp, gulp.

"Wild guess."

Whiskey is miraculous. I can now talk to Strand without feeling self-conscious.

"Do you want to try my beer?" he asks me.

"Sure."

It's silly, but when I raise Strand's beer bottle to my lips, I can't help but blush at the fact that his lips have touched the same spot. It seems intimate, sharing a drink with a guy I barely know. Then the beer washes over my tongue, and I almost choke on its metallic taste.

"Blech! Oh sweet lord!" I shudder and hand the bottle back to Strand, then reach for a napkin to dab at my tongue.

Strand's smirk shifts into a real smile. "Are you always that dramatic?"

"It's disgusting," I say.

"To you."

"No. There's no way anyone actually enjoys that taste."

"Is that so?"

"Yeah," I challenge. "I think you drink it to look cool."

"You think I'm concerned with looking cool?"

"Of course you are. Isn't everyone?"

Strand fingers the rim of his beer bottle and sets it back down on the table. "To an extent, maybe."

Strand's new groupie looks me up and down, her expression turning cold. Wow. She views me as competition. Like I would waste my time vying for Strand's attention.

"I'm Victoria," I say to her, trying to look as friendly as possible.

"Diana." She forces a smile.

"Victoria is our potential lead singer," Strand tells her.

She looks less than thrilled at the prospect. "Oh. What happened to the other one?"

"Long story," Strand replies hurriedly. His eyes dart over to Krina, who is preoccupied with the karaoke book.

Levi slaps his hands on his knees and gets up abruptly. "I'm getting another drink. Victoria? Whiskey sour?"

"Sure," I say. "Why the hell not."

I'm a few sips into my second drink, and looking at the stage doesn't intimidate me as much anymore. It helps that the person up there now, screeching through the chorus of "Total Eclipse of the Heart," sucks. I can do better than that. People should *hear* me do better than that. Why do I settle for singing in the shower?

Strand slings an arm around me and leans in so close that our foreheads are practically touching. I try to ignore the annoying fluttering sensation in my stomach.

"Want to know something?" he murmurs in my ear.

The fluttering intensifies. He's sexy, and I'm weak. I can't help it. For a moment I think Strand is about to ask me out or start making out with me, and, maybe it's the whiskey sour, but I am 100 percent okay with both of those things.

"Yes," I say. I'm breathing too hard, like I finished a 5k. Every inch of my skin is overheating in anticipation of what is about to happen.

Strand cups a hand over my ear and says, "He likes you."

I pull away from him. "What?"

"Levi. He likes you," Strand repeats. "How do you feel about that?"

I feel . . . duped. Stupid. Disappointed. It takes me a second to regain my composure after the fluttering stops.

"How do you know?" I ask Strand.

"I know him."

I watch Levi at the bar, trying and failing to get the bartender's attention. He's good-looking enough. Not a sex god like Strand, but maybe that's better. Someone like Strand is too much work to catch, and even more work to hold on to. Would it be so bad, to be liked by Levi?

"What do you think?" Strand watches me intently.

"Why do you care?" I counter, and he looks taken aback. He takes another sip of disgusting beer, still watching me.

"He's my friend," Strand says. "I don't want him to waste his time if you're not interested."

The sad truth of the matter is that I was still hoping for Strand to show a hint of what I was feeling, because I can't believe that kind of chemistry can be one sided. Then again, that's probably how all of his other girls have deluded themselves. The reality is that Strand could have chemistry with a brick wall. Chemistry means nothing.

"I *am* interested," I say with impressive conviction. I turn away before I can overanalyze Strand's reaction.

When Levi comes back with my drink, I try to give him my full attention. No boy has ever shown much interest in me, with the exception of Ryan Arevalo in the first grade. He gave me a valentine that read "i lik yu," and that's been the extent of my relationship experience.

"Having fun yet?" Levi asks, handing me the glass.

I nod vigorously. "Yup," I add for good measure. "You?"

"Yes. I'm glad you came." He gives me the sweetest smile, and I know giving him a chance is the right decision. Chemistry doesn't always have to be instant. It can be learned.

When I look back at Strand, he's blocked by Diana, who has climbed on top of him and is kissing him like she wants to devour his entire face.

Yeah. I definitely made the right decision.

Levi is someone who will focus on me. Strand is someone who will play with my head and make out with another girl seconds later. I can never let myself forget that.

By the time I've finished my third glass, I've fully transitioned from shy Victoria to fearless Natasha. I talk to Levi and Strand as though I've known them my whole life. I tell them about how the first album I ever bought was David Bowie's *Hunky Dory*, and how I sing under my comforter when I feel sad, and how when I'm home alone sometimes I'll dance naked to Beyoncé songs.

That last fact gets me a raised eyebrow from Strand.

I start to realize that my verbal diarrhea could mean I'm a tad drunk, which I didn't think was possible after only three yummy candy drinks. The next thing I know, someone with a microphone calls my name.

"Huh? What?" I say aloud.

"You're up!" a voice in the crowd yells.

"Victoria Cruz to the stage!" the man with the microphone bellows. How the hell does he know my name?

"Yeah, Vi!" Annie hoots, clapping her hands, and I know she's somehow responsible.

"I'm going to kill you!" I yell back at her, but she and Krina just laugh.

I must float onto the stage because I don't remember walking. A haze blankets my mind and my body moves on its own, free to manage itself. Even as I look down on the crowd in front of me, they don't seem real. Instead of hiding from their attention, I absorb it. I drink it up like my whiskey sours.

The pumping riff to "Freedom" begins and I don't need to think or look up at the lyrics on-screen. The song is ingrained in me, and even through my alcohol-induced fog I remember every word. I strut around the stage like I would in the privacy of my own bedroom, and the crowd starts to cheer. The crazier I get, the bigger their response.

It's amazing.

I think I can hear the band yelling my name, and it propels me higher. I need to show them all that I'm not the Victoria who blew her audition last week. When the bridge hits, I sustain my note, holding it until my throat is raw. And then the guitar kicks back in. I jump up and down, whipping my hair around and spitting out every lyric. For the first time in my entire life, I stop caring. I empty all of my frustrations onto the stage until there's nothing left in me.

It feels like I'm only onstage for ten seconds, but I'm panting by the end of the song, and the crowd is screaming for an encore. They love me. When I look over everyone's heads at Annie and the band, they're all standing and pumping their fists into the air. They love me too. And for once, I love me. The real me, not the one in my head.

Chapter Ten

"SUNDAY MORNING"
—THE VELVET
UNDERGROUND

I open my eyes to a room with pale-pink wallpaper and fancy crown molding. This isn't my bedroom. My walls are painted a faded blue. Then the dull ache in my head brings everything back to me. Well, most of it. I don't remember how we got back to Annie's last night. Or what time we left the bar.

My mouth is sticky and dry, my saliva like glue. It's far too bright in Annie's room. The sunlight pierces through the slats in her blinds, projecting fuzzy stripes across the floor. I lift myself off the bed and the room revolves around me—what I can only assume is my first hangover.

"Ugh, this sucks," I say out loud, my voice hoarse. "Annie?"

"Good morning, rock star!" She enters the room, fully dressed and carrying a glass of water. She's annoyingly perky. And loud.

"What time is it?" I ask groggily. "Why is my throat so sore?"

"It's nine in the morning." She sets the water down next to me on the nightstand. "And your throat is sore because you regaled us with five karaoke performances last night."

I squint at her. "I did not. I only sang once."

"False."

My head feels as massive as a beach ball. "How much did I drink?"

"Not nearly enough compared to how wasted you were. You're a real lightweight."

"God." I cover my face with my hands. "What did I do?"

"Well, you sang Beyoncé and then . . ." She smiles fondly, like it's a treasured memory.

No, no. God, please no. Things happen to me when I'm singing Beyoncé. I lose control of my body and mind, I fuse with her spirit. And that's when I'm sober.

"Annie," I demand. "Tell me. Now."

"You got really into it, like belting out the chorus, and then you threw your chicken cutlets into the crowd."

I sink back into the bed and bury my face in a pillow. "You're messing with me."

"I'm not. It was kind of amazing. One of them hit Levi in the face."

I give a muffled groan.

"Don't worry," she says. "Strand and Krina thought it was hilarious."

"While Levi will never let me in the band."

"He looked really impressed up until he was hit . . ."

I feel my breath, warm and reeking of alcohol, against Annie's pillowcase. Not only did I blow the audition, I failed my do-over, too.

"Do you want anything to eat?" Annie asks. "We can go get some bagel sandwiches."

"I can't eat. My life is ruined."

"Hey." Annie pokes the back of my head. "Stop freaking out. You were really impressive last night."

I turn my face to look at her. "Seriously?"

"Yes," she says emphatically. "You were being yourself onstage. No shyness. Now you just need to do it without the alcohol."

Like I've mentioned before, Annie doesn't lie, so I know that whatever comes out of her mouth is the Bible truth.

"I'll work on it," I say.

She gets up, crosses the room, and sweeps open her blinds. The sunlight stabs me in the eyes.

"Time to get up," she says. "You look like hell."

I get home later that afternoon. I'm worried that when I walk through the front door, Mom will immediately know I drank last night. I've hidden every piece of evidence—scrubbed the makeup off my face, brushed my teeth and tongue, taken an aspirin for my headache— and I'm still terrified.

"Did you and Annie have fun?" she asks, taking a seat next to me on the couch.

"Yup." Not a lie.

"I hope you two didn't keep her parents up."

"We didn't." Still technically not a lie. The Lins could sleep through a hurricane.

"You're not very informative today."

"Sorry. I guess I'm just tired." I stare at the TV. She has a telenovela on, and a beautiful woman on-screen slaps a man across his face.

"So what did you girls do?"

My heartbeat quickens. Does she know something, or is this her usual interrogation routine?

"We watched a movie, had some pizza," I say, my voice slightly high-pitched. "Nothing that interesting."

Liar, liar, pants on fire.

"That's nice. You and Annie haven't had a sleepover since middle school."

"Yeah. It was fun."

"I like Annie. She's a good girl."

I'm sure Mom would change her tune if she found out her precious Annie encouraged me to partake in underage drinking last night. I don't say a word, though. As long as Mom believes in Annie's perfection, I am perfect by association.

My cell rings in the middle of dinner on Sunday night. We're eating takeout, except for Matty. He's eating a peanut butter sandwich because Mom said it wasn't worth the fuss tonight. If my parents keep letting him eat whatever he wants because they're too lazy to fight it, he's going to become even more spoiled. Of course, no one will listen when I tell them that.

I freeze when I hear my ringtone, fork halfway to my mouth. Levi. They made a decision.

"Can I take this?" I ask my parents. "Please?" Dad hates when anyone interrupts sacred family dinnertime.

Dad looks annoyed. "Can it wait, Ria?"

Mom shushes him. "Go ahead," she says to me. No one ever calls me, and she looks ready to combust with curiosity.

I carry the phone into my room, unfortunately situated next to the dining room. "Hello?" I answer in a voice slightly above a whisper.

"Hi, Victoria. It's Levi."

"Levi, hey. Listen . . . I'm sorry about—" I glance over my shoulder to find my parents staring at me. When they're caught looking, they guiltily go about eating their food.

"Who's Levi?" Matty calls as I close the bedroom door behind me.

"I'm sorry about your face," I continue.

"Oh, that. It's okay. No big deal." He sounds embarrassed.

"Did it hurt?"

"My cheek's a little red, but I'll survive."

"Okay. Good." It's strange to talk to Levi like this after being so open with him on Friday night. We both sound so stiff and . . . sober.

"Anyway, I have some news for you," he says. "We all talked and we decided we want you to join the band . . . if you're still interested."

I have to squelch the squeal rising in my throat. My energy level is suddenly off the charts, as if I've been held down by an anchor and released with Levi's words. I want to dance around my room, jump on my bed, scream as loudly as I can.

"Victoria?" Levi asks.

"Yes, sorry! I zoned out."

"So . . . you're still interested?"

"Yes! Definitely. Yes."

"Cool. We usually practice in the band room after school. Can you come by tomorrow?"

"Sure." I'll have to figure out a way to bail on cross-country practice.

"I'm looking at the set list," Levi remarks, "and I was thinking that maybe we should add some of what you sang at the Cave."

"Good idea," I agree. "No Beyoncé, though. We can't risk any more cutlet-related violence."

Levi laughs. It's a hacking, coughing sound, like he's trying to expel a piece of food lodged in his throat.

"If we want to stand a chance at Battle of the Boroughs, I need to find the perfect song," he says.

"What exactly *is* this Battle of the Boroughs?" I ask.

"It's the biggest music contest in the city." Levi's voice quickens in excitement. "Hundreds of music acts enter. The winner gets tons of prizes, like a recording session with award-winning producers, a music video, a photo shoot, and a magazine spread."

"Wow," I say, but I fail to match his excitement. All I can muster is fear. I've only recently learned to sing in front of high schoolers. I'm nowhere near ready for professionals.

"Don't worry," he assures me. "The Battle isn't until the end of March, so we have plenty of time to prepare."

"You know," I mention, eager to change the subject, "I can look over my music and see if there are any other songs we might want to work in to our set list."

I expect him to ask me which ones, but he just says, "Oh . . . sure. I can think about it."

"Awesome." I'm already on my computer, adding potential songs to a brand-new playlist.

Levi turns silent for a moment. I check my cell's display to make sure the battery didn't run out.

"Hello?" I say into the phone.

"I'm here. Sorry. Hey, I was wondering something."

"Yeah?" I click on the *The Rise and Fall of Ziggy Stardust* album. There probably aren't any Bowie songs on our set list, and that needs to be rectified.

"Do you have any plans on Saturday?"

"No plans. Why?"

"My parents have tickets to see the London Symphony Orchestra at Carnegie Hall."

"Oh . . . wow." I'm not sure how to respond, because he didn't directly ask me a question. Is he implying he wants me to come with him and his parents? I'm not sure about a family outing. The Schusters sound so refined and sophisticated. So very unlike Jorge and Gloria Cruz.

"They're going out of town this weekend, though," he continues. Ah. "Have you been to Carnegie Hall?"

"No, never. I would love to go."

"Great."

"Is this, like, a band field trip?" I ask.

Levi pauses. "No . . . I think Krina and Strand are busy. Is that all right?"

I realize that Levi is making his move, in the slowest way possible.

"Yeah, no problem," I say, careful not to betray any hint of over-analysis, because this is what normal teenage girls are supposed to do. They go out with boys like it's no big deal. So that's exactly what I'll do too.

After I hang up, I calmly sit back down at the dinner table even though every muscle in my body is vibrating. My parents try very hard to be casual. I can practically see their mental clocks ticking.

After a reasonable amount of time passes, Mom scoops some stir fry onto her plate and asks, "So is this Levi a friend of yours?"

I shrug. "More like an acquaintance."

"Or a boyfriend," Matty chimes in, his mouth full of soggy bread.

"Don't talk with your mouth full," I tell him. "It's gross."

He sticks his tongue out at me, speckled with sandwich crumbs.

"Matty," Mom says sharply.

"You can tell us if you have a boyfriend, you know," Dad says to me. "We'd be cool about it." His tone is light, but he's clutching his fork in some kind of kung fu death grip.

"Levi is not my boyfriend," I say. "No one is my boyfriend."

Dad relaxes the grip on his fork. "Good for you. Teenage boys are a waste of time."

"Oh God, Dad."

"I'm serious. They're only interested in one thing, *tu sabes?*"

My dad can be a total caveman sometimes.

"But we'd rather you tell us if you're dating someone," Mom adds.

"Right," says Dad. "Even though you shouldn't be."

"What is the one thing?" Matty asks.

Mom nudges Matty's plate toward him. "Finish your sandwich, *anda*."

"I was a ladies' man in high school," Dad says to me. "I know what I'm talking about."

I drop my fork onto my plate. "I've officially lost my appetite."

"Does Levi get good grades?" Mom asks me.

"Can we talk about something else?"

"*Ay*, Victoria, you get so worked up. We're just having a conversation."

"I'll be sure to bring you a copy of Levi's report card tomorrow. I'll get his social security number too; that way you can perform a full background check."

"You two must be dating, because you're getting very defensive." Mom eyes me as she takes a sip of her wine.

I press my thumbs against my temples.

"We don't care if you're dating," Dad insists.

"Sure," I say. "You guys could not be more easygoing . . ."

"What happened to his face, anyway?" Mom asks.

"What?"

"You said you were sorry about his face."

I stare back at her. "Seriously? You were eavesdropping?"

Mom and Dad exchange a look. "Not at all," she says. "Don't flatter yourself." She looks away when she lies, just like I do.

Chapter Eleven

"EVERLASTING LIGHT"
—THE BLACK KEYS

I have to quit cross-country. I've missed two practices so far, and now that I'm in a band (I'm in a band!), I'll have to miss a lot more. My parents will never be okay with it. Today I shove these thoughts aside and hide them in the corner of my mind. That can be a problem for Future Victoria. Present Victoria is in a band.

Annie walks me to band practice after school. We're striding across the quad to the Paul Fridman building where band, orchestra, choir, and all other music-related activities are held. Annie informed me that Levi is to the school band what she is to the orchestra. The bandleader loves Levi so much that Levi gets unrestricted access to the Evanston band room when it's unoccupied.

"When are you planning on telling your parents?" Annie pesters me. I've been in a band for about a day and she's already killing my buzz.

"That would be never."

"You have to tell them, Vi. They're going to find out."

"Then I'll make something up."

Annie's face reeks of disapproval. "I think you should tell them tonight and get it over with."

"Not happening."

"Did you at least tell Coach B you're quitting cross-country?"

I stay silent.

"Victoria Cruz, you didn't quit the team? They're at practice right now! Probably waiting for you!"

The thing about Annie is her tendency to drag into the open everything I want to hide. We reach the music building and I pull open the front door. "I'll tell Coach B tomorrow. Give it a rest, okay?"

The Fridman lobby is designed with plush carpets and velvet sofas to soak up noise, and heavy soundproof walls surround each music room. As soon as we walk in, I immediately feel the need to speak in hushed tones.

"I know you," Annie goes on in a whisper. "You're going to put it off, and it's only going to make things worse in the end."

"Which way is the band room?" I interrupt her.

"This way." She heads for the metal staircase that winds three floors up. "Are you listening to me, though?"

"Yes, Annie. For the love of all that is holy."

She doesn't reply, just stalks ahead of me and up the steps. I follow her to the second floor, down the carpeted hallway until we reach a corner room.

This is it. Band practice.

The walls of the practice room are stacked with chairs and lined with arched windows half-covered by drapes. Krina and Levi are already inside setting up. My nerves tingle even though the hard part is supposed to be over. I auditioned already. I'm in. I'm here. So why am I on edge?

Levi gives us an awkward wave. "Hi, Victoria. Hi, Annie."

Thankfully, there's no cutlet-shaped imprint on his cheek. I'm not sure if I'm supposed to go over and talk to him, this boy who asked me out on a date. What are we if we haven't yet gone on said date? How should we act with each other in the meantime? Are we telling everyone else about our plans? I settle for waving back at him, like we're two acquaintances passing each other in the hallway. I immediately feel stupid about it.

Krina mutters a hello. Today her Mohawk is covered by a patterned scarf and she's padding around the room in ripped tights. Her boots are sitting by the doorway.

I say hello to her, keeping my distance, but Annie walks straight up to her without hesitation and says, "So I listened to that Sleater-Kinney album."

I'm surprised to hear this come out of her mouth. Annie never listens to my music. She says she doesn't have time to listen to music for fun, only for educational purposes like violin practice.

Why are Annie and Krina recommending music to each other?

Are they buds now? How is Annie suddenly friends with someone so scary?

I'm not sure what it is about Krina, whether it's the rumors or the Mohawk or the hulking black combat boots. Maybe it's all those things. But mostly I think it's because Krina can look at me and make me feel like I'm five years old playing dress-up in Mom's heels.

"I told you to listen to Sleater-Kinney months ago," I say to Annie.

"I don't remember that."

"Did you like it?" Krina asks her.

"I loved it!" Annie twirls a lock of hair around her finger. "So much rage."

"If you want real rage, listen to 'Rebel Girl.'"

Annie has rage? Since when? I try to edge my way into the conversation. "I love Bikini Kill."

"Yeah," says Krina. "Who doesn't?"

"I'll try them next," Annie replies. Her eyes dart to the mounted clock above the door. "Shoot. I'm late to rehearsal."

"You're what?" I look at her in shock, but she doesn't look back at me. Annie has never been late to anything in her life.

"See you guys later," she calls as she heads toward the door. When she opens it, Strand is framed by the entryway, guitar case in tow.

"Bye, Strand," Annie says as she brushes past him.

Strand nods at her, then catches sight of me. His face brightens. "Chicken Cutlet! Welcome to band practice."

"Can we please not make that a thing?" I glance at Levi.

"It's already a thing. Probably the best moment of my life," Strand says, popping open his guitar case. "I'm almost sad I peaked so young."

"Again, I'm so sorry," I tell Levi.

Levi points to his cheek. "Look—no permanent damage."

"Don't be sorry, be proud," Strand says. "When you whipped out those cutlets and snarled at the crowd? Performance of our generation."

Strand might as well be describing a stranger. Maybe I get a strange Jekyll-Hyde complex when I drink. In my sober reality I don't snarl at people. I smile pleasantly, never wanting to make waves, always seeking approval.

"Was that supposed to be a feminist statement?" Krina asks.

I want to say yes, a feminist statement, not a drunken mistake. Then Krina can stamp her approval on my coolness. Instead, I admit the truth.

"I don't even remember doing it. Annie forced me to wear the cutlets so I'd look older."

"The crowd did love it when you threw them," Levi points out. "Maybe that should be your trademark."

"It could be a protest against the impossible standard of beauty that society forces on women," Krina says.

"I don't think Victoria needs to resort to a gimmick," says Strand as he tunes his guitar in the corner. "Gimmicks are for people without talent."

Was that a compliment?

Krina lets out a small snort and Levi looks at her questioningly.

"Sorry," she says. "I just pictured you getting hit in the face again."

That gets Strand going, and Levi closes his eyes like an exhausted parent.

"Moving on," he says. "We need to talk about our set list." He hands me a thick packet and when I open it, I find a stack of papers clipped together and a flash drive. "The first page is a list of the songs we've been playing. The flash drive has the music in case you're not familiar."

"Wow. Thanks. You're very . . . well prepared." I scan the set list. I'm familiar with most of the songs, but I don't know all of them by heart.

"You have a say in the set list too," Krina cuts in. "Nothing's written in stone."

"Yeah, feel free to chime in." Strand finishes tuning his guitar and looks up at us. "We haven't changed our set list since—"

Abruptly, he stops talking and looks over at Krina, whose face turns stoic.

"It's fine," she says. "Go on."

". . . since she who will not be named," he finishes.

Levi claps his hands together. "Back to the set list. Strand, what's going on with that song you're working on?"

"Not finished," Strand says.

"It's been about a year now . . ."

"Can't rush the process." Strand's voice sounds odd, clipped. He clears his throat, and his normal voice returns. "Have you given any more thought to my other suggestion?"

Levi exhales loudly. "We're not covering Billy Joel."

I raise my eyebrows at Strand. As someone who embodies cool, he doesn't strike me as a Billy Joel fan. Are cool kids listening to Billy Joel now? Or does everything Strand touch become cool, like a King Midas thing?

"Cutlet, what do you think?" Strand asks me.

If he calls me Cutlet one more time, I may actually have to throw one at him. I don't care how good-looking his face is. It could stand to get hit.

"You'll have better luck if you stop calling me that," I reply.

"Billy Joel isn't our sound," Levi protests.

"We can make it our sound," Strand says. "We could do a harder cover."

"Let's just try it so Strand will shut up," says Krina.

"Fine." Levi takes off his glasses and rubs his palms against his eyes. "We'll try it later this week."

Strand raises a triumphant fist in the air.

"Glad that's settled. Can we play now?" Krina spins a drumstick around and around her finger, looking like a sullen baton twirler.

"All right," Levi agrees. "Let's go with 'Just Like Heaven.' You know it, Vi?"

I nod. It's on my Future Wedding playlist. I don't tell the others that whenever I hear it, I imagine myself in a vintage rose-colored wedding dress, dancing with my future husband on a starlit rooftop terrace. In fact, no one knows of my bizarre habit of making mental movies to go with my playlists. Unless my embarrassing alter ego revealed it when I was drunk.

Strand plugs his Fender into the amp, which sounds like it's buzzing in anticipation. Levi and Krina get their instruments set up, and Levi hands me a mic.

I clutch it with both hands and practice breathing through my diaphragm like Annie taught me. My stomach flutters slightly, but it's nowhere near as queasy as it was during my audition. There's still some fear in there, but it's mixed with a large dose of excitement. That dose only grows when Krina smacks her drumsticks together and counts off.

"One, two, three, four!"

The three of them play in unison, and the space is filled to the brim with music. That feeling rises inside of me again, but instead of playing a music video in my head, I feel like I'm living in one. The music bounces off the floor and reverberates through the walls, surrounding me in a loud happy bubble.

My face slips into a smile. Now that I've made it into the band, maybe I can actually enjoy this.

Strand's guitar trails off as Levi handles the bass line before my intro. I take one more gulp of air and open my mouth, not sure what exactly will come out this time.

Miraculously, my voice is steady. No shaking. I look over at Levi, who bobs his head to the music, and my voice grows louder. When Strand's guitar kicks in again, we sound . . . like a band. I didn't expect us to sound like this. Like they could play us on the radio and no one would change the station. My smile grows wider. I possibly look idiotic, smiling so much, but it feels good knowing I can do this. Even when I stumble over some of the lyrics, no one flinches and the music charges forward.

I'm not 100 percent confident. I can't imagine hurling any chicken cutlets or rolling around on the floor like I do in my room—but I'm not the stiff, shaky version of myself from the audition. So . . . that's progress.

When the vocals, drums, and bass fade, Strand ends the song with an improvised guitar riff before strumming the last chord. It lingers in the air long after he releases the strings, and Krina lets out a hoot.

"That was fucking great," she says. "Can we talk about how great we just sounded?"

Levi frowns, loosening his shirt collar. "I think the rhythm could be a little tighter. We were all a little out of sync on the second verse."

Krina waves him off with her drumstick. "You're way too critical."

"Yeah, man," Strand agrees. "Cutlet came to play. We've never sounded better on that."

"I wasn't talking about Victoria," Levi says.

"You should know that Levi is an insatiable perfectionist," Strand says to me. "He'll have you bleeding on the stage."

Being friends with Annie has made me an expert at handling insatiable perfectionists. Because I want to impress Levi, I suggest we run it again. Even though I think we sounded awesome.

Levi looks pleased with my dedication. "Yeah, let's run it again."

We run it five more times. I don't hear much of a difference, although I become more comfortable every time we play. I even put some of my own vocal inflections into the song so it doesn't sound like a carbon copy of the original.

By the end, even Levi, the insatiable perfectionist, seems satisfied. I leave Evanston Academy smiling, which is a first for me.

Chapter Twelve

"NORMAL PERSON"
—ARCADE FIRE

Coach B has never looked more imposing than she does today, her white teeth hidden behind glossy pursed lips. Cross-country practice starts in fifteen minutes, but I'm still in my Evanston uniform, sitting on the other side of her impeccably organized desk.

"We missed you yesterday," she says in her semisweet tone, and I know she wants an official explanation for why I skipped yet another practice.

I look down at my plaid skirt, ironing out the wrinkles with my hands.

"Is everything okay?" she asks.

It's hard to look her in the eyes, all widened with concern, but I force myself to meet her gaze.

"I . . . I wanted to let you know that . . ." I swallow so loudly I swear the whole team can hear it from outside. "I'm quitting cross-country. And I won't be joining track in the spring."

She stares back at me, blank faced.

"I'm sorry," I add.

Coach B leans back in her chair, assessing me. Her lack of reaction is worse than the lecture I imagined in my head.

Finally, she speaks. "I have to say I'm surprised, Victoria. May I ask what led you to decide this?"

I shift around in my seat. "I don't have the time anymore. With homework and stuff. And to be honest, I . . . I never really enjoyed running."

"Your teammates will be disappointed."

I say nothing, but her guilt trip is working on me. Maybe I'm being selfish. Still, I've lived my entire life in fear of letting people down . . . my parents, Annie, my teachers, my team. In the process, the one person I end up letting down is myself. Can't I put me first this once? Can't I hang on to the happy feeling I had after band practice yesterday?

"Is there anything I can do to change your mind?" Coach B asks.

Don't back down now. I think of snarling Victoria hurling her chicken cutlets across a crowded room.

"I don't think so," I say. "I'm sorry."

"I'm sorry too."

I leave Coach B's office, and my rule-following instinct is to change into my workout clothes and join my teammates out on the field. But instead of walking to the locker room, I turn decisively in the opposite direction, toward Fridman, where my bandmates are waiting for me.

Levi sighs when Strand arrives fifteen minutes late to band practice. "Come on, man."

"Sorry." Strand unlocks his case and leisurely sets up his guitar. "I got caught up in something."

"Yeah, Brianna DeVito's throat," Krina murmurs from behind her drum set.

Strand bends his head over his guitar to avoid Levi's glare. I can't believe his nerve, delaying practice to tongue-wrestle another admirer. Strand has no right kissing anyone when we're stuck here waiting for him.

He catches me frowning in his direction. "Did I offend you, Cutlet?"

"No," I reply evenly. "I couldn't care less who you suck face with."

"Then why the schoolmarmy stare?"

"I wish you wouldn't do it on our time, that's all. It's rude and inconsiderate."

Levi's head pops up from behind the music stand, and Krina lets out a low but audible laugh.

I'm a little surprised at the sharpness in my tone. As a people pleaser, I've never chastised anyone but Matty. But I don't back down. I'm filled with an unexplainable bitterness toward Strand and his legion of groupies.

He doesn't speak right away, but he studies me like I'm one of Mr. Davis's equations on the chalkboard.

"Okay," he says finally. That's it. Okay. And he continues to tune his guitar.

Levi gives me a little nod of approval and I swell with hope. Then I look at Strand and feel slightly bitchy. But why should I feel bitchy? I didn't say anything that wasn't true. Maybe it's good for me to put him in his place. Maybe now he'll stop calling me Cutlet.

The rest of the practice goes okay, but one of our songs, "Lithium," needs a lot of work. I hold back on the high notes instead of slicing through them. My voice is limp and my rasp is too contained.

"Take five," Levi calls after we run through the song seven times.

Krina accompanies me to the water fountain outside the room. I need to get some distance from Levi. And Strand.

"What's with the newfound sass?" she asks me as I lean over the fountain and take a mouthful of lukewarm water.

"Do you think I was too mean to him?" I ask, wiping a few drops off my lips. "I feel mean."

"Nah. He's a big boy. And I've never heard a girl talk to him like that. I'm impressed."

"Maybe I shouldn't have snapped at him."

"He'll be fine. Strand's pretty resilient."

"Yeah, but—"

"Okay. Breathe." She raises her palm to stop me. "Has anyone ever told you that you worry too fucking much?"

I consider this. "No, actually. I'm pretty tame compared to Annie."

"Well, no arguments there." She lowers her hand back down. "Has Annie always been so . . ."

"Intense?" I finish.

"I was going to say bat-shit crazy, but sure. Let's go with intense."

"Pretty much," I say. I give Krina a quick history of our friendship and tell her about the time Annie visited a teacher at home to argue her way from an A– to an A.

"Remind me to hook her up with some Xanax," she says.

Back in the room, Levi wants to practice the song one more time. Krina groans and points up at the clock with her drumstick, but Levi ignores her.

"And, Victoria, don't be afraid to let loose on this one," he says to me.

I quietly bristle. I know Levi's trying to be constructive, but I'm reaching my breaking point. He's in full-on dictator mode, and it's throwing me off.

"This is the eighth time we're playing the song," Strand points out. "Not that I'm counting or anything . . ."

"We'll play it five hundred times if we need to," Levi replies.

When his back is turned, Strand pretends to wallop him over the head with the guitar. I try not to smile.

The great thing about being in a band is that when the music is loud enough, it can drown out your thoughts. When Strand strums his guitar and the chords buzz straight through my brain, I can let out my feelings without stopping to process. I spit the frustration and confusion into the mic. And boom, it's instant therapy. The others might be working through their own issues, because we're playing harder than before.

All of us—even Levi, which is saying a lot—are smiling by the time the song ends.

"That'll do for today," he says. It's equivalent to high praise from a normal person.

Strand doesn't say much as he unplugs his guitar, and I almost go over to apologize to him for my earlier comment. Almost. I stop myself.

He *was* being rude, and why should I feel bad for pointing it out? I was being honest. There's only so much I can hold inside of me at once, and some frustrations are bound to slip.

While everyone's packing up their instruments, I let it slip to Krina that Levi and I are going out on Saturday.

"Really," she says. "You and Levi?" She looks surprised by this revelation.

"Yeah."

"Huh."

"What does that mean?" I ask. "Why 'huh'?"

"I don't know. I just didn't see you guys together. Don't you think he's a little . . . tightly wound?"

I study Levi and Strand from across the room—Levi's hair cleanly slicked back, Strand's wild and unruly; Levi's shirt pressed and tucked into his khakis, Strand's tied around his waist, revealing a black undershirt. A rock 'n' roll odd couple.

Levi's traditionally cute. He looks like he could have been an extra on a fifties sitcom. The kind of guy who would buy a girl a dozen long-stemmed roses on Valentine's Day. The kind of guy who would keep your heart safe.

"I like him," I decide out loud to Krina. I feel like I'm convincing myself as much as her.

She gives me that look again, the one that makes me feel small.

"What?" I ask.

"Oh, nothing." She slips her feet back into her heavy black boots. "I have to go meet Annie."

"You do?" I ask in surprise. "Doesn't she have violin practice?"

"Not today. Her teacher's sick."

I feel an unexpected, unexplainable pang of envy. I'm not sure if it's the fact that Annie is bonding with one of my bandmates faster than I am, or if it's the fear of Annie replacing me with a much cooler, more interesting friend. Either way, it's a stupid feeling, and I swallow it down and force a smile.

"Have fun," I tell Krina. Ugh. What a mom thing to say.

She gives me a lazy wave as she heads out the door. When she's gone, Strand wanders over to me, his guitar strapped over his shoulder.

"You were right earlier," he says, looking surprisingly contrite. "I'm sorry I held you guys up."

I have the urge to apologize too, but I stand my ground, remembering what Krina said about Strand's other girls.

"I'll let you off with a warning this time," I say, giving him a mock stern look. "But don't let it happen again."

"Never again, Ms. Cruz." He crosses his heart for good measure.

I want to ask whether he really was tonguing Brianna DeVito, but I think I already know the answer. Brianna's gorgeous, and Strand's gorgeous, so what's to stop them? Besides, it's none of my business.

"So," Strand says. "Any exciting weekend plans?"

"Actually, yes. Levi and I are going to Carnegie Hall."

Levi looks over at the sound of his name, and Strand's expression stiffens before settling into a strange smile.

"What the hell, man?" he says to Levi jokingly. "Why wasn't I invited?"

Levi laughs, but it doesn't reach his eyes. "Only two tickets."

Strand looks at the two of us for a moment.

"Got it," he says. "I guess I'll take a rain check."

There's a sudden tension in the air, and I wonder if Strand is feeling some of the jealousy I felt about Krina and Annie.

"Maybe you two should go instead," I offer, but Strand shakes his head and laughs and I feel stupid for even suggesting it.

"I was kidding," he says. He ruffles the top of my head like I'm five years old. "Enjoy yourself, Cutlet."

Chapter Thirteen

"ARCHIE, MARRY ME"
—ALVVAYS

Levi insists on picking me up at my apartment on Saturday and riding the train with me to Carnegie Hall. This is a terrible plan for a couple of reasons. Levi lives on the Upper West Side, twenty blocks north from Carnegie Hall, so coming farther north to Washington Heights is out of his way. But the bigger reason I'm against his coming here is because he'll have to meet my parents. Which means I have to tell my parents about him.

Levi is a parent's dream, clean-cut and polite, but I think the Cruzes are a potential boyfriend's nightmare.

I fess up to Mom and Dad while they're watching TV in the living room. I wait until they're watching a *Seinfeld* rerun so they'll be at their most happy and unassuming. Mom lets out a loud guffaw at something Kramer says. Then, right when they're mid-laugh, I sit on the couch next to them and drop the bomb.

"Just so you know, I'm going out with Levi tomorrow night."

Their laughter stops abruptly, like they've been put on mute. So much for the casual approach.

Dad grabs the remote and shuts off the TV. Jerry Seinfeld's face dissolves on-screen and we're engulfed in silence. "Excuse me? Just so we know?"

"You have a date?" Mom asks.

"If you want to call it that."

"What else would you call it?" Dad asks tersely.

"An outing between friends?"

Dad scratches the stubble on his chin. "Is this the Leo kid who was stalking you?"

"Levi," Mom corrects him. She turns to me. "Is Levi your boyfriend, Victoria?"

"No. We're just . . . hanging out."

While she and Dad eye me with suspicion, I snatch up the remote and click the TV back on. The silence is making all of this too intense. I need a laugh track to pepper the conversation so I can pretend this is all a good-natured sitcom.

"Where are you two going?" Mom asks. Her voice is measured for optimum feigned indifference.

"We're going to a concert at Carnegie Hall."

Dad's eyebrows almost shoot up to his hairline. "*Coño.* He has the money to take you to Carnegie Hall?"

"They were his parents' tickets."

"I assume he's picking you up here," Mom says. "We need to meet this boy, and you're not going downtown at night by yourself."

"*¿La vamos a dejar salir con ese muchacho?*" Dad mutters to her, like I'm not sitting two feet away from them.

"Hello?" I wave my hand in front of his face. "I'm right here. And I'm fifteen years old. Totally appropriate age for dating."

"So it *is* a date," Mom says.

Whoops.

"Maybe?" I shrug. "I don't know."

"You like this guy?" Dad asks.

I shrug again. Miranda rights.

"We expect you home by eleven," Mom says. "And we're giving you money to take a cab. No arguments."

I sit up a little straighter and try to hide the smile spreading over my face. Does this mean I officially have my parents' permission? Dad slumps in his seat with his arms crossed, and even though his body language doesn't scream enthusiasm, he's not objecting.

"I promise," I say, raising three fingers in a scout's-honor salute. "Home by eleven."

"Does this look okay?" Mom strikes a pose in the middle of my doorway. She's wearing jeans and a black cardigan. Levi is set to arrive any minute.

"Yes, for the umpteenth time," I reply. This is the third outfit she's tried on. Meanwhile, I picked out my cotton lace dress last night. Mom let me borrow her makeup, and I'm sitting in front of my mirror, drowning the zit on my forehead with liquid concealer.

"I want my outfit to look casual, but still say 'I'm the mom,'" she continues.

"Congratulations, you've achieved that delicate balance."

Now one spot on my forehead is two shades lighter than the rest of my face. I pat the edges of the concealer to blend it into my skin.

"Do you need help?" Mom comes over without waiting for an answer, then clicks open her powder and dabs it all over my face. I scrunch my eyes shut so the powder doesn't get into them.

"Don't make me look like a ghost."

"*Ay*, Victoria, I know how to put makeup on."

"I'm just saying."

She pauses, brushing the powder on my cheeks in quick, circular motions. "Can I ask you something?"

It's never a good sign when she prefaces a question with another question.

"Yeah?"

"Have you and Levi . . . kissed?"

She closes the powder jar and my eyes flutter open. Mom and I never had the birds-and-the-bees talk when I was in middle school. All she told me was that when a man and a woman got married, God blessed them with a baby. The whole "having sex" factor was completely omitted. I always worried that she would try to fill in the blanks when I got older. I pray that now isn't that time.

"Mom, can we not talk about this?"

"You can't tell your own mother whether you kissed a boy?"

I busy myself with adding more concealer to invisible blemishes on my face. Anything to avoid Mom's anxious stare. "No, we haven't kissed."

"You'll tell me, right? When it happens? If it happens tonight?"

I lay the concealer on the vanity. She sounds so desperate, like her entire world will come crashing down if I kiss a boy without telling her. It makes me a little sad, so I say yes. Even though I'd rather pull my teeth out than talk to her about my blossoming sex life.

Before our conversation can get worse, the buzzer at the front door goes off.

Dad and Matty rush into my room, and Mom clutches her chest like she's going into cardiac arrest. "That's him!"

"He's here!" Matty shouts.

"Who answers the door?" Dad asks Mom. "Do we both answer? Should I hug him or give him a handshake?"

"A handshake, I think?" she answers. "Or is that too formal? Victoria?"

"How should I know?" I ask.

The four of us are all jittery, and no one is moving to get the door.

Bzzzz. Levi buzzes for a second time.

"*Bueno*, he's a little impatient," Mom observes. "Not a great quality in a boyfriend."

"Answer the door!" I hiss at my parents.

Matty runs to follow them, but I pull him back by the shirt collar.

"Not you," I instruct. Levi doesn't need to be ambushed by the entire Cruz clan.

"But I want to see him!"

I hush him and listen as the door opens.

"Levi, hello! So nice to finally meet you!" Mom gushes in a fake June Cleaver tone.

Dad's voice comes out more stern. "Nice to meet you, Levi. I'm Jorge." He says his name the American way, so that it sounds like "George," not "Hor-hay."

"I think he went with the handshake," I whisper.

"Can I go out now?" Matty whispers back. "I want to see what he looks like."

"Fine," I concede, "but don't embarrass me. You say hi and that's it."

"Okay," Matty agrees.

"Pinky swear it."

We hook our pinky fingers together and Matty bolts out of the room. I take one last look at myself in the mirror. My hair looked big and fuzzy this morning, so I wrangled it into a messy braid.

I bought my dress last year for Matty's school concert, and I haven't had another excuse to wear it until today. It hugs me in the right spots, then turns loose and flowy to conceal some of my bubble butt. Annie has always envied my butt because hers is pancake-flat, but at least she has an easier time finding clothes that fit.

I take a last deep breath, then walk out to the entryway, where Mom, Dad, and Matty are surrounding Levi. When they see me, everyone falls silent.

Levi gives me a small smile. He looks like a fancier version of himself, with a button-down shirt and V-neck sweater. Nerd chic. Cute.

"You look really nice, Victoria," he says. I can't tell if he means it, or if he says it because it's obligatory and my parents are staring us down.

"Thanks," I reply.

He strides over to me and puts his arms around my shoulders. I realize this is a limp attempt at a hug, and in return I give him a stiff pat on the back. If this is what our hugs are like, it doesn't bode well for future body contact. The night is off to a shaky start.

"Well, we should get going," I say after Levi and I unwrap ourselves. My parents gape at us. They've never seen me so much as talk to a boy, and here I am hugging a stranger. I tug on Levi's sleeve, eager to escape their prying stares.

"Levi, do you want something to drink before you go?" Mom asks, regaining her composure. "Water? Tea?"

"No, thank you, Mrs. Cruz."

"Yeah, Mom," I say. "We don't want to be late . . ."

"Here." Dad thrusts a wad of cash into my palm. "For the cab ride home."

"Oh, no, Mr. Cruz," Levi says, holding a hand up. "It's on me."

I see Dad's brain waging an inner battle: take the money back and lose your pride, or save yourself thirty dollars?

"No worries," I tell Levi, slipping the money into my purse. The two of use edge toward the door like trapped zoo animals.

"Good meeting you all," Levi says to my family as I drag him out of the apartment. Mom and Dad hold hands as they watch us go, looking overly sentimental and misty eyed. I can't escape fast enough.

Chapter Fourteen

"BETA LOVE"
—RA RA RIOT

Levi's parents have first tier seats at Carnegie Hall, and I feel like a member of the elite as the ushers lead us past the flocks of people headed for the upper tiers.

I settle into my red velvet seat and swivel around to check out the curved, lit balconies looping around us.

"This is beautiful," I say to Levi.

"It is." He follows my gaze up and grins. "I guess I take it for granted. My parents are members, so we come here pretty often."

"Must be nice." I look up around the venue, racking my brain for something to talk about. I should have Googled first-date topics.

What do Levi and I have in common? In my head I tick off our mutual interests: Evanston, music, Strand, and Krina.

"So what's the rest of the band doing tonight?" I ask.

"I think they're going to the Cave."

The Cave sounds like fun, and I feel a flicker of envy that Levi and I aren't with them, like we're missing out on something. I shake the feeling away. I'm in Carnegie freaking Hall. I should be enjoying this.

I wonder if Strand will sing karaoke tonight. Krina did praise his vocals. More than likely he'll be mashing tongues with another groupie.

When I mention this to Levi, he grunts in agreement.

"How are you two even friends?" I ask. "You're so . . . and he's . . ."

"He's a good guy," Levi says. "Once you get to know him."

"How long have the three of you known each other?"

"I've known Strand and Krina since freshman year. Krina and I were in the school band together, and she and Strand have been friends since grammar school."

"Wait a second. Krina was in the school band with you?" I can't picture Krina in the Evanston band, playing "Louie, Louie" during football games. It all seems too rah-rah for her.

"She quit last year," Levi says. "After she got the Mohawk."

"So you met Strand through Krina?"

"Right."

Our conversation is interrupted when the lights dim and the orchestra swells in a discordant warm-up. I wiggle around in my seat to settle in, gripping my armrests like I'm on a plane about to take flight. I shoot Levi a smile, and he awkwardly pats my shoulder.

When the music starts, it might be the most beautiful sound

I've ever heard. It fills the pockets of space between the seats and rumbles through the ground and up the walls.

I close my eyes and inhale like I can smell it. Listening to music like this is way better than hiding under the covers with my headphones on. This is the way music should be experienced.

"What do you think?" Levi whispers, and I'm yanked out of music dreamland and back into my date. For a moment I forgot he was sitting there next to me.

"Incredible," I murmur. "I'm so happy you brought me."

The music rises around us, but I'm not listening anymore because his hand is sliding onto my armrest and closing around mine. It's a nice feeling, holding hands with a boy who's actually interested in me. We hold hands for the rest of the performance, until our palms are clammy and warm, finally unclasping when the concert ends. By the time we follow the crowd outside of the theater, it's ten o'clock.

"You're taking a cab home?" Levi asks.

"Yup. Parents' orders."

"I'll hail it for you."

But he doesn't move, and neither do I.

"We might have time for a quick walk by the park," he suggests.

"Sure. Yeah. As long as I make my curfew."

In theory, a walk around Central Park is a romantic experience. The trees, the moonlight, the clip-clop of horse-drawn carriages. Reality hits about the same time as the smell of horse shit.

"God, that's powerful," I remark, pinching the edges of my nose together.

Levi does his coughing laugh and takes my hand, the one not

holding my nostrils shut. He leads me to a wooden bench away from the odor.

"Better?" he asks when we're seated.

I let go of my nose. "Just the smell of car exhaust now. We're good."

"Good."

The silence between us could be considered romantic, meditative. It could also be a sign that we have nothing to talk about. But that can't be true. We go to the same school, we're part of the same band. Conversation should flow easily.

I'm nervous, that's all. I need to think of something to say. I can pretend I'm here with Annie.

"Did you look at the music I sent you?" I ask, fiddling with a loose string hanging off my dress.

"Not yet," Levi says. "I'll get to it soon."

"Check out the PJ Harvey song first. Don't you love her? Her voice is so raw."

"She's great."

Whenever I speak, Levi's eyes flicker down to my lips. I'm suddenly self-conscious about how I move them and whether the lipstick I'm wearing has ended up on my teeth.

"Your voice has that edge to it, like hers," he continues.

"Thanks." I smile a closed-lip smile. "I take that as a high compliment."

"You should."

He scoots closer to me on the bench so that our legs are touching. His face is inches away from mine. It wouldn't take much to fill the distance between us. I tilt my face up to his, his tilts down to mine. There's no fluttering in my belly, only a persistent nagging sensation that this moment isn't right, it's too forced, like we're following a script.

"I should probably go soon," I say right before his lips touch mine.

Why? Why did I choose to say that right when I'm about to be kissed? Who cares if I don't feel the fluttering? I should just get it over with and stop expecting everything in my life to be a freaking movie.

Levi straightens up. "You have to go now?"

"Not right this very second . . ."

"Oh, okay." He swallows hard, his Adam's apple bobbing in his throat.

"So . . . ," I start.

"So . . ." He leans toward me again, closing his eyes this time.

Suddenly, his lips are on me. It's what I was waiting for, but it still manages to take me by surprise. I feel a strange sense of relief, like I can check something off my bucket list. I'm finally kissing a boy. In this moment, I am a real, desirable girl. Then it hits me how little I know about Levi. Where did he grow up? What do his parents do? He's practically a stranger to me, yet here he is on my mouth.

The absurdity of it all makes me laugh.

Levi pulls away self-consciously. "What's so funny?"

"It's not you!" I say midlaugh.

"Well, what is it then?"

"It's—" I only laugh harder when I try to speak. "It's me."

"What do you mean?" He looks at me, slightly horrified, so I draw in my breath and suck in my cheeks to try to stop the laughter.

"I'm sorry." I force the corners of my lips down. "It took me by surprise. Let's try it again."

He slumps against the bench. "I can't now. The mood is ruined."

"No! I promise I'll be good. Go."

"I can't just *go*, Victoria."

Shit. I've ruined everything. I see myself in the future, recalling the horrific story of my first kiss. When someone asks me about it, I won't be able to describe it as magical. No fireworks, or poetry, or sparks lighting up in our hearts. Just me: Victoria Cruz, boy-repellant. In an attempt to salvage the moment, I cup Levi's smooth chin in my palms and plant my lips on his. He gives in easily.

Levi does all the right things, which shouldn't surprise me given his perfectionism. He moves his tongue in a clockwise direction and he opens his mouth at a precise forty-five-degree angle. He's all about attention to detail when we rehearse, so why wouldn't that concept apply to his kissing?

We kiss for a few minutes, and when we pull away, Levi has my lipstick smeared over his mouth.

"See? No laughing," I say.

"Thank you." His cheeks turn pink, but he's smiling.

I use my thumb to wipe my makeup off his face. Most of the powder Mom applied so carefully is now a collection of splotches on his nose, chin, and jaw.

Levi glances down at his watch. "You'd better get going if you want to make your curfew."

Krina was right about Levi's dedication to punctuality. He's like a male Annie. I let him pull me up from the bench, and he lifts his arm to hail me a cab. The action strikes me as a classic New York gentleman thing to do. He's perfectly going through the motions of dating, whereas I'm stumbling through them.

As the cab screeches to a stop beside us, Levi opens the door for me and says formally, "I had a good time tonight."

"Me too."

"Even though you think my kissing skills are hysterical."

"I don't," I protest, and I kiss him again to prove him wrong.

"Come on, sweetie," says the cab driver, shattering our picturesque good-bye moment. "You getting in the car or not?"

"Sorry." I squeeze Levi's arm and climb into the backseat. He gives me a bashful wave as he closes the door. When the cab lurches forward, I gaze at him from the car window until he's lost in a crowd of tourists.

When I get home, Dad is already asleep and Mom is waiting for me in the living room, cradling a bowl of popcorn in her lap.

"Well?" she asks.

"Well . . . it happened." I say.

She pats the spot on the couch next to her, and, even though I want to huddle under my covers and fall asleep, I oblige.

"That's all I get?" she asks. "It happened?"

I don't feel like rehashing the details. In all honesty, my first kiss was underwhelming. I think I'm the problem. Too many love songs, too many fantasies. I had unrealistic expectations, so of course Levi couldn't live up to them. Story of my life.

"When?" she asks when I sit down.

"After the concert. We walked by Central Park."

"That's a nice setting for a first kiss."

"It is."

Her eyes turn distant. "You're growing up too fast."

"I'll try to stop."

"I'd appreciate that."

I nod at the TV. "What are you watching?"

"*Anchorman*. It's terrible."

"*Anchorman* is a masterpiece." I stuff a giant handful of popcorn into my mouth, suddenly famished. I wonder how many calories a person burns by kissing.

We watch the movie in silence, the only sound in the room coming from the TV speakers and our random spurts of laughter at Will Ferrell's cartoonish facial expressions.

"He's a nice boy, right?" Mom asks suddenly.

I swallow down my popcorn. "Will Ferrell? I'm sure he's great."

"Funny."

"Oh, *Levi*," I say in mock realization.

"Yes, Levi. He's nice? He's not . . . pressuring you to . . . ?"

"Mom," I groan. "No. He was a perfect gentleman."

"Good." In a show of surprising restraint, she doesn't say anything more. No questions about the date, no mention of kissing, no belated birds-and-bees talk. I'm thankful for the quiet. We sit and watch *Anchorman*, and I start to think that the best part of a date night might be when the date is over and you don't need to work so hard anymore.

Chapter Fifteen

"GIRL"
—JUKEBOX THE GHOST

S trand's hands are clasped behind his head, his long legs propped up on the folding chair in front of him. His face slips into a smile when I walk into the band room.

"*Finally . . .*," he remarks. "I've been here for ages."

"Yeah, yeah." I drop my backpack onto the floor. "Congrats on making it to practice on time, something the rest of us do every day."

"As long as you acknowledge my efforts, I'm satisfied, Giggles."

"Giggles?" I ask, slipping out of my blazer and hanging it on the chair beside me. "What happened to Cutlet?"

He doesn't respond, still smiling, waiting. And then I piece it together. "Oh my *God*. Levi told you?"

"I didn't think the kid was *that* bad." The grin expands, threatening to take over his face.

"He's not bad," I insist. "I don't know why I laughed. And frankly, it's none of your business anyway."

I shove his feet off the chair (even his feet look smug, flopping across the seat) and plop down onto it.

"You're getting defensive," he observes calmly.

"No I'm not. Levi is a great kisser. Thus, I have nothing to defend."

"I believe you."

I roll my eyes at him. "You're trying to pacify me."

"Well, yeah, but that doesn't mean I don't believe you."

"I can't believe he told you . . ." I glare at him. "Wipe that smile off your face, please. It's so annoying."

"Don't lose heart. There's more to a relationship than the physical."

"And as resident man-whore, you would know that how?"

He looks taken aback for a second before his face shifts into a neutral expression. "Maybe I'm not the man-whore you think I am."

"If it looks like a duck and walks like a duck . . ."

Strand gives a short laugh. "Let me see if I understand. Because I enjoy the company of women—"

"Oh God," I scoff. "The company of women? Are you Hugh Hefner?"

"Because I enjoy the company of women," he repeats, "that makes me a bad person?"

"I never said you're a bad person."

"Man-whore doesn't have the best implication."

"When you lead women on, use them, and dispose of them . . . well, it doesn't make you a *good* person, does it?"

"That's what you think I do? Use them?"

"How else would you spin it?"

"I'm up-front and honest with anyone I meet. They know I'm not looking for a relationship."

I think about Janine, and the worship in her eyes when she watched Strand onstage. Even if Strand does tell these girls the truth, some part of them might hold out hope for something more than a one-night stand.

"Not every girl wants a relationship like you do," he says.

"Who are you to assume I want a relationship?"

"Come on . . ."

"What?"

"You're a relationship girl. It's so obvious."

"Maybe your other girls don't want a relationship," I reply, "but I'm sure they at least want their names remembered."

Strand stops, as if considering this. Then, surprisingly, he says, "Point taken."

The swish of the band door interrupts our conversation. Levi enters the room, and my stomach tightens at the sight of him. We haven't seen or talked to each other since Saturday night. Krina comes in behind him, and she does an exaggerated double take when she notices Strand in the room.

"You're on time," she states in disbelief. "Sign of the apocalypse?"

"Ten minutes I've been waiting for you slackers," says Strand.

Levi slaps hands with him, then looks at me. "Hey."

"Hey." I suddenly don't know what to do with my hands. I tuck a strand of hair behind my ear, then pull at the hem of my skirt. I feel Strand's eyes on me.

Levi walks over and gives me a peck on the lips, right in front of the others.

Krina pinches my cheek. "You guys are so damn cute together. Aren't they, Strand?"

"Adorable." Strand gets up from his seat to set up his guitar.

Levi and I smile at each other. There's a difference in me, pre- and postkiss. I feel as though I've been injected with a shot of sex appeal and confidence. I am a kissable person. It's a proven fact.

It comes out in my singing, too. When we rehearse "Lithium" this time, my voice growls and glides at all the right moments. I crouch down during the verses, making myself look demure, pretending there's an audience I'm fooling. Then during the chorus I spring up, jumping around so that my hair flies over my face.

When practice ends, Levi offers to walk me to the subway. The two of us zigzag through the suits and tired-looking nannies cramming into the uptown train entrance.

"So when people ask me about you," Levi says, pulling me away from a stroller hurtling toward us, "what should I tell them?"

"What do you mean?"

"Do I call you my friend or the girl I'm dating or . . . my girl-friend?"

"Do you *want* to call me your girlfriend?" I ask.

"Yes. If you're okay with it."

I hate to admit it, but I think Strand is right. I *am* a relationship girl. A relationship girl who has never had a real relationship, which now strikes me as sad. I've always wondered what it would be like. Why wouldn't I try it with Levi? He's cute, and he's smart, and we both love music. My family approves. There's nothing wrong with him, as far as I can tell.

"I'm okay with it," I say. Then, noting the way his smile wavers, I say, "I'm *more* than okay with it."

Levi places his hands on either side of my face and gives me one of his forty-five-degree angle kisses. When he pulls away, his glasses are foggy.

"I have to get home," he says, glancing down at his watch.

"Okay." I try to hide the disappointment clouding my face. Punctuality bests me again.

"Believe me, I would love to stay and do this"—he motions between our lips—"but I have an essay due tomorrow."

"I have a lot of homework too," I admit grudgingly.

We kiss one more time, right outside of the subway entrance, until a homeless man barks at us to get a room.

Chapter Sixteen

"THE KNOCK"
—HOP ALONG

Something bad is about to happen, because when I walk through the front door of my apartment, Matty bellows, "She's here! Victoria's here!"

Mom comes rushing out of the kitchen, her hair in disarray, cell phone in hand. "Where the hell have you been?"

I stand dumbly in the foyer with my backpack still strapped on. "You're home early," I offer by way of explanation.

"Where were you, Victoria? I was worried sick."

"Does this mean we don't have to go see Dr. Ferber today?" Matty asks happily.

A hazy memory takes form at the mention of Dr. Ferber. Mom

mentioned something yesterday about a doctor's appointment after school. I was supposed to come straight home and skip cross-country practice. Or, what she thought would be cross-country practice.

"I'm sorry," I say, sliding my backpack off my shoulders. "I forgot."

"I don't think you should be mad at her, Mom," Matty says in the tone of a kid who believes his opinion will be taken seriously.

Mom grips the phone so tightly her knuckles are white. "Matty, go play in your room."

He mutters something under his breath as he makes his exit, leaving me cornered by the wild beast.

"Can't you just reschedule the appointment?" I ask meekly.

"That's not the point."

"I'm sorry I forgot. It won't happen again. I'll come straight home."

"I called Coach B looking for you."

A miniature atom bomb explodes in my chest, destroying the remains of my happy mood. It's been ticking away so quietly I forgot that it existed, that I had braced myself for this detonation to happen sooner or later.

Mom's voice comes out eerily quiet. "She said you quit cross-country last week."

"Oh."

"You owe me an explanation."

"I don't want to talk about it." I sweep past her and walk toward my room, on the off chance that she'll leave me alone. But it's silly of me to think that when she's had two hours to stress and worry about my whereabouts. That's a lot of pent-up emotion that needs to be fired at someone.

"Do not walk away from me, Victoria," she says, her voice right behind me.

I stop and face her. "What do you want me to say?"

"I want you to explain yourself, for starters. Why did you quit the team? Why did you keep it a secret?"

"It wasn't a secret . . . I was going to tell you . . ."

"What the hell have you been doing after school for the past two weeks?"

"Nothing."

"Nothing my ass. Is this about Levi?"

"No!"

"Then why did you quit the team?"

"Because I hated it, okay? I hate running, and I was sick of doing something I hated, so I quit." I turn back around, stalking over to my room.

"We'll talk about this when your father gets home!" she yells after me.

"Fine!" I shut my bedroom door and flop onto my bed. I'm too wired to do my homework at the moment, even though I have a chem test on Thursday and Dr. Miller's tests are notoriously brutal. I slip on my headphones, crawl into bed, and snuggle under my comforter. I won't quit the band. I don't care what my parents do to me. My life is finally starting to feel like mine, and I won't give that up.

I make it through an entire playlist before Dad gets home. When I pull the covers off my head, I hear muffled Spanish outside my door. My parents still believe Spanish is this indecipherable secret language to me. Even though I don't speak it fluently, I've been around it my entire life and can understand it almost perfectly.

Mom is telling him I quit the team, and I can't make out Dad's reaction, but I hear the confusion in his voice.

There's a light rap on the door before my parents enter without waiting for a response, which in my opinion renders knocking unnecessary anyway.

"Hi, Ria," Dad says, taking a seat on the edge of my bed. He's still in his work attire—jeans and a polo shirt emblazoned with the company logo.

"Hi." I sit up against my pillows.

Mom sits next to him, hands folded in her lap. "We want you to know that we're not mad you quit the team."

"You're not," I repeat doubtfully. She sounds like she's reciting from a parenting book.

"That doesn't mean we agree with your decision—" Dad starts.

"But that's not why we're mad," Mom finishes.

"Look, I'm sorry I didn't tell you." I study the faded floral pattern on my comforter. "I was worried you'd force me back on the team."

"Victoria, you've lied to us for two weeks," Mom replies. "That's unacceptable."

"Yeah, but I thought—"

"We raised you to tell the truth," Dad says.

"I understand that, I just . . ."

"It's the dishonesty that's disappointing to us," Mom adds.

This is obviously a firing squad, not an exchange. I'll have to let them run out of ammunition. "Okay. I get it."

"I want to know why you quit," Mom says. "And I want to know what you've been doing after school for the past couple of weeks."

I have two options here, each carrying a certain risk. I can lie (again). Make up an excuse for where I've been spending my time. Find another lie to hide the band. Tutoring underprivileged youths? Volunteering at the local homeless shelter?

Or I can tell the truth.

I go for the latter, and I wish I could say it's because of my strong moral compass, but it's because I know my parents' reactions will be that much worse if I'm caught lying again.

I look them in the eyes and I say it. "I joined a band."

It sounds like a joke. The equivalent of telling them I joined the circus or the Harlem Globetrotters. My parents' faces go through multiple stages of confusion.

Dad looks to Mom, then back at me. "What?"

"The school band?" Mom asks. "But you don't play an instrument."

"Not the school band. I sing lead . . . for a rock band. Called Debaser."

"A *rock* band?" Mom's eyes look ready to pop out of their sockets. I can see the associated images flitting through her brain: underage drinking, unprotected sex, hard drugs.

"You sing?" Dad asks in surprise.

"People seem to think so."

Mom gnaws on her pinkie nail, silent for a moment.

"Levi plays bass," I explain, "and there are two other members, Strand and Krina."

"That's . . . not what I expected," Dad says. He has a decisively calm look on his face, but his eyes are a giveaway. They're blinking a little too hard, too rapidly.

Mom's face is nowhere near calm. She's not one to hide her emotions. "I don't understand. Why?"

"Because I like it," I reply simply. "It's fun."

"I'm not sure it's appropriate for a young girl to be in a *rock* band."

"It's not the kind of band you're thinking of, Mom."

"But Mr. Adams said you should have a sport for your college application."

"It's not a necessity."

"What about track?" Dad asks. "You're still going to run track, right?"

"No."

That shreds through his calm. "What do you mean no? You're going to drop everything for a band?"

"I'm not dropping everything. I'm still going to school, getting good grades . . ."

"Good grades aren't enough," Mom says. "And the lying, the quitting . . . I don't like how this band is influencing you."

A rush of heat runs through my body. My voice comes out a couple notches too high. "This is exactly why I didn't tell you guys! I knew you'd react this way!"

"Don't you yell at us," says Dad.

"How can I not yell? You're both sitting here attacking me!"

"No one is attacking you," Mom says. "We're your parents. We have to think of what's best for you."

"The band *is* what's best for me! I'm finally feeling happy, and you're trying to take it away from me!"

"*¡Ya basta, Victoria!*" Dad barks. "You don't raise your voice at us."

Why do parents get to decide when it's enough? And they can raise their voices at me, but I'm not allowed to do it back? What kind of hypocrisy is that?

I'm shaking suddenly. I want to kick them out of my room, smash things around, run away from these control freaks, and never come back. I can't do any of that, so I curl myself up into a little ball, physically shrinking away from them, and glare.

"Your father and I will discuss the situation," Mom says. "For now, you're grounded until we say otherwise."

"What?" I snap.

"You're going to have to earn our trust back," she says. "You'll come straight home every day after school."

I squeeze my eyes shut, feeling the sting of oncoming tears. The last thing I want is to give Mom and Dad the satisfaction of seeing me cry. They're not going to win this.

"You can't ground me," I try to reason. "I have band practice. They're counting on me."

Dad looks at me with a mix of disbelief and anger. "You heard your mom. You're grounded. End of discussion."

That's when I lose control. I think about the band finding a replacement singer. Someone cooler, more confident. Singing with my band. My boyfriend. The tears trickle down my cheeks and along my jawline. I wipe my face off with my shirtsleeve.

"It's not fair," I blubber, reverting back to a little girl.

"We're doing this for your own good," Dad says. The cliché makes me rage. If this is for my own good, why does it feel so miserable? Why are my parents taking away the only thing that's made me happy since enrolling at Evanston?

My mom reaches out to comfort me, but I jerk away. She looks stricken. I don't care. She did this to me, and she'll have to deal with it.

"I'd like to be alone right now," I say coldly. I'm surprisingly calm considering what I really want to do is scream profanities at them for destroying everything.

I turn my back to them without waiting for a response, and they wordlessly exit my room. After the door closes, I turn my music back on, and it feels like the tiniest of victories. They can prevent me from making music, but they can't prevent me from listening to it. Angry music, with lyrics that would make them clutch their imaginary pearls.

I fall asleep before the music stops.

Chapter Seventeen

"I'M NOT PART OF ME"
—CLOUD NOTHINGS

The next morning I slip a note into Levi's locker, calling for an emergency band meeting at lunch.

Annie notices something's wrong as soon as she spots me in the hallway. I know I look rough. I got three hours of sleep last night. My eyes are bloodshot, my hair knotted and wild.

"Are you okay?" she asks, reaching for my shoulder.

"My parents found out," I say in a flat voice. "About the band."

Her eyes widen. "What did they say?"

"Let's see. They're disappointed in me, they think I'm a liar, I'm grounded for the foreseeable future . . . oh, and I might have to quit."

Annie fiddles around with the ends of her hair the way she does when she's deep in thought. "There has to be something you can do. A way you can change their minds."

"I'm working on it, but . . ." I raise my shoulders in defeat.

"They'll come around. You have to let them calm down a little."

Annie's gotten to know my parents well during the course of our ten-year friendship. She was there for the Battle of 2007, when I ate all my Halloween candy after Mom told me not to and I threw up all over our newly remodeled living room carpet. She also witnessed the Hair Debacle of 2010, when I decided to cut my own bangs and ended up with a crooked slump of hair sitting on top of my forehead. Even the hairdresser who we paid to fix it helplessly suggested a strategically placed headband.

My parents and I were due for another blowout, I guess. But this time I have more at stake.

At lunch I wait until we're all seated together. Levi takes my hand underneath the table and my stomach sinks. Will I still have a boyfriend if I'm forced to leave the band? Or is the band destined to be our only shared experience? The sole reason for my appeal to Levi?

"What's this about, Cutlet?" Strand asks. He actually looks somewhat concerned.

Maybe Strand and Krina will vote me out of the band, thinking I'm not worth the trouble. Greg is probably still available to sing lead. Greg with his stupid beard and perfect pitch.

I stare at Krina's sandwich, hummus and red pepper, and say the words quickly, avoiding their faces. "My parents found out about the band and I, um . . . I'll probably have to quit."

121

There. The words are out there, floating in the universe. The possibility of me leaving is real now.

Levi lets go of my hand. "But I just booked a gig in two weeks!"

"Screw that," Strand says. "We can cancel the gig. Or reschedule."

"Yeah, the bigger issue is keeping Vi in the band," Krina adds.

I look at each of them in surprise. I wasn't expecting either to rush to my defense. Not Krina, who is perpetually indifferent, and Strand, who I nag and scold.

Meanwhile, my boyfriend stays silent. I look to him for support, but he won't meet my eyes.

"We need a plan," Annie says.

Krina chews thoughtfully on a piece of her sandwich. "Give your parents a few days to cool down. You need to prove to them that nothing's changed."

"And then what?" I ask.

"Negotiate," Krina replies. "It worked on my parents. They freaked out when I joined the band. I studied medicine in India over the summer so they would think I was still on the PhD path."

"But you're not?"

"Hell no. But they don't need to know that."

"In the meantime, try not to piss them off," Strand says. "Be the model daughter for a few days."

Levi has turned his body slightly away from me. His fingers are intertwined, except for his index fingers, which are resting on his chin. He looks deep in thought. What those thoughts are, I wish I knew.

"I can help you practice for when you talk to them," Annie offers.

"Thanks, guys," I say. "I appreciate the advice, but I don't see them backing down."

"Hey." Krina points her sandwich at my face. "Failure is not an option here."

Strand offers me half of his chocolate chip cookie. It tastes like wax and sugar. "Yeah, Cutlet. You're stuck with us whether you like it or not."

"You guys are so cheesy," I tell them, but I feel strangely sentimental, like I'm seconds away from crying.

For the rest of the week I follow their advice. I rush home after school, even getting a head start on my homework while I'm sitting on the train. I help my parents cook dinner at night. I make Matty peanut butter sandwiches for dinner. I hand him his sandwiches without calling him a spoiled brat, which takes plenty of restraint.

When we're finished with dinner I stay in the kitchen to help Dad handwash the dishes. He passes me a freshly rinsed plate and I dry it with a terry-cloth rag, peering up at him for some indication that the tide has turned, that my good deeds have earned me back my band.

I spend the weekend in my room, catching up on schoolwork. As much as I hate to admit it, I've let some things slide in the wake of joining the band and dating Levi.

Levi sits with me and Annie at lunch now. So do Strand and Krina, most days. It's my only contact with them now that I'm missing band practice. I update them on my interactions with my parents, and we analyze the data for signs that they're giving in.

They seem confident that my parents will let me back in the

band before our gig. Well, except Levi, whose face crumples with worry whenever the subject is brought up.

I want to go on a real date with Levi again. Since the grounding, the only real time we have together is our lunch period and any free pockets of time in the school day. If we're in the library, we'll head to a section that people rarely visit, like Linguistics, and make out against the stacks. Levi's anxiety about the band seems to make him more passionate.

Our make-outs are still prudish by most standards. Levi's hands run over my waist and lower back, but never below the belt. I keep mine clamped around his neck. It seems wrong to go farther when there's a chance that Mrs. Hester, our seventy-year-old librarian, could find us groping each other against *The Changing English Language*.

On the whole, I've been a respectful and well-behaved young adult. My parents seem to have cooled down. They're back to smiling at me, calling me their syrupy Spanish nicknames. It's me I'm worried about. Underneath my perfect child exterior, I'm ready to crack.

My life is quickly reverting to the bleak, stodgy routine it was a couple of months ago.

The band is practicing without me, and we're still adding new songs to our set list. I know it has to be done. They need to hash out chord changes, and Levi is checking for kinks in his arrangement. Strand is taking over the vocals until I come back.

"Don't get too used to it," I tell him, only half joking.

He reassures me that he's strictly a guitar guy and would never be able to pull off the chicken cutlets like I do.

Still, I worry.

Chapter Eighteen

"CLASS HISTORIAN"
—BRONCHO

At dinner Mom mentions that Jessica is in a tough spot. Matty is eating at a friend's house tonight, so the three of us are spared the usual headache that goes along with our meal.

"Who's Jessica?" I ask.

"You know Jessica," Dad says.

"Jessica," Mom stresses, like repeating her name with more emphasis will help jog my memory.

"Again, who's Jessica?" I ask.

"Your dad's second cousin's daughter."

"We went to their house in Jersey a few years ago," Dad reminds me.

I vaguely remember a two-story colonial with a pool in the

backyard. A girl with wide-set black eyes and silky dark hair hanging down to her waist.

"Anyway," Mom continues, "Jessica's having a quinceañera in February."

I can't help the roll of my eyes, which luckily goes unnoticed, because perfect daughters don't roll their eyes.

A quinceañera is the Latin American equivalent of an American sweet-sixteen party on crack, except we celebrate when a girl turns fifteen years old. It's a cheesy, overpriced spectacle involving tacky ballroom gowns, towering hairstyles, and video montages set to sappy Spanish ballads.

Krina would find it all horribly sexist. I may find it sexist too, among other things.

Mom and Dad gave me the option of having a quince when I turned fifteen last year, and without a second thought, I turned it down. I think they were both relieved at not having to scrounge up thousands of dollars for an overblown birthday party.

"What's the problem?" Dad asks Mom in between mouthfuls of mashed potatoes.

"She needs more couples for the court. Clarita asked if I knew anyone."

Mom innocently pats the corner of her mouth with a napkin, training her eyes on Dad before letting them drift over to me. Then, as if it's just occurring to her and not a thought-out manipulation, she says, "Oh, Victoria, maybe *you* can volunteer!"

I open my mouth, ready to argue, and then snap it shut. The perfect daughter doesn't argue. If I put up a fight, there's no chance my parents will ever let me back in the band. Besides, if I know Mom, she's already told Clarita yes on my behalf. Refusing would make her look bad.

"What would I have to do?" I ask cautiously.

Mom tilts her head in feigned nonchalance. "Go to a few rehearsals, dance with a partner, wear a princess dress . . . it could be fun."

I take a sip of water, swirling a piece of ice around with my tongue. Fun. Sure.

"Would we have to buy the dress?" Dad asks, frowning.

"Of course," Mom says.

"Sounds expensive," he mutters.

"Jorge, *por favor*." She silences him with a death stare and turns back to me. "Ria? What do you say?"

I mentally adjust my perfect daughter halo and slap a smile on my face. "Sure. I'm happy to help *Jessica*."

"Good," she says. "Ask Levi tomorrow."

I take a piece of Cuban bread and slather it in butter, pretending not to notice the way Dad shakes his head in disapproval. "Ask him what?"

"To partner with you."

I'm having trouble processing her words. "Partner . . . wait, what?"

"*Por dios*, Victoria, you can't dance in a quince by yourself."

"I thought Jessica only needed girls."

"No, no, no. She needs couples. I thought you could ask Levi."

"I can't ask Levi to be in a quince with me!" I try to imagine Levi surrounded by powdery pink dresses and old women kissing his cheeks while rattling off Spanish. The two images refuse to merge.

"Why not? He's your boyfriend, isn't he?"

"Well, yeah, but—"

"But what?" Mom presses. "These are the kinds of things that boyfriends are supposed to do."

"We've only been dating for a few weeks," I say. "I don't even think Levi knows how to salsa dance."

Mom tears off a chunk of my bread, even though she's on a diet this week. She claims it's not cheating when it's my food she eats.

"You don't know how to salsa either," she points out, popping the bread into her mouth.

"Yes I do!" I act affronted.

"You can move your hips, but you don't know the steps or the turns. That's why you guys will have rehearsals."

A perfect daughter would ask her boyfriend to do this. She would smile and nod like it's no big deal. I stuff more bread into my mouth, eating away my annoyance, filling up the pockets of my cheeks so I can't talk back. The imaginary halo above me dims and fades.

Chapter Nineteen

"STRANGE"
—BUILT TO SPILL

I wait until the end of lunch to ask Levi about the quince. For some inexplicable reason, the idea makes me nervous. I can't predict his reaction. He might laugh in my face or freak out and break up with me on the spot.

"I have a huge favor to ask you," I say to him while the others are talking, my voice low.

"Sure, go ahead."

I lick my lips, which suddenly feel cracked and dry. "Have you ever heard of a quinceañera?"

"Oh God, don't tell me you're having one of those." Krina looks over at us with an expression of deep disgust.

"It's not mine," I say defensively. "I'm already fifteen. It's my cousin's."

"Okay, hold on." Levi raises his palm. "What is a quince-whatever?"

Annie opens her mouth to explain, but Krina cuts her off. "It's a party that signifies a teenage girl is on the market, ready to be purchased for marriage."

I bite down on my cheek. The last thing I need is for Krina to go on a rampage against quinceañeras and turn Levi against them.

"That's not what it is anymore," I tell her.

"That's how it started. That's what's behind it."

"Easy, Krina," Strand says, but the corners of his lips twitch like he's fighting a laugh.

"Can you put a lid on the feminist agenda for one second?" I ask. The sentence flies out of my mouth before I can distill it.

Crap. No one talks to Krina like that, especially not me. I don't talk to *anyone* like that. The thing is, I partly agree with her. The quince tradition is firmly mired in sexism, yet somehow I have turned into its defender. It's one thing for me to bash my culture—it's another for Krina to do it.

I brace myself for the fallout, but Krina doesn't say a word. Her face dips into a scowl.

"It's kind of like a sweet sixteen," I explain to Levi. "I'm one of the girls in my cousin's court, and I need a partner."

"Okay . . . ," he says slowly.

"A male partner."

"Ah."

I try to analyze his expression. Not thrilled, but not completely horrified.

"So . . . what exactly would I have to do?" he asks.

"You get to wear a tux!" I say with scary enthusiasm. "Like James Bond!"

I fail to mention that the tux will probably be white and paired with a tacky pastel-colored tie. Decidedly unlike James Bond.

"I wear a tux and walk you around?" Levi confirms.

"Walk . . . dance . . ."

"Dance?" he echoes.

"Huh?"

"Dance?!"

"Okay, yes, dance," I admit. "But there will be rehearsals!"

"Rehearsals?"

"Why are you parroting back everything I say?"

"Levi doesn't dance," Strand comments, plucking a blueberry muffin off his plate. "He despises it."

"It'll be easy," I tell Levi. "It's all choreographed."

He sinks down into his chair and lowers his chin to his chest. "When is it?" he asks without looking up.

"February twenty-seventh."

The date is still a couple of months away. By committing to this, Levi is essentially committing to us, to staying together at least until then.

He lifts his head, and his facial features loosen in relief. "Oh. I can't do it, Vi. I'm sorry."

I'm keenly aware of Strand, Krina, and Annie still watching us, an audience to my current humiliation. I knew Levi wouldn't love the idea of a quince, but I never dreamed he would outright reject me in front of everyone.

"Why not?" I ask, my voice wilting a little.

"Evanston Band competition," Levi answers. "We're going to be in DC for a week in February."

"You can't . . . I don't know, leave early? Or anything?"

"I can't, Vi. I'm the only bassist they have. I'm sorry." He shifts his face into an appropriately sorry expression, but I see the relief seeping through the knitted brows and downturned mouth.

Strand clears his throat. "I can partner with you."

We all whip our heads around in unison to look at him. He's slouched in his seat and flashes me a bright, possibly mocking smile.

"Not funny, Strand," I reply.

"Who's being funny? I'll do it."

I stay silent for a beat, waiting for the punch line, but it never arrives. "You're serious?"

"Yeah, why not? Could be fun."

"You realize you'll have to salsa dance. Come to rehearsals. Learn choreography."

"I'm not a half-wit, Victoria. I can handle a few dance steps."

It's not the dancing I'm worried about. It's Strand's inability to commit, as evidenced by his flavor-of-the-week dating style.

Levi is fully on board with the idea, since now he's off the hook and can reject me guilt-free. "Great!" he says. "So if Strand is in, everything works out."

"It sure does," Strand agrees. "Right, partner?" He turns to me with a positively gleeful expression.

"Right," I mutter.

I refuse to call him partner. I'd be better off partnering with Matty.

Chapter Twenty

"BONES"
—RADIOHEAD

It hit me this morning, while I ate my peanut butter toast. While Dad poured soy milk over his cereal, and Matty tried to play his 3DS under the table before Mom snatched it up from his skinny fingers.

My parents will never let me sing in the band. I've been fooling myself this whole time.

Everything is exactly how it was, the way they want things. I even asked them, point-blank, if they came to a decision. They made their excuses, like how Dad's been busy with work and they haven't had a chance to talk about it. Then they exchanged a look, a look that gave me my answer. In fifteen years, I've become an expert at reading my parents' faces. I know when they're biding their time, waiting me out in the hopes that I'll forget. Like this band thing is some dumb teenage phase that I'll grow out of.

"Victoria?" Mr. Davis's voice interrupts my thoughts. He's wearing his white button-down shirt today, the one that accentuates the sweat stains. "Can you find the value of x?"

It's been twenty minutes since I stopped paying attention. I can always find the value of x without a problem, but today the equations on the board blur together in a jumble of unrecognizable symbols. Next to me, Annie cups a hand around her lips and mouths the answer, but I can't focus on her long enough to interpret it. I'm so *tired*. It's like I've used up all my strength being the perfect daughter, and I don't have enough left to be the perfect student.

"No," I say.

Mr. Davis blinks slowly at me. "Would you like to try?"

I take a deep breath and squint at the board, then sink back into my seat. Still gibberish. I'm exhausted from the effort it takes to wake up, to sit through eight periods of school and pretend I care about any of this.

"No." The word pops out of my mouth again before I can stop myself. Snorts of laughter hit my back. I'm not trying to be a smart-ass, but I know that's what it sounds like.

It's horrible the way Mr. Davis stands there, staring at me like I've let him down. I am the girl who finds x. I take diligent notes and pretend to laugh at his math puns. Sometimes the laugh is genuine, like when he came back from a weekend in the Bahamas and said,

"What happened to the pasty math teacher who sunbathed too long? He became a *tangent*."

I'm *that* girl, not the slacker who makes his job harder.

Annie's hand pops into the air, but he ignores her. I shoot her a grateful look for her failed distraction attempt.

Mr. Davis doesn't say anything. He rips a slip of paper from a pad in his pocket, scrawls something onto it, and drops it onto my desk. I know what it is without looking at it. A detention slip. The only detention slip I've gotten in my entire life. My face burns in shame as I fold the paper into a tiny triangle. I make it smaller and smaller, wishing I could make it disappear like a magic trick.

Detention at Evanston means sitting in complete silence for an hour after school. No cell phones, no books, no access to the outside world.

"I still don't understand," Annie says as she walks me to Mr. Holmes's classroom. He's the detention monitor today. "Didn't you see me mouthing the answer? Twenty-seven!"

"That's not the point, Annie," I answer, picking up my pace. It's impossible to lose her. She's like a tiny Chihuahua nipping at my heels.

"Why didn't you tell him you didn't know the answer?"

"Because I'm an idiot."

"You're lucky that detentions don't go on your record," Annie goes on. Her short little legs struggle to keep up with my long strides. "Otherwise, kiss Harvard good-bye."

Yeah, that would be a shame, wouldn't it.

I still feel awful about what happened. I didn't mean to disrespect

Mr. Davis like that. He's a nice man, even though he'd benefit from a stronger antiperspirant. It's not his fault I'll never care about the value of x. I apologized to him after class, hoping it might make me feel better, but it didn't. When he asked me what happened, I told him the truth—that I don't know what came over me. I still don't know.

Annie and I round the corner, stopping in front of Mr. Holmes's classroom.

"Text me when you're out," she says, giving my arm a squeeze.

"I will," I promise.

She runs off to live her responsible life, and I turn the doorknob, ready to fulfill my new destiny as a juvenile delinquent. I step into the classroom, which is uncomfortably warm and smells of discarded tuna salad. Mr. Holmes is half-asleep at his desk, his face hidden behind a giant hardcover. I jot my name down on the sign-in sheet in front of him. When I turn around, I spot Krina and Strand right away, slouched in the back row and giving off deep *Breakfast Club* vibes. They look too comfortable here.

Strand straightens when he notices me, his mouth falling open in surprise. Krina practically chokes with sudden laughter.

With my face tipped toward the ceiling, I march to the back of the room and take a seat at the empty desk between them. I zip open my backpack and take out my math homework, ready to find the crap out of x and make things up to Mr. Davis.

Immediately, Strand leans over and whispers, "Didn't know you had it in you, Cutlet."

I stare straight ahead. "Shut up."

"What happened? Get caught with a sherm stick?"

I have no idea what a sherm stick is, but I'm not giving Strand the satisfaction of asking about it. Instead, I fix Strand with a menacing stare. Or, my best attempt at one. It clearly doesn't work. He can't stop grinning, and Krina has to put her head down on her desk to muffle her laughter.

"I don't find any of this funny," I whisper to them.

"Relax," he whispers back. "Everyone gets detention at some point. It's practically a rite of passage."

"Not for me."

Mr. Holmes peers at us from behind his book. Strand and I clamp our mouths shut, staring at different spots in the classroom. When Mr. Holmes goes back to reading, Strand scoots closer to me.

"It's all right," he says in a low voice. "He'll go to the bathroom in two minutes and stay there for a while."

"How do you know?" I murmur.

"Twice a day. Once right before first period, and once in the afternoon. He's freakishly regular."

"Gross."

Sure enough, two minutes pass by and Mr. Holmes rises from his desk. He takes the book with him, so it seems he's in it for the long haul.

"Okay," Strand says in his normal volume when the door closes behind Mr. Holmes. "Let's hear it."

I bend over my homework. "I don't want to talk about it."

"Oh, come on," Krina says, finally calm enough to speak. "It's *you*. It couldn't have been that bad."

The words send a flare of annoyance through me. I'm good at underestimating myself, but I don't like when other people do it. It makes me feel predictable.

"I get it," I say. "You guys are the badasses, and I'm the good girl."

"Good girls don't sing Zeppelin like you do," Strand says, leaning back in his chair. "But you're right about me and Krin. We're total badasses."

I meet his eyes, and they're twinkling in amusement. He's mocking me again. Wonderful.

"Well, what are *you* guys in here for?" I ask. I know Krina's reputation, but I'm curious to hear what the newest addition to the Evanston rumor mill will be.

Krina lifts an eyebrow at Strand.

"Go ahead," he says with a wave. "Tell Cutlet what badasses we are."

Krina motions for me to come closer. "Strand and I were caught . . ." She lowers her voice dramatically. I find myself leaning in to her, bracing myself for the impending shock. Caught what? Having sex? Doing drugs? Stealing a test? "We were caught . . . *eating*. In the *library*."

I narrow my eyes, looking from her to Strand. "You're messing with me."

"Nope." He pulls a Ziploc full of cereal from his blazer. "Cheerios. You want?"

"You two got detention for eating Cheerios in the library?" I confirm in disbelief.

Krina shrugs. "We were hungry."

My face cracks into a small smile. Getting detention for such a dumb reason makes Strand and Krina a little less untouchable. I reach my hand into the bag and pull out a handful of cereal.

"Okay," Krina says. "Your turn."

I look down, pausing to break a Cheerio in half, straight down the middle. "I'm here because I refused to do a math problem in class. 'Talked back to a teacher' is what it says on my slip."

Strand gives a low whistle. "Damn, Cruz."

"Who do you have?" Krina asks. "Davis?"

I nod.

She flicks her hand. "Asshole with a micro penis."

"He's not so bad," I say. "I deserved the detention."

She twirls a multicolored string bracelet around her wrist and looks at me pensively. She's uncomfortable. The sight of an uncomfortable Krina is foreign to me.

"What?" I ask.

Krina shifts around in her chair. "Nothing, just . . . look, I'm sorry for what happened yesterday."

"What about yesterday?" I ask.

"I was an ass to you. About the quince. Annie says sometimes I can come across as 'insensitive' or some bullshit."

"You weren't an ass," I reply automatically.

"I was. It's fine. I know I can be."

"Maybe a little. Like the cheek of an ass."

"Okay, then I'm sorry for being an ass cheek."

"I get it," I say. "I mean, I chose not to have a quince for the reasons you mentioned. It's totally sexist, and it's a huge waste of money."

Krina lifts her shoulders. "But I shouldn't have been so harsh.

I've never even been to one. And besides, just because quinces started for terrible reasons doesn't mean they're terrible now."

"I have to wear a hoop skirt," I say.

"Jesus. Now I'm really sorry."

"I told you. But I appreciate your efforts to be positive."

"I try. I can't promise I won't mock, though."

"You and me both," I say, and a hint of a smile peeks through her dark painted lips.

Krina being nice to me is something I didn't expect. She's not supposed to be a nice girl, according to the general consensus. Fierce? Yes. Tough? Without question. But when someone you've pegged as unapologetic goes and apologizes to you, it makes you rethink your assumptions.

Strand, who has been silently observing me throughout our conversation, suddenly says, "I've never met anyone who eats Cheerios like you."

"What do you mean?" I ask. I'm cradling a handful in my palm.

"You break each one in half before you eat it."

"So?"

"So one Cheerio is too large?"

"I'm savoring it."

"It's ridiculous. I can't even watch."

"Then don't," I say, tossing one at him. He swiftly catches it in his mouth, because he's Strand, and everything he does is effortlessly cool.

Krina throws one at him for good measure, and we both laugh when it gets caught in his hair.

"Dude," he protests.

"What?" she asks. "You can't even see it in there. Your hair is like a black hole."

I come to his defense, fluffing up my own frizzy hair. "Don't worry, Strand. I get your struggle."

"We're gonna have to get Mohawks so we can be super cool like Krina," he replies.

Krina runs her hand over the top of her hair's spiked edges. "You losers wish you could pull this off."

Strand and I take turns trying to land a Cheerio perfectly on top of her Mohawk's highest point until Mr. Holmes walks back into the room, readjusting his pants. I try not to laugh out loud and end up making a strange choking sound, which sends Strand and Krina over the edge.

"Is there a problem?" Mr. Holmes asks us.

I shake my head while they answer, "No, sir," in strained, polite voices.

When Mr. Holmes sticks his nose back into his book, the three of us exchange secret smiles. I think if there's one good thing that's come out of detention, it's feeling slightly less intimidated by them both. Like when you're a kid and you're old enough to realize the monster by your bed is really just a coatrack.

Chapter Twenty-One

"RAISING THE SKATE"
—SPEEDY ORTIZ

It's never a good sign when both of my parents ambush me at the same time. I'm in the middle of my newest playlist, headphones lodged in my ears, when I notice them standing over me. Their faces are closed curtains drawn tight, and I know what's coming.

"We got a call from Principal Tishman," Mom says.

My chest tightens, like a bowling ball is crushing my sternum.

"*Detention*, Ria? Detention?!"

I can't bring myself to look at either of them.

"Explain yourself," she says. "Right the hell now."

"I should have told you," I say in the world's smallest voice, "but—"

"Detention," she says again. "For talking back to a teacher."

"I didn't," I say. I want to explain what happened, that I was tired and the word "no" came out without thinking, but Dad stops me.

"You're going to sit and listen," he says firmly.

I obey. I can't argue with my dad when he's on a power trip. Mom throws her hands up into the air, her eyes brimming with tears. Dad's are watering as well, and I have to look away.

I now know what the worst feeling in the world is. It's making your parents cry. I am officially a monster.

"I don't even know where to start, Ria. When your school called, I thought there was a mistake." She paces around my desk. "Your teachers have always loved you. You're a sweet girl, you're polite . . ."

I nod dumbly. "I messed up. I'm sorry."

"We didn't raise you to talk back to an adult. Not to us, not to your teachers."

I wish that I could explain to them how I've been feeling, but I know they won't understand. They didn't grow up in a world with Evanston in it.

Mom gives Dad a nudge, and he rubs his hands together. "Ria, your mom and I talked about . . . things."

"The band," I clarify.

He nods, his lips forming a straight flat line. I don't want to hear him say it, so I say it for him.

"No band." My voice sounds strange, expressionless. They look sorry, which should make me feel better. Instead, it makes me more depressed. They're sorry for something they can fix.

"It's inappropriate," Mom fills in. "I don't like what it's making you become."

I look down at my toes, scrunch them against the carpet. "The band has nothing to do with any of this."

I know it's not true. The band has everything to do with how I'm acting, just not in the way they think. When I have it in my life, I feel better. When I don't, I turn into someone I don't like.

"But we were thinking," Mom continues, "that if you insist on singing, maybe you can find a healthier outlet. Did you know that the Evanston school choir competed at Disney World last year?"

She pauses, expecting me to lose my shit over Disney World. As though I'm five years old.

"Or think about getting back to running," Dad says. "Now that you've taken your little break."

The pain in my chest sharpens. That's what he thinks I was doing? Taking a little break?

"You're too good to give up on your running, Ria. Coach Bridget told us you could go to Nationals."

Mom brightens. "You could even do both! Track *and* choir!"

Dad snaps his fingers. "Great idea."

"G-A-A-S," Mom recites. "Your grades are good. You'll have athletic and artistic. We just need to find you some community service. Maybe over the summer."

"She can tutor," Dad says. "There's that school on a hundred and sixty-eighth."

"No, you're thinking of the one on one sixty-second."

"Glo, I pass it every morning on my way to work."

"Jorge, it's on a hundred and sixty-second. Daniela works there."

Oh my God. I can't listen to this anymore. I stand up and close my laptop with excessive force, and they jump, like they forgot I was still sitting there. They don't need me to have this conversation anyway. What would I know about my own life? They could ask, but they don't.

"I'm tired," I announce. "Can I go to bed?"

"Are you . . ." Mom doesn't finish the sentence. Okay, she wants to ask. I'd rather her not, because I'm not up to lying at the moment.

Dad cracks his knuckles, and each popping sound threatens to send me over the edge. "Get some sleep. We'll finish this tomorrow."

"I know this is hard right now, but you'll see that we're doing what's best for you," Mom says. "It's a mistake to throw away your future for some . . . some *rock band.*"

She says "rock band" like it's word garbage. The most important thing in my entire life is trash to them.

"Good night," I reply. It's the most polite way I can think of to shut down this conversation.

"Good night," Dad says. They each give me a kiss on the forehead before they leave my room. Dad thinks the problem's solved, but Mom knows better. She looks back at me before shutting the door behind her.

I put on my pajamas and wriggle into bed, but I don't fall asleep. My parents are out in the living room, talking in soft murmurs that drift through the walls. They're probably patting themselves on the back for their excellent parenting skills. Go team. Obstacle avoided. The path to Harvard is still clear.

I didn't cry. That was good. From the way my parents winced, I think they expected me to cry, or beg, or even yell. Instead, I knew what I had to do. Act okay. Say nothing. Remain calm, even if it hurts.

I was able to do all of these things surprisingly well, because as soon as my parents walked into that room, I made an important choice.

I'm staying in the band. With or without their permission.

Chapter Twenty-Two

"COMPOUND FRACTURE"
—MY MORNING JACKET

I call Levi that night and lay out my plan. He'll secure the band room during lunch, so we can have our practices then. It'll require scarfing our food down on our way to Fridman, but it's a sacrifice we'll have to make. There's no hope of having practice after school now that my parents expect me to come straight home.

At practice I focus instead on getting my voice back in shape. We attack each song with a new ferocity, like wolves devouring a carcass. Our time is limited, so we're extra focused on getting things right. The instruments, my voice, everything fits together seamlessly even after our separation. The separation may have actually made us stronger.

It's not until Friday that my happiness devolves into full-fledged panic. Somehow, my mind had tucked away the fact that bands do more than practice. That they actually perform, and I'm supposed to sing in front of actual people tomorrow.

I've gotten comfortable with myself as a singer, but only in the privacy of our now-familiar little band room. I haven't tested my comfort level outside of that shared space and in front of people who aren't my fellow band members. Not since the drunken karaoke night at the Cave. Annie is covering for me to make it to the gig on Saturday. She has me tell my parents that we're working on a group project in the library. Because she's Annie, she's prepared me to handle my mom's interrogation.

"Which library?" Mom asks me.

"The one on tenth street," I say. "Some of our group members live in Brooklyn, so it's really the most convenient meeting place."

"And what project is this?" Mom asks. She glares at me preemptively.

"It's for science class," I say, reciting the lines that Annie e-mailed me. "We're studying the effect of sleep deprivation on cognitive abilities."

Mom looks impressed, and I say a silent "thank you" to Annie. I am officially free on Saturday.

Two hours before the gig, Annie, Krina, and I are staring into Annie's intensely organized closet. Her clothes hang off satin hangers, grouped by color and style. The task at hand is figuring out what I should wear. I don't trust myself to make the decision alone, since I lack Krina's innate sense of cool and Annie's attention to detail.

"I don't know why you're stressing," Krina says to me. "Wear a T-shirt and jeans and call it a day."

"Krina," Annie chides. "That's so frumpy."

"That's what I'm wearing."

"Yeah, but you're hidden behind a drum set."

"So? The boys wear jeans too. Because Vi's a girl she needs some sparkly look-at-me outfit?"

"Uh, no," says Annie. "But Vi is the lead singer, so she should stand out. It has nothing to do with gender."

"How about this?" I interrupt, pulling out an all-black ensemble. Black top, black pants, and black boots. I imagine the audience will perceive me as a woman shrouded in mystery.

Annie's lip curls. "Are you planning a heist?"

"What?" I dangle the clothes in front of her. "It's chic."

"It's my orchestra costume," she says.

"Oh."

"What about your hair?"

I tighten my ponytail. "My hair isn't working today. It's too poofy."

"Poofy is fine." Krina slides off my hair tie. "Poofy is you."

"Poofy but styled," Annie corrects.

She sets to work, producing an empty spray bottle from her drawer and filling it with tap water. Then she instructs Krina to coat sections of my hair in gel and wind them around her finger.

"I'm going to look like a chola," I warn, but neither of them listens.

I try to ignore the heavy stone rolling around in my stomach. In all the time I spent playing the good girl, trying to cement my spot in the band, I focused only on the happy things, not the scary things. But the scary thing is here, today. In mere hours.

"You're quiet," Annie comments after my hair is finished. She pats at my face with a powder puff, and I try not to inhale the particles rising from it.

"Nervous," I say.

Krina's rummaging through Annie's drawers, looking for accessories like Annie instructed. "Those don't go away," she says, shuffling through folded clothes. "The nerves."

"You get nervous?" I ask her. I can't see it. Girls with Mohawks aren't nervous.

"We all get nervous," she says. "Strand was the worst. He used to throw up before going onstage."

I'm not sure if I feel better or worse knowing this. If Strand, confident sex god, gets nervous, what hope is there for me?

Annie opens a tube of red lipstick and tells me to pucker up. "I can't imagine Strand that nervous," she says, carefully outlining my lips.

"He just hides it well," Krina says. "Hey, what about these?" She pulls out a pair of red suspenders from Annie's drawer.

"What about those?" I ask.

"These will give you the perfect pop of color," Annie says, snatching them from Krina and clipping them onto my waistband.

"Aren't those from your Doctor Who Halloween costume?" I ask skeptically. "They don't exactly scream rock star."

"Here. Wear them slung over your hips, like this," Krina says, pulling the suspenders off my shoulders so they dangle at my sides.

They bring me over to the mirror, looking pleased at the end result. Examining myself in the reflection, I have to admit the suspenders are a cool touch. It takes me a while to adjust to the Victoria staring back at me. I look almost as fearless as Krina, if you ignore the queasy look on my face and my skin's sickly yellow tint showing through the layers of powder.

My hair is still poofy, but it's purposely poofy. It's unrestrained, not confined to the limits of a hair tie.

Annie taps a finger against her chin. "I don't know . . . it's missing something."

"It's not missing anything," Krina argues. "She looks perfect."

"Hold on." Annie rustles through her bag and her hands emerge clutching a pair of chicken cutlets.

"Oh my God," I say. "No! No. This is not becoming my thing."

"Come on," Annie says, laughing. "Just in case you feel the urge to throw them."

"You never know when desire will strike," Krina says.

I sigh and stick them into my bra, even though I have every intention of pulling them out before I get to the gig. Then I shoot Krina and Annie the finger, which makes Annie laugh and Krina smile in approval.

Chapter Twenty-Three

"FALLING AWAKE"
—KAISER CHIEFS

We're playing at Country Lanes bowling alley on Staten Island. It's not exactly Madison Square Garden, but a gig is a gig.

Country Lanes is two hours from my apartment. I meet the band there, entering a bare, cavernous building teeming with kids and old Italian men wearing bowling shirts, the old-fashioned kind with name patches. It's noisy and overwhelming. Every time I hear the clattering of bowling pins it's like a jolt to my nervous system.

When I get inside, a man named Vinnie with a thick New York accent leads me down to the basement where the rest of the band is waiting. Everything—the walls, the table, the floor—is sticky from dried beer.

"You okay to perform?" Levi asks me when he sees me descend the stairs. "You look nervous."

He doesn't kiss me hello or compliment my hair or makeup or outfit, which makes me feel insecure. I hate that I'm a girl who feels insecure because her boyfriend doesn't compliment her appearance.

"I think I'm going to puke," I say, "but I'm otherwise fine."

"If you're going to puke, the bathroom's upstairs," says Strand. He looks up at me from his guitar, his eyes flicking to the top of my head. "Your hair . . ."

I reach up to touch it. It's still puffy and stiff with product. "What about it?"

"It's big."

"Okay?" I knew I should have brought my hair tie.

"I like it."

"Really?"

"Yeah."

"Vi, did you bring the earplugs?" Levi asks me.

I look away from Strand. "Krina has them. Hey, should we be concerned that there's no one our age here?"

"We still have an hour before we're scheduled to play," Krina says, handing the earplugs to Levi. "And a few people I invited said they were definitely coming . . ."

"We get paid either way, right?" Strand asks.

Levi is a blur, zipping around the room, playing with the equipment and tinkering with extension cords. I stand around helplessly.

I warmed up in my room with Annie earlier, but my vocal cords are now seizing in my throat.

"He's in preshow mode," Krina says, tipping her chin in Levi's direction. "You can't talk to him until after. Nothing you say will register."

I wish I would register with him, even a little bit. I need him to hold my hand and reassure me that I won't blow chunks all over the audience.

By the time we're set up, we have half an hour to practice. We run through the first song on our set list—"Reptilia" by the Strokes, and my voice manages to hold steady because no one is focused on me. They're frowning over their instruments, pausing once in a while to retune.

"One more time," Levi says before the final note of the song fades, so we play it again.

I grip the microphone tightly, staring at the cinderblock wall, trying not to imagine performing upstairs where actual living beings will be listening to me. When I imagine that, I stop breathing.

When we finish playing, Levi taps my arm and says, "So after the first couple songs, you'll introduce us."

My blood runs cold. "What?"

"You'll introduce us," he repeats.

For some reason, this idea terrifies me more than singing. At least when I sing, I have a melody and lyrics, both forming a lighthouse to guide me through my fear.

"What do I say?" I ask. "Can you write it down for me?"

He gives me a strange look. "All you say is, 'Hey, we're Debaser.'

Then you say your name and everyone else's. You talk to the crowd."

He might as well ask me to recite *The Iliad* while I'm at it. Both seem equally impossible. I'm not the confident bandleader who can rile up a crowd. They're strangers to me. Strangers who will smell my insecurity and pounce on my mistakes.

But I nod and say, "Sure. Fine."

Like it's nothing. Mostly because I want Levi to stop staring at me like I've grown three heads.

"I can do it," Strand offers.

I point to him. "Sold."

"No, Vi has to do it," Levi argues. "She's the lead singer. The face of the band."

"Who gives a shit?" Strand replies. "There's no rulebook."

Levi sighs, rubs at his eyes underneath his glasses.

"Oh, just let Strand do it. It's Vi's first gig," Krina says behind us, tapping on the snare drum.

Levi clenches his jaw. "Fine."

I've disappointed him, but my relief wins over my desire to please my boyfriend.

We rehearse a couple more songs before Vinnie pokes his head in and tells us we can go up in a couple minutes.

"What do we do now?" I whisper to Krina.

"We wait," she says.

The waiting is the worst part. I pace the length of the room, chewing on my bottom lip before I remember the lipstick Annie applied to me so carefully. It's probably smeared all over my teeth. I rub them with the side of my finger and wonder if I should wipe it off.

"Hey." I feel two hands clamp onto my shoulders to stop me from moving. Strand spins me around to face him. "Think of it as a practice."

"I can't," I say, my voice cracking embarrassingly. "There are people . . ."

"And?"

"And . . . I can't sing in front of people!"

"Look at me, Cutlet."

I do. Right into those midwinter sky eyes, which still make my legs go weak even though I'm supposed to know better.

"They're all going to be dead one day." Strand flicks his hand toward the door. "So will we. This is a tiny moment in time that will one day be lost forever."

I laugh, in spite of myself. "Morbid much?"

"It helps though, right?"

In a weird way, it does.

Krina is drumming her fingers against the wall. Every part of her body seems to move. Her toes tap, her head bobs. Levi sits with his eyes closed on the teeny couch against the wall. Krina tells me that Levi always meditates a few minutes before heading onstage.

Levi is unflinchingly calm, while every muscle in my body quivers.

Vinnie's voice upstairs breaks the silence, amplified by the microphone. "Hey . . . uh . . . how's everyone doing?"

"This is it, this is it, this is it," I mutter to myself.

Krina smacks her drumsticks against the wall. "Bring it in, guys."

Levi opens his eyes and springs to life. The four of us circle up and each place a hand in the center. Mine goes last, on top of Krina's.

"Since when do we 'bring it in'?" Strand asks her.

She glares at him. "Since now. It's Vi's first show."

It's surprisingly sweet for Krina, but at the moment I'm too nervous to appreciate the gesture.

"Hurry up," Levi urges.

Krina frowns at him. "On the count of three . . ."

But after she counts, no one says anything.

"Well," Strand says, "that worked out well."

When we head upstairs, the crowd is smaller than I expected. I can't decide if that's better or worse. On the one hand, fewer people to see me perform. On the other hand, I can see each and every one of the faces in the audience. They aren't an anonymous mass. I see a freckled girl from my English class. A boy with translucent white skin who sits near us at lunch.

I see Annie, who is wearing her paperclip nose ring. She holds up a sheet of paper that says I ♥ DEBASER in thick purple marker. The sign is big enough that we can see it, but not so blatant that it's embarrassing.

Krina takes her seat behind the drums. Strand and Levi pick up their instruments.

"Please welcome . . ." Vinnie checks the index card in his hand. "Debaser!"

What would happen if I ran off the stage? Strand would probably take over, pulling double duty—guitar and vocals. The groupies would be all over that.

Our set is only supposed to last forty-five minutes. As Krina counts off, I think about how good I'm going to feel forty-five minutes from now.

And then the music starts, and I stop thinking.

I soak up the haunting sound of Strand's guitar, the building thumps of Krina's drums, and the sudden burst of sound when everything collides. What I love about this song is how it kicks off at full speed.

A few cheers ring out when some people recognize the guitar chords, and the intro is too quick for me to think about what my voice will sound like and how I'm not sure what's going to come out when I open my mouth.

It's only my voice. It doesn't squeak or wail or do anything embarrassing like I expected. It just sounds like me. A more timid version of me, but at least it's not as shaky as it was during the audition.

Annie lets out a whoop when I start the first verse. The crowd is smiling, drinking, . . . and moving. I'm doing this. I'm making them move. I'm like an all-powerful puppet master.

I move too. As much as I can without bumping into Strand or Levi, since there isn't much room on the stage. I don't move like I do when I'm alone in my room, or even the way I do during band practice, but I manage to do something besides stand still.

Strand takes the mic after we play our third song and introduces us. He saves me for last, and I wait for him to call me Chicken Cutlet or Giggles, but he says, "And please give it up for our immensely talented lead singer, Victoria Cruz!"

My face warms, and I look down at my Doc Martens. I have to

mentally remind myself that lead singers don't look down at their feet. When I raise my eyes to the crowd, they're all smiles. They're like a pack of dogs, hungry for music, lapping at each new song we offer. They feed us, too. We eat up their energy as we play. It reminds me of Super Mario after Mario eats a mushroom and doubles in size. I feel doubled.

Pale boy is jumping around, and the girl from my English class is swaying her hips off rhythm. When we end our set, the group shouts, "Encore, encore, encore!" before the words devolve into inarticulate screams. It's the most beautiful sound I've ever heard. Better than the London Symphony Orchestra at Carnegie Hall. I want to record the crowd and listen to them every day.

We play the encore, and they roar with delight. Everyone jumps up and down in perfect unison, and we match the action onstage. The stage is set low, so if you looked at all of us from above, you would see us as one leaping, fleshy blob.

When we leave the stage, my skin is slick with sweat. I jump on Levi like a tree frog and wrap my legs around his waist.

He laughs. Postshow Levi is much more fun than tense, preshow Levi. I kiss him hard, adrenaline still coursing through my veins.

"Should we leave you two alone?" Krina asks.

I hear a frown in Strand's voice as he says, "Gross. You're killing my buzz."

Levi and I pull apart and he lowers me back onto the floor. I feel euphoric, like a helium balloon barely tethered to the ground.

"I can't believe it," I say. "I can't believe how awesome we sounded."

Strand pokes his shoulder against mine. "You did it, Cutlet. You pulled it off."

"Fucking right she did," Krina says. Even Krina looks happy, which for her means a less deep frown.

"That being said, I do have some notes," Levi announces, and we groan. Krina smacks him lightly on the head.

I kiss him, fully on the lips and tell him, "Monday. Let us have today."

Chapter Twenty-Four

"MODERN GIRL"
—SLEATER-KINNEY

work hard at making out, the way I work hard at school and singing. I study, and I apply myself. I adjust my moves to fit Levi's. But
maybe studying isn't enough to make up for my lack of experience.

When do you move forward from kissing, anyway? There should
be some kind of time line. Month one, kissing. Month two, groping.
Month three, hand job. And what is a reasonable amount of time
before sex should occur? If you have it too soon, you're a slut. If you
wait too long, you're a prude. There's no winning if you're a girl,
and when I decide what to do with Levi and when to do it, I will
inevitably make the wrong decision, because everything is the wrong
decision. Thinking about it too long gives me a migraine.

My parents would insist that sex should come only after marriage, which is easy for them to say. They were each other's first big relationship and married at eighteen. It's not like they had to suffer without sex for long. A few years ago, I let them sucker me into signing a purity pledge at church. My Bible-beating peers and I solemnly swore that "true love waits," and I used my most grown-up cursive handwriting to sign a (thankfully) nonbinding contract.

That was then. Now I'm not sure how long true love is supposed to wait. Or what it feels like. Does Levi love me? Do I love him? He has all the ingredients of someone I'm supposed to love. Smart, responsible, ambitious. Great husband material. We both have the same dark hair and dark eyes that would match nicely in a wedding photo. I can imagine us living in a mansion in Westchester with two children and a golden retriever. We'd celebrate both Noche Buena and Hanukkah, and our kids could light a tree and a menorah every winter.

I ponder all of this as I take a long shower, the bathroom overflowing with steam.

"Victoriaaaa!" Matty pounds at the door. "You've been in there for half an hour! Mom and Dad say to get out!"

"Go away!" I shout back over the running water, but I'm out of the shower two minutes later.

I turn and face the foggy bathroom mirror, completely nude. I want to see myself the way Levi will when/if we ever we have sex.

I inspect myself at new angles—flexing the backs of my legs, jiggling my breasts around, clenching my butt. My neck craned, I stare in horror at the dimpling skin along the outer edges of my butt cheeks. Apparently being young and painfully skinny does not make me immune to cellulite. I make a mental note to start doing daily squats and lunges.

Turning around again, I zero in on my breasts. Back in middle school, Annie and I had a great debate over ideal areola size after we watched a movie that featured a topless Scarlett Johansson.

"Those are perfect," Annie sighed, rewinding the scene to admire them again.

They *were* perfect. Perky and round and with an ideal areola-to-boob ratio. According to Annie, some girls barely have an areola.

"It's mostly nipple," she says. "Like a pencil tip. But then some girls have giant areolas that take over their boobs, like slices of baloney."

I'm not sure what Levi would think of my boobs. They're not round like Scarlett's. They're pointier, like they didn't grow as much as they intended to in order to round out. My areolas are colored a soft pink, and they measure about the size of a pepperoni slice. I wouldn't mind them being a little smaller, especially when my boobs barely have any surface area to offer.

My boobs are smaller than both Annie's and Krina's. Krina's body is all curves, not a straight line to be found. And Annie's breasts have grown into glorious C cups since we watched Scarlett on-screen.

In the mirror my reflection stares at me with palpable disgust. My breasts have a game of catch-up to do with my pear-shaped hips and bubbled rear. Annie calls my lower half my *sabor*, my latinassence. She jokingly offers to trade me—one of her C cups for a slab of my butt cheek.

"Then we would each be perfectly proportioned," she says. I think she's only trying to cheer me up. Her body is already perfectly proportioned, because despite what Nicki Minaj claims, most guys I know seem to prefer smaller rears.

I imagine Levi lifting up my shirt and gazing down at my naked torso. In this mental film, my breasts are not my breasts. They're Scarlett's, pasted onto my body. Levi smiles at them appreciatively.

In reality, if and when Levi does take off my shirt, he'll probably call foul after removing my heavily padded bra.

"That's it?" he might let slip. And he'd be within his rights. It's false advertising, walking around with an extra inch of foam.

I mentally devise my own sex guidelines:

Levi and I are ready to have sex when . . .

1. I get rid of the cellulite on my butt.

2. My boobs fill out.

3. I'm okay with Levi seeing me naked.

4. Levi and I say "I love you" for the first time.

It doesn't matter at the moment, anyway. Levi is having a love affair with school. Whatever bases he and I decide to cross, the game is on hiatus until finals are over. I trace a frowning face into the mirror's condensation before tucking my little breasts into my towel and exiting the bathroom in a trail of steam.

Chapter Twenty-Five

"JUNK OF THE HEART (HAPPY)"
—THE KOOKS

This is impossible," I moan, tossing my pencil across the table at Annie.

She rolls it back to me. "Very mature."

It's the weekend before finals and we've taken over my dining room table. Its surface is covered with strewn loose-leaf paper and open binders. It's been two hours, and my crankiness is kicking in.

With finals on the horizon, Levi has canceled band practice so we can use the extra time to study. The problem is that band practice was the one thing keeping me afloat. A life preserver in a tidal wave of pressure.

"When in life are we ever going to use quadratic equations anyway?" I ask.

"Never," Annie replies. "That's not the point."

I scribble some calculations into the margins of my notebook.

"Do you realize," I say, "that if we live to eighty-five, our lives are only thirty-one thousand and twenty-five days long?"

"Stop distracting yourself."

"It's so much shorter than I thought it was. I mean, I know 'life is short' is not an original revelation . . ." I trail off as I figure out my numbers. "Out of those measly thirty-one thousand twenty-five days, five thousand, six hundred, and seventy of them are spent cooped up in a classroom! And that's not counting study days, or grad school."

Annie shrugs. It's an insufficient response considering all the extensive math I just did.

"I don't understand our world," I lament.

"Oh geez." Annie shuts her textbook. "If I humor you for five minutes, can we get back to quadratic equations?"

"Yes."

"Fine. Go ahead and finish your rant."

"I'm just saying. We all agree life is short. So why do we spend it behind desks? Why don't we all come together and decide to do things differently?"

"This is the way the world works, Vi," Annie says. "You study hard so you get into a good college. You get into a good college so you find a high-paying job. Then, when you earn enough money, you can travel and retire and enjoy the rest of your days."

I play with the metal rings of my binder, popping them open and shut. "You sound like my parents. And Levi."

"You say that like it's a bad thing. He *is* your boyfriend, you know."

"Yes, my boyfriend who I never ever see."

"He's studious."

"He's worse than you. I didn't even know that was possible."

Pop, pop, pop.

"You're going to break that," Annie warns me.

I ignore her. "Aren't teenage boys supposed to be all about sex?"

"You're complaining that Levi isn't a sex fiend?"

"I don't want him to be a sex fiend. I would like him to find me attractive is all."

"Levi is into you, Vi. You know that."

"He's just so . . ." I try to find the right word. "Practical. He writes himself a color-coded daily schedule every day."

"So? You could use something like that. You never schedule your time wisely."

"So sometimes I want him to rip up the schedule and say 'to hell with it.' And . . . I don't know, take me."

"That's not Levi."

"I know."

"You have to accept him the way he is."

"I know that, too."

"It's simple," Annie says. "Does he treat you well?"

Levi has never snapped at me. We've never argued or criticized each other. Sometimes he offers me half of his cookie at lunchtime, and I don't even need to ask him.

"Yes," I decide. "He does treat me well."

"Then don't create a problem where there isn't one."

I pop open my binder and the metal tab snaps right off.

"I told you it would break," Annie says sagely.

We finish our finals on Wednesday afternoon. My mind feels like a puddle of goo, but I'm pretty confident that I did well enough on all my tests that my transcript will remain untarnished and Harvard-ready. Around me the hallway spills with students who have way more energy than I do.

"School's out, bitches!" hollers Nate Greenbaum, banging his hands against the locker door. A teacher immediately pokes her head out of a nearby classroom to scold him.

The band members plus Annie are going to Cafe Lalo to celebrate the end of finals and the beginning of winter recess. We share a table in the back of the café, against the exposed brick wall. I order hot chocolate with a dollop of fresh whipped cream and nestle against Levi.

"I have some news," Levi says as soon as we get our orders. He takes a dramatic pause, stopping to look at each of us in turn.

"Yeah?" Krina asks. "Do you need a drumroll?"

Strand raps his fingertips against the table and we all follow suit, to the annoyance of the customers sitting around us.

When Levi raises his hand, we stop. His lips curl into a smile as he says, "Clear your schedule for March twenty-sixth."

At first his words don't register. Then Annie shrieks, and Krina's fork clatters onto her plate.

"We made it in?" Strand asks.

"We're in," Levi confirms. "Battle of the Boroughs. The youngest band ever to make it."

Now everyone's full-on screaming, and our waitress has to rush over and ask us to keep it down.

"Miss, you're talking to future Rock and Roll Hall of Famers here," Strand tells her, shooting her a glimpse of his dimple. Because he's Strand, she stops scolding us and lets out a girlish giggle.

"Barf," Krina mutters as the waitress scurries back to the kitchen. I wholeheartedly agree.

"We'll start rehearsing every day after break," says Levi. "We need to practice longer and harder."

In spite of the excitement around me, dread worms its way into my stomach. It's not the longer practices in my future. Practice tends to be the bright spot in my day, so I have no problem extending it. It's the Battle. It sounds so intense. Not like performing in the band room or a bowling alley. We're singing in front of industry people and fellow musicians—people who know what good music is supposed to sound like. People who will know I'm a total fraud.

"Speaking of break, what are you fuckers up to?" Krina asks. She scrapes the edge of her caramel cheesecake with her fork and slides it into her mouth.

Strand looks at me sideways and says, "Victoria and I will be very busy with quinceañera rehearsals." I feel myself blush. Everything Strand says sounds inherently dirty, especially when he throws in some Spanish.

"I'll be skiing in Vermont," Levi reveals.

I place my mug on the table and try to swallow my surprise. "You will?"

"Yeah. My family goes every year."

This is news to me. I was hoping to spend some quality time with Levi in all his postfinals glory. It's my fault for assuming he had nothing else to do, but I'm disappointed all the same. No Levi, and as an additional crappy bonus, no band practice. I straighten up and shift a couple of inches away from him in my seat.

"What about you, Annie?" Krina asks.

Even in a predominantly dessert café, Annie still manages to order a salad. She pokes a piece of lettuce with her fork and says, "No plans."

"Thank God," replies Krina. "Me either. Let's hang out."

"You guys should come watch our rehearsals," Strand suggests. "Get a taste of the magic."

I shake my head at him. "No one wants to witness that train wreck."

"Excuse me, Cutlet. I can only speak for myself, but I happen to be an excellent salsa dancer."

"Riiight," I say, blowing ripples onto the surface of my hot chocolate, which is still piping hot.

"I'm serious. I went out with the captain of the dance team last year."

"He did," Krina affirms. "For, like, two weeks."

Of course he did.

"Well, I look forward to seeing your supposed moves," I say. I turn to Levi. "And when are you leaving for Vermont?"

"Four days," he says.

"I wish you had told me you were going."

This comes out a little more severe than I intended, so I force a laugh at the end of my sentence. Then I end up sounding maniacal instead. The rest of the table falls silent.

"I'm sorry," Levi says. "I should have told you earlier. I was wrapped up in studying."

The apology should satisfy me, but it doesn't. It's not that I want him to apologize for going on vacation. He should feel free to ski down a few mountains without me. But would it kill him to give me some notice? Maybe look a little disappointed at the thought of leaving me over break? Is that very codependent of me?

"It's fine," I say, busying myself with stirring my drink. "No worries."

I'm silent for the remainder of our outing. I focus on downing my hot chocolate and avoiding eye contact with Levi. As much as I realize I'm overreacting, I can't deny the annoyance bubbling in my chest. Levi doesn't seem to notice, which only annoys me further.

As we walk out of the café, Strand nudges me. "You okay?"

"Yeah, totally."

"I recognize that look. The signature annoyed Cutlet expression."

"Or it's my natural resting face."

"It's not. I should know. It's usually reserved for me." He hangs back with me while Levi, Krina, and Annie walk ahead. "Don't take it personally. Levi's forgetful when he's in the zone."

Okay, but when does a zone stop becoming a zone and start becoming a person's normal state?

I button up my jacket, which doesn't do much against today's thirty-degree weather. "I'm fine, Strand."

"Right." He looks at me like he's reading my mind, and I have to break my gaze away.

"I am."

"I totally believe you," he says, but his tone suggests the opposite. "See you Saturday?"

"Yup. Come by at eleven."

Strand is coming to my house so my mom can drive us to Jessica's for quince rehearsal. The thought only adds to my bitterness. Levi should be the one at my house on Saturday. Levi should be the one accompanying me into a decked-out banquet hall on February twenty-seventh.

When Strand leaves, I catch up to the group. Levi tries to take my hand, but I slip it into my pocket.

"I'm cold," I explain. My voice comes out icier than the wind.

He shrugs. "Okay."

I'm quickly learning that Levi is not a master at reading subtlety, so I sigh and add, "I'm also kind of annoyed with you."

"Annoyed?" He blinks. "Why?"

"I was hoping to spend some time with you over break."

"Oh. Well . . . we still have some time before I go . . ."

"I guess."

"Want to come over on Friday night?"

I frown. "To your place?"

"Yeah. My parents said I should invite you over for dinner."

My frown gives way to a trace of a smile. "Really? They want to meet me?"

"Yeah. I mean, if you're free."

"I'm absolutely free!" I throw my arms around his neck. "That's so exciting!"

He kisses me on the cheek. "It's not a big deal, Vi."

"In what world is meeting your boyfriend's parents not a big deal? I don't even know their names."

"Steven and Shira."

"Steven and Shira Schuster . . . very alliterative. Do I call them Mr. and Mrs. Schuster?"

"I would, yeah. They're pretty old-fashioned sometimes."

"What do I wear?"

Levi winds his arm around my waist. "Wear a dress. You look nice in a dress."

I know he doesn't mean to be insulting, but I wish he had said I'd look nice no matter what I wore.

Chapter Twenty-Six

"NUMBER ONE BLIND"
—VERUCA SALT

The great thing about being in Debaser is that my tolerance for anxiety has grown much higher. Performing onstage in front of a sea of strangers will have that effect. So on an anxiety scale of one to ten, meeting Levi's parents ranks about a five. Parents tend to like me. I don't have any tattoos or unorthodox piercings, and I always remember to say my pleases and thank-yous.

Before I leave my apartment, my parents offer some gems of advice.

Mom: "Remember to offer Mrs. Schuster help in the kitchen."

Dad: "Relax. You don't have to impress anyone. They'll love you. And if they don't, they're idiots."

Mom: "No, Jorge. She still needs to be polite."

Dad: "I never said she didn't."

Mom: "You basically told her not to try."

Dad: "I just want her to be herself."

Mom: "Yes, but an extra polite version of herself."

They discuss the issue at length as though they're determining the fate of the free world. Finally, I cut them off with a harried goodbye and hustle to the train.

"Don't listen to your father!" Mom shouts after me.

In my purse I have Levi's address saved on my phone, and a tube of lip gloss. A natural pink lip gloss that tells the Schusters I am a respectable young woman. Every inch of my body is sensibly dressed.

The heat is blasting on the subway train. Sweat soaks into my dress and my hair bristles with frizz. An hour of blow-drying all for nothing. I can only hope the Schusters will appreciate my inner beauty.

Twenty minutes later, I'm standing in front of their apartment building on the Upper West Side. No, not a building. More like a sprawling Gothic palace, so imposing compared to my squat brick abode. The building wraps around a private courtyard with its own marble fountain. There are two doormen, one stationed outside the entrance and one behind the desk in the front lobby. It seems excessive. But then, so does everything about this place.

I knew the Schusters would have to be well-off. Any family that sends their child to Evanston, without the help of a scholarship or financial aid, has to be. Still, I didn't expect this much. Annie's family pays full Evanston tuition, but they live in a modest brownstone in Queens. To say the Schusters are sitting in the lap of luxury is an understatement. They're straddling it.

The doorman points me to the elevator, and when I step inside, there's an elderly white-haired man whose purpose, it seems, is to push the elevator button for me. When I thank him, his face crinkles into a smile.

The elevator zooms up twenty stories and stops at the very top. The penthouse floor. Oh my freaking God. Levi lives in a penthouse? I look down at my dress, which is suddenly the rattiest looking scrap of fabric I've ever seen.

The elevator man nods at me as the doors slide open. "Have a great night, ma'am."

It's an unsettling feeling when a man at least sixty years your senior calls you "ma'am."

I step off the elevator into a dimly lit hallway that leads to the Schusters' front door. My anxiety level increases a notch as I ring the doorbell. Inside, a dog emits a high-pitched yelp before the door clicks open and Levi is there, grinning his chipped-tooth grin. He kisses me, then pets the small white dog trying to nip at my shoes.

"Princess, hush," he scolds her.

I shut the door behind me. "I didn't know you had a dog."

"Yeah . . . it's my mom's dog, technically."

"She's cute."

I'm lying. Princess isn't cute. Her tiny pointed teeth jut out in a severe underbite, and she's baring them at me now. When I reach over to pet her, a low growl emanates from her belly.

"She takes a while to warm up to strangers," Levi assures me, scooping her up in his arms.

"Of course." I shrug off my coat and hang it on the rack by the door.

Princess wiggles around in Levi's arms until he lowers her back onto the floor. "Follow me," he says. "My mom's in the living room."

I start to follow him, but he stops short. "Oh. Would you mind taking off your shoes first?"

I look down at my high-heeled boots, chosen specially to complete my sophisticated, elegant look. The tights I'm wearing underneath have an inelegant hole by my right pinky toe. Levi is wearing argyle socks with no discernible holes in them.

He shows me the shoe rack inside a hallway closet.

"Sorry," he says as I try to peel off my boots as gracefully as possible. "My mom's anal about tracking dirt inside the apartment."

"No problem." When I bend down to put my boots on the rack, a snarling Princess runs around Levi's leg to face me, her eyes bugging out maniacally.

"She's feisty, isn't she," I comment. Inconspicuously, I try to fold my tights over my toes to conceal the hole on the edge.

"She's really sweet once you get to know her."

Right.

When we walk into the living room, my first thought is that the area of this one room is larger than my entire apartment. There's an overwhelming amount of neutral color . . . beiges, creams, and taupes. And there's nothing on the floor but carpet. No Xbox discs in sight. Not even a dog toy of Princess's, which might explain her aggressive personality.

Mrs. Schuster rises from the couch when we enter the room. She's small and frail and heavily doused in perfume. Her hair is black like Levi's, and she wears it in a low bun.

"Hello, Victoria," she says, grasping my hand. "Lovely to meet you."

"Nice to meet you, too, Mrs. Schuster."

"Come have a seat, please. Steven should be home soon. He's running a little late at work."

The three of us form a semicircle with Levi and me on the loveseat and Shira on the couch. Princess gives a yap and snuggles against Shira's side.

"That's my good girl," Shira coos at her. Then she turns to me and asks, "Do you like dogs, Victoria?"

I sense this is the first test of Shira's approval.

"I love them," I say. I do love dogs. Most of them, anyway. Princess may be the exception.

"Princess is a bichon frise. Levi and his dad gave her to me as a birthday present a few years ago."

"That was very sweet of them," I say.

"She's the best present I could have gotten." As if understanding our conversation, Princess closes her eyes contentedly. "Does your family have any pets?"

"Unfortunately not. Our apartment building doesn't allow them."

Shira clucks her tongue and wiggles her French-manicured toes. "How awful."

"I've always wanted a cat, though."

She wrinkles her nose. "Levi's allergic to cats."

"Oh . . . well then, it's a good thing I never got one." I give an unnatural chuckle.

"I never liked cats," Shira says. "I don't trust them. They're so withholding."

Annie had an old cat named Larry, and he was the most affectionate pet I've ever known. He used to crawl onto my lap and fall asleep, heavy purrs thrumming through his body. I don't want to bring him up though, in case Shira thinks I'm arguing with her anti-cat stance.

The phone rings, and Shira excuses herself to answer. I give Levi a backhanded slap on the shoulder when she's out of sight.

"Since when are you allergic to cats?" I ask him.

"Ow." He rubs his shoulder. "What difference does it make?"

"It makes a difference. It seems like something I should know. Kind of like the fact that your mom hates cats."

"You don't have to hate cats just because my mom does."

"Is there anything else your parents hate that I should know about?"

He scratches his eyebrow. "Um . . . the Mets?"

"Great, Levi," I reply, voice hard. "My parents love the Mets."

"Relax, Vi. I don't think your family's favorite baseball team is going to come up tonight," he says, rubbing me on the knee. Then he stares down at my feet. "You know you have a hole in your tights?"

When we sit down for dinner, the table is set for four even though Mr. Schuster is still at work. The silverware is wrapped in ivory linen napkins and the china sparkles under an antique glass chandelier.

A round woman in a blue cotton dress brings out a salad bowl. I think back on my mom's advice to help Mrs. Schuster in the kitchen.

It seems Mrs. Schuster already has all the help she needs in that department.

"Thank you, Rosa," Shira says to the woman. Rosa gives a quick nod and shuffles back into the kitchen. She comes back a moment later to fill our water glasses.

"Gracias," I say to her. She smiles at me, and Shira looks surprised.

"Do you speak Spanish, Victoria?" she asks me.

"Only a little."

"It's a useful language to know these days . . . do you take it at Evanston?"

"No," I say. "My parents are Cuban, actually, so I learned from them."

"Cuban!" Shira remarks. "How interesting! Rosa is Cuban too, isn't she, Levi?"

"Dominican," Levi says.

Shira shrugs off the error and takes a sip of her water. "I assumed you were Italian. You look very Italian."

"Do I?" I say. I never know how to respond to comments like this. Evanston is a predominantly Caucasian school, and it's like when people find out I'm Hispanic, they expect me to turn five shades darker, don a sombrero, and speak with a Sofia Vergara accent.

"I think so. You look like a young Isabella Rossellini."

"I don't know who that is," I admit.

"She's pretty," Levi assures me, giving my arm a squeeze.

"Well then . . . thank you," I say. I take a bite of my salad and chew as silently as possible. I'm not used to eating without the TV on in the background. I'm also not used to eating dinner on fine china.

My family has a set that we only use for Thanksgiving, and the rest of the time we use mismatched plastic plates collected from various department store sales.

When we finish our salad, Shira sighs and announces that we should start our main course so it doesn't get dry.

"Shouldn't we wait for your dad?" I whisper to Levi, but he shakes his head.

"He usually gets home late."

I now see where Levi gets his workaholic nature. My mind flashes forward to my possible future, where I'm sitting alone in an exquisite beige living room, waiting for him to come home for dinner. The portrait inspires me to feel a flicker of pity for Shira.

I'm snapped out of my daydream when Rosa enters the dining room with a platter of sliced meat. I try to mask my horror.

Levi has to know I'm a vegetarian. We eat lunch together every day.

"Is something wrong, Victoria?" Shira asks as Rosa plops a pile of dead animal carcass on my plate.

Levi looks at me questioningly. Obviously he doesn't know, and I can't make a scene now. What will Shira think if I refuse to eat the meal? Then again, it's not as though she spent the time and effort preparing it. I would possibly offend Rosa.

"Nothing's wrong," I reply, giving her a tight smile. "It looks delicious."

"It's veal piccata," she says. "Levi's favorite. Go ahead and start."

Levi doesn't need to be told twice. He sticks a huge chunk of veal into his mouth with almost unnecessary gusto. I stare down at my plate and try to ignore the voice in my head telling me that I'm a horrible human being who neglects her morals to impress her boyfriend's mom. The meat is covered in a glop of brown sauce.

"It's delicious," Levi says to me.

It's a baby calf, I think to myself. *What kind of a monster kills and eats a baby calf?*

Shira cuts her meat into tiny pieces and chews for a long time before swallowing. I force myself to cut a piece, and it slices easily under my knife.

Tender baby meat, that's why.

Then I stick the meat into my mouth. I don't taste the flavor, only the overwhelmingly chewy texture. I chew until my gums ache, then swallow it down.

"How is it?" Shira asks me. She probably thinks it's rude that I haven't complimented the food yet.

"It's very good," I say, gearing up for the second bite. I eat about a quarter of the cutlet before my stomach jolts in protest.

"Where is the bathroom?" I ask Levi.

"Up the stairs to your left."

"Excuse me," I say, then do a half walk, half sprint to the bathroom, feeling the sour taste of bile rising in my throat. Just as I kneel in front of the toilet, my body forcefully expels the five bites of veal along with everything else I ate today. I cough and gag, clutching the porcelain edges of the toilet seat until my stomach stops contracting.

I slump against the wall, eyes closed. I should have reminded Levi I was a vegetarian as soon as he extended the dinner invite. I could have sworn he already knew. How could he not? I feel irrationally angry. He's my freaking boyfriend, and I've been a vegetarian for three years. Hasn't he been paying attention?

I rise to my feet and my entire body feels sore, the same way I used to get after a cross-country meet. I rinse out my mouth with tap water and wipe off any leftover traces of vomit sticking to my lip gloss. So much for elegant and sensible.

When I get back to the dining room, I tell Shira that I'm very sorry but I'm not feeling well. She cocks her head to the side and presses her lips together like she's trying to diagnose me.

"No, you don't look well," she decides, then insists on paying for me to take a cab home.

When I protest, Levi rubs my upper back with one hand and uses the other to scoop more veal into his mouth. The smell makes my stomach lurch.

"I agree. Take a cab home," he insists between mouthfuls, and I'm too tired to politely argue anymore, so I accept the crisp pair of twenties that Shira slips me. As I slink out of the Schusters' penthouse suite, Princess follows me to the door, yapping at my back. I stick my tongue out at her before leaving.

Chapter Twenty-Seven

"WITH A GIRL LIKE YOU"
—THE TROGGS

The next morning I wake up to the sound of laughter drifting in from the living room. I blink my eyes open and for a second I'm seized by hope. Was my disastrous dinner at the Schusters' only a dream? Then I look and see the dress I so carefully picked out discarded on the floor, along with my holey pantyhose. No. This is real life, and it sucks.

I need to call Levi and make sure his mom doesn't hate me. I sit up too quickly and have to wait for my post–wake up dizziness to subside. Then I hear it again. The laughter. My mom's laugh is easily recognizable, but there's another voice joining hers. A deep male voice that is not my dad's, because he's working this Saturday. Oh God, is Mom having an affair?

I creep out of my room in the direction of the laughter and the first thing I see is a mop of messy brown hair poking up against the couch.

Strand, of all people, is sitting in my living room, cracking jokes with my mother. Mom spots me first, and before I can motion for her to keep quiet, she calls, "Good morning, sleepyhead!"

Strand turns to look at me, a smile already playing at his lips. "Cute pj's," he says in lieu of a good morning.

I look down at my Pokémon T-shirt, which I don't remember picking out last night, or even purchasing in the first place. It's so large it hangs over my polka-dot pajama pants, which, like my pantyhose, also have a hole.

I really need to buy new clothes.

"What time is it?" I wonder out loud, rubbing the sleep out of my eyes.

"It's ten thirty," Mom says.

I glower at Strand. "You're early."

He stretches his arms out in front of him and gives a lazy shrug. "I overestimated how long the train ride to your apartment would take."

"You're never early. To anything."

Mom looks between the two of us, then zeroes in on my shirt. "Ria, why don't you go get dressed so you can keep Strand company?"

"Ria?" Strand asks with interest. "Is that a nickname?"

"Oh, it's one of our pet names for Victoria," Mom replies.

"How lovely," Strand says. "I'm quite fond of giving Victoria nicknames myself."

"Really?" Mom sounds thoroughly fascinated. I cut in before Strand can open his big smirking mouth. None of the nicknames he's given me contain a backstory appropriate for my mother.

"Nothing out of the norm," I say, shooting him a warning glance.

He bats his eyes angelically in response, then says, "Gloria was just telling me some stories about your childhood."

I stare back at him. "Gloria?"

"Yeah . . . your mother? Gloria?"

"I know my mom's name, thanks."

"Oh, good, because you sounded confused."

"That's because you should address her as Mrs. Cruz."

Mom furrows her eyebrows at me and says, "He's welcome to call me Gloria. Mrs. Cruz sounds old."

"Which you are anything but," Strand says to her. "You're, what? Twenty-eight?"

"Oh, please," Mom replies, but she's grinning like a fool.

"I'm serious. I can see where Victoria gets her looks."

Mom tips her head back and laughs so hard I can see her fillings. "You're too much, Strand."

Good freaking lord. I'm about to vomit for the second day in a row. Strand is flirting with my mother. Has he no shame? Does he have to flirt with everyone in possession of a vagina? Worse, she seems to be enjoying it.

I excuse myself to change, throwing on a pair of jeans and my least wrinkled sweater. I pray that I won't come back into the living room to find Strand and my mom taking it to the next level, since it seems most women, regardless of their age, are helpless against his spell.

When I emerge from my room, neither of them has left the couch.

"Is that what you're wearing?" Mom asks. I try to ignore the obvious implication in her voice, that I should about-face and make myself look more presentable.

"Yes."

"Do you want me to iron it for you?"

"Nope."

She flattens her lips together, and I know she would pursue the issue further if Strand weren't here. Who do I have to impress, anyway? It's a rehearsal for a quince I was suckered into. There is a long list of better ways I could spend my Saturday. Things that are much more preferable than spending the day with Strand stepping on my toes in an attempt at salsa.

"So, Cutlet, do I get to see your room or what?" Strand asks.

"My bedroom?" I say. "I don't think so."

Even Levi hasn't been inside my bedroom. I would assume my parents aren't okay with me having a boy in there, but then Mom says, "Go ahead. Show Strand your music collection."

Apparently, all rules fly out the window when it comes to Strand.

"My room is a mess," I protest.

Strand hops off the couch. "I don't mind."

"I do," I say, but I lead him down the hallway anyway. We pause outside my door. "Count to thirty before you come in," I instruct him.

"You're serious?"

"Yes."

"I didn't realize you thought I was worth impressing."

"It's not about that," I say. "It's just common decency."

"You're a ridiculous person."

"Count."

"Thirty . . . twenty-nine . . ."

I slip into my room and close the door, then rush around to scoop clothes off the floor, throw breakfast bar wrappers into the trash can, and hastily make my bed.

"Two . . . one," Strand calls through the door. "Ready?"

"Yes, come in."

He steps inside, almost hitting his head on the doorframe. He's so damn tall, it's like my room can barely contain him. It's odd to have a boy in here, in the space that I take up every day. He looks so out of place with his grungy jeans and Converse sneakers.

Strand peers around, inspects the posters on my walls, and says, "It's pretty much what I imagined."

"Why are you imagining my bedroom?"

He smiles innocently, then notices my wall of music, partially hidden from view inside a little nook by my desk.

"Is that your collection?" he asks, striding over. His steps are so heavy that the floor trembles under their force.

"Yes." I hover behind him. He smells like vanilla. I wouldn't expect someone like Strand to smell like baked goods. Leather, maybe. Or pot.

He inspects my vinyls, pausing to nod in approval or pull one out to examine it more closely. Then he glances at my laptop, open to my online music account.

"May I?" he asks.

My biggest source of pride isn't my seven-minute-mile 5k split or my 3.8 GPA. It's my music collection. I have everything from Bach to Metallica to Kendrick Lamar. I invest a lot of time and effort into crafting the perfect playlist for every occasion. There's a playlist for skinny-dipping, for sleeping under the stars, for driving a convertible on a hot summer day. Not that I've done any of these things . . . but if I listen to my music while I think about it, I can pretend I have.

I've never let anyone look through my playlists. Not even Annie. For some reason, though, I give Strand permission. "Okay."

Strand plants himself at my desk, scrolling through my never-ending succession of playlists.

"That's a good one," I say. I lean over his shoulder to point at the screen. Crap, he smells delicious. "My Staring Out the Window on a Rainy Day mix. Slow, mopey . . . there's some Portishead, the Smiths, Nick Cave . . ."

I scoot to share the seat with Strand. I can only fit half of my massive butt on the chair. "And this is my Lying on a Hammock on a Sunny Day playlist."

Strand laughs. "That is so specific."

"And this is the Stargazing playlist. Gustav Holst, Brian Eno . . ."

"Pink Floyd?"

"Obviously."

"Have you actually done this stuff while you listened? Stargazing, lying on a hammock?"

"No, but when I listen it gives me the feeling of doing them. I can imagine it."

Strand is the first person I've ever admitted this to. I'm not sure why I decided to tell him.

"You," he says, "are the most unique person I know." He smiles when he says it, and it's the genuine smirk-free kind, so I don't feel offended. I smile back at him for maybe the first time in the history of our semifriendship.

He continues to scan my music collection. Sometimes he stops to nod appreciatively or run his finger along his chin. He hums as he scrolls, in his soothing baritone. The melody is interesting. Beautiful, actually, in a sad way.

"What's that?" I ask.

"What?"

"That song you're humming."

"Was I humming?" He rises from the chair, his back to me as he walks over to my vinyls to inspect them for a second time. "Got any Pixies?"

"You were definitely humming." I walk over to him and slide the Pixies' *Doolittle* from the top shelf. "I liked it, whatever it was."

His fingers graze mine as he takes the album from my hands. "It's something I'm working on."

"I forgot that you wrote music."

"I don't. Not physically, I mean. I come up with a melody and record it."

"Why don't you ask Levi to arrange it? We could use some original songs."

Strand rakes his fingers through his hair. "I've never actually shared my stuff with anyone. It's kind of . . . personal."

Color me surprised. I pictured Strand writing the type of songs that involved strippers and pole dancing, à la Def Leppard or Warrant.

"Personal means it's good," I say. If I didn't know better, I would think Strand is actually being shy. Which is impossible, because Strand is the most confident person I know.

"Coldplay is personal."

"Coldplay is unfairly maligned. My point still stands. Anyway, all I'm saying is that I'll listen to your song . . . if you want."

His eyes drift from the album up to my face. "Yeah?"

"Yeah."

At that moment Mom yells that we have to leave for Jessica's.

"Next week?" I press.

"Maybe."

"Strand, come on! I want to hear it."

His cocky swagger is back in full force as he bows for me to walk in front of him.

"Please?" I ask.

"Maybe."

Jessica is much more developed than I remembered. She's wearing a tight long-sleeved shirt that clings to her round bosom. Suffice it to say that my small breasts don't come from this side of the family. When Strand and I walk into the house, she grazes my cheek with a kiss and then focuses her attention on Strand.

"Who's your boyfriend?" she asks, tugging on the bottom of her shirt to reveal more cleavage.

"Friend," Strand corrects, and I'm slightly annoyed at how quickly he clarifies that fact. Like it would be inconceivable for someone to think we were together. "I'm Strand."

"Nice to meet you!" Jessica kisses him on the cheek, shamelessly rubbing her chest against him in the process. Or maybe her chest is so big it has nowhere else to go. "Any friend of my cousin's is a friend of mine."

"Isn't that nice," Strand says.

She smiles, exposing a glittering set of braces. "Well, come on in. We're practicing in the living room."

As we trail behind her, Strand leans into me and whispers, "She's very friendly."

"Don't get any ideas," I reply.

"Do you seriously think I would?"

"Wouldn't you?"

"No," he says, sounding annoyed. "She's your cousin."

I don't see what that has to do with anything. I mean, he was openly flirting with my mother not an hour ago.

Jessica's living room is packed with couples. The furniture has been pushed against the perimeter of the room so that the large rug in the center has become a makeshift dance floor. A boom box is set on the floor by the large glass doors leading out to the pool.

"¡Ya estamos listos, Eduardo!" Jessica says to an old, gray-haired man bedecked in sunglasses and a bright-red pashmina.

Strand pokes me for a translation.

"She's telling the old man we're ready," I whisper to him.

Eduardo claps his heavy hands together, and in a husky smoker's voice, rasps a stream of directions in Spanish. He does this too quickly for me to understand, so I mimic the way the other couples are gathering into a straight line, and in response Strand mimics everything I do.

As flamboyant as his fashion sense is, Eduardo seems like a person who demands respect. He doesn't bother to officially introduce himself or ask us our names. He immediately launches into the steps, barking directions in Spanish.

"*¡Adelante!*" He steps forward with his left foot, lifts his right foot slightly off the ground, then plants both feet back in their original spot.

"*¡Atras!*" He performs the same move, but reversed, stepping back with his right foot and shifting the weight off his left foot.

"Now you," he says in heavy accented English.

So we dance. He continues to shout commands, and we follow his footwork like an army of salsa soldiers. Eduardo sways his hips in the direction of whichever leg moves, so I try to do the same. The movement feels natural to me. I look over at Strand, and he's not as awful as I expected. He even adds these tiny arm flourishes.

"I see you admiring my moves," he says without missing a beat.

"I kind of am."

We dance in unison. One-two-three, one-two-three.

"I told you I could dance," Strand says.

"I had to see it to believe it."

"Maybe you should take me at my word more often." He swivels his head to give me a meaningful look.

I turn to face forward, staring at the way Eduardo's shirt lifts to expose a mound of back fat. "Maybe I should."

Chapter Twenty-Eight

"SMOKE GETS IN YOUR EYES"
—THE PLATTERS

It's the day before Levi leaves for his ski trip. His dad is at work and his mom is at a charity function, so we have his entire apartment to ourselves. Mom and Dad don't know that part, otherwise I would be under house arrest instead of sitting on Levi's puffy blue comforter and striped sheets.

"Is it lame to say I'll miss you?" I ask as I watch him pack the suitcase flopped open beside me. With him leaving in less than twenty-four hours, everything he does is suddenly adorable. Even the way he packs. He tucks his shirts under his chin, then flips the sleeves first in a very methodical approach to folding.

"No," he says, layering the shirt onto the others in his bag. "It's sweet."

There's a certain expectation hanging over us. We don't usually have the chance to be alone, unsupervised like this. As adorable as Levi's packing style is, I secretly wish he would be a little less careful about his folding so we can get on to things.

"Do you *have* to finish packing now?" I ask him, leaning back on my elbows.

He looks down at his half-filled suitcase. "I just hate putting it off."

"Maybe you can put it off for a little bit . . ."

"Maybe, but . . ."

I sit up and hook my fingers onto his belt loops. "A ten-minute break will make your packing skills even stronger."

"I'm almost finished, I swear," he says, undoing my grip on his jeans.

"Well, at least let me help you."

As I get up and start to fold a sweater, Levi openly cringes.

"What?" I ask.

"Nothing," he says, scrunching his lips together. "Your folding style is a little different than mine, but it's okay."

I groan, flopping back onto his bed and covering my face with my hands.

"Never mind," I say through my fingers. "Just let me know when you're done."

A few minutes later, I hear the zip of the suitcase and feel the bed descend under Levi's weight. I look over at him hopefully.

"All finished?" I ask.

"All finished."

And then he leans in, and that nerve-wracking pressure is back. The apartment to ourselves, a week-long separation approaching. I want our good-bye to be perfect, so the memory will linger on in his mind as he descends the slopes of Vermont.

There are steps to Levi's kissing, just like there are steps in the way he folds his shirts. He starts with small closed-mouth kisses, then he slowly moves in with a purposeful, precise tongue.

"I'll miss you," I say when we break apart for breath.

"Me too."

I pull him on top of me and we continue where we left off. This is new, this horizontal making out, but it also feels instinctual. Whether it's biological engineering or years of watching romantic comedies, something has contributed to my not being inept at sexiness.

Then I feel *it*. Through Levi's jeans, against my thigh.

At first I think maybe it's the remote control wedged between us. But when I gaze downward I see the bulge pressing against Levi's jeans. This is the only real-life erection I have ever come across. Here lies (or rises) physical proof that I have turned Levi on, that I possess the capacity to do so. I feel proud, powerful, and winningly feminine. And then the feeling passes and I wonder whether now I have to do something with *it*.

My hands are fixed onto Levi's waist, and even when I will them to migrate downward, they don't budge. The idea of a penis kind of freaks me out. I wouldn't know what to do with it. I've never even pictured one, really. I view most men as real-life Ken dolls. I don't usually think about whether they wear boxers or briefs, or what lies beneath the layers of clothing. If I don't see it, I don't believe it's there. Or in this case, as I'm reminded by the weight on my thigh, feel it.

Levi's hands begin to play with the bottom of my shirt, grazing the skin underneath. They slide upward, onto the small of my back, then stroke the skin between my shoulder blades. I should be lost in a wave of passion at this point, but all I can think about is how quiet it is in the room, and the fact that a boy's hands are officially up my shirt.

The hands creep around so that they're almost on my breasts, and that's when I remember with a slight panic that my bra is packed with more padding than a mattress showroom. Flinching, I grab Levi's hands and our lips smack together as I pull away.

Levi blinks his eyes open, startled out of a heavy daze. "Sorry. Was that not okay?"

"Oh! No. I mean yes . . . it wasn't not okay," is all I can manage, brilliantly. "I wasn't ready for it, that's all. Maybe we can—"

"Take things slow."

"Right."

I feel disappointed in myself, like I've failed an important test. It's not that I don't like doing this stuff with Levi, but something stops me. Maybe it's the fact that he's going away. Or that stupid purity pledge I once signed.

The two of us sit in silence. He has a disquieting look of concern on his face that I avoid returning. My eyes flit to a framed picture of him when he was a little boy. I think about Levi as a little boy, watching his future self trying to find his way under my bra. I glance down to Levi's crotch, where his erection forms an awkward bulge through his jeans.

"Do you want to go home?" he asks.

I jerk my head up. "Do you *want* me to go home?"

"Of course not. You just seemed uncomfortable."

"I'm fine," I say. "Do you want to watch TV or something?"

"I'll do whatever you want, Vi."

What I want is to stop overthinking the situation. I want to move forward in this relationship and prove to Levi that my feelings are real. It doesn't seem like something I can do today, though. He grabs the remote control and clicks on the TV. The bulge in his jeans has disappeared. The moment has passed.

"What do you want to watch?" he asks as he flips through the channels.

We lean back against his pillows and I curl into his chest.

"I'll watch whatever," I say.

He settles on CNN, which is pretty much as unsexy as it gets. You can't be in the mood when a chubby middle-aged news anchor is lecturing you on the state of affairs in China.

As exciting and scary as making out is, sometimes I prefer this. I like the sexual stuff too. But there's something nice about closeness without sexual expectation. I trace my finger along Levi's arm, admiring how it's slender yet toned, enjoying the feeling of his chin resting on my head.

I soak in all his Levi-ness, because I'll be going without it for ten days. A record for us. I want to give him an exciting send off. I want to show him I could be sexually adventurous. I want to tell him that I'll be ready to do more soon, just not today. But when I look up at him, he's fallen asleep.

Chapter Twenty-Nine

"GIMME ALL YOUR LOVE"
—ALABAMA SHAKES

I'm surprised to realize that I'm looking forward to the second quince rehearsal. I haven't spoken to Annie all week, and Levi hasn't called from Vermont, so I've been living hermit-style. Cut off from the outside world. I wake up before my laptop has a chance to belt my morning wake-up playlist from its speakers. I straighten up my room, even making my bed properly, decorative pillows and all.

Since I have some extra time, I put a little more effort into my appearance, brushing my lashes with mascara and blotting on some lip gloss. When the doorbell buzzes, I beat Mom to the door to open it.

Strand grins at me and strides into the apartment. He's wearing the same thing he wore last week except for his shirt. Today it's a faded Pixies T-shirt with a picture of a bull terrier on it.

"Ready to serenade me?" I ask him, and his grin falters.

"Not sure what you mean."

"Don't play dumb with me, Strand."

He groans as I push him by the shoulders into my room. It takes some effort. Strand is heavier than he looks. "I was hoping you'd forget."

"I could never." I shut my bedroom door almost completely, leaving a small enough crack to placate Mom. As much as she likes Strand, she's still my mother. It's an unspoken but understood rule that thou shall not hang out with boys behind closed doors.

"Shouldn't I say hi to Gloria?" Strand asks, his eyes flitting to his escape route.

"Mrs. Cruz. And you can say hi to her after you sing. Stop stalling."

"Not stalling, just demonstrating my impeccable etiquette."

I flop onto my bed and look at him expectantly. He swallows. I'm loving this rare moment, when the tables are turned and I'm the one making him anxious.

"All right," he says. "So you want me to just . . . start?"

"Yes."

"You're a pain in the ass, you know that?"

"Yes."

"All right," he says again. "Here we go."

He clears his throat. And . . . nothing happens. I've never seen Strand so undone. Any trace of ego has diminished, leaving him looking exposed. For once, he doesn't look like an all-confident sex god. He looks like . . . I don't know. Like Strand.

"I have an idea," I say.

"Yeah?"

"What if I close my eyes? You can pretend I'm not here."

"Thank you, yeah, let's try that. Good thinking."

I shut my eyes, and I hear him clomping around my room. I feel the weight in my bed shift as Strand lies down next to me. Then I lose all concentration.

There's a boy in my bed. This has never happened before.

Mom would freak out if she saw us. *Levi* would probably freak out if he saw us. It's purely innocent, though. We're not even touching. I open my eyelids halfway to peek at Strand. His eyes are closed, his hands resting on his stomach.

His chest rises as he takes a long breath.

"Ready?" My voice comes out in a whisper.

And then he starts. His voice is smooth and warm. Honestly, he should consider singing for a chocolate commercial, because that's what his voice reminds me of. Chocolate truffles with dark cherry filling. That could be the name of his playlist. He really is lovely when he uses his mouth for singing and not annoying me. His brown curls frame his forehead, and his lashes are long and dark. He almost looks angelic.

I shut my eyes again. Strand sings about things I wouldn't expect from him. Love. Yearning. Awakening. Right when I think I can predict where the melody will go, it takes me by surprise by veering somewhere else, bending lazily to create a dreamy, sensual effect. With the music lingering in my ear, my other senses grow overwhelmed. I smell the vanilla on Strand, feel the heat radiating from his body. Even though I stay still, the energy coursing through me is wildly intense.

Strand's voice swims in and out of my ears. Usually when I listen to music, I do it to escape. To be transported to an alternate life, where I'm much cooler than I actually am and do exciting things. But now, lying next to Strand, listening to his voice, I am fully here. I don't think about how I would perform this, or what a music video to the song should look like. I just listen.

I'm vaguely aware that Strand's hand has slid off his stomach and now lies next to mine. I don't need to open my eyes to sense this. We're still not touching, but it almost feels sinful, the way my body responds to what we're *not* doing.

I must miss Levi.

Strand gets to the chorus, and I'm not prepared for the longing that rips through his voice . . . it's so beautiful that a tear leaks from my eye, and if I weren't so filled up with the music, I would have room for some embarrassment. The never-ending buildup was worth it, for this song.

Before I know it, Strand's hand is touching mine. I don't remember moving mine closer to his, or him moving his closer to mine, but they're touching, and the edge of my pinky where my skin meets his is on fire. We leave our hands there, resting against each other's. I should move mine away, but I stay still. We're not really doing anything wrong, I guess. It's accidental hand grazing. Still, I feel as though something's verging on inappropriate.

I must really miss Levi.

When his voice fades, it's like waking up. None of that was real. The feelings I had—they were a product of the song.

Strand's eyes flutter open. The expression on his face is slightly dazed. He starts to speak, but then Mom calls for us.

"Are you and Strand ready to go?" she yells from the kitchen.

"Yes!" I reply quickly and loudly, too loudly. I jump out of the bed and smooth out my hair, keeping my eyes on anything but Strand. The air feels thick and heavy in here. I feel Strand watching me, even though I have my back to him. I'm suddenly too aware of what my hands are doing. I wring them together, then reach up to my hair again.

"Did you like it?" he asks, finally. When I turn to look at him, he quickly clarifies. "The song?"

I stare at him for a moment. Was Strand in the same strange state that I was in? For once, there's no trace of a smile on his face. Or maybe I'm projecting my own weirdness onto him. He looks at me, his eyes silently pleading. I decide it's my imagination working overtime again.

"The song was . . . amazing, actually. You're amazing." I hate to say it, but I mean it. Strand is a natural-born songwriter.

"Oh, *really*?" He folds his hands behind his head and stretches back against my pillows.

Ugh. It was a mistake to compliment him. Now he has to get all annoying about it. He gives me his dimpled grin, the one Krina has termed "the panty-dropper."

"Shut up," I say. "Don't let it go to your head."

"I won't." The panty-dropper grin grows wider. He's such a liar.

Chapter Thirty

"FROM EDEN"
—HOZIER

A small part of me is okay with not having Levi around, and I think that might make me a terrible girlfriend. It's not that I don't miss him. He's my boyfriend. I *have* to miss him. It's obligatory. The thing is, I don't feel as incomplete as I thought I would with him gone. It's a relief to stop dreading him leaving. I prepared myself for the worst, and what I got instead is okay.

It's nice not to have to worry about what we'll do when we're alone together. Wondering how far we'll go or how to fill the pockets of silence in our conversations. No need to shave in case he touches my legs, or choose the clothes and makeup that I think will make me more attractive to him. I can wake up in the morning and stay in my pajamas all day. I can lip-synch to pop songs without judgment.

I haven't seen Strand since he sang to me. It's not like anything happened. There's nothing to feel awkward about, but the awkwardness is there anyway. My stomach is off, like I ate some of Shira's veal before practice. It doesn't help that I can't get his song out of my head. I hear it while I'm lathering my hair up in the shower. I hear it while Dad lectures me on dairy during dinner. I hear it before I fall asleep at night.

Sometimes I'll try to sing it, but I don't know all the words. I'll lie on my bed and try to recreate the experience of hearing it. I can almost smell the vanilla. But it's not the same.

When Strand comes over for the next rehearsal, he looks like he always does—T-shirt, dimple, perpetual bed-head.

"Hey, you," he says, and my skin prickles at the sound of his voice.

"Hi." He's early again.

Today he asks to hear one of my playlists, and I pull one up called Sipping Hot Chocolate in Front of a Fire, since it's twenty-seven degrees outside and drizzling cold, wet snow.

"We should do it," Strand says. "Do you have any chocolate syrup?"

"I think so." I duck out to check the kitchen and return to my room a couple minutes later with two steaming microwaved mugs.

"It's soy milk," I warn him as I hand him the personalized VICTORIA mug my parents got me at the Jersey shore. "My dad's lactose intolerant."

"That'll do," he says.

My apartment lacks a fireplace, so we sit in front of my chipped, rusty radiator. I keep a safe distance from him. There's no touching when we listen this time. I make sure to keep my eyes wide open.

My belly is still warm when Mom drops us off at Jessica's house. It's not just because of the hot chocolate. I would never admit this to my parents, but I find myself looking forward to quince rehearsals. I can be the girl in the rock band, swishing her hair around onstage, but then this—happy, hip swaying, salsa Victoria—is another part of me too. It's a part of me I neglect, so much so that I forget it exists sometimes. Levi has never even seen this Victoria.

Today, Eduardo arranges all the partners in a circle. We're rotating partners in this dance, launching into our basic salsa steps with each new pairing.

"¡Vuelta!"

At Eduardo's command, the girls are spun, like tops, into the arms of the next waiting guy in the circle. When Strand lets go of me, I'm caught by a boy named Chris. He has sprinkles of acne across his forehead and is well-meaning but stiff, and he apologizes profusely every time his knobby knees bash into mine.

"It's okay," I assure him for the fifteenth time.

"I still can't get the steps . . ."

It doesn't matter, because twenty seconds later, "¡Vuelta!"

And I'm spun into the next boy. So it goes, again and again. Gangly boys, short boys, boys with clammy hands, boys with rhythm, boys who can't count in time with the music.

Fourteen turns and I'm back to Strand. His hands, rough and calloused from playing guitar, clasp mine firmly. Strand moves forward as I step back. We're not exactly great performers. I stare down at my feet to make sure I don't step on him, and he swings his hips in a wildly exaggerated fashion to make me laugh.

"You're so frowny," he comments. "I can practically hear you counting in your head."

"I'm not," I say, even though I'm doing exactly that. "You're too loose."

"Um, I am not loose."

"Your steps are gigantic."

"I have long legs."

"Excuses, excuses."

Strand's eyes glint with mischief and he asks me, "Want to do a trick?"

My eyes dart over to Eduardo, who is running his fingers across his pashmina and staring the group of us down.

"He's watching," I warn.

"Oh, I'm sorry, I was confusing you for someone else. I know this badass who got detention for talking back to a teacher."

"Fine," I relent, allowing Strand to pull me into the center of the circle. It's only a rehearsal, after all. The other couples slow down their salsa dancing to watch us. No one is supposed to escape the circle.

Strand loosens his wrist, then spins me around, over and over again, around ten times. Jessica's living room whirls by until I lose my spotting and collapse into him.

"Sorry," he says, steadying me by the waist. "Too much?"

"A little ambitious," I say breathlessly.

I wish he would stop staring at me with those stupid blue eyes, and I wish I would stop having these ridiculous thoughts about how their hue perfectly matches the sky today.

The couples around us break into loud applause.

Eduardo lowers the music and bellows at us in Spanish to stick to the choreography.

Strand asks me how to say sorry in Spanish, and when I tell him he calls back to Eduardo, *"¡Lo siento, lo siento!"*

Eduardo glares back at him. I think he's the only person I've come across who is immune to Strand's charms, and it makes me like him more.

After the song ends, I sweep my hair off my neck and fan myself. It's ridiculous. Former cross-country runner loses breath after three minutes of salsa dancing. There's no reason for me to be this winded.

Jessica rushes over to us, her eyes shining. "You guys looked great! Tyler and I are going to have to step our game up."

Tyler, her freckled white boyfriend, looks less than thrilled at the prospect. He stares down at his sneakers.

"Victoria . . . are you okay?" Jessica asks.

"Yeah, I'm fine," I reply, melting onto the couch pushed against the wall. "I didn't have breakfast today, so I'm a little lightheaded."

"Do you want me to get you something?" Strand offers.

"No, no. It's really all right."

The reason I feel sick is not because I skipped breakfast today. The reality sets in. An epiphany of sorts.

Ever since Strand's song, I've been a little queasy. I can't stop thinking about what could have happened with us, lying together on my bed. Did Strand feel something too? If I gave into what I was feeling, how would he have responded? Would he have kissed me? The thought of his lips on mine sends my stomach into my throat.

Finding Strand attractive physically sickens me.

I'm stronger than this. Yes, Strand has charisma. And confidence. And lots and lots of sex appeal. So what? He could never meet my emotional needs. I'm not an idiot. I know Strand has a cornucopia of available women at his disposal, and I would never choose to be one of them. *He* would never choose me to be one of them. Besides, I'm lucky to have Levi. My responsible, patient boyfriend. And Strand's best friend.

"You're looking a little pale," Jessica says. "We have Fig Newtons in the kitchen if you want . . ."

"Relax, guys." I force myself up and almost jump when Strand reaches out to help me. "Let's go dance."

It's only when the music starts that my brain shuts up.

Chapter Thirty-One

"A MULHER DO FIM DO MUNDO"
—ELZA SOARES

My parents have used this time off to plan an excursion to the exotic land of Cambridge, Massachusetts. They're bouncing-off-the-walls excited to finally see Harvard in person. This is their big plan to get me back on track. If I see Harvard, I'll remember that this is the reason for all of our hard work. The late nights spent studying, the tears over ten-page essays, all of the bullshit will disappear because . . . HARVARD. I looked into their big smiley faces when they announced the trip—it was the happiest I'd ever seen them—and I realized that saying no was not an option. I'm not sure it ever will be. Getting out of NYC might be good, though. It'll give me some much-needed distance from Strand.

So, four Cubans pack themselves into a car, and Mom and Dad argue about directions during the entirety of the three-and-a-half-hour drive.

"I have the map on my phone," I try to shout over them. They don't care, because for some ridiculous reason they don't trust technology. Mom got written directions from her friend Jeannie, whose son went to Harvard. Apparently, Jeannie is way more reliable than Google.

"You have to take Putnam Avenue!" Mom shrieks.

"There is no Putnam Avenue!" Dad hollers back.

Matty and I roll our eyes at each other.

"Stay on River Street," I say, zooming in on the phone map.

Mom shakes her head and peers at her pencil scrawls. "Jeannie didn't say anything about River Street."

"Can I have my 3DS?" Matty asks.

"No!" Dad replies. "No phones, no 3DS. We are going to talk like a goddamn family, *coño*!"

And so it goes. We finally make it to Cambridge, twenty minutes later than we would have if we'd followed Google's directions, and I jump out of the car as soon as Dad parks.

I bend over to stretch my hamstrings while Matty tries to grab his 3DS from Dad's pocket. Dad smacks his hand away.

"So," I ask. "What specifically are we going to do? Wander around?"

"What do you mean?" Mom asks. She squeezes my shoulders and plants a giant kiss on my cheek. "We're going to see *everything*!"

"Yeah, but like . . . for how long?"

"All day, baby," Dad says. "We're doing this all day."

Matty rests his head against the car, closing his eyes. He suddenly looks ten times his age.

They decide we should explore Cambridge first. The town of Cambridge is utopia to the Cruz family. We walk through narrow streets of bookstores and restaurants (all things we have in New York, but you wouldn't think so, listening to my parents).

Everything is charming, or, as it sounds in my parents' heavy Cuban accents, "sharmeen." The trees are sharmeen, the drugstore is sharmeen, the garbage cans are sharmeen. They have morphed into living heart-eyed emojis.

"*¡Mira, Ria!*" Dad says, stopping abruptly in front of Algiers Coffee House. "Look at this! Look how—"

"Charming?" I cut in. He skips over my sarcasm.

"*Coño,*" he breathes, scanning the menu posted on the window. "They have soy milk lattes."

"So does Starbucks," I say dully.

"Look at all the Harvard kids in there! Want to go get coffee and check it out?"

"I don't like coffee."

"You'll like it when you're in college. You'll be in there, drinking coffee and reading a book for class. Right, Glo?"

And Mom does the same thing. "Look, Ria, they have all these vegetarian options! You and your Harvard friends could come here for lunch!"

They drag Matty and me inside. The shop is nice, I hate to admit.

It's two stories, decorated in a Middle Eastern style, and has a terrace overlooking the sharmeen Brattle Street. My parents order soy lattes for themselves and mint hot chocolates for me and Matty.

Mom and Dad sit on one side of the table, sipping their lattes and poring over Jeannie's recommendations. According to Jeannie, we have to rub a statue's foot, visit the art collection at Sackler Museum, and walk along the Charles River. They're so loud about everything that people in the café start to stare at us over their laptops.

"Can you guys lower your voices?" I whisper. "You don't need to tell the entire café our plans."

"We're not being loud," Dad says in his booming voice, and it practically thunders through the floorboards. I sink down in my seat. This is what sucks. Some days I'm the lead singer of a rock band, and some days I'm a little girl embarrassed by her excessively loud family. Cuban volume is roughly the same decibel level as a jet engine.

"Nobody cares what we're talking about, Victoria," Mom adds. "They have important *Harvard* things to worry about."

"How's your hot chocolate, Matty?" Dad asks.

Matty gives a giant grin. "This is the best hot chocolate I've ever had."

Matty has become one of them. I feel betrayed.

We set off for Harvard at the slowest pace imaginable. I grumble about why we couldn't do this in the summer when it's warmer out, and Mom and Dad ignore me. I hate everything about this. I hate that Cambridge is, in fact, a cute town. It would be much easier if it were ugly. Even the winter weather isn't as awful as I'm making it seem. The sun is peeking out from behind fluffy white clouds, like it's determined to make me look petty.

We stop when we get to a pair of respectable brick pillars at an entrance to Harvard Yard. My parents ooh and aah, but it's underwhelming to me. It looks like a bigger, more intense version of Evanston. All I think can think is, *I might be walking between these pillars every day for four years.*

"Let's get a picture of you, Victoria!" Mom says. "Give Dad your phone."

"Do we have to?"

She practically shoves me into the pillars and I stand there, smiling stiffly while Dad jabs at my phone, muttering to himself.

"Just press the camera icon," I say through my teeth.

"*¿Donde?*"

"On the home screen."

"I think I did something wrong."

My smile falters. "Give the phone to Matty."

Matty takes the phone and Mom reminds him to get the pillars in the picture, and throughout the process I feel my life slowly winding to its end.

Mom makes Matty take pictures of everything. Statues and crimson flags and the Harvard seal. Dad stands in front of the seal, giving the camera a dorky thumbs-up. He puts his arm around me and gazes around the campus wistfully.

"Want to trade places?" he asks me.

Gladly, I want to say.

When my parents make comments like that, I feel like a colossal bitch. They would have done anything for the chance I have. What's wrong with me that I don't want this? Why don't I just suck it up and do it for them?

Our last stop is the Harvard gift shop, where my parents buy themselves overpriced crimson sweaters with giant *H*s on them.

"I want to go to Harvard too," Matty says with a certainty I'll never have. My parents glance at each other, and I see the happiness on their faces wane. Matty is smart, but he's not exactly school smart. Which sucks, because he works harder than I do at practically everything. They buy him a T-shirt anyway.

"What about you, Ria?" Dad asks me.

"I'm good," I reply.

"You have to get something. We're at Harvard!"

"It's so overpriced."

"Don't worry about the price."

This means something, coming from Jorge Cruz. He's one of the stingiest people alive. Reluctantly, I pick out the cheapest T-shirt I can find. It's gray.

"Family picture," Mom says before we leave.

I bite down on my lip to keep from screaming. Mom hands my phone to a student in glasses. The girl probably has way more important things to do than take a picture of us, but she agrees anyway.

"Smile," Harvard girl says, holding the phone out in front of her. She looks studious and nice, like the daughter my parents deserve.

I try to smile, and my eyes sting with tears. All the guilt I've been holding in all day—no, scratch that, for fifteen years, threatens to spill out of me.

Do not cry in front of the Harvard girl. Do not cry in front of your parents or they will flip a shit. Go to your happy place.

My mind goes to Jessica's living room, and I think about Strand's arms around my waist, and then I feel guilty for entirely different reasons.

Click, goes my camera phone.

Chapter Thirty-Two

"PAY ATTENTION"
—COLLEEN GREEN

The rest of the break comes and goes in a blur of video games, TV marathons, and Noche Buena at my aunt Rita's house in Union City. Fifty of my relatives crammed into Aunt Rita's small slab of backyard. I cringed at the helpless pig injected with mojo juice and splayed inside a roasting box known as *La Caja China*. The entire process is what led me to turn vegetarian three years back. Then I had to deal with Abi chasing me around with a forkful of pork to try to get me to fatten up. Abi is relentlessly stubborn about my vegetarianism. Luckily, Aunt Rita bought a block of tofu especially for me, and I had that with my rice and beans instead. I told Abi it was chicken, which met her approval.

In the midst of the chaos, I wondered what Strand would think of this crazy Cuban version of Christmas Eve. I shuddered to think about Levi's opinion. He didn't call me that night or the day after. I could excuse it because he's Jewish, after all.

But then New Year's came and went. Abi served us each twelve grapes, one for each month of the year. We gathered around the TV to watch the ball drop in Times Square, and I was so sure Levi would call to wish me a happy New Year. Instead, I got a mass text and a smiley face emoji.

It's the first day of school since break ended, and I'm nervous about seeing my own boyfriend. It makes zero sense. He should be the one person who makes me feel safe and comfortable, but I haven't talked to him since our failed make-out session before he left for Vermont.

Has he changed his mind about me? Maybe he realized during his time away that he's too busy for a girlfriend, and I'll have to face the new year as a single woman. The thought turns my blood cold. Levi is the only boy who's ever shown a real interest in me. He may be the only one who ever will.

I spot him as soon as Annie and I enter the cafeteria, and in that second I see him, I forget every question I had about us. All thoughts of Strand's sexiness and that fleeting bedroom moment vanish. I don't know what I expected Levi to morph into during his time away, but he's the same Levi, sitting there with Krina and Strand, munching on his tuna sandwich. He's so cute with his glasses and short hair that I want to cry. I really did miss him.

When Annie and I get to the table, he stands up and pulls me into him. I'm still his girlfriend. I feel it in the way he grips my waist so tightly. Being touched like this after two weeks apart makes it feel like the first time. I inhale the scent of his hair gel and it reminds me of holding hands and Carnegie Hall. We kiss in front of the others, without shame. Krina and Annie aww, while Strand groans.

"Jesus, enough," he says.

I break away from Levi and take a seat at the table. "Strand, I've seen far worse from you."

As the king of inappropriate PDA, he can't argue with that. He mutters something under his breath and takes a bite of his wrap.

"So, I got you some stuff," Levi says, dragging a gift bag out from under his chair.

"You did?" How could I have doubted this man?

"It's all maple syrup related," he says, handing the bag to me. "That's pretty much Vermont's main thing."

I pull out the items. There's a bottle of maple syrup, maple sugar candy, and . . . a wrapped maple-cured sausage. Phallic imagery aside, I'm not sure what to say. It seems too late in the game to tell Levi I'm a vegetarian, especially since I didn't tell him when I went to his house for dinner.

Then Strand opens his big mouth and does it for me. "Dude, Victoria can't eat that."

"What?" Levi looks at me. "Why not?"

Annie and Krina exchange a glance, and I can practically hear Annie's lecture in my mind.

Levi doesn't even know you're a vegetarian? Everyone knows you're a vegetarian! How do you think you're ready to get intimate with this guy when he doesn't know the basics about you?

Even in my head, she's shrill. I place the items back into the gift bag, avoiding eye contact with everyone at the table. "I, um . . . I don't really eat meat."

"You what?" And even though I'm not looking at him, I can already picture his baffled expression as he adjusts his glasses.

"I'm kind of a vegetarian." I look up now, and add, "But thanks for the gifts . . ."

"Why didn't you tell me?" Levi asks in an accusatory tone.

"Duh, man. She's mentioned it before," Strand says. "And she eats pizza for lunch every day. You should have known." I look at him, and he can't even conceal his enjoyment of this moment. So much for our newfound friendship.

"But you ate veal at my apartment," Levi says.

Annie's hands fly up to her mouth. "Vi, you didn't!" Her words are soaked in disapproval.

"What is this, a firing squad?" I ask. "You guys are all meat eaters!"

"But *you're* not," Annie says.

"Is that why you got sick?" Levi asks. "Were you actually sick?"

"Yes," I admit. "I didn't want to insult your mom."

Levi shakes his head. "I feel terrible."

I put my hand over his. "It's my fault. I should have said something."

"You have," Strand says, and I cut him off with a glare.

Krina casts a strange look over all of us, like she's suddenly found herself sitting with a group of strangers. "So . . . I'll take that sausage if you don't want it, Vi."

"Oh, Krina, you have no interest in sausage," Strand says. Krina punches him on the shoulder.

Chapter Thirty-Three

"CUT YOUR HAIR"
—PAVEMENT

At band practice Levi mentions that Kaitlyn Fielding invited the band to play at her party next Saturday.

Kaitlyn is a senior at Evanston, and probably the most untouchably beautiful girl I've ever seen in person. She has auburn hair the color of fall leaves, and it spills in perfect layers around her face. Kaitlyn's parties are a big deal. There's a hot tub and catered food, and someone is always cheating on someone else. I've never been invited to a Kaitlyn Fielding party. No sophomore has.

At the sound of Kaitlyn's name, though, Krina's head springs up from behind her drum set. Her face turns a violent shade of crimson, perfectly matching Harvard's school color.

"What the *fuck*, Levi," she says.

"She offered to let us play a short set," he replies as we pack up to leave.

"Why are you even talking to her?"

"She came to me. Besides, we should play whatever we can get."

"What's going on?" I ask. "What's wrong with Kaitlyn?"

Strand sets his guitar against the wall and wipes his forehead with the back of his shirtsleeve. "We won't do it if you don't want to, Krina."

"It's been a year," Levi says. "Kaitlyn's extending an olive branch."

Krina glares at him. "Fuck her branch."

"What happened last year?" I interrupt.

"Kaitlyn revealed herself to be the spawn of Satan," Krina replies, then she promptly turns back to Levi. "I love this band, Levi, but I'm not lowering myself to play at Kaitlyn's request."

I shoot Strand a confused look and he motions me over.

"Kaitlyn sang for Debaser before you," he whispers, keeping his eyes on Krina.

"What?" I whisper back. "As in Kaitlyn Fielding?"

"Yes."

"Perfect hair, legs that don't quit?"

"Yes."

"Kaitlyn Fielding, of the Fielding Dining Hall?"

"Yes."

Girls like Kaitlyn Fielding don't sing lead for rock bands. They just don't.

"Why the bad blood?" I ask.

"CliffsNotes version? They dated, Kaitlyn didn't want to come out, dumped Krina, quit the band, fucked the wrestling coach."

"What?!" I shriek. Krina and Levi glance over at me before resuming their conversation, which seems to have grown progressively more heated, based on the way Krina is waving her drumsticks around.

I should have figured it out long before now.

Krina's a lesbian. Out of all the rumors spread about her, this is the one thing I hadn't heard or even considered.

How could I have missed this? What's wrong with me? All the signs were right there, glaring and bright. The rainbow bracelets adorning her wrist, Strand's joke earlier that week about her having no interest in sausage, the fact that she's never, in all the time that I've known her, mentioned an interest in boys.

"The answer is no!" Krina yells at Levi, and I duck as a drumstick flies over my head and crashes against the wall behind me.

"Aaand, that's our cue," Strand says, strapping his guitar onto his shoulder. He places a hand on my back and guides me out of the band room as the second drumstick goes flying.

We don't say anything as we walk down the stairs and out of the building. I feel a million miles away from Krina all of a sudden. We've been friends for months, and I didn't know this giant part of her life.

"No idea, huh?" Strand says in his weird psychic way, and I'm ready to snap at him until I look at his face and see that he's not laughing at me. He's simply stating a fact.

I sigh. "I'm an idiot."

"Hey now. No one talks about my partner like that." Strand sticks his hands in his pockets and stares at something straight ahead. "You're not an idiot, Victoria. You're just . . . sheltered."

"Gee, thanks."

"That's not an insult. I like that about you."

"Why?"

"Because. Things are new to you. Things surprise you. That's a good quality to have. You're sheltered, but you're still open to trying things."

"You're basically describing a child. And I'm not open to trying things. I'm a wuss."

Strand rolls his eyes. "Will you stop doing that, please?"

"What?"

"Insulting yourself. Take a damn compliment."

"I'm being honest!"

"You tried out for a band. You performed in front of a bunch of strangers. A wuss wouldn't do that."

My instinct is to disagree with him, but when he says it out loud, it does sound brave. Impressively brave. Maybe I don't give myself enough credit.

"Fine," I say begrudgingly. "So I'm not a total wuss."

"That's better."

We walk a couple blocks and when I see the subway entrance, I suddenly wish it were farther away.

"Is Krina going to be all right?" I ask.

"I have no doubt."

"I don't know why Levi would agree to it."

"He was thinking of the band."

"But what about Krina?"

"You know Levi," Strand says. "He can lose sight of things."

Boy, do I know this.

"Can I ask you something?" Strand says, not looking at me. My heart palpitates like it's been jump-started.

"Okay . . . ," I say in my best casual voice.

"When you're kissing Levi, and you try to run your hand through his hair . . . does it get caught in his hair gel?"

"Strand!" My heart slows back to its normal rate.

"What?" he asks, eyebrows raised in innocence. "It's an honest question."

I suck in my cheeks to keep from smiling, because making fun of Levi's hair is not a girlfriend-y thing to do. "It's more crunchy than sticky."

We've reached the subway, but Strand leans against the entrance without making any move to leave.

"Once on a field trip," he says, "our class went into this tornado simulator. We had to wear protective goggles and everything. So we get into this simulator, and it's, like, hundred-miles-per-hour winds. Everyone's clothes are rippling, hair is flying everywhere. And I swear to God, not one hair on Levi's head ever moves."

"That can't be true," I say, letting myself smile this time.

"I'm serious." Strand looks pleased at my reaction. "Levi's hair is like the eighth wonder of the world."

"I'm sure it looked better than yours," I say. "Do you even brush it?"

I reach up to tousle his hair, which is soft and miraculously untangled despite its messy appearance. My fingers slide right through it.

Strand clamps his hand around my wrist, and when he looks at me, his smile fades. I pull my hand away from his grip, suddenly feeling self-conscious.

"You need a haircut," I say, to relieve the tension.

He shakes his hair out so it flops from side to side. "Girls like something to hold on to."

I shove him on the shoulder, and the spell is broken.

Chapter Thirty-Four

"SUPERSTAR"
—SONIC YOUTH

My parents insist on having Levi over for dinner, both to get to know him better and to return the favor after Shira had me over. Mom thinks it's rude if we don't. She's really concerned with what the Schusters will think of us. Heaven forbid they consider us middle-class immigrants. She makes spaghetti with canned tomato sauce and heats frozen garlic bread in the oven. For her, this is the pinnacle of culinary ambition. Tonight we use our special occasion matching plates with little blue flowers along the borders.

With Levi coming over, I see our apartment through a rich person's lens. I see the chip on the edge of my glass, the worn fabric of our dining room chairs, all kinds of things I never noticed before. I'm ashamed that I feel ashamed.

Levi wears a button-down shirt and khakis while everyone else in my family wears jeans. I wish I'd made them dress up a little. He gives me a quick kiss in greeting, as quick as possible under Dad's hawk-eyed stare.

"Mr. Cruz, Mrs. Cruz," Levi says, shaking everyone's hand again even though they've met before.

He's so polite that my family becomes stiff. They're all on their best behavior, including Matty. He eats the spaghetti without complaining, and he doesn't even bring his 3DS to the table. Each of them is pretending to be someone they're not, someone more in line with the typical Evanston family.

When we're all seated, Mom nudges me to pour everyone's drink, which is something we never do. Usually each person in our family fills their own glass.

"So, Levi," Dad says as I pour him a glass, trying not to splash. "Victoria said you play the bass guitar?"

"Yes, sir," Levi replies.

He doesn't elaborate, and Dad doesn't really know what to say to that.

Mom jumps in. "How long have you been playing?"

"About five years," Levi says.

"He's really good," I tell my parents. "He's going to regionals with the school band in February."

"What songs do you know?" Matty asks him.

"Well . . . ," Levi says. "A lot . . . too many to name." He talks to

Matty in a slow, measured way, like he's dealing with a foreign species instead of a ten-year-old kid.

"Can you play any AC/DC?" Matty asks.

"Sure."

"Like, which songs?"

I sit down next to Levi. "Matty, stop badgering him. He can probably learn any AC/DC song."

"Cool!" Matty says. "Can you bring your bass over and play next time?"

Levi takes a sip of water and looks to me for help.

"We'll see," I tell Matty, which usually works in getting him to shut up.

Mom asks Levi what his parents do, and Levi answers. The entire dinner is a strange interview. The conversation isn't flowing, and there are moments of silence that last too long. It bothers me that Mom isn't more taken with Levi. I can tell she approves of him, but she doesn't laugh and joke around with him the way she does with Strand. It's like everyone's too busy trying to impress him to act like themselves.

When we finish dinner, I show Levi my room. I don't tell him that Strand's already been inside. Not that it's a secret or anything. I just decide not to. I keep the door open, and Mom and Dad find any excuse to pass by and poke their heads in to make sure we're not up to anything scandalous.

"This is my vinyl collection," I announce to Levi, posing in front of it like a *Price Is Right* model.

Levi looks around and nods in approval. I can't help puffing up with pride.

"And these are my playlists," I say, pulling them up on my computer. I tell him about how my playlists are specially crafted for each mood, and how, depending on what I want to imagine, I know exactly where I can find some matching songs. I wait for him to laugh and kiss me and marvel at my excellent taste in music.

"Interesting" is all he says, and I can tell from his tone that he doesn't find my system endearing or unique, like Strand did. Just confusing.

Chapter Thirty-Five

"R U MINE?"
—ARCTIC MONKEYS

Against all odds, Krina agrees to play at Kaitlyn's this Saturday. "But," she informs us as we stand shoulder to shoulder in front of her. "I will not speak to her. I will not look at her. I'm there to drum and leave. Understood?"

"Yes," we say in unison.

"You shitheads owe me."

Annie and I sneak out of her apartment at nine o'clock and take the train to the Upper East Side. Kaitlyn lives in a large apartment, even larger than Levi's, next to Central Park. It has high vaulted ceilings and brightly polished tiles. Professionally photographed portraits of Kaitlyn hang delicately on the walls. Kaitlyn on a horse, Kaitlyn reading a book, Kaitlyn posing with a violin.

I'm nervous to perform tonight, more nervous than I was at the bowling alley a couple of months ago. This is different. I'm not performing in front of strangers, I'm performing in front of people I pass in the halls every day. If I mess this up, I have to face them for the rest of high school.

Thankfully, we're not playing too long. Kaitlyn's hired a DJ, and according to Levi, we're only playing a twenty-minute set during the DJ's break.

This is my first real high school party. I would never choose to spend my free time with the Evanston population, but I'm sacrificing myself for the band. Swarming around me are actual drunk high schoolers. People I know are transformed. Shy, sweet Erin Wheaton with the big eyes and the Minnie Mouse voice is dancing against a wall. Math Club president Kevin Young is straddling a keg like he's riding Seabiscuit. It's eerie the way alcohol brings out people's inner selves.

Annie and I find the others right away when we enter, except for Strand.

"Are you okay?" I ask Krina. She's sitting stiffly on Kaitlyn's Chanel couch, her eyes darting around the room.

"I need a drink" is her response as she gets to her feet, leaving me, Annie, and Levi on the couch by ourselves.

"Do you want me to come with you?" Annie offers.

Krina's eyes stop moving for a second. "No thanks. I'm okay."

When Krina's out of earshot, Annie says, "I've never seen her like this." Her brows scrunch together. "Do you think she's really okay?"

Krina is swigging a bottle of beer on the opposite side of the room, eyeing Kaitlyn, who is giggling in a corner with a group of lacrosse players.

"Krina's always okay," I tell her.

"She's not," says Annie. "She just pretends to be . . . God, I can't stand her."

"Krina?"

"No," Annie says. "Kaitlyn. The way she started those rumors about Krina . . . she's a terrible excuse for a human being."

"Kaitlyn started the rumors?" I ask. "Even the one about the wrestling coach?"

"Of course," Annie says. "Krina wouldn't do any of that stuff."

I feel guilty for believing anything when it comes to Krina. It turns out that the more I learn about her, the less I feel I really know her.

Annie looks distressed, but I can't keep my gaze from drifting around the room.

"Where's Strand?" I ask Levi.

Levi jerks his thumb over his shoulder. "Talking to some girl over there."

I look past him and, sure enough, Strand is chatting up a girl— my former cross-country teammate and captain, Rachel Levine. It hits me how annoying I find Rachel. She always runs in a sports bra that shows off her flat, toned stomach, and she's always tan, even in the dead of winter.

"I'm going to get a drink," Levi says. "Do you guys want anything?"

I figure a little booze might soothe my nerves. Plus, since I'm staying at Annie's tonight, there's no danger of my parents waiting up for me to get home and smelling alcohol on my breath. I ask Levi to bring me a shot of tequila.

"Isn't that a little much?" Annie asks. "You don't want to get sick again." She's in a mood tonight.

"I won't have much," I assure her.

"If you say so . . ." Her lips tighten as she takes a sip of her ice water. Honestly. Who drinks water at a party? Annie can't even loosen up enough to have a soda, because of the sugar content.

I look over at Strand and Rachel again. She's taking a sip of his whiskey and laughing at something he said. She looks pretty when she laughs. It's the contrast of her teeth and her tan.

"Rude," I say aloud.

Annie, who is openly staring at Kaitlyn, tears her eyes away to follow the direction of my gaze. "Who? Strand?"

"Yeah. He hasn't even come over to say hi."

"He probably didn't see us come in."

"He saw us."

Annie shakes her head. "Look at her."

"Who? Rachel?"

She sighs in exasperation. "Krina."

I look. Krina's hair is extra spiky tonight, her liner painted in thick circles around her eyes. But if I pay close attention, I can almost see Krina without the haircut, makeup, and snarl. She looks less terrifying tonight, despite the extra effort she put into her appearance. She looks depressed.

Before I can respond, Levi comes back with a beer for himself and a tequila shot for me. I sniff at it and wrinkle my nose.

"You've never had one?" he asks me.

"No, she hasn't," Annie replies for me.

I frown at her. "Stop making it such a big deal."

"Just take it in one gulp and chase it with the lime," Levi says.

I tip the glass so the liquid goes straight into my throat and my tongue burns with the sharp, metallic taste. My body coughs and shudders involuntarily as I reach for the slice of lime in Levi's hand to end this assault on my taste buds.

"I told you, that's too much for you," Annie says, and she's so satisfied at being right that I turn away from her and say to Levi, "I'll do another if you do it with me."

Krina comes back to the couch empty-handed. She must have downed her beer in about five minutes. She looks down at the empty shot glass and lime rind on the table. "Are we doing tequila shots?"

"No," Annie says.

"Yes we are," I reply. "Do you want one?"

Kaitlyn laughs loudly at something one of the lacrosse players says, and Krina squares her shoulders. "Hell yes." She nudges Annie. "Come on, Annalise, don't be a party pooper."

"I'm fine," Annie says, lifting her chin.

"Bring her one," Krina says to Levi, and Annie sucks in her cheeks but doesn't protest.

Levi is back in a flash, trying to balance two shot glasses in each hand. He places them on the coffee table in front of us.

Krina recites a toast in Spanish that I've never heard before. *"¡Arriba, abajo, al centro y adentro!"*

I laugh, already light like I'm filled with helium, and the four of us down the shots together. It doesn't take long to kick in. I recognize the feeling of being slightly dizzy but happy.

"I want to dance," I decide. There's a group of people dancing near Strand and Rachel.

"Levi doesn't dance," Krina reminds me.

I pull him up off the couch and offer, "I'll dance, you can just stand."

He does exactly that once I drag him onto the floor. He stands there and looks uncomfortable while I move with the music, matching my hips with the thumping bass line. I dance with people I've seen in the halls but I've never spoken to before. Levi bobs his head but doesn't join the action.

After a few minutes I'm sweaty and flushed. I look over to find Strand openly staring at me, his expression unreadable. When I meet his gaze, he looks away and says something to Rachel.

"You look good when you dance," Levi says.

"Really?" I smile at him.

"Yeah," he says. "It's sexy."

Sexy. This is the first time Levi, or anyone in the world, has used the word in relation to me. I wonder if Strand thinks I look sexy when I dance or if he still considers me a sheltered little girl. When the DJ starts a new song, I get even more into the music, dipping my hips low, desperately trying to solidify my sexiness. I've never danced like this in public, but I've practiced plenty of times in my room, and I know I look good.

See, Strand? I'm not so sheltered now, am I? The two sides of my brain are at war, one insisting that I stop worrying about what Strand thinks, the other wanting to prove him wrong. Out of the corner of my eye I glance at him, but he's not looking at me anymore. Instead, he's kissing Rachel. She has her hands wrapped around his neck, her fingers caressing his hair. The same hair that I was touching a few days ago. It bothers me that she knows how soft it is.

And Strand had the nerve to tell me he wasn't the playboy I thought he was. How could I ever have felt an attraction to him?

"Do you want to sit back down?" Levi asks. His face is beet red even though he hasn't moved much, just bobbed back and forth like a water buoy.

"Nope." I look away from Strand. "I want another tequila shot."

"Are you sure that's a good idea? We're up soon . . ."

"One more," I promise.

Levi ventures to the kitchen for another shot while I continue dancing alone, uninhibited. I realize that guys are looking at me, smiling at me. Maybe Strand doesn't find me desirable, but other people might. Including my boyfriend. My sweet boyfriend who is obediently fetching me a drink.

When Levi returns with the shot, I take it quickly, my tongue barely registering the taste this time. Then I make out with him, right there on the dance floor in front of everyone. I run my hands under his shirt, pressing my fingers against the dimples in his lower back.

"Let's go somewhere," I tell him in my sultriest voice, trying hard not to slur my words.

His eyes widen. "Where?"

I take his hand and lead him even though I'm not sure where we're going. As I drag Levi behind me, I purposely bump into Strand and Rachel so they have to break apart.

"Sorry!" I say innocently.

Strand rubs his lips, stained pink from Rachel's lipstick. "Where are you going, Cutlet?"

"Somewhere *private*," I say pointedly, gripping Levi's arm.

Strand narrows his eyes at Levi. "Is she drunk?"

"She had a few tequila shots," Levi says.

It's infuriating, the way they speak to each other like I'm not there.

"I'm perfectly fine," I tell them both. "Don't treat me like a kid."

Rachel fiddles with a charm on her gold necklace and looks at the three of us. "Hi, Victoria. Haven't seen you in a while."

"Hi, Rachel," I reply coldly.

Then I feel bad because she looks confused, and she really hasn't done anything wrong. No one's done anything wrong. Strand owes me nothing, and I have no say in who he kisses. He's not my boyfriend, after all.

I look at Levi, and my heart floods with affection. Good old Levi.

"Why don't you get her some water?" Strand says, again to Levi.

Levi nods and leaves me there with Strand and Rachel.

"Don't worry about me," I tell them both breezily. "Carry on with the kissing."

For some reason, I add a salute to show them how okay I am with it. It's one of those moves that makes sense in my drunken mindset but fails in real-world execution. I turn to follow Levi to the kitchen, but my ankle twists and I wobble unsteadily. Strand's hands are around my waist before I have time to stand up again.

"I'll be right back," he tells Rachel, then he pulls me into an empty hallway. I let him guide me, reluctantly.

"Strand, I don't need a babysitter." I close my eyes to stop the walls from tilting.

"I'm not babysitting you."

"Then what are you doing?"

"I'm making sure you're okay."

"Why?"

"Because . . . I'm your friend."

"Well, thank you, *friend*," I say sharply. "I appreciate you looking out for me."

When I open my eyes, Strand looks slightly wounded. "What the hell, Victoria. Are you mad at me or something?"

"Why would I be mad at you?"

"Great question."

I look down, and his hands are still on my waist. We're standing so close that I can see the bits of stubble on his chin and smell the whiskey on his breath.

"I'm not mad," I say quietly.

Our eyes lock, and it occurs to me that it would be so easy to reach up and close the distance between our lips. I want to know what they feel like. They look soft, like little pillows. His eyes flicker down my face. Is he wondering the same thing about mine?

"I'm glad," he says.

"What?"

"That you're not mad."

"That rhymes," I blurt out stupidly, and he laughs. "I'm a little drunk."

"You don't say."

"I should go find Levi."

"Right." He lets go of my waist. "I should get back to Rachel."

Even though I told him I wasn't mad, a flare of anger burns through me.

"Are you going to have sex with her?" I ask abruptly. He doesn't answer right away, and it bothers me. "Is that a yes?"

He's looking at me in that way he does, like his mind is constructing a theory. "Is there a reason I should say no?"

"Ugh. You're disgusting."

"I'm sorry we're not all as chaste as you, Victoria."

"I'm not chaste. Levi and I have done plenty of stuff."

"What do you care anyway?" he asks. "Why don't you stop concerning yourself with what I do?"

"Why don't you stop acting like a disappointment to the male species?" I shoot back.

"Oh, get over yourself. Go back to your boyfriend." He practically spits the word out, *boyfriend*, and it slices through me. He's never talked to me like that before.

"I will," I say in a similarly harsh tone. "I'm lucky to have Levi. He's nice and he makes me feel safe and—"

"Are you describing a car seat or a person?"

"Stop it." Either I'm swaying, or Strand is. Or maybe it's the room.

"I mean, it's an odd way to describe someone you love. You do love him, right?"

"I don't need to explain myself to you, Strand. Or my choice of words."

"No, you don't."

Still, I want to. I *have* to, for some reason. "There's nothing wrong with being safe."

He presses his thumb between his eyebrows and closes his eyes. "I know that." He sounds tired.

"But you're too cool to play it safe, right, Strand?" I say, and there's a stop sign going off in my brain but my mouth ignores it, charging ahead. I'm infuriated at what Strand is implying. To prove my point, I blurt out, "At least Levi doesn't have to screw every girl in sight."

He opens his mouth like he's about to speak, but he doesn't. I keep going.

"It's disgusting," I say. My brain shouts at me to stop, but I'm tired of censoring myself. I deliver my final words with a flourish. "*You* disgust me, Strand."

There. I wounded him like he wounded me. It's written all over his face.

"Hey . . ." And Levi is suddenly here, standing in the middle of the hallway with my glass of water. "I couldn't find you two. Is everything all right?"

Strand's expression shifts from hurt to disdain.

"She's drunk," he says bitterly, and leaves us behind, probably to head toward Rachel.

"What happened?" Levi asks.

"Nothing." I snatch the water out of his hand. "Let's go back out there."

We skirt past the swarms of Evanston students grinding against each other and bump into Annie back in Kaitlyn's living room.

"Where's Krina?" Levi asks her. "We're up in twenty minutes."

"I can't find her," Annie says, her eyes scanning the room. "She went to get another drink and never came back." Worry creeps into her voice.

"Wonderful," Levi says, tapping his fingers against his thigh. "Now we don't have a drummer."

Annie folds her arms over her chest. "Well, maybe you shouldn't have pressured her into playing tonight. Kaitlyn treated her like dirt."

"She should put the band before her personal issues," Levi says.

"Or maybe you should put your friend before the band."

"Okay, okay, okay," I say, raising my hand like I'm in a classroom. "Let's focus on finding Krina."

Strand, too, has disappeared, but I'm in no mood to run into him.

"I checked the kitchen," Annie says, "but I didn't go into the bedrooms."

"You do that," I say. "I'll check the bathrooms. Levi . . . you stay here in case Krina comes back."

Annie takes off down the hallway, and I ask a broad-shouldered football player where the bathroom is. He points me up the spiraling staircase, looming above me like Everest. Shit. I go up slowly, clinging to the railing. Tequila shots and spiral staircases are not my friends tonight. When I make it upstairs, the bathroom door is closed, so I rap my knuckle against it. No answer.

"Krina?" I call, knocking harder.

Still nothing. I grimace and push the door open, hoping not to walk in on anything too traumatic. The bathroom is massive, all sparkling white tiles and sleek chrome fixtures. Huddled in the corner is not Krina, but Kaitlyn, sitting against the wall, looking glassy-eyed. Her beautiful auburn hair hangs in a tangled mop around her face, looking unstyled for the first time ever.

I start to back out, but she says, "Come in. Close the door."

"Sorry," I say. "I was looking for Krina."

Kaitlyn doesn't acknowledge my statement. "You want?" she asks, lifting a small plastic bag of weed.

"No." I touch the door handle, trying to make my exit. All I want is to get away from Kaitlyn, looking so lifeless and scary. "Do you know where Krina is?"

"Sit down," Kaitlyn says, patting the space next to her.

"I'm okay."

"You're the new lead singer, right?"

"Yeah."

"Sit down," she repeats. I can tell she's not giving up until I listen to her, so I sit cross-legged across from her. The bathroom tiles are icy cold through my clothing.

"Krina's gone," she says.

"Gone where?"

"Out. Out of this apartment." She waves her hand around and I catch a whiff of her scent, a mix of lavender and weed.

"What happened?"

"I tried to apologize to her. She just left. She didn't even talk to me."

"Well . . . she kind of hates you."

"I guess I deserve that." She rubs her eyes, and mascara smears around her lids. "I miss her. I thought if I invited you guys to play, she would maybe . . ."

Her voice trails off, and she stares into space.

"So why did you do it?" I ask. "Dump her, I mean."

"Come on."

"Come on, what?"

"What was I going to do? Fall in love? Get married, have kids, tour the country like a gay Partridge Family?"

"Yes. Why not?"

"You have no idea what people expect of me."

Ha. I know a thing or two about living up to people's expectations, but I don't argue with her.

"Did she make you happy?" I ask.

She doesn't answer me. She takes a giant sniff, and I can't tell if she's crying or on something. Then she says, finally, "Yes. But I was scared. I'm not like you."

"You don't even know me."

"I can tell." Kaitlyn leans her head against the wall and closes her eyes. "You're a brave one."

The door bangs open, and I jump up. Levi is standing there, looking exhausted. "Vi, come on. We found her."

Chapter Thirty-Six

"HOT AND COLD"
—EX HEX

K rin, where's your coat?" Annie asks. Even though the rest of us are bundled up, the cold still penetrates straight through our bones. Krina doesn't seem aware of the freezing temperature, or anything at all, really. She's stumbling around, drunk off her ass, mumbling something about rocks.

"I can't believe this," Levi mutters.

"What?" I ask, catching Krina before she face-plants. Krina shoves my hand away, lurching forward to grab a small black stone from the pavement outside Kaitlyn's building.

"This!" Levi waves his arm in Krina and Annie's direction. "Strand takes off, Krina gets completely trashed . . ."

Annie turns on him, furious. "And whose fault is that?"

"Certainly not mine," Levi says.

"Oh, no," Annie replies. "You just pushed her into playing at her ex-girlfriend's after Kaitlyn dumped her, cheated on her, spread rumors about her—"

"If Krina wasn't ready, she shouldn't have agreed to do it."

"You pressured her into it!"

"Whoa, whoa, whoa!" I interrupt as Krina hurls the stone at Kaitlyn's building, slurring profanities at the top of her lungs. She spins around as she throws it, slipping on her heels and landing squarely on her rear.

"Fuck!" Krina groans. "That fucking hurt, fucking Kaitlyn!"

Annie gives Levi a glare and goes to pull Krina up. Levi shakes his head at the two of them.

"I'm gonna go tell Kaitlyn the band's not playing," he says, moving toward the building's entrance. "You two get Krina home before someone calls the cops."

"Great," Annie calls to his back. "Thanks for the help!"

"Annie," I warn.

"I'm sorry, Vi, but he's being a real—"

"Dick," Krina mutters, resting her head on Annie's shoulder.

"Jerk, I was going to say." Annie sighs. She wipes some smeared liner that's ended up on Krina's cheek.

I pull the hood of my jacket over my head and scan the street for open cabs. "Well, he's right about getting Krina home."

"No," Krina moans, still slouched over Annie. "I don't want to."

"We'll take her to my place," Annie says.

"And how are we going to explain her to your parents tomorrow morning?" I ask.

"We'll get her out before they wake up."

"Fine," I reply. I'm too tired to argue, and Annie has her determined face on. "Follow me."

I walk uneasily to the street corner, not totally sober myself, and hail the first cab I see. It squeals to a stop against the curb as Annie hurries over, dragging Krina alongside her. The cabbie, a middle-aged white man, turns his head and glares at the three of us as we slide into the backseat.

Annie gives him explicit directions to her apartment in Queens, telling him to take the Grand Central Parkway and explaining, unnecessarily, why it's superior to any other route. The cabbie, meanwhile, looks at Krina through the rearview mirror.

"Hey," he says. "Your friend doesn't look so good."

"Sir, we have it under control," Annie says, but she gives Krina's hand a squeeze and whispers to her, "Let me know if you have to throw up."

I lie back against the headrest, letting my eyes flutter closed, wishing this nightmare could just end. I'm in that strange, half-drunk, half-sober state where you just become groggy and sad. The only thing I want right now is to curl up in Annie's bed and never wake up.

I was *mean* tonight. I was mean to Strand for no reason except that he was kissing a girl. I can still see how he looked at me, like he'd been slapped. I didn't know anyone could make him look like that, let alone someone like me. The longer I close my eyes, the more his sad face is seared into my brain.

"Um, Vi?"

I'm yanked awake by Annie's panicked tone. I didn't even realize I had fallen asleep. We're still in the cab with Krina between us, completely passed out. She's snoring loudly with her mouth hanging open.

"Are we there?" I ask. "Are we at your house?"

"Vi, where is your phone?" Annie asks, her voice rising.

"It's dead. Why?"

She groans and puts her fingers over her eyes. "This is bad. This is very, very bad."

"What's going on?"

"I turned my phone off after we found Krina."

"And?"

"And I just turned it back on."

I don't know what Annie's talking about or why it matters when she turned off her phone. Every time the cab flies over a bump in the road, I feel my stomach leap with it. I try to breathe slowly in and out through my nostrils.

"I don't understand, Annie."

"What I'm telling you," Annie says, growing hysterical, "is that I have fourteen voice mails from our parents!"

Now I need to throw up for multiple reasons. If Mom and Dad are calling Annie at this time of night, they must have somehow found out what we were doing.

"Shit," I mutter. I'm fully awake now. I lean forward in my seat to look at Annie. "How far are we from your house?"

"A couple of minutes."

"All right. Let's not panic," I say, but my voice is high and flimsy and the cabbie keeps braking too suddenly, sending me smacking into the seat in front of me.

"We're dead," Annie says. "We're completely dead."

"We're not dead! We just need an alibi."

"An alibi for why we snuck out of my apartment on a Friday night? Literally the only excuse our parents will accept is if someone had a gun to our heads."

"Just think, just think," I mutter as the cab turns the corner onto Annie's street.

"Oh. My. God." Annie's face pales as she looks out the window. "Vi."

I look, and there, standing in Annie's front yard, are the police, Annie's parents . . . and my dad.

He doesn't say a word to me when he sees us getting out of the cab. I see him turn to Annie's parents and say something to them. Then he marches toward me and grabs my wrist, his thumbs digging into my skin.

"Ow," I whimper, but he doesn't loosen his grip.

He yanks open the car door for me before walking around to the driver's side. I get in the passenger seat and shut the door, looking through the window at Annie and a wobbly Krina standing in front of Mr. and Mrs. Lin.

As soon as Dad pulls out of Annie's driveway, I wait for the yelling to start. Instead, he stays quiet for a long time. I slide out of my coat and peek over at him, but he's staring at the traffic ahead, jaw clenched.

After a few minutes he finally speaks. His voice is low and stiff. "Your grandmother is in the hospital."

"Abi?" I clutch the side of the car, feeling my pulse in my stomach. I knew something horrible had happened. This is karma. Because of my lying, my overall shittiness, everyone around me is now going to suffer. This is why I can't step out of bounds. I'm not made for it. "What's wrong? Is she okay?"

"We think she's going to be fine."

"You think? What happened?"

Abi has never had any health problems. She's seventy-two years old, but she lives on her own and takes aerobics classes at the Y.

"We thought she had a stroke, but the doctor says it could be TIA."

"What is—"

"It's a blood clot that blocks blood flow to the brain. Same symptoms as a stroke, but temporary. Slurred speech, facial paralysis, loss of movement . . ." Dad rattles off other scary symptoms in the same way someone would read a grocery list. His face is pulled tight, like it's made of elastic.

Everything he lists, I picture happening to Abi. Strong, stubborn Abi, not being able to move, feeling scared and confused because her body isn't working right. I swallow hard. *God*, I pray. *If you make Abi all right, I'll be the perfect daughter again. I'll quit the band, I'll be a good girlfriend to Levi, I'll do anything.*

"We've been trying to reach you for over an hour," Dad goes on.

"We called Mr. and Mrs. Lin when we couldn't get you or Annie on your cell phones."

"Oh," I say in a small voice.

"Imagine how your mom and I felt when the Lins told us you were missing from their house."

I lean my head against the window and keep my eyes on the flashing lights of traffic. I know I deserve the guilt trip, but I feel horrible enough already.

Without looking at Dad, I start to say, "We weren't—"

"Don't. We're not talking about it right now." His accent comes out harsh, his voice spitting out words like a stream of bullets. He pulls his cell phone from his pocket and hands it to me. "Text your mom that we're on our way to the hospital."

I quickly text my mom that we'll be there soon. I will myself not to cry, but the enormity of the night crashes into me all at once. How I hurt Strand, how I let my parents down, how I could have lost Abi. All this horribleness in one night.

Dad doesn't say another word to me until we get to the hospital. It's one of the rare moments I want to be yelled at. Anger is easier to take than the silent treatment.

The waiting room is quiet and practically empty. Matty is strung across two chairs, asleep. Mom stands up as soon as Dad and I get out of the elevator. As we approach, I can see the exhaustion etched in her face. Her eyes are pink and watery, with heavy bags. Fresh guilt overtakes me, because I'm part of the reason she looks like this.

"How's Abi?" I ask immediately.

"Abi's okay," Mom says. "She's asleep." Then she stops and stares at me in a way you would look at a stranger you can't place. I remember I'm wearing my band makeup, all heavy black eyeliner and rouge red lips.

"You smell like alcohol," she says, her voice cracking.

"Come on." Dad leads her back to the stiff vinyl chairs in the waiting area. I trail behind them, choosing the seat across from theirs. Mom collapses into her chair. Her eyes don't leave my face.

"I need you to start explaining yourself," she says. "Right now."

Under his breath, Dad asks her in Spanish if she really wants to bring it up tonight, and Mom snaps back, "Yes, Jorge. Our daughter is going to tell us exactly where she was and why she reeks of booze."

"I'm sorry," I whisper.

"You should be. Do you realize what you put us through tonight?"

I lower my head and nod at the floor.

"No," Mom says. "You have no idea. You have no idea what it's like to hear that your child isn't safe in bed. To spend half the night worrying about your sick mother and your missing kid."

"I didn't mean for this to happen," I say feebly. "There was something I had to do, and—"

Dad shakes his head. "Bullshit, Victoria."

"Where were you?" Mom asks quietly.

"At a party." It sounds so inadequate right now, out of context.

"Drunk at a party," Dad cuts in. Mom starts crying now, like a parent who's found out their kid is a heroin addict. I know what I did tonight was wrong. I'm not saying it wasn't. But my parents don't get that every other student at Evanston does this kind of stuff on a weekly basis. I'm supposed to be better, somehow, because I'm Victoria Cruz. When I do what everyone else does, I'm automatically worse than all of them.

"I had a little to drink," I admit. It's not a secret anymore. Mom smelled me coming off the elevator.

"You're *underage!*" Mom snaps. The only other person in the waiting room, besides Matty, gives us a narrow-eyed stare. I wish I could teleport right now. To Hawaii, or to Japan, or to Neptune. Yeah, Neptune would be good.

"I know . . . I . . . ." The tears spill down my cheeks. It's a Cruz family trait to cry too much, too easily. We're not weak, we just feel a lot. And tonight I'm feeling like my heart's been hit with a mallet over and over again. "I really am sorry. I don't know what to do."

"Why did you do it?" Dad asks. "What did you have to do at this party?"

Before I can answer, Mom's face clouds over, and I know she's figured it out.

"You're still in that band," she says. "Aren't you."

"Yes, but . . ."

She bites her lip and closes her eyes, then opens them to look up at the ceiling. I feel like she's looking to God, asking him what she did to deserve such a crappy daughter.

"But it's not like that," I say desperately. "It's not what you think. I'm not this girl who parties and gets drunk all the time or anything."

I want them to get it, to know that I'm still me. I don't like lying to them, but I did what I had to do.

"Did you or did you not sneak out to a party?" Dad asks.

"Yes," I say, "but—"

"Did you or did you not drink?"

"I just—"

"Did you or did you not lie to us about quitting the band?"

I stop. I look at Mom, and she's crying as much as I am. It seems like all I do these days is make my parents cry.

She turns to Dad and says, "I don't know her anymore."

The words rip me apart.

When I was little, every fight with my family seemed like the end of the world. I would cry so hard that I couldn't speak or catch my breath. There would be snot and hiccupping and all kinds of messiness, but I wouldn't care because I was so overwhelmed by sadness. This is how I feel now. I don't know how I ended up here. All I wanted was to sing and be a part of something that made me happy, and suddenly it became this. My parents don't know who I am, and I'm not sure I do either.

Mom can't look at me, but Dad faces me straight on.

"Here's what's going to happen," he says. He's calm, which is surprising because he's usually the most temperamental of us all. The effect is unsettling. "You'll continue to come straight home after school."

I nod.

"And you're grounded every weekend. All day, all night. No more . . . *sleepovers* . . . at Annie's." He doesn't physically make the air quotes when he says sleepovers, but his tone does it for him.

"Except for quince practices," Mom says. She glances at me now. "Your cousin is counting on you and Strand."

"Except for quince practices," Dad confirms.

I'm not resisting anymore. It's over. I've been running and hiding from this moment, but I'm tired. Fate has caught up to me.

Levi will probably call Greg to replace me, or some other singer who doesn't have a family like mine. Someone who doesn't have to sneak around and lie and hurt people. It'll be better for everyone. In the meantime, I can go back to being normal. Go to class, go home, finish my homework, repeat. Being normal will mean I don't feel anything, but it beats feeling like this, this horrible mix of disappointment and misery.

"You're going to have to earn back our trust," Dad says. "It's going to take a long time."

I nod again. "I understand."

Mom gets up from her seat. I get the feeling that she can't stand to be near me anymore. "I'm going to talk to the doctor again."

"Glo," Dad says to her. He cups his hand over hers. "Everything's okay."

Her lower lip quivers like Matty's does when he gets scared. I have the strange urge to get up and hug her, because she looks so small and pale under the hospital lights. But I don't do it. I don't think she would hug me back tonight. She leaves to talk to the doctor, and Dad watches the TV overhead with a glazed, unresponsive expression.

I burrow into the waiting room chair and close my eyes, drifting off to the sound of Matty's snores.

Chapter Thirty-Seven

"BIRDHOUSE
IN YOUR SOUL"
—THEY MIGHT BE GIANTS

Abi is released from the hospital the next morning with instructions to take it easy over the next few days. She'll be monitored by a neurologist and treated with anticlotting medication. Mom lectures her about taking it every day, and in a stream of Spanish, Abi insists to all of us that she's fine, that she could go to the Y tomorrow, that we're all paranoid and she just had a slight fever.

Even though she's at her most difficult and stubborn, I want to cry with relief. My parents don't tell her what happened with me last night, so she still calls me her *corazón*, her heart. She's the only person who treats me like me.

Back at home my parents are freezing me out. Mom still won't look at me, and Dad doesn't say a word to me, even when I eat cereal with a generous serving of whole milk.

I spend the day listening to playlists alone in my room. I put on one of my favorites, called Running Away. I made it halfway into my first year at Evanston and have been adding to it ever since, with songs like "Born to Run" by Bruce Springsteen and "Let's Dance to Joy Division" by the Wombats. When I listen to it, I imagine ripping off my royal-blue Evanston blazer and sprinting out of the campus's wrought-iron gates. Today I imagine leaving this apartment, suffocating me with its disapproval. I could hop on the train to Greenwich Village and kill time at a café (even though the taste of coffee makes me retch) or go to Sam's Records and stock up on vinyls from the dollar shelves.

Annie calls me late in the afternoon, speaking through the phone in a low, hushed tone.

"I can barely hear you," I say.

"I'm trying to be discreet."

"Why? Are your parents around?"

"Not right now, but it's been full Big Brother around here. Yours?"

"No," I reply. "They're avoiding me. I'm pretty sure they're going to hate me forever."

"Please, Vi. Your parents are obsessed with you."

"Not anymore."

"Have you told Levi what happened yet?" Annie asks.

"No," I say. Levi's going to freak when he finds out what happened. The Battle of the Boroughs is only a month away, and now the band is out a lead singer.

"What about Strand?"

Just hearing his name sends a cold wave of guilt down my body.

"No," I say again. I don't want to tell Annie what happened between me and Strand. She'll ask me a bunch of questions and make me relive the moment all over again. I don't need to feel any crappier than I already do.

"I think they'd let you play in the Battle," Annie says.

"Do you know my parents at all?"

"Yes. Very well, actually. You might try talking to them, Vi."

"I think it's finally over," I say. "The band."

"They'll come around. I promise."

I don't tell Annie the truth: that I don't think I'll come around.

I'm devastated to lose the band from my life, but the Battle of the Boroughs still terrifies me. The idea of not doing it makes me feel a lot of things—regret, sadness, guilt. But the sensation of relief overpowers everything else. I'm relieved to have a reason to back out of the Battle. That if someone questions my decision, I can point to my family and say it's not my fault.

The fear of my Battle debut has lurked inside of me for weeks, a cold, black fear that runs through my veins. I picture myself onstage in the Battle, freezing up under the lights the way I did during my audition. Letting everybody down, including myself. I wasn't ready for it. It's too big, too scary.

"Right," Annie says loudly. "So he wants it in MLA format and a bibliography included."

"What?"

"Yes, it's due next week."

"Oh," I realize. "Your parents are there?"

"Right. Let me know if you have any other homework questions, okay?"

"Very smooth. Talk to you tomorrow."

We hang up, and as if on cue, Matty bounds into my room.

"Were you eavesdropping?" I ask him, grabbing him by the earlobe. It wouldn't be the first time Matty played undercover agent.

"Ow!" he laughs. "No! I swear!"

"Uh-huh." I give him a little push and he falls back onto the floor dramatically. "So what do you want?"

"I'm bored."

"Go play a game."

"I don't want to."

"Go talk to Mom and Dad."

"I don't want to." He rolls onto his back and blinks up at the ceiling.

"Well, I'm not going to entertain you. I'm busy."

"You're listening to music," he says, pointing toward my computer.

"It's for school."

He says nothing in response. His body, usually a blur of moving limbs, stays perfectly still.

"Matty . . ."

"Can I just stay in here? I won't make any noise."

I roll my eyes. Fat chance. Matty has the attention span of a fruit fly. "Whatever. But if you get annoying, I'm kicking you out."

He nods solemnly.

About a minute passes in silence. Then, still looking at the ceiling, Matty asks, "Is Abi really okay?"

My heart thaws a little bit. In the midst of all Matty's usual brattiness, sometimes I forget that he's just a kid. I remember what it was like to be his age, to constantly feel like everyone but you is in on some big secret. I don't know if you ever grow out of that stage, really. You just pretend to know the secret as you get older.

"Abi's okay," I say firmly. "I promise."

"Well, Mom and Dad are acting weird."

"That's not because of Abi."

"Oh." He flops over on his side and begins to trace patterns on my rug. "Are you guys in a fight?"

"Kind of. I guess."

"Why?"

I would usually throw Matty out of my room at this point, but I know he's freaked about Abi, so I sigh and slip off my headphones. "They don't want me to sing in a band."

"Why?"

"They want me to do other things."

"I think you should sing," he says decisively. "You like it."

Typical Matty, boiling everything down to its simplest point.

"Maybe if you sang for them, they would change their minds," he says.

I laugh, even though I find my situation far from funny. "I don't think so, Matty."

"They might. Strand says you're the best singer he's ever heard."

"What?" I look at him. He has my full attention now. "When did he tell you that?"

"I dunno. The other day."

It takes everything in me not to grab Matty by the collar and interrogate the crap out of him. Exactly what day? What was the context of their conversation? Was Strand just being Strand, or did he really mean it?

Except the conversation took place before Kaitlyn's party, when Strand didn't hate me. Thinking about him now, especially considering the way I treated him, hurts. And as much as I want to know more, I also don't. I keep my mouth shut and face my computer so Matty can't witness my internal dilemma.

"Hey, Matty," I say, clicking through my playlists. I think a change of subject will be the best thing for both us. If I think about Strand or the band right now, it might just break me. "Want to hear one of the greatest songs ever made?"

He jumps up from the rug, energy fully restored. "Yeah!"

"You sure you're ready for this?" I ask.

"*Yes.*"

I put my headphones on him, and they immediately slide off his small ten-year-old head.

"I don't know . . . ," I say, readjusting the band. "You're so young . . ."

"So?"

"So your brain is undeveloped. If I play this song for you, it could literally explode."

"Come on!" he's moving again, back to Matty mode. Every limb is jittery and excited. It's nice to know that I don't have to cause pain to everyone in my life, that I can still make someone happy.

I hit the play button and hear the muffled noise flooding through his ears. I watch Matty's face move through a dozen microexpressions all at once. Curiosity, wonder, awe, calm. When he smiles, I smile. I can temporarily forget how much has been taken away from me.

Chapter Thirty-Eight

"GIVE IT UP"
—ANGEL OLSEN

You're *what?*" Levi asks me, but it sounds more like an accusation than a question.

I predicted that he'd be upset when he heard the news, but I didn't predict the eyes bulging out of his glasses or the vein pulsing in his temple.

I try to repeat myself in calm, dulcet tones, like you use for trauma victims. "I'm out of the band."

"You can't be serious, Victoria. You can't do this to me right now."

This is a new, angry Levi. His anger doesn't scare me. The fact that I've never seen it before scares me. It makes me wonder what else he's holding inside.

"My grandmother's okay, in case you were wondering," I can't help but add, because he didn't ask me once how Abi's doing. I told him about getting the news from my dad, about fighting with my parents in the hospital waiting room, and his only response was to fixate on the band.

Levi blinks, the color returning to his face. "Vi, I . . . of course I'm glad she's okay. This is just . . . a lot to take in right now."

Annie and Krina pass by. They shoot me a wave and pointedly ignore Levi.

"What's their problem?" he asks.

"We're all in trouble."

"That's not my fault."

"I know it isn't," I say, but I think he deserves some of the blame. Krina was clearly pushed into something she wasn't ready for. Then again, he didn't force us to perform at Kaitlyn's. He didn't force Krina to drink too much or insist that Annie and I sneak out of the house when the Lins went to bed.

I don't tell him any of this, and he doesn't ask.

"I can't do this right now," he says, avoiding my eyes. "I have class."

"We still have a few minutes," I say. "If you want to talk."

"No." He shakes his head, and all his anger is back in its cage. "I mean, no thanks. I just have to sort this all out."

"Okay." I give him a kiss on the cheek, but it barely registers. I can almost see his mind computing all of the weekend's events, trying to figure out a way around them and orchestrate a miracle.

*　*　*

I spot Kaitlyn from a distance at lunchtime, sashaying across campus, her hair back to its perfectly styled former state. It's different now. I can see past the mirage of perfection. Kaitlyn Fielding, of all people, thinks I'm brave. She was obviously drugged out of her mind. Brave people don't sit in their rooms making playlists all weekend.

But then, Strand thinks I'm brave too.

I feel shivery all over when I see him at lunch. Levi's catching up on work in the library, so it's the three of us, and we don't talk about what happened over the weekend. We're all in silent agreement to pretend none of it ever happened. We don't talk much at all, actually. The worst thing is that Strand doesn't completely ignore me. He's polite, and he uses my proper name. He says Annie told him about Abi and he's glad she's okay.

He treats me like an anybody.

I used to think Strand had a perpetual grin on his face. Sometimes I wanted nothing more than to smack it off him. But when I see him frown, it's all wrong. I would give anything to restore the grin to its rightful location.

"Maybe it's better like this," Krina says unconvincingly while we're silently picking at our food. "Maybe we all need a break from the band."

No one argues with her.

On Friday night, after a full week of Strand's irritating politeness, I have an idea. I shut myself in my room, eyes glued to the computer, frantically plucking songs out of my sprawling music collection. I don't realize how long I've been at it until my mom walks into my room and flicks on the lights. My eyes need to readjust to the sudden brightness. The glare of the computer screen has been my only light source for two hours.

"Dinner in half an hour," she says.

"Okay." I look at her, but her face is impassive. "Thanks."

She nods and closes the door. This is what now passes for conversation between me and my parents. They command, and I obey.

Annie calls a minute later with a homework question.

"Why are you doing your homework on a Friday night?" I ask.

"Because I have nothing better to do. And I know for a fact that you don't either."

"Still," I say. "I haven't gotten that desperate."

"And what are you doing that's so much cooler?"

"Making a playlist." I don't look up as I scan my selection of artists. I'm only on letter N.

"Ah," she says knowingly. "Valentine's Day gift for Levi?"

I stop scanning. Shit. I forgot about Valentine's Day, only four days away.

"Yes," I say. I don't explain that all of this is for Strand. She'll get the wrong idea.

After we hang up, I eat a silent dinner with my family and return to my incarceration. I spend the rest of the night crafting a masterpiece of a playlist. It's filled with songs of regret, like "All Apologies" by Nirvana, "Swallow My Pride" by the Ramones, and "So Sorry" by Feist.

My apartment is dark by the time I'm finished. I upload the songs onto a flash drive and label it VICTORIA'S APOLOGY.

Chapter Thirty-Nine

"O BABY"
—SIOUXSIE AND THE BANSHEES

I'm half expecting Strand to be a no-show for quince rehearsal the next morning, but he's at my door twenty minutes early, charming my mother and regarding me with detached politeness. He has a new Pixies shirt on, black with a monkey wearing a halo.

"Follow me," I say to him when Mom heads to the kitchen for snacks.

He looks at me, silent.

"Please?" I add. He motions for me to go first.

I take him straight to my room so I can give him the playlist in private. He stands in the middle of my chevron rug with his hands in his pockets. We're both stilted and awkward and not us. I clear my throat a couple of times, but my voice still comes out fuzzy.

"I want to apologize," I say. "For how I talked to you at Kaitlyn's party."

"It's okay. You'd had a lot to drink," he says, but he won't look at me. His eyes rest on a spot directly above my head.

"It's not okay. I had no right to criticize you. You're single. You should do whatever you please with whomever you please."

On a practical level, I believe those words. I don't have to like that Strand flirts, that women flock to him like bees to pollen, but I have to accept it. There's no reason not to.

I hold out my peace offering. "Here."

Strand takes it, but he still doesn't look at me. I want so badly for him to go back to normal, even if it means dealing with the smirking and the nicknames.

His expression changes slowly as he takes it from me and reads the label. The corners of his lips twitch. "What's this, Cutlet?"

For once, I love the way the word sounds. I'm Chicken Cutlet again. The natural world order is restored. "You should know I've never made a playlist for anyone before. Not Levi. Not Annie."

He twirls the flash drive between his fingers, then looks at me. "Thank you."

"No biggie," I say, suddenly embarrassed.

Strand smiles his vague little half smile and sticks the drive into his back pocket.

"So all is forgiven?" I ask. I can't help but feel that if Strand isn't mad at me anymore, things will be the slightest bit more okay.

"How else would you make it up to me if it weren't?" His smile grows wider, showcasing two straight rows of teeth. That's when I know he's back to his old self.

"Oh, shut up." I check the time on my cell phone. "We should get going. Are we . . . good here?"

"We're good."

As he follows me out of the room, he says to my back, "I didn't sleep with Rachel. In case you were wondering."

I pause, unsure of how to respond.

"Good to know," I finally reply, and I keep my back to him so he can't see the look on my face.

Chapter Forty

"DO YOU"
—SPOON

It's impossible to find a Valentine's Day gift for Levi. What do you get for a boy who has everything? How much should you spend on a boyfriend you rarely see anymore? When the sole thread holding the relationship together is snipped apart? Without the band, Levi has devoted all of his free time to not being around me. He's usually holed up in the library or practicing his bass alone in the band room. Our relationship has been reduced to routine pop kisses between classes and a recitation of all the work he has to do.

When I ask Strand's opinion on a gift, he says to buy Levi a wholesale tub of hair gel. I don't know why I ever go to Strand for advice.

In my desperation, I ask Mom if I can go to Sam's Records to find Levi something. I have to gear myself up to ask her the question, because talking to her feels unnatural these days.

"You're grounded," she reminds me immediately. "Remember?"

As if I could forget. Ever since the night of Kaitlyn's party, I've no longer been playing the model daughter—I *am* the model daughter. You could stick me in the middle of a 1950s family sitcom and I would fit right in. Well, except for my massive ass, wild hair, and ambiguous ethnicity. Still, my efforts aren't enough for my parents, who continue to regard me as the spawn of Satan.

"I wouldn't be going for fun," I say, even though Sam's is one of my favorite places in all of New York City and I haven't set foot in there since the grounding. "As soon as I find Levi a gift, I leave."

I see the tug-of-war going on inside her. As much as she wants to punish me, she still cares about what people like Levi, in the upper echelon of society, think. In her eyes I'm a reflection of our family, and our family is a reflection of all Cuban immigrants. The reputation of the motherland rests squarely on my shoulders. No pressure or anything.

"Please?" I add pitifully.

She looks at me, and I can see her resolve waning.

"You can go," she says finally.

I sigh in relief. "Thank you."

"But I'm going with you."

"You want to come with me?"

"Yes."

"You want to come with me to Sam's."

"Yes."

"Or you don't trust me to go to Sam's?"

Her silence gives me my answer.

Sam's Records is owned by an old potbellied hippie whose name is actually Fred. Why he named his store Sam's is one of life's eternal mysteries. Fred has a curvy naked woman tattooed on his forearm and a freakish memory for music. You can hum him a song, any song, and he'll identify it in thirty seconds or less. I've tested him on this.

Taking Mom to Sam's feels like letting her into this secret part of myself. The appeal of Sam's can be lost on some people. It's a cramped, split-level space in dire need of cleaning, and smells like a combination of mothballs and weed.

Mom lets out a giant sneeze as soon as we walk in. In Spanish, she mutters something about the dust, pinching her nostrils together.

I look around the space appreciatively. When you get past the layers of dust, you can find all kinds of treasures here. We're surrounded by cassettes, CDs, and vinyls. They line the walls and sit inside boxes heaped on wooden tables. A fat gray cat lounges on an unopened box next to the staircase.

"Do what you have to do," Mom says dramatically, still holding her nose, like the store is an affront to her entire existence.

I spend about an hour listlessly wandering through the stacks of vinyls. I'm itching to buy something for myself, but I know without being told that this is forbidden under my current punishment. It goes against my parents' goal of making me wallow in my own misery.

Levi loves Sigur Rós, but he owns all their albums already. Sam's has some other great albums, but none that would be meaningful enough to merit buying for him. Then, when I pass the Classical Music section, I'm struck by inspiration. The perfect gift. I find a copy of Tchaikovsky's *Romeo and Juliet*, the music we listened to during our first date at Carnegie Hall. It's poignant, it's musical, and it's under twenty dollars.

I have the album cradled under my arm when I go to get Mom, but she's not in the spot I left her.

"Mom?" I call. I check my phone, thinking maybe she went to get some coffee and I missed a text, but I have nothing.

I finally find her at the back of the store, clutching Blondie's *Parallel Lines* on cassette and looking at it in wonder.

"What have you got there?" I ask with forced casualness. It's a standard question, one I wouldn't hesitate to ask under normal circumstances, but we haven't had a normal conversation in weeks.

She doesn't look at me, just turns the cassette over in her hands. "What?"

"Are you buying something?"

"No, of course not. It's just . . . I haven't seen this in years," she says. She stares at Blondie, almost like she's talking to Debbie Harry more than to me. "It was the first album I ever bought here."

It takes me a second to realize that by "here," she's not talking about Sam's, she's talking about the US. It's weird to think of my practical, focused mom, feet firmly planted in reality, as a little girl who sang along to Blondie in broken English. Mom doesn't listen to music now, doesn't own any old CDs or have an online music account. I assumed she was always like this, too determined to prove herself to waste her time with frivolous hobbies like music.

"I like Blondie," I say, although truthfully, I only know a few of their songs.

Mom is barely listening. It's like touching the album has transported her back to 1979.

"Abi threw it away after I married your dad," she says, brushing her fingers over the cover. There's a reverence to the way she's holding the cassette. "I forgot all about it."

"You should buy it," I suggest.

She looks at me now, and her face changes back to the stoic mask she's been wearing since our fight at the hospital. It's like she forgot she's supposed to be mad at me.

"Ay, por favor," she says, shoving the cassette back onto the shelf. "What the hell would I do with it now?"

The next morning I wait for Levi by his locker. He greets me with his usual quick peck on the lips. Always efficient.

"Happy Valentine's Day!" I say so loudly that he flinches. "So what are we doing tonight? Dinner? A movie? Dinner and a movie? The world is our oyster!"

I don't know if it's the Blondie effect, but Mom and Dad have lifted one night of my parole so Levi and I can have a Valentine's Day date. It's like Levi exists in a sphere outside of the band. My parents consider him my responsible, intelligent, white boyfriend savior. In any case, I'm beyond excited to see a world outside of Evanston and my bedroom.

Levi opens his locker and shoves his books inside. "I don't know. What do you want to do?"

"Why don't we go to Celeste?" I suggest. "We always talk about going."

"We won't get a table at Celeste on Valentine's Day. The wait will be crazy."

I fight the pang of annoyance ringing through me. If Levi had thought to make a reservation somewhere, we wouldn't have to worry about the crowds. As a noob to this whole boyfriend thing, I assumed Levi would have something planned.

Krina would say that's not progressive of me. Why is it Levi's responsibility to make all the plans? It takes two to be in a relationship, after all. I tuck a strand of hair behind my ear. I blow-dried it for two hours last night so I could be frizz-free for our date.

"What about Casa Nueva?" I say.

"Also a ridiculous wait."

"Not if we go early."

"Yeah, but I have some homework to do."

"I was thinking . . ." I reach out and play with the sleeve of his blazer. "Maybe we postpone the homework today?"

"Victoria," he says, practically recoiling from my touch. "You know I have Mr. Yager's essay due Friday."

Maybe I did know. Since the band's semipermanent hiatus, there's been a drought of conversation between Levi and me. He's taken to filling in the silence by telling me every last detail of his workload. This has become our daily ritual. My job is to nod, give the occasional "that sounds rough," and look sympathetic.

Between his tests and essays and SAT-prep courses, I'm stressed out just listening to him. I don't know why he's so concerned about his grades. He has the highest GPA in his class, and his parents have a building named after them at Yale. I would say his future is entirely secure.

"We'll figure it out," I say brightly. "Here. This is for you." I hand him the gift. He unwraps it carefully, turning the album over in his hands.

"Tchaikovsky?" he asks.

"Think back."

He scratches his eyebrow before turning his attention back to the album. "Ummmm . . ."

"Our first date?" I press. "Carnegie Hall?"

"Oh! Of course! I'm sorry. That's really sweet."

"Now you can relive it. We can listen to it today, if you want."

Levi looks a little guilty as he hands me a squashed gift bag from inside his locker. "This is your present. It's not much, but . . ."

When I take the gift out of the bag, my first thought is that it must be a joke.

I dig around the bottom of the bag in case I missed the real gift. There's nothing else inside. Which means this isn't a cruel gag, this is the hard truth: all my boyfriend has gotten me for Valentine's Day is a set of drugstore tights.

"I noticed the pair you wore to my apartment had a hole in them, so I figured you could use some new ones," he explains.

"That's very . . . practical of you."

"I like to give practical gifts. It's better to get something you'll actually use, don't you think?"

"Definitely," I say, even though I firmly disagree. I'd much rather get something impractical and romantic. Hands down.

The gift is thoughtful, in a Levi sort of way. It was observant of him to remember the hole in my tights, even though I would love for him to forget it. It's one of the many reasons I felt out of place in his home. Tights are a perfectly fine Valentine's Day gift.

Besides, I should be grateful to have a valentine at all.

I repeat this in my head over and over again, like a mantra, then smile at Levi. "Thank you. I love the tights."

I have a weird feeling that if I stop smiling, I may start to cry.

— *Chapter Forty-One* —

"STONEMILKER"
—BJÖRK

Our last quince rehearsal takes place the day Levi leaves for the Evanston Band competition, so Levi and I don't have time to say good-bye. It's better this way.

Ever since Valentine's Day, I've been on edge. I've become someone I can't stand—someone who wants constant affirmations of love from their significant other. It's like without the band, the only identity I have left is Levi's girlfriend.

Strand is spending the night at our apartment so we can leave early the next morning for the quince. Surprisingly, this is my parents' idea. If I were a parent, there's no way I'd allow a boy, especially one who looked like Strand, to spend the night with my teenage daughter.

We order pizza for dinner, marinara slices for Dad, and eat from our old mismatched plates. I guess my family doesn't feel the need to impress Strand with our fine china.

"Are you Victoria's new boyfriend?" Matty asks. He peels the cheese off his pizza and sticks a glob of it into his mouth.

I rest my head in my hands and close my eyes, but Strand laughs it off.

"Your sister and I are friends," he answers.

"Then why are you her quince partner instead of Levi?"

"Levi had something else he had to do," I say, raising my head. "Stop being so nosy."

"Were you in the band too?" Matty asks Strand.

My parents become incredibly awkward at the mention of the *B* word. Dad coughs suddenly, taking a big gulp of his water. Mom clears her throat and digs her nails into the dining room table.

"I was," Strand says.

"What do you play?" Matty asks.

"Guitar."

Matty grins. "Awesome!"

"Do you play an instrument?" Strand asks.

"No. I wish I could play guitar, though."

Strand folds his pizza and takes a large bite, then says, "I'll teach you."

Matty hops up and down in his seat while I say to Strand, "You don't have time for that."

"Sure, I do. Right, buddy?" He high-fives Matty. "You'll be a regular Jimmy Page."

Figures. Strand sits down for five seconds and he and Matty are best friends.

"Or Slash," Dad says. I stare at him.

"You like Guns N' Roses?" Strand asks.

"*Use Your Illusion* was my shit."

"Jorge," Mom says sharply. "Language."

"Sorry. My jam." Dad rolls his eyes at Strand like, *Women, right?* I would be offended, but I'm too busy digesting the new information about my dad. I mean, I knew he had eclectic taste in music, but I can't imagine the man in front of me, wearing his salmon-colored company polo shirt with a Rodriguez Appliances logo on his chest, listening to a Guns N' Roses album.

Mom steers the conversation to safer topics, like reality TV and new restaurants opening in the neighborhood. Somehow, Strand's presence turns my parents back into themselves. They look at me without contempt. They even smile—not at me, not directly, but it's progress nonetheless.

After dinner Strand rushes to help put the dishes away. Everyone is under his spell. Mom says she wishes she could adopt him. Dad teaches him about the hidden dangers of dairy, and Strand listens intently, saying things like, "You can barely taste a difference with soy milk." And Matty follows Strand around like a lost puppy.

We all watch TV on the couch like a big, happy family, and an unpleasant thought pops into my head.

This should be Levi.

Levi should be the one charming my family, helping clean up

after dinner. Has he ever cleaned a dinner table, or is he used to Rosa doing it all for him?

It's ten o'clock when I excuse myself to go to sleep. I'm not tired. Mainly, I'm weirded out by my friend who is a boy, but not my boyfriend, sleeping over at my apartment and making my family feel normal again.

I brush my teeth, put on my pj's (the ones without any holes in them), and crawl into bed. I pick up a copy of *High Fidelity*, which Annie lent me a couple of months ago. It's been sitting on my nightstand collecting dust.

An hour into reading, the house has become quiet. I'm about to start a new chapter when I hear a soft tap on my door, so soft that I think I must have imagined it. I stick my nose back into the book, but then I hear an actual knock.

I open the door to find Strand standing there in a T-shirt and boxers.

"I can't sleep," he says. "Entertain me."

Don't look down. Do not. Look. Down. His boxers are blue with white pinstripes.

"Entertain yourself," I say.

"Wow. Is this how you treat a guest in your home?" He feigns shock. "Come on, you can't sleep either. I saw your light on."

"I am not doing anything with you unless you put some pants on."

"Seriously?" He looks down at his underwear. "It's not like I'm wearing tighty whities. They're practically shorts."

"They are not practically shorts. They have a little slit in the front where your . . . thing can pop right out."

"My thing?" Strand presses his forehead against the doorframe and starts cracking up.

I give him a shove. "Go put on your pants! I'll meet you in the living room."

He's still laughing when I close the door. I wait a few minutes before I go out, because I don't want to see Strand putting his pants on. It's too weird. Intimate. The act of getting dressed. Like we just . . . you know. After a reasonable amount of time has passed, I tiptoe into the living room, where Strand is waiting for me, fully clothed.

"Does this outfit meet your standards?" he asks.

"It does, thank you very much." I sit on the far side of the couch so there's a cushion of space between us. Strand's eyes crinkle up, but he doesn't say anything.

"Okay, so." He leans back and appraises me. "What do you want to do?"

Why is it that everything he says sounds like a come on? I sit up straight, refusing to melt into a puddle of uselessness like most girls would. I tap my finger against my chin. "Want to play a game?"

"Always."

I grab a sheet of paper from the end table and scrawl MASH on the top.

"MASH?" he asks. "As in the TV show?"

"No . . . as in Mansion, Apartment, Shack, House. You've never played MASH before?"

"Nope."

"You're kidding me."

"I would never."

"Annie and I played this all the time when we were younger." I write out the categories: Wife, College, State, Job, Kids.

"You get to pick two options per category and then I pick the third for you," I say. "First is Wife, so you pick two girls. I know it'll be hard for you to limit yourself."

"Two girls . . ." Strand ignores my dig and props a throw pillow under his neck. "So it has to be a girl I like?"

"Does such a creature exist?"

"I'm capable of feelings, you know."

"For Rachel Levine?" I make a gagging sound.

"Very mature, Cutlet." He looks at me in an uncomfortably direct way. "Serious question?"

"Shoot."

"What do you have against Rachel?"

"She's just so . . ." I suddenly don't know what I have against her. "Blargh."

"Oh yeah, I know," he says, rolling his eyes. "She's so totally blargh."

"She always runs in a sports bra even when it's cold. And during races she runs with her elbows out so people can't pass her."

He gasps. "That *monster*."

"You can learn a lot about someone by paying attention to the little things."

"You're a harsh critic."

"I'm just looking out for you."

"Anyway . . . it's not Rachel."

"What's not Rachel?"

"The girl I like."

"So there *is* a girl!"

"There might be a girl."

"Who is she?"

"No comment."

"Oh come on, why?" I tuck my legs under me. "I'm proud of you, having a little crush."

A twinge of . . . something flutters in my chest. Probably pity for this supposed crush of his. She should be warned that no girl could possibly hold Strand's attention for longer than five minutes.

"Next category, please," he says.

I sigh. "Fine. We'll skip Wife."

When we get to the College category, Strand's top choice is "the College of Life."

"What does that mean?" I ask.

"It means I'm not sure if I want to go to college. At least not right away."

I've never heard anyone from Evanston consider life without college. It's practically incomprehensible, but that's Strand. Living like all these things that have been drilled into us don't actually matter.

When I say this out loud, he says, "They *don't* matter."

"But—" I stop myself. Why am I arguing with him? Doesn't that mean I'm no different from my parents, or Levi, or Annie? I'm spouting back everything they've said to me.

"What about you?" he asks. "Have you thought about college?"

I wiggle my toes in my socks and lean my head against the couch. "Harvard, I guess."

"You sound thrilled by the prospect."

"I kind of freak out if I think about it too hard."

"Freak out how?"

"You know . . . pit in my stomach, sweaty palms, sometimes crying."

"You realize that's not normal, right?"

"I'll get used to it. At some point. I hope."

"Why are you acting so powerless?" he asks.

"What do you mean?"

"I mean . . . if the thought of Harvard makes you physically sick, don't go to Harvard. You're the one who decides your own future."

"No," I say. "It's not that simple. My parents—"

"You," he corrects.

I run my hands across my pajama pants. "So what am I supposed to do, then?"

He pauses, then looks at me closely. "Consider your options. Maybe it's not Harvard, maybe it's a different college."

I've never considered other colleges, really. My parents have suggested some others as acceptable options. Yale, Princeton, Columbia. Each and every one just as unappealing to me.

"Or," Strand adds, "come join the College of Life with me. They have a very high acceptance rate."

"I don't know if I can be happy if it means making everyone else so miserable."

The dimple in his cheek deepens. "It's your life, not theirs. They want you to be happy."

"Happy at Harvard."

"No," he says. "Just happy. Come on, Cutlet. Anyone with eyes can see how much they love you."

"You make all this sound easy."

"Not easy. Doable."

I twirl my pencil between my thumb and index finger. "What do your parents think about your decision not to go to college?"

"My dad doesn't know yet. He'll deal with it when the time comes."

"And your mom?"

"My mom passed away when I was little."

I stop twirling my pencil. "I'm sorry. I didn't know."

"I don't talk about it a lot."

"What was her name?"

"Emilie."

"That's pretty. Sorry, should I not ask questions?"

"Feel free." Strand extends his legs onto my lap. "Is this okay? My legs get sore if I sit for too long."

"Yeah, go ahead."

I barely notice. My mind is too busy replaying all the snide comments I've ever made to Strand. Poor Strand, living life without his mother. Did his father have to learn to do everything by himself? Did Strand have grandparents to help raise him?

As if reading my thoughts he says, "You don't have to feel sorry for me. I was young when it happened."

"Well, that's a relief. I hate feeling sorry for you."

He laughs. His laugh is smooth, like the tinkling of piano keys.

For kids, Strand wants two. "A boy and a girl. Like me and my sister."

"I thought you were an only child."

"Nope."

Come to think of it, why did I assume Strand was an only child?

"How old is your sister?" I ask.

"She's twenty. She studies acting at NYU."

"Acting?" I ask. "That's so cool."

"She *is* cool."

"Are you guys close?" I ask.

"Very. She knows everything about me. She knows about you, too."

"Me?" I look up, startled.

"Yeah. I sent her your audition video."

My hands fly up to my face. "Strand, no. You didn't."

"She loved it."

"The Princess Leia buns? The metal mouth?"

"So?"

"That video is so embarrassing."

"You're your own toughest critic, do you know that? I love that video. I've seen it about fifty times."

"No you haven't." I look down at his jeans and play with the rip across his knee.

He crosses his heart. "Fifty times, if not more."

"Why?"

"Because you're amazing?" He says this as though it's plainly obvious, like I'm an idiot for not understanding. "Even as an orthodontically-challenged Princess Leia."

"Whatever," I say. I need to remember not to take Strand's

compliments too seriously. This is his MO with women, spitting out compliments like a Pez dispenser.

"You should meet her," he says.

"Who? Your sister?"

"Yeah."

"Why?"

He shrugs. "I think you'd like her. And you'd like NYU. I bet you could get into their theater program."

He's spouting complete nonsense. I've always had this mental image of college as sitting in a big lecture hall, listening to stuffy professors who wear jackets with elbow patches. It's Evanston on a grander scale. Going to school for something I actually love, like singing, has never occurred to me.

My parents would shoot it down immediately. Singing isn't exactly the college experience they have in mind for me. To them, college isn't about finding yourself, or even learning. It's checking something off the list. It's a guarantee of a future that won't be spent scrimping and saving. I can already hear them. Their voices are a permanent part of me, filtering every experience though their eyes before mine. *This is why we came to this country? This is what we sacrificed everything for? You're getting a degree to become a waitress at the Stardust Diner?"*

So I ignore the tiny seed that plants itself inside my brain. I'll starve it, stick it in a dark windowless room with no air circulation.

Strand and I talk for hours. I learn several interesting facts about him. I learn that his mom's side of the family is white, his dad's side is black, and his maternal grandparents didn't approve of the marriage. I learn that Strand is named after the bookstore where his parents first met. I learn that his favorite song is not by the Pixies. It's by Billy Joel. He swears he isn't joking, and he won't tell me which one.

It's so late that I start to feel drunk from lack of sleep, all dizzy and happy and lacking a brain filter.

"Sing me your song again," I command him while my eyes are half-closed.

"Dance, monkey, dance."

"Seriously. I want to hear it."

He doesn't fight me on it this time. I guess it's because the scary part is over—I've already heard it. As he launches into the melody that's gnawed at me for weeks, I close my eyes. But I don't fall asleep. I'm not even close.

"One more time," I say as soon as he finishes.

He laughs. "Sing it with me."

"I don't know all the words."

"So? You'll learn."

We keep our voices soft, so we don't wake up my parents. Our voices are different—his smooth, mine scratchy—but they blend perfectly together. With both of us singing, it's like his song takes on a bigger shape. I can feel what he's feeling. I wonder why we haven't done this before.

We finish, and the silence pulses in my ears.

"Wow," Strand says finally.

I glance at my phone, and the time reads 4:47 a.m. We need to wake up in a few hours to get to Jersey. "I should go back to my room."

"You should."

But neither of us moves.

Chapter Forty-Two

"OTHER PEOPLE"
—BEACH HOUSE

My hair looks like a lollipop. It's piled into a tight bun perched on the crown of my head. All the girls in the quince have the same towering matching hairdos, but Jessica is wearing her hair half up since it's her "special day." We're all packed into a dressing suite like a herd of cattle as we primp.

"It's fine," Mom says about my hair when I complain to her. "It balances out the fullness of your dress."

The dress is a whole other disaster. It's Pepto-Bismol pink and speckled with glitter. Underneath it I'm wearing a slip made up of what looks like three hula hoops. I yawn as Mom tries to apply my lipstick. Things still aren't okay between us, but Strand and the quince are acting as a Band-Aid, temporarily patching up our relationship.

"Why are you so tired?" she asks me. "You went to bed early last night."

"I didn't sleep well." Truthfully, I'm not sure what time I went to bed. Strand and I talked for so long that I dozed off at an unknown hour while we were on the couch. He must have carried me back to my room. I try not to think about it, because I've heard from Annie that I'm not the most beautiful sleeper. I snore with my mouth hanging open and sometimes there's drool.

When Mom is finished beautifying me, she hurries back inside the main hall to wait with Dad and Matty. The court hasn't made its official entrance yet. Eduardo lines us up next to our partners on a marble staircase outside of the main doors. This is the first time we're seeing each other all dressed up.

I try not to gawk at Strand in his rented tuxedo. I pretend that my heart doesn't rattle in my chest, but it's hard when he looks prettier than I do.

His face breaks into a smile when he sees me.

Clearing my throat, I take my place beside him on the staircase and tell him, "Don't say a word. I know I look like a human cupcake."

His eyes glimmer, or maybe that's the reflection of my sparkles as he looks me up and down. "You say that like it's a bad thing . . ."

"It is."

Eduardo shushes all thirty of us and the hall goes silent as he presses his ear against the doors to listen for our entrance cue. When the opening horns of Celia Cruz's "La vida es un carnaval" begin, he throws open the doors. From my position on the stairs, I can see past the heads of the quince court and straight into the crowded hall. It looks like we're about to enter a concert arena filled with colored lights and smoke.

The DJ announces the first couple in Spanish. They shuffle awkwardly onto the dance floor to the applause of all the families in the hall, smiling and linking arms the way Eduardo instructed. Strand and I are the thirteenth couple in line.

"This is a little intense," he whispers to me, his breath tickling my ear.

"I know," I whisper back. My stomach is doing an aerobics routine as if I'm about to take the stage with the band.

When we reach the bottom of the staircase, Strand takes my arm and weaves it through his. I look past the couple in front of us and can see my family toward the end of the hall, seated at a round table with Abi. I almost cry when I see Abi, wearing her blue sequined jacket and matching skirt. Matty points at me and waves.

"Ready, partner?" Strand says as the couple before us sashays onto the dance floor.

I'm clawing into his arm. "Ready."

"Strand Connor *y* Victoria Cruz!" the DJ bellows, and Strand and I strut in unison down the dance floor like it's our personal runway, my dress ballooning out with every step I take. My family cheers loudly when we pass their table, and Matty pumps his fist in the air. An unstoppable smile forms on my face.

We gather into our formation, a line of girls facing an opposite line of guys, and start our choreography. It's nothing too complicated, mostly grape-vining and cha-cha-ing with some scattered turns as we face our partners. Strand makes silly faces at me so I'll laugh, while most of the other boys look deadly serious, concentrating on not stepping on each other's toes.

I'm surprised to realize that I'll be sad when the quince is over. This is the last time we'll all perform this choreography together. It's the last time I'll salsa dance with Strand. Even though I was upset when Levi couldn't be here, now I can't imagine another partner.

Jessica makes her grand entrance to thunderous applause and shimmies through the space between our conga lines. She's wearing a toothpaste-white dress with ruffles down the skirt and a pink sash tied around her waist. And even though the whole affair is as tacky as I predicted, I have to admit she looks beautiful.

When we start our salsa circle, Mom and Dad whip out their phones.

"We're being filmed," I warn Strand.

He dips me so low my head almost touches the floor, then whips me back up and shoots the cameras a movie star smile.

"Eduardo's going to kill you!" I warn him. "How dare you corrupt his choreography!"

"I can take Eddie," he replies.

After we cycle through the choreography, the quinceañera turns into a full-on party. The DJ plays all the Top 40 hits, the ones that I can't admit to anyone but myself that I secretly love. Strand and I dance with my parents, Abi, and even with Matty. They're exhausted after half an hour, but I am the Energizer Bunny when it comes to dancing, relentlessly untiring.

Here's the thing—I'm in between two worlds, but I can't fit into either one perfectly. I can round my words when I speak English so that there's no trace of my family's accent. Pull my hair up into a bun so you can't see how wild and unconfined it is. My skin is pale enough to make me ethnically ambiguous—I can pass for Italian or Greek or French. But when I'm around all my Cuban relatives, I don't feel quite right either. My Spanish is clunky, and I've never spoken it fluently so I opt to keep my phrases short, a barely passable Spanglish. I don't bother with quinces or feel any nostalgia for a country I've never visited.

When I dance with Strand, it's like I'm bridging the gap. I can be here, feeling the connection to this world, my family's world, and still be me. I think he appreciates it. It's the same way I feel in the band, a connection to something larger than myself. This music connects me to where I come from, and the band's music connects me to where I want to go.

Strand and I show each other the nerdiest dance moves we know. As a former athlete, I've perfected the running man, while Strand teaches me the Bernie. I launch into the Carlton dance from *Fresh Prince*, and Strand fights back with the lawnmower. I'm about to attempt the worm when "Shake It Off" comes on and Strand accidentally lets out a whoop of excitement.

I widen my eyes at him. "Oh. My. God!"

"Shut up," he says quickly. "Let's never speak of this."

"You like Taylor Swift! You!"

In all the time I've known Strand, it's taken me until today to realize the truth about him: that underneath the dimple, the smirking, the groupies, and the guitar . . . Strand is a dork. He knows every single word and sings without shame. I join him for the chorus, cracking up the entire time.

"You so practice this alone in your room," I say.

"I do not," he says in between lines.

"I'm telling everyone we know. I'm going to shatter your illusion of cool."

"I'll show them the footage of you doing the Carlton. Your parents recorded it all."

"You can't get my family's help to blackmail me."

"Why? They like me better anyway."

I laugh. "That might actually be true."

The song ends all of a sudden, and the DJ announces a couples dance. I start to leave the dance floor, but Strand holds me back.

"Come on," he says. "I still have energy to burn."

I hear the opening bars of "Other People" by Beach House, one of my favorite songs, and I'm torn.

"Levi won't mind," Strand insists.

"Fine," I say, allowing him to place his hands around my waist. I stare up at the ceiling and drag my arms over his shoulders.

"If it makes you that miserable to dance with me, we don't have to," Strand says, a smile playing at his lips. "I know how much I 'disgust' you."

"It's fine," I say. "Not a big deal."

I want to make sure Strand knows that dancing with him under the glow of the lights has no romantic effect on me whatsoever, so I fix my face into a scowl.

"Good song," he says.

"It's okay," I mutter.

"Don't act like you don't love it, Victoria."

I narrow my eyes at him as we sway side to side. "I don't."

"I can picture you listening to it under the covers with your eyes closed."

How the hell does he know I do that?

"All right, so I like the song," I admit.

"Uh-huh. And how do you categorize this one?"

I stare away from him, into the dark crowd surrounding us. "It's in the Moonlight Over a Lake playlist."

"You are so bizarrely specific."

"I see what I see."

"Are you swimming in this lake?"

"No. I'm in a rowboat, obviously."

"Right. Of course. By yourself?"

"No . . ."

"With Levi?"

The heat of his palms warms my lower back, even through layers of taffeta.

"With . . . I don't know," I reply. "A faceless man, I guess."

"Creepy."

"Why do you care who's in the boat?"

"I'm just trying to get a visual, that's all," he says. "Do you miss him?"

"Who?"

"Levi."

"Of course I miss him," I say indignantly. "He's my boyfriend."

"So why isn't he in the rowboat with you?"

"What is your fixation with the damn rowboat?"

"It seems to me that if he's your boyfriend, you would visualize him with you in this rowboat under the moonlight."

I shrug in response.

"Do you still laugh?" Strand asks. "When he kisses you?"

"Is this an interrogation?"

"No interrogation. We're friends, right?"

"Yes," I say firmly. "Friends."

But he's pulling me closer now so that we're dancing cheek to cheek and I can feel the hair on the back of his neck tickling my fingertips. Friends don't dance like this. I hope my parents aren't watching. I should probably pull away, dance like there's a Bible between us. It's so hard to do when the song is so beautiful and my dress is twinkling like Strand's stupid blue eyes.

"The answer to your other question is no," I say. I hope he gets the message that Levi and I are serious, and I'm no longer this dumb schoolgirl who laughs when she's getting kissed.

"Which one?" Strand asks. His breath is warm in my ear.

"When Levi kisses me," I say. "I don't laugh anymore."

It sounds sad when I say it out loud.

Chapter Forty-Three

"DEATH OF COMMUNICATION"
—COMPANY OF THIEVES

It's the day after the quince and Levi hasn't called me. I know he's back from the band trip by now because I saw their schedule in the school newsletter. At first I decide to wait it out and play it cool, but then I turn irrationally angry.

Why didn't he call me as soon as he returned? Why should I play a stupid little game and wait for him to call? Why can't I call him without worry of being labeled clingy or needy?

So I pick up the phone and dial his number, because I'm his girlfriend and girlfriends like to talk to their boyfriends after an absence, and this isn't something I should be ashamed of. After two rings, my call goes straight to his voice mail. I try again, three more times, each with the same result.

Okay, Levi. If that's how you want to play it. I find his home number in the school directory and let my righteous fury take over as I stab at the numbers on my phone.

Shira answers. I can hear Princess barking in the background.

"Victoria, how are you?" she chirps.

"I'm good, Mrs. Schuster," I reply. "How are you?"

"Oh, you know . . . same as ever."

I think of the sameness in Shira's life. How all of her days must consist of her sitting alone in the beige living room, with only Princess to keep her company. Steven Schuster at work, Levi consumed with school and the band. It might be the only connection between the two of us, but it suddenly feels profound.

"Is Levi back from his band trip?" I ask.

"Yes, he got back a couple of hours ago. Let me go grab him for you."

I wait on the line for a couple of minutes, entertaining myself by performing the quince choreography in front of the mirror.

"Victoria?" It's Shira's voice again.

"Yes?"

"Levi is taking a nap. Poor thing is exhausted from the trip. Should I have him call you back?"

"Um . . . no thanks, it's okay. I'll talk to him in school tomorrow."

"Okay, dear. Talk to you soon."

I hang up the phone and sink into my bed. So Levi's been back from the trip, probably for hours, and he didn't call, even though we haven't spoken for days. I try not to read too much into it, but when I stop and think about it, it could really mean a lot.

Levi's nowhere to be found the next day at school. He wasn't at his locker early this morning and he's missing from the cafeteria at lunch. That's when I know something is wrong.

I bolt to his locker as soon as my last class ends, ducking past opening doors and streams of students exiting their classrooms. I spot him bent over his backpack, hurriedly stuffing books inside.

"Levi!" I call, breaking into a jog.

He looks up and smiles a lukewarm smile when he sees me. I slow down and stop in front of him. After hunting him down all day, I've found him and now I'm at a loss for words.

"Hi," I say idiotically.

He stands up and slings his backpack over his shoulder. "Hey."

I kiss him, aiming for the lips but getting his cheek instead. "I was hoping you would call me when you were back."

"Yeah. Sorry. My mom told me you called." He shuts his locker and grips his backpack strap with two hands. "How did the quince go?"

The quince feels like years ago. "It went well. Strand and I had a lot of fun."

He nods, shifting his gaze to the floor.

"Of course, I still wish you could have been my partner," I add quickly, because it seems like the right thing to say.

"Do you?" He drags his eyes back to me.

"Yes!" I say. "You're my boyfriend. I would have loved it if you'd been there."

Then he gives this little sigh, one I can't interpret. I remember my vow that I wouldn't play any games.

"Is everything okay?" I ask him.

"What do you mean?"

"You're acting . . . different . . . I don't know, maybe I'm imagining it."

I'm not imagining it. I know I'm not. His eyes are darting around like they're tracking a fly.

"How was the band trip?" I ask.

"It was good. Phenomenal, actually." There's a fondness in his voice that makes me feel betrayed.

That's ridiculous, though. Why should I feel betrayed? I had fun at the quince without him. There's no dating rule that says you can only have fun with your boyfriend.

"Phenomenal, wow. That's a strong word," I say.

"We had a lot of fun," Levi replies with a shrug. "I was sad to leave."

I've been so proud of myself for keeping my cool, but at that statement, the floodgates open and my rage rushes through, wanting to drown him.

"Sad to leave? Are you kidding me?" I start. "I would think you'd be glad to come home and, oh, I don't know, see your girlfriend."

Levi's mouth flops open, and I realize that this is the first time he's ever seen me angry. Throughout our whole relationship, I've tried to be a lighter version of myself, a version without any bitterness, sarcasm, or negativity. And less flavor, I now realize. Like Diet Victoria.

"You know what else?" I go on, embracing the emotions rising to the surface. "It would have been nice to get a phone call so I knew you made it home alive."

"Vi . . ." He stares at me. "I told you I was sorry."

"That's not the point," I sigh.

"Okay . . . what is the point, then?"

"The point is that you didn't *want* to call me. It wasn't number one on your priority list."

Levi takes his glasses off to rub them on his shirt. I want to snatch them and break them in two. "I was tired. I knew I would see you in school today."

He really truly doesn't understand.

"Did you miss me?" I ask. I'm not asking in the clingy way. I genuinely want to know.

"Did I miss you?" he repeats. "Sure, I missed you."

"Levi . . . be honest. Did you miss me while you were gone?"

He looks down at his feet, silent. I already have my answer, but I want to hear it from him. When he looks up at me, his eyes are glazed with tears. This is one of the first times I've looked into his eyes, not through the glasses, but really looked into them.

"No," he says, his voice one notch above a whisper. "I didn't."

Now I'm the one who has to look away, because I know I'll start crying at any moment. I hate crying. Especially over a boy. I've become a living cliché.

"Did something happen on this trip?" I ask, staring at the vents in the locker beside me. My vision turns blurry as the tears start to form. "Is there someone else?"

"No," Levi says firmly. "This isn't about another girl."

"Why didn't you tell me you were feeling this way?"

"You didn't say anything either," Levi points out quietly.

"I was committed. I thought things were working between us."

"Vi, come on . . . we've never done anything more than kiss."

I whip my head around to face him.

"I don't mean it like that," he clarifies. "I just mean . . . we had more of a friendship than a romance."

"I don't kiss my friends, Levi," I say icily.

He slides his glasses back on, and my heart inadvertently pangs against my chest. I remember thinking how cute he was in those glasses.

"I think I need some time," he says. "Maybe a break or something."

This can't be Levi, saying these things to me. He wasn't supposed to do this.

"A break," I state. "How long of a break? A break so that you can see other people?"

"Vi, I told you this isn't about other people."

"Then what exactly is this break supposed to achieve?"

He exhales through closed lips. "I don't know."

"Well, I don't do breaks," I say.

When the words come out, they surprise me, too. Sometimes you're not sure how you feel about something until you say it. There's a huge part of me that wants to wrap myself around Levi's leg and hold him down so he can't walk away. And then there's a small but strong voice inside that tells me I deserve better. I shouldn't be with someone who's willing to risk losing me because he needs a break. Like I'm a chore or an exam. And if I'm going to be honest with myself, didn't I sometimes feel the same way? Was spending time with Levi ever fun for me, or was it something I felt like I should do?

Levi bites his lower lip. There's barely a pause before he says, "Then I guess we're done."

It's like he's taken a pocketknife straight to my gut.

"You realize this is it, right? I'll never take you back," I say.

I wish he would take a second to think about things, to make me feel like I was worth some consideration. Surely he values something about me.

"I know," he says with finality.

There's something in me that wants to argue with him and plead my case, but somehow I scrounge up the remains of my pride and keep quiet.

He coughs and says, "I hope this won't affect . . . the band or anything. You know?"

"The band." My voice is laced with disdain. Not our relationship, or even our friendship. The band. I stare at him, and I realize that for the past four months, I've been dating a robot. Is he honestly talking about the welfare of the band right now? After breaking up with me?

"I need to tell you something, Levi, and I want to be very clear," I say with as much calm as I can muster.

"Okay." He nods, waits.

"Fuck your band."

───── *Chapter Forty-Four* ─────

"FEEL THE PAIN"
—DINOSAUR JR.

At first, I'm emotionally numb, like I took an ice cube to my feelings. I'm almost convinced that the breakup didn't happen. Or it happened to me but I'm watching it from a faraway distance.

My family and I are eating another dinner in silence. Without Strand here, we all remember that we currently don't like each other. Matty plays his 3DS at the table, and my parents let him. I think dealing with me has drained them of all their energy.

"Levi and I broke up," I say without feeling, midway through my bowl of spaghetti.

Even as I say the words, it still seems made-up, like it couldn't have actually happened to me.

Before our fight at the hospital, Mom would have reacted to the news by squishing me into a tight hug and calling me *mamita*. She would have asked me if I was okay and looked into my eyes and known that I wasn't.

Now she looks at me, but I can see that there's still something standing between us.

"I'm sorry," she says softly, and we all go back to eating in silence.

After saying the news out loud, things begin sinking in. I won't feel Levi's glasses against my face when we kiss. I won't be able to listen to Tchaikovsky without thinking of our first date. What happens to us now that Levi and I as a couple cease to exist? What happens to me now that the band is officially dismantled?

Maybe I was naive, thinking I could do the whole high school boyfriend thing. I was so obsessed with the idea of having someone that I didn't care who it was. But why? Since when am I the girl who needs a boyfriend? What was I trying to prove?

There's a pit in my stomach and the few bites of dinner I can eat won't fill it. Later, when I'm lying in my bed, I'm surprised that I am starting to feel. The numbness is fading, the ice cube has melted. An overwhelming fear grabs hold of me.

What if this was it? What if Levi was my one shot? He's the only guy who's ever shown an interest in me, and I ruined it. Yesterday, I belonged to someone. Today, I have no one. How can you be with someone and then cut them out of your life forever? How can Levi discard me like an old T-shirt? That's what feels worst of all—that Levi was willing to let me go. Even if, I can admit to myself now, we weren't right for each other. It's like he saw nothing in me that was worth staying for. It's confirmation that I'm not all that special, really.

I only let myself cry because Levi isn't there to see me, and I don't think I can stop it now. I stick my face into my pillow and let out every gutted sob. It's painful, but it's better than feeling numb. It's almost a relief, knowing I can feel something this deeply.

I don't realize Mom's entered the room until my bed dips under her weight. She sits next to me and strokes my hair like I'm three years old again. She doesn't say anything for a while, just lets me cry everything out. The silence is different now, less hostile. When I lift my head from my pillow, it's soaked in tears and a little bit of snot.

"This sucks," I say finally, sniffling and wiping my nose. And it does. Everything about this sucks right now—the breakup, the dissolution of the band, our fight.

"I know." She dabs the corner of my nose with a tissue. "But you won't feel like this forever."

My brain understands that fact, but my body doesn't. The pain of losing everything feels like I've been sucked into a permanent black hole.

"Do you want to know what I think?" she asks, lying down next to me.

I nod and scoot over to make room for her.

"I think," Mom says, "that one day you'll find someone who really makes you happy."

"I think I'm the problem," I counter. "Levi *should* have made me happy."

There are plenty of things that should make me happy, but don't.

All the things in life that are supposed to satisfy me, that satisfy everyone else.

Mom wipes the tears from under my eyes. She looks at me for a long time, in that really unnerving way that moms can. I can't even meet her eyes. I look down at the crumpled, snotty tissue in my hands.

"I really am sorry," I say, and I start to cry. Again. Because I'm not just apologizing for that night at the hospital. I'm apologizing for being me, for what I'm sure will be a lifetime full of future disappointment for them.

"I know," she says. She puts her arm around my shoulders, and I cry until I have nothing left in me.

Later, Dad comes into my room, drags my desk chair over to the bed, and sits down. The chair creaks underneath him.

"This chair sucks," he says.

"Yeah."

"Why don't you get a new one?"

I shrug. He glances around my room, his gaze lingering over the door. I know Mom pressured him to come in and offer me some words of wisdom.

"The guy's an asshole," he says finally.

Even though the giant hole in my gut is still there, I laugh. "Levi?"

"There's something I don't like about him . . . I never trusted him."

My instinct is still to defend him, but when I open my mouth, nothing comes out.

"You know," Dad says, "I had a bad breakup right before I met your mom."

"Really? You dated someone before Mom?" I always assumed my parents were each other's firsts, since they met in high school.

"Her name was Melissa Soto. We dated for a year."

My jaw drops. "You dated someone who wasn't Mom for that long? Why didn't I know about this?"

"I don't talk about it much," Dad says. "She broke my heart. Dumped me for another guy."

"Did you cry?"

"I bawled my eyes out, but that's not the point. The point is that if I hadn't gone through that sh—that stuff . . . I wouldn't have met your mom. I wouldn't have known how much better it could be."

"Yeah, but . . . what if there isn't anything better?"

Dad looks down his nose at me. "Are you telling me you don't think you can do better than this Leo kid? With that stupid hair of his?"

This time when I laugh, I forget all about the hole in my gut.

Chapter Forty-Five

"NO THE END
IS NOT NEAR"
—BENNY HESTER

I learned something important. If you are going through a breakup, the people you love will bend over backward to make you feel better. Mom and Dad let me skip school for the day because when I wake up, I'm crying all over again. I'm crying because I'm bound to see Levi around school, and I don't know how to act when I do. I'm crying because I've let someone make me feel worthless, and that's a dumb thing to do, but the feeling still remains. More than anything, I'm crying because I knew from the start that being with Levi felt wrong. I knew it, and I ignored it, and now I've lost myself.

The one good thing that's come out of all of this is that my breakup with Levi has unexpectedly brought my parents back to life.

Dad actually buys me a pint of ice cream at my request. Real, lactose-filled ice cream.

"This won't make you feel better," he warns, but he's wrong. It helps.

I spend the morning in bed, still wearing my robe, watching Netflix and scarfing down spoonfuls of mint chocolate chip. Then I create a new playlist for my music collection: Breaking Up. I sing Bonnie Tyler at the top of my lungs. I eat more mint chocolate chip ice cream. I watch more TV. I sing and dance to Carly Simon and Pat Benatar.

I take a nap with the TV on, because I don't like the silence. When I wake up, I'm not sure what time it is, if it's day or night. I hear the front door slam and Mom shouting, "Victoria! Look who I found!"

"Huh?" I shout back. My voice is sore from my female empowerment songfest.

Annie bursts through my door, still in her Evanston uniform. I don't know what surprises me more, that she made the long trip up to my apartment, or that she's putting off her homework to make me feel better.

"You have chocolate all over your face" is the first thing she says to me. She licks her thumb and aims for my cheek, but I duck away.

"What are you doing here?" I ask in disbelief.

"I heard about you and Levi."

I sit up and blink the sleep out of my eyes, finally taking note of my surroundings. My room is a disaster. *I'm* a disaster. My comforter is falling off the bed, there's an empty pint of ice cream on my nightstand, and my clothes are scattered all over the floor.

Annie is already tidying up my desk area, humming to herself.

"How are you feeling?" she asks, organizing my notebooks into a neat pile.

"Crappy."

"I'll bet."

"How is Levi doing?" I ask, feeling a pang as I say his name aloud.

She hesitates. "I didn't really see him today."

"He didn't sit with you guys at lunch?" I press.

"Nope," she says shortly. She sweeps my empty ice-cream carton into the wastebasket. "He's an idiot."

"He's got the highest GPA in the eleventh grade," I point out.

"He's still an idiot."

"Can you stop cleaning my room, please?" I ask.

Annie pauses, her arms full of my clothes. "Let me just put these in the hamper. You don't realize how much a mess can affect your mood. It's all about the feng shui."

"All right," I sigh, too drained to argue.

"Do you want to talk about it? Or do you want me to tell you everything I hate about Levi? I'm prepared to do either."

"There's not much to say about it," I say. "He didn't like me enough. He dumped me."

"Stop it, Vi. This isn't about him not liking you enough. You guys weren't right for each other." Annie puts my clothes away, then rummages around in her backpack and pulls out a sheet of notebook paper and a pen. "Time to make a list."

Annie believes that any problem can be solved with organized thinking.

"I want you to think of everything you didn't like about Levi," she instructs.

"This isn't going to help . . ."

"Yes it will. You need to stop thinking of yourself as the problem."

"All right, all right." I fluff the pillows behind me and lean against them. "I guess . . . it kind of bothered me how he always put work first."

"Good start," Annie says, jotting it down.

"And he never listened to any of the music I recommended. Only Sigur Rós. He's obsessed with Sigur Rós."

"What else?" Annie prods.

"He's spoiled," I say. My mind is dusting off its wheels and slowly grinding back to work. "He bought me tights for Valentine's Day."

"You can't be serious," Annie says.

"Sadly, I am."

"I have one," Annie says. "No passion. Remember? You said you wished he would just take you."

"Levi would never take anyone," I say. "And he was an okay kisser, but nothing amazing. Add that to the list."

We work diligently on the list for another few minutes. When Annie reads it aloud, it says:

Why Levi Sucks

1. Puts work first

2. Boring taste in music

3. Spoiled

4. Not romantic

5. No passion

6. Probably bad at sex

7. Kissing skills are mediocre

8. Terrible dancer

9. Bossy

10. Critical

11. Self-centered

"Uses too much hair gel," I add, thinking of Strand.

Annie writes it down and tacks the paper onto my wall, right above my desk. "To be continued," she says. "It helps, right?"

"It does. But he wasn't all bad . . ."

"Vi, hush. You don't talk about the good stuff when the breakup is this fresh."

"Right."

She pauses, then, "Can I ask you something?"

"I guess so," I reply, because I know Annie and she'll ask me what she wants, with or without my permission.

"Were you with Levi because you liked him or because you were scared?"

"Scared?" I repeat. "Scared of what?"

"I don't know. Scared of being alone, scared of going after something you really want."

"I was with Levi because . . ." It's something I don't know how to explain. Annie sits there, waiting as I try to put my thoughts into words. "I thought it would be enough."

She flattens her lips like she's holding herself back.

"I wasn't scared," I insist. "Stop looking at me like that."

"If you say so . . ." She pauses, then asks hesitantly, "What's going to happen with the band?"

I look around my room, anywhere but her eyes. "There's no more band."

"For now, I know—"

"No, Ann. For good."

"I still think if you sat down with your parents and explained everything, they would come around."

"No, they wouldn't."

"You have to *try*, Vi. And what about the Battle of the Boroughs?"

"It's not gonna happen."

"But you love the band! And you guys have a shot at winning. Krina said—"

"Annie."

"What?"

"I really don't want to talk about it."

For the first time in the history of our friendship, Annie listens. I'm grateful, because the hardest part of breaking up with Levi is breaking up with the band. There's a finality to it this time, like the window I always kept open is officially shut and locked.

We sit in silence for twenty minutes, and she leaves my apartment right before dinner. I think to myself that even though Levi doesn't love me, I have plenty of other people who do. And that can be good enough.

Chapter Forty-Six

"NOBODY'S EMPIRE"
—BELLE AND SEBASTIAN

Of all the scary things I've done, walking into school the next day might be the scariest. I don't know how I'll act when I run into Levi. I'm not sure if I should smile at him or ignore him. My hands fumble with the combination lock when I attempt to open my locker. I'm on edge, the star of the horror movie that is my life. But the thought of facing Levi is ten times scarier than encountering Michael Myers or Freddy Krueger.

I grab my books as quickly as humanly possible, because my best bet in making it through today is to avoid public spaces such as hallways. When I close my locker door, Strand suddenly appears next to me. I let out an ear-piercing shriek.

"Hey, partner," he says, unfazed. "Did I scare you?"

"What the freaking hell, Strand?" I hug my books against me protectively and scan the hall. No Levi in sight.

"Are we looking for *him*?" Strand follows my gaze around the hallway.

"He's not high on my list of people I want to run into."

"Understandable."

"So he told you we broke up?" I ask.

"No. Annie did."

"Of course . . . I suppose you feel sorry for me."

Strand scoffs. "Why would I? It's his loss, not yours."

"Are you even allowed to be talking to me? Aren't you supposed to be on *his* side?"

"Why?" he asks. "Because I'm a guy?"

"No, because you're, like, his best friend."

"Levi and I may be friends, but you and I have a sacred bond stronger than friendship . . . we're quince partners."

"I have news for you . . . the quince is over."

"So what? We're done, then?"

I'm not sure what Strand and I are now. Were we ever friends, or were we bandmates and quince partners? Or something else entirely? All I know is that there's no longer any reason for him to come to my apartment and lie in my bed and sing with me.

"Things are complicated," I say.

"What about the band?" he asks.

The question makes me want to scream, because first it was Levi, and now it's Strand placing the band above my feelings.

"What about it?" I ask coldly.

"We'll still play at the Battle, won't we? I can try to talk to your parents, if you want."

"Forgive me if the band isn't my number-one concern at the moment."

Strand looks taken aback. "I just meant . . ."

"I know what you meant. I'm sure you and Levi are very concerned about who you'll find to replace me."

"Will you stop being so dramatic? We're not replacing you, Victoria. There's no band without you."

I think about having to sing next to Levi, like nothing ever happened between us, like we've never made out or held hands, and it makes me sick. Then I think about not having to perform at Battle of the Boroughs in front of all those people, and I feel that familiar sense of relief.

"Then I guess there's no band," I say to Strand.

"You don't mean that."

"I can't do it, Strand. I can't be in a band with him and pretend nothing ever happened. I can't lie to my family anymore."

"So don't," he urges. "Talk to them. Talk to Levi."

"I'm sorry," I say.

I realize that maybe I wasn't the only one saved by Debaser. Maybe it was saving Strand, too. Maybe it means more to him than he lets on. I can't stick it out for him, though. It hurts too much.

"This isn't about Levi or your family, and you know it," he says.

I don't answer. Partly because he's right. It's not all about them. It's a lot about me.

"The Battle's in two weeks," he says. "You have time to change your mind."

My stomach knots. "I can't . . ."

Strand shakes his head at me, and for a second his disapproval hurts as much as any part of the breakup. "You're braver than this."

"I'm not," I reply. "I told you. I'm a wuss."

In class I make myself as invisible as possible. It's easy and familiar. My life preband. I keep my head down and take detailed notes, shaking out my hand every few minutes. If I stop writing, I think of life without the band. So I don't stop writing.

Annie keeps checking up on me throughout the day, and as much as I love and appreciate her, I don't feel like being reminded of how sad I should feel.

"How are you doing?" she asks, knitting her eyebrows together in concern. She's acting like I've been diagnosed with a fatal disease.

"Oh, you know," I say, forcing a smile. "I'll survive."

"The key is to keep yourself busy. You should take up a new hobby or something."

"I plan on watching hours of TV and eating a pint of ice cream for dinner tonight. Is that enough of a hobby?"

She ignores me. "Ooh, I know! How about crochet?"

"So I can cement my future old-maid status? No thank you."

"Track's starting up soon . . . why don't you sign up? Then you'll have two seasons to put on your college applications next year."

"I can't, Annie."

"Why not?"

"Because it'll be like none of this ever happened. I'd be the same Victoria I was at the beginning of the year."

"That Victoria wasn't so bad. She made rational decisions to help herself get into a good college."

"I'll think about it," I tell her. I won't, though, because that Victoria was miserable. To go from lead singer back to that girl is all too depressing.

I avoid everyone the rest of the day. I layer a sweater under my coat and eat lunch outside, even though it's still cold. I sit against a gnarled tree trunk on the opposite side of campus, far away from the cafeteria. The tree's just large enough to shield me from the biting wind. I'm the only one outside today. It's too cold for normal people, but today the outside perfectly matches my inside.

Chapter Forty-Seven

"YOUTH"
—DAUGHTER

Enough of this moping around," Annie declares before math on Monday morning. "You're eating lunch with us today."

"I have plans," I say.

"With whom?"

"My tree. I named him."

"You named a tree," she repeats incredulously.

"Yes. Roberto de la Fuerte, because he's sturdy and always there for me."

"See?" Annie latches onto my shoulders. "Look what this lack of human contact has done to you! You can't avoid society forever, Vi. It's a small school. You're bound to run into Levi sooner or later."

"I only have to avoid him for another year and a half until he graduates."

"I haven't even seen him in the cafeteria. I think he's eating with the band students. Come on. It's just me, Krina, and Strand."

"Fine," I say, because she has a point. I can't live in fear forever. If I see Levi, I'll nod and go about my day. Even if it feels like I'm dying inside.

Annie claps her hands in delight.

"You're in a good mood," I note.

"Sorry." She lowers her hands. "Am I too cheerful? I shouldn't be cheerful when you're so sad."

"Don't be sorry. I'm glad my misery isn't rubbing off on you."

Then she physically blushes. Her cheeks turn a perfect shade of peach. Annie does not blush. She makes lists and studies and applies herself. She does not blush.

"Oh my God," I say, struck by something through my fog of depression. "You like someone!"

"Don't be silly," she says, the color in her cheeks deepening. Her second lie to me in the entire time I've known her, after the eraser theft of third grade. Annie isn't good at lying to me.

I sit up and gawk at her. "You do!"

"I do not." She opens her book up to a random page and pretends to be deeply invested.

I wait her out, knowing that she can't keep the lie up for long. Sure enough, she shuts the book and blows a strand of hair out of her face.

"There *might* be someone I *might* be interested in," she confesses.

"Oh my God, that's great, Annie!" I don't even need to force my enthusiasm. Annie hasn't liked anyone since Danny Palermo in the fourth grade. She's always claimed that she isn't interested in dating until med school, where she will find an aspiring brain surgeon to marry.

"I didn't tell you, because . . . well, you know. Besides, I doubt anything will happen."

"You don't need to worry about me," I promise. "I'm happy for you. Really."

"Thanks, Vi."

"So . . . who is it?"

Annie shakes her head. "I don't want to jinx it."

"Oh, come on," I beg. "Let me live vicariously through you since my love life has turned to ashes."

"You've only been single a week!"

"It's okay. I'll be fine alone. I've accepted my fate."

Mr. Davis clears his throat to start class, and I lean forward to whisper to Annie, "Do you want to go to Lalo after school today? I could use some cheesecake. And we can discuss your mystery man."

"I can't," she whispers out of the corner of her mouth. "Homework."

Lie number three. I can tell by the way she stares straight down at her shoulder without looking at me. But this time she doesn't admit the truth.

Thankfully, Levi is absent from the cafeteria during lunchtime. That doesn't stop me from looking for him. My body stiffens each time the cafeteria door swings open.

"You're making *me* nervous," Strand says.

"I think it's too soon for me to be here," I reply. My tray of pizza sits in front of me, untouched.

"You're making it harder on yourself," says Krina. "Why should you be the one avoiding places?"

"Because I'm the one who was dumped. Where has he been eating, anyway?"

I'm filled with curiosity as to how Levi's been filling his time for the past week. Krina and Strand are his good friends too, but they haven't seen or spoken to him. It feels like I've been granted full custody after a divorce.

"Maybe he's avoiding *you*," Annie offers. "He could have found his own lady tree."

"Did you guys know he hasn't tried to contact me since we broke up?" I ask. "Not once."

"It's better that way," Annie says. "A clean break."

"I don't understand it, though. I don't understand how you can date someone, see them every day, meet their parents, and then drop them like they never meant anything to you."

"Some people need the distance," Krina says.

"Levi doesn't. I'm convinced he was born without the capacity to feel."

"Don't you think you're being a little harsh?"

"No, actually."

"There are two people at fault in a breakup, Victoria," Krina says. "No matter who does the dumping."

"That's not true." I refuse to believe that I deserve any blame in this situation. Levi is the one who pulled away.

"Drop it, Krina," says Strand.

"It's true," she maintains. "I'm not saying one person can't be more at fault than the other. But, Victoria, you need to ask yourself what role you played in things."

"I didn't!" How dare she accuse me of playing a role in the breakup? I'm the victim here. I was the loving, understanding girlfriend who put in the effort. I ball up my paper napkin and throw it onto my plate. Appetite officially lost. I want to be alone again, outside in the quiet.

"I'm not saying Levi didn't act like an ass," Krina says, "because he did. I'm just saying it's not that simple."

"I tried so hard to make things work with him," I say. "How can you say that it's partly my fault we broke up?"

Krina looks up at me with narrowed eyes. "Because it is. You both played a part. Even if you won't admit it."

As I'm packing up to go home, I think about what Krina said. Despite my indignation, I wonder if she's right. I wonder if I'm to blame for the breakup too. I was never fully myself with Levi, always worried about messing things up. Maybe that did us in. Maybe it was how fast I jumped in before asking myself if he was the right guy for me. Or . . . and this is what really scares me . . . maybe I'm just a massive screw-up. I shun the things that normal people would want, and, in the end, I lose everything.

I slam my locker shut. Out of the corner of my eye, I see Annie rushing down the hall. She usually meets me at my locker after school, but today she's speed-walking toward the stairwell. What is she actually doing after school? She wouldn't lie to me unless it was something big.

In my desperation for a distraction, I decide to do something shameful. Something beneath me.

I'm going to follow her.

I'm almost sure her lie has something to do with her current crush; otherwise she'd be honest with me about what she's doing after school. I'm dying to see who's managed to capture Annie's affections and alter her five-year plan.

Hiking up my backpack, I keep my eyes trained on her jet-black ponytail and the way it swings from side to side when she walks, like a beacon amidst the crowd. When she starts down the stairwell, I make sure to slip in and out of a group of students directly behind her. She exits the building and turns right, heading through the quad and out the campus gates.

Luckily, there's a steady stream of students pouring out, so I'm able to go unnoticed. Annie's walking pace is unnaturally quick to begin with, but it's accelerated now, like she's purposely trying to lose someone. After a few blocks she reaches the uptown subway train, but instead of going inside, she turns right.

I duck behind a tree, waiting for her to walk farther down the street before I follow. She continues walking, past Columbus and Amsterdam, then stops outside of Artie's Diner.

Does she actually have a date? In a *diner*? Annie hates diners. She thinks they're grimy and rat infested. But in she goes, through the swinging door and out of sight. I creep up toward the smudged front window. I want just one glimpse of her mystery man. Then I'll stop.

Through the window of the diner, I see her take a seat in the booth at the back, but I can't see who she's sitting with.

I stand on my tiptoes, trying to peer over the heads of the other diners, mostly groups of high school students. A crotchety man sipping a coffee scowls at me through the glass. I back away. If I move to the other window, I'll get a better view of the back of the diner. The problem is I'll also have a better chance of getting caught.

I decide to take the risk. If Annie had been honest with me from the beginning, I wouldn't have to resort to stalking. I move to the other window, hunching over Quasimodo style. If I lean a little to the right, I can get a view of mystery man's head.

Stretching my body to the side, I catch a glimpse of wavy dark-brown hair. I tilt my head farther, ignoring the incoming muscle crick in my neck.

Then I freeze.

I recognize that hair. The way it pokes up every different direction like it can't make up its mind.

An embarrassing choking sound rises from my throat. Simultaneous panic and terror seize my body, paralyzing me from head to toe. When I try to breathe, my throat tightens, cutting off my airflow. My body turns to ice, and I truly, 100 percent, think that I might die right here outside this filthy diner.

My thoughts spin around me, and the only one I can hang on to is the one that makes me feel worse:

Annie's on a date with Strand.

Chapter Forty-Eight

"GIDDY STRATOSPHERES"
—THE LONG BLONDES

'm sitting in my room that night, mulling over what I saw. I've been mulling ever since I trudged home from Artie's. I mulled about it on the train, mulled about it while eating spaghetti with my family for dinner, and I'm mulling about it now instead of finishing *Pride and Prejudice* for English homework.

Strand and Annie? When? How? Most important . . . why? I try to reason away their secret rendezvous, but nothing I come up with makes sense. Nothing explains why Annie would lie to me.

They don't match as a couple. Can't they see that? They're all sorts of wrong for each other. I know opposites attract, but Annie and Strand together is a little extreme. She's all schedules and plans, while Strand is . . . well, a mess. Annie could never handle it.

She does like to clean, though. She might consider Strand the ultimate project, like those home makeover shows she watches on HGTV. God knows I'm hard on Strand sometimes, but he deserves better than someone who sees him as a fixer-upper. He's spontaneous and funny and lives in the moment. I don't want Annie to take that away and turn him into an Evanston robot. He's different from the others.

Yes, he's dated a lot of girls. Way too many girls. He obviously has a plethora of commitment issues. Unless . . . what if Annie's using him for sex? Does she want someone with experience to pop her cherry? Does she want to be one of the many in his harem of women? Or are they embarking on an honest relationship?

If they're dating, really and truly dating, I should be happy for them—"should" being the operative word. Instead, I feel betrayed. My best friend and my . . . whatever Strand is.

And ew, what if they publicly display their affection all over school? Make out during lunchtime? Hold hands in the halls? Is Annie going to—God forbid—sit on his lap? I physically won't be able to handle that.

But they're my friends, and I should want the best for them. End of story. If they want to date, good luck to them.

Despite all the peace and love my brain is spouting, I pick up my desk chair and hurl it across my room. It slams against the wall with a crash louder than I anticipated.

Oops.

Moments later, Dad bursts through the door, halfway through

the act of undressing, wearing his polo work shirt and pajama bottoms. "Ria! What the hell happened? Are you okay?"

"*¿Qué pasó?*" Mom shouts behind him.

"Sorry." I'm in a state of shock after my Hulk transformation. I stare at the chair now lying helpless on its back. "Just an accident."

"An accident?" Mom squeezes past Dad and notices the desk chair. She looks at me in disbelief.

I pray that she doesn't ask me what kind of accident would end with my chair flying across the room.

"I'm okay," I say, feeling my cheeks warm. "Sorry for the noise."

"Do you . . . Is there something you want to talk about?" Mom asks, head swiveling from me to the chair.

"Is this about Leo?" Dad asks. "He's not worth it."

"It's not about Levi," I reply, grabbing the chair and planting it in front of my desk. It's a little wobbly, but not broken. "Anyway, I have a lot of homework to do, so . . ."

They hesitate for a moment, then slowly back away from me.

"We're here if you need to talk," Mom says as they shuffle out of my room. Before closing the door, she looks back at me as though fearful I'm having a psychotic breakdown. Maybe I am. Throwing my chair against the wall is not exactly a normal reaction to finding out my two friends are dating.

Okay, fine. If I'm being honest with myself, I'm not happy about it. Strand needs someone who can appreciate his music. Someone imaginative, someone who can call him out on his crap but still be open to his point of view.

No. No, no, no, no, NO. This can't be happening.

I can't be in love with Strand. There are so many reasons why I can't be in love with him.

Except . . . what were those reasons again? Because I was with Levi? Or was it that Strand's too good-looking? Too confident? Too experienced?

None of those reasons seem to matter like they used to. Or is there another reason at the root of all the others? Do all my excuses boil down to the fact that I'm a giant wuss? That I had to make excuses to cover my fear of going after who I wanted?

Of course, there's no point in overanalyzing now. Not when there's a larger, more pressing reason looming above all the others.

Strand is dating my best friend. And that's the reason I can't argue against.

Chapter Forty-Nine

"UNDER A ROCK"
—WAXAHATCHEE

I won't be another member of Strand's female fan club, one of the many clamoring for his affections. That's not me. I won't let on to what I'm feeling. It's all about the power of self-control. After all, emotions are only chemical reactions in the brain. I can beat them. And if I can't, I'll lock my feelings in tight and shut them away until I forget they exist. Simple, right?

I try to act as normal as possible the next day at lunch, even though he sits right next to me and my skin shivers every time his arm brushes against mine.

Snap out of it, Cruz.

"Scoot over," I tell him, wrenching my arm away.

"I'm not even near you."

"You're in my personal space."

"Okay . . ." He scoots his chair over about an inch. "Is this better for you, Princess?"

"Yes." I look away from him. Do not engage. Those blue eyes of his are dangerous.

"What's with the mood?" Krina asks me.

"There's no mood."

She looks over at Annie, and Annie shrugs in return before taking a bite of her salad. Salad. Again. She even eats it the same way, picking out the blue cheese and dicing up the hardboiled egg into four equal pieces before pouring on the dressing. I hope Strand is ready for a lifetime of predictability.

Stop it. Annie is your friend. Be happy for her.

"Shit," I hear Krina murmur. When I look up, she's staring across the cafeteria. "Wait, Vi," she starts to say, but I turn my head in the direction of her gaze.

Levi has entered. And it's not just Levi. Attached to his arm is a small, pale girl with freckles and chestnut-brown hair.

My first thought is, shamefully, that I'm prettier than her. Even though I'm over Levi, I feel a strange sense of ownership, as though this girl is trespassing on my property.

I tear my eyes away before Levi can catch me staring. I feel everyone waiting for my reaction, not just at our lunch table, but throughout the cafeteria.

When I look at Krina and Annie, they wear matching expressions of guilt on their faces.

"Did you guys know about this?" I ask them quietly.

"We weren't sure," Krina says. "We wanted to tell you, but we didn't want to worry you if it was nothing."

"Clearly, it's something," I say.

Levi and the girl are standing in line with their trays now. They've stopped holding hands, but she has her head on his shoulder.

"Asshole," Strand mutters. He gives me a face, one I've never seen from him before. I recognize the expression. It's pity. And it's the last thing I want him to feel for me.

"Do you want to talk about it?" Annie asks. "We can take our food somewhere else so we don't have to look at them . . ."

I have to remind myself not to hate my best friend of ten years. So her love life is taking off with the person I've liked all along. The guy who is now looking at me like I'm an unwanted shelter pet just as I've discovered my ex has quickly moved on to someone else like I never mattered.

Nothing worth getting riled up over.

"I'm fine," I reply. I take a sip of water to moisten my lips, which are suddenly dry and cakey.

Now the pity is on all of their faces, and no one is speaking.

"Actually," I go on, "I remembered I have some homework to finish for class. I'll see you guys later."

I leave my tray in the middle of the table and rush out of the cafeteria, away from the stares and the girl with her head on my ex-boyfriend's shoulder. I'm worried I'm going to start crying at any moment. I hustle down the hallway toward the bathroom, when I hear a voice behind me.

"Vi!"

When I stop to turn around, Annie is pumping her arms and speed-walking to catch up with me.

"You liar," she says. "You always finish your homework before class."

Sometimes it sucks that she knows me so well.

"I didn't feel like staying for the show," I mumble.

"Do you want me to punch him in the face for you? Because I will."

"Yes. Right on the mouth so this new girl will have to kiss it when it's swollen and bloody."

"I'll go buy some brass knuckles after school."

I smile a little. It feels foreign.

"I swear I was going to tell you," Annie says. "I wanted to make sure they were dating before I said anything."

"How long have you been seeing them together?" I ask.

"A couple days after you broke up. She's in the school band with him. I think she plays the flute."

"Oh." According to that time line, Levi either works very quickly or this girl played a role in our breakup.

"I'm sorry, Vi. I should have told you sooner."

"It's okay," I tell her, because her face is scrunching up like she's going to cry.

"I hate him. I really do," she says.

"Ann, you don't hate anybody."

"I do so. I hate people who throw trash out their car window, and people who man-spread on the subway. And people who hurt my best friend."

I can't deny the blaze of anger that jolts through me when I think of Levi. I might hate him. I look at Annie, prepared to hate her now too. Then I notice how close she is to tears, and it puts a damper on my hate.

Annie is one of the few people in my life who has always been there for me. She always wants the best for me, even though to her, the best usually means a perfect college application and a future high-paying job.

If she knew what I felt for Strand, she would stop seeing him in a heartbeat.

I don't want Annie to hate Levi or feel my sadness, because she deserves to be happy. Maybe dating Strand will help her escape normal life, like joining Debaser did for me.

"How are things going with your mystery crush?" I ask.

She bends her head so that her soft black hair falls over her face. She's wearing it loose today. It used to be tied back all the time for optimum efficiency. I wonder if she's trying to look prettier for Strand or if she's growing out of her old style.

"You don't want to talk about this," she says. "Let's talk about how much we hate Levi."

"I don't want you to hate Levi. I can hate him fine on my own."

"Yeah, but—"

"Seriously. We always talk about me. I'd rather talk about you."

"Are you sure?"

"Positive."

"Okay." Annie draws in her breath. "Things are going well with my crush. So well that it's freaking me out."

"Why would that freak you out?"

"Because . . ." Her face clears. "I don't know what I did to deserve to feel this good. Especially when you're so miserable."

"Of course you deserve it," I say. "I think it's great. And . . . I'm happy for you. Really happy."

Yes, this is a lie. But I once read that if you say something enough, you can will the statement into being. As Annie's friend, I'm supposed to be happy when she's happy. I'm not there yet, but I think that sometime in the faraway future, if I keep saying it enough, I can be.

Chapter Fifty

"FRIENDS WITH BENEFITS"
—JIM O'ROURKE

With Levi dating someone new, I can finally close the casket on our relationship. It's strange to see him with someone else and suddenly become an outsider in his life. Sometimes I'll make comparisons, like whether her hair is softer than mine when he runs his fingers through it. Whether he's gone under her bra yet. Whether he's brought her over for dinner. Whether she likes that damn dog of Shira's. He doesn't have lunch with the rest of us anymore. He and that girl sit with a few of the band kids on the other side of the cafeteria.

I think about all of these things, but it doesn't hurt like it used to. It's subsided to a dull ache now.

Annie and Strand haven't gone public with their relationship yet, but I know it's still going on because Annie walks around school with a dopey, dreamy look on her face. She also forgot to bring her notebook to math class, which has never happened in the history of Annie. Her hair is always down now, like she can't be bothered to style it anymore.

Whenever I ask her about it, she presses her lips into a little smile and says, "Nothing's definite yet."

"You don't have to spare my feelings," I say. "I'm over Levi now."

She keeps smiling in that distant way of someone who is sickeningly in love. How are you supposed to function in life when you want to slap your best friend?

There's a difference between the way I think about Levi and the way I think about Strand. One causes me a small twinge of bitterness, and the other feels like a machete has split me in two.

Chapter Fifty-One

"SEASONS (WAITING ON YOU)"
—FUTURE ISLANDS

Today is my birthday, and the Battle of the Boroughs is in two days. I remember thinking, only a few months ago, that this would be the most important week of my life. Now it's here, and it's empty.

I wouldn't have remembered my birthday if not for Mom, Dad, and Matty crowding around my bed to sing me awake. Matty pushes down on the edge of my mattress to the rhythm of the birthday song. When I sit up, Mom positions our old, stained breakfast tray onto my lap with a plate of Cuban *pastelitos* that my dad bought. They're my favorite—crackling pastries filled with cream cheese and guava. *Pastelitos* are a Cruz birthday tradition that I usually look forward to, but today they make my stomach turn.

"Happy sweet sixteen," she says, squeezing me in a hug. Dad plants a wet kiss on my forehead.

"Thank you, thank you." I stretch my eyelids open, secretly wishing I were anywhere but here.

"Do you feel older?" Matty asks, studying my face as though I'm about to sprout wrinkles.

I think about it for a second. "A little bit, I guess."

I feel weathered, like a bike that's been left outside for too many years. Although that has less to do with being older and more to do with losing my band, my boyfriend, and the boy I like, all in one fell swoop.

"Finish your breakfast," Mom says. "You still have to go to school, even if it's your birthday."

I take a tiny bite of my *pastelito*. "Or you can give me the best birthday present ever and let me skip school."

"*Sigue soñando,*" she says. Keep dreaming.

I'm not at all hungry, but I force myself to finish my breakfast. Instead of beautifying myself for school, I grab the cleanest-looking shirt from my floor and scrape a brush through the rat's nest on my head. Who cares what I look like today? It's just like any other day.

After I put on my uniform, I examine myself in the mirror. I do look older. Not only older, but tired. Defeated. Sad.

I'm sixteen now.

I'm more than halfway to thirty. I can drive a car by myself . . . well, if I didn't live in NYC and actually needed a car. I'm old enough to get married (with parental consent). I'm practically an adult. So why can't I smile?

This is a new year of my life, and in this new year, it's time to stop letting others dictate my well-being. For weeks I've been wallowing in self-pity, straying further and further from how I used to imagine myself. For what? A stupid boy? A high school band?

I make the decision, standing shoeless with my shirt half-tucked, that my sweet sixteen gift to myself is to be happy with me. Just me.

At school Annie greets me with a perfectly wrapped present. The edges are crisp, and a little pink bow is tied neatly on top. Annie can wrap a gift like it's her job.

"You didn't have to—" I protest, and she shoos my words away.

"Yes, I did," she says. "Open it."

I carefully unwrap the gift without tearing the paper, so Annie doesn't scold me for ripping up her hard work. Underneath the paper is a small velvet box. I open it to find a delicate silver chain attached to a music note. It's beautiful, not at all gaudy, and perfect for me.

"I know you don't like wearing jewelry," Annie begins, "but I thought it was so you . . ."

"I love it." I blink back tears, embarrassed I'm getting so emotional over a necklace. "Thank you."

Annie helps me fasten the chain around my neck.

"It suits you," she says approvingly.

I try to smile at my reflection in the locker mirror. The music note twinkles against my skin. It does suit me, and it's not surprising that she knew it would.

* * *

At the first hint of spring, there is a mass exodus of Evanston students eating outside today, sunbathing on the lawn, uniform shirts lifting to expose ghostly white skin.

"They say it's your birthday," Strand sings in a high-pitched falsetto when I lower myself onto the grass.

Krina hands me a thin present, also perfectly wrapped. "Annie did it for me," she explains. "I suck at that stuff."

"Aw, Krina!" I tip my head and place a hand over my heart. "You got me a gift?"

"Shut up."

I open her present and it's a framed cartoon drawing of me, with my eyes closed and my headphones on. Watercolor swirls and music notes circle my head.

"Oh my God!" I exclaim. "You drew this? You can draw?"

Krina shrugs, but she's smiling. "It's just a doodle."

"Isn't she talented?" Annie says. "I told her she should go to art school."

Krina tears a blade of grass from the ground. "My parents would disown me."

It means something that even someone as fearless as Krina is scared to go against her parents. The two of us are completely different in so many ways, but we share more than I realized. She gets me in a way that other people don't, and once I sift through her scary exterior and all the rumors that come with it, I start to get her, too.

"You should come out to them first, then the art school thing won't seem so bad in comparison," Strand suggests with a grin.

Annie throws a crouton at him and he tosses it back at her. It's nauseating.

I know I shouldn't expect everyone to get me presents on my birthday. It's spoiled, bratty, and entitled. Still, I'm disappointed not to get anything from Strand. Did he think Annie would get jealous? What's more likely, knowing Strand, is that he didn't remember my birthday in the first place.

"So are we watching the Battle this weekend?" Krina asks me.

I'm surprised to hear anyone mention the Battle now that Debaser is no more. I thought that, together, we would all pretend the Battle of the Boroughs didn't exist. All three of them turn to look at me, like the decision rests in my hands.

"Still grounded," I say. Right now I'm thankful to be grounded, because I'm not sure I could stomach a whole night of what might have been.

I also don't want to face an outing with Strand and Annie. Eating lunch with them is hard enough on me. I keep imagining what they're doing in private, and as much as I try to be happy for them, I'm only human. It sucks even when it's in my imagination.

"We have to go," Annie decides. As usual, what I say is of no importance to what she wants to do. "Your parents will definitely let you for one night. It's your *birthday*, Vi."

"Yeah, Cutlet." Strand is already taking her side of things. "It'll be fun."

It's interesting, this newfangled definition of fun, because it seems a lot like torture.

* * *

As the day goes on, I hide my birthday-girl status. It's not something I like to draw attention to. There's usually singing involved, or a teacher asking me in front of the entire class what my plans are, or something similarly embarrassing.

When I get to my locker near the end of the day, though, I'm struck by a confusing sense of disappointment. My birthday is practically over. I thought sixteen would be a bigger deal, but it's really any other day in my boring existence. Is this going to be my life from now on? A continuous string of disappointing events?

I shut my locker door after I pack up, and Strand is standing there. Like he was magically conjured by my mind. Happy birthday to me.

"You need to stop doing that," I tell him, zipping up my backpack. "Popping up out of nowhere. . . . It's creepy."

He taps the tip of my nose with his finger. "You should be more observant."

God. He is both unbearably beautiful and consistently annoying. It's a confusing combination.

He leans against my locker. "Wanna get out of here?"

"Out of here? Like, out of school?" I can't entirely tell if he's kidding.

"Out of school, yes. What do you have next period?"

"Study hall." With Annie, but I don't mention her name to Strand.

"They don't take attendance, you know."

I look furtively from side to side, like Principal Tishman has spies stationed around the building. "But . . . how do we . . . ?"

"Come on." Strand grabs my hand before I can finish. He leads me out of the hallway, down the stairs, and out of the building. So simple. No overthinking, no second-guessing. Strand just *does*.

The burst of sunlight is jarring when we step out the door. My eyes are still in cloudy winter mode. I've never skipped a day of school in my life, but if there's any day that demands skipping, it's this one. It's too beautiful to be trapped inside a classroom.

"Strand, wait!" I whisper as we near the front gates. I yank my hand out of his grasp. "What about the security guard?"

"You mean Rip Van Winkle over there?"

Sure enough, the security guard, enclosed in a glass booth behind the gate, is slumped over in his chair. His chest rises in slow, sleepy breaths.

"Point taken," I say. "So we . . . we just leave?"

"Yup."

"We walk right out, huh?"

"Correct."

My legs freeze in place. I picture the security guard jolting awake as soon as we enter his line of vision. I imagine heavy handcuffs slapped onto my wrists. Phone calls to Mom and Dad. Suspension. Or worse, expulsion. Good-bye, Harvard.

"Cutlet." Strand's face appears in front of me. "Don't do that. Follow me."

So I do.

We walk with purpose as we exit the school. Surprisingly, no one gives a second look to two teenagers in uniform wandering outside in the middle of a school day.

"Oh my God, oh my God, oh my God," I say when we're a safe distance away from Evanston. "I'm skipping school. I, Victoria Cruz, am skipping school."

"Congratulations, Cruz. You are officially a badass."

It feels good to be a badass for a day. Unfortunately, my anxiety levels are too high to ever do this again.

"Where are we going?" I ask, keeping rhythm with Strand's long strides.

"Central Park?" he suggests.

Central Park is only a couple blocks away from Evanston, yet despite its close proximity, I rarely go. I'm always rushing to get home from school. I've never actually been inside the park, only around the periphery.

When I say this to Strand, a determined look crosses his face. "How is that possible? You're a New Yorker!"

"Yes, but I live above Harlem. We have our own parks."

"Still unacceptable. Sorry."

He takes me to Strawberry Fields first. We stand over the John Lennon memorial, a black-and-white mosaic with the word IMAGINE at its center. We're quiet for a moment. I look around at the tall elm trees surrounding us, at the fork in the path when you pass the memorial. I remember that John Lennon quote: "Life is what happens while you're busy making other plans." I'm suddenly very, very glad I skipped school to come here with Strand. Maybe he's reading my mind again, because he catches my eye and we both smile.

"Not my favorite John Lennon song," I say when we continue walking.

"Mine either. I mean, hello? 'Instant Karma'?"

"Or 'Mind Games.'"

"'Jealous Guy.'"

"I miss him. Isn't that weird? To miss someone you've always known as dead?"

"No. I think it's worse, in a way, to always know them as dead. We never got to live in the same world as they did. All we know is their legacy."

Strand drops his gaze, and I wonder if he's thinking about his mom. I try to steer the conversation back to a safer topic. "'Imagine' is still a good song, though. It's not his fault it's overplayed."

I stop talking when I see the Bow Bridge in front of us, a series of interlocking circles stretching over Central Park's lake. I've never seen the bridge before, outside of movies. It's iconic New York. Strand's right. It's unacceptable that I've never done this.

"Let's go!" I say to him. Struck by a sudden burst of energy, I run up the bridge's wooden planks. I reach the center and he's a few feet behind me.

"Jesus, you're fast," he says when he catches up. I don't point out the fact that it's been almost six months since I quit cross-country. I consider myself out of shape at this point.

"Look," I say. I point down at the lake below. "Isn't it beautiful?" The water is a shimmery reflection of trees and buildings. I wish I could hold on to this moment so I could revisit it over and over. The smell of fresh grass, the warmth of the sun, the way the entire city surrounds us.

"You're so excited right now," Strand says, looking thoroughly amused.

"I totally am." We're standing next to each other, arm against arm. Only the two of us. Away from Evanston, from the band, from my family. I feel the familiar electric tension crackling between us. I can't have electric tension with my best friend's new boyfriend, but he's like a lightning rod.

"I got you something," he says, and my heart flip-flops in my chest. I try not to betray my emotions through my face.

Strand remembered my birthday.

"Is it a pair of tights?" I joke.

"Do I look like Captain Hair Gel to you?" He reaches into his back pocket and pulls out a palm-sized box tied with a silk ribbon. He hesitates for a second before handing it to me.

I bite my lower lip to keep from smiling. "You bought a box *and* a ribbon? How crafty of you."

"Yeah, yeah. Open it."

I untie the ribbon and slide the lid off the box. I don't know what I expect to find, but I'm surprised to see a small flash drive sitting inside. Written on the label in Strand's chicken-scratch handwriting are the words KNOWING VICTORIA.

"It's a playlist for your collection," Strand explains. He rubs his hands together, then sticks them in his pockets. "I know it's cheesy."

"It's not," I say, swallowing a lump forming in my throat.

"I've worked on it for a while. It's made up of songs that remind me of you. Some from the band, some random ones. It's a little long . . ." He looks out across the lake. "Turns out a lot of songs remind me of you."

I close the box and put it in my blazer pocket. I don't have the words right now. This is everything, this gift, and as much as I wish it didn't change my world, it kind of does. I can't pretend otherwise.

"You hate it," Strand says. "Don't spare my feelings."

"Will you shut up already?" I reach out to give him a playful push and he grabs my wrist to stop me. Still clinging to my wrist, he looks at me in a way that I can't fully interpret. A way that he shouldn't be looking at me.

He's not letting go, either. Not that I'm putting up much of a fight.

There are a million reasons why I should pull away. Among them is the very big reason that is Annie. My best friend. When I look at him, though, all these reasons fade away, and, in one moment, I do something I never thought I was capable of doing: I go after what I want.

I kiss Strand, yanking on his collar to pull him toward me. Right in the middle of the park, surrounded by New York City.

For a good five seconds, I don't care about my list of reasons. I'm like a hungry child who finally got into the cookie jar. I want to devour those cookies, every crumb. Strand's lips are even softer than I thought they would be, fuller and stronger than Levi's. We kiss against the bridge, and I tug on his hair, pressing my body against his. I feel the kiss all the way in my stomach. Kissing Levi was never, ever like this.

Then my brain catches up with my mouth.

"Oh my God," I say, pulling away from him. I reach my fingers to my lips, still tingling from contact.

His expression reflects my shock. I mean, I'm Victoria Cruz. I don't throw myself at pretty guys with inviting lips and thoughtful playlists and histories of breaking hearts. When Strand doesn't say anything, I fully realize what a huge mistake I've made.

"Pretend it never happened, okay?" I say before he can speak. "Promise me."

His voice finally begins to work. "Victoria . . ."

"Promise me," I repeat sharply. "Unless you want to ruin everything."

Strand inhales and presses his lips together. The lips that were just on mine a second ago. "That's what you want?"

"Yes."

"Really."

What does he want me to say? That I'm another helpless groupie, falling for someone I can't have?

"That's what I want," I say, examining my shoelaces. One look at his face and I'll pass out. Or attack him again, since apparently I have lost full control of my faculties.

I can feel him deflate next to me as he says, "Then I promise."

With that promise, I break into a run, leaving a confused Strand in my wake. The gift box thwacks against my hip with every step, a continuous reminder of my humiliation. My only solace is that the kiss happened here in Central Park, away from any witnesses that would report anything to Annie.

As I race home I think about a lot of things: how horrible I feel, what led to my moment of weakness, how many people might have seen what happened. But the one shameful thought that overpowers all others is the one thing I know for sure: Strand kissed me back.

Chapter Fifty-Two

"SATELLITES"
—MEW

I refuse to listen to the playlist. I shut the flash drive away in my underwear drawer and take three steps back. There must be some hidden voodoo magic in that playlist. That's the only possible reason for why I would ruin a friendship over a boy.

I need to tell Annie.

This isn't something I'm looking forward to, but it's something I have to do. For one, I can't keep a secret this big. How can I sit across from Strand every day at lunch, chewing innocently on my pizza like nothing ever happened? That would be an Oscar-worthy feat, to pretend a kiss like that meant nothing to me.

I'm a terrible friend. Scratch that, a terrible human being. The worst part is not that I kissed Strand. Kissing Strand is a mistake I can rub away. The worst part is that I liked it. That it will probably be the best kiss of my life, and I can never have it again. It must be the whole forbidden love aspect. There's no way kissing Strand under normal conditions could feel that good.

How do girls function in everyday life after kissing him? How do they brush their teeth and tie their shoes without becoming overwhelmed by the memory of those lips?

I get the groupies now. I am deeply, spiritually connected to them. Even though I still find most of them intolerable.

And there's still the fact that Strand kissed me back. There was passion behind it. It wasn't like Levi and his textbook precision. The way Strand kissed me, I could almost swear it meant something to him, too. And if it did mean something to him, shouldn't Annie know that?

I can't believe how stupid I'm being. It was one kiss. That's all. I kiss Strand once and turn into a mindless idiot. Meanwhile, Annie experiences touching his hair, holding his hand, kissing him every day. This is the difference between Annie and me. She realizes what she wants, and she gets it. I shrink from what I want, and by the time I decide to take my chance, it's too late.

The more I think about it, the more I realize Strand has a lot of nerve, kissing me back. Yes, okay, I made the first move. I'm not saying that was the right thing to do. But he could have pulled away. I'm not even supposed to know that he and Annie are a thing! Technically, *no one* has told me. As far as the world knows, I'm an innocent in this situation.

I stomp over to my dresser, grab the flash drive, and plug it into my computer. I'll listen to the first song, but that's it. One song won't hurt. My laptop rumbles to life as the playlist loads, a burst of music that gives me a temporary escape from today's events.

Except I don't stop after one song. I physically can't.

I listen to each and every song on that playlist. I listen with my legs against the wall and my head propped against a throw pillow. I listen sprawled on my rug like a snow angel. I listen until the last song fades and all I hear is the silent whirring of my computer. Then I click on the first song and start from the beginning.

I lose all concept of time. Each song rolls through my ears and I imagine kissing Strand again and again as the music plays. Because something about these songs makes me believe that Strand sees me, really sees me.

The next day at school, I know I have to tell Annie. As much as I want to blame this all on him, and as much as he does deserve some of the blame, it doesn't change the fact that I did something wrong. Annie is *my* best friend, not his. My mistake is the larger betrayal. I have undeniable feelings for Strand, but I need to will them away.

It's just that there's never really a good time to tell her. What am I supposed to say, anyway? The truth? *Sorry, but I knew who your mystery crush was all along and I happen to be in love with him. I also attacked him with my lips yesterday. Then I fell asleep listening to the playlist he gave me and dreamed that he did unspeakable things to me.*

I freeze up during math class and instead of talking to her,

I pretend to make careful corrections to my homework. When the bell rings, I sprint to my locker and get to my next class five minutes early to avoid any chitchat. By the time lunchtime rolls around, an all-consuming guilt eats away at my stomach. I've spent so much time thinking about telling Annie that I forgot I'd have to face Strand, too.

My lunch tray wobbles in my hands when I step outside. I can spot Krina and Annie in the distance, already sitting at a bench. There's no sign of Strand yet. I mentally command my legs to move, one step at a time, and grip the lunch tray to force my hands still.

When I take a seat, Annie and Krina are in the middle of a conversation about the Battle of the Boroughs tomorrow. In all my postkiss hysteria, the band's lost moment of glory slipped my mind.

Instead of listening to them, I stare at the cafeteria doors, expecting everyone who comes out of them to be Strand.

After a few minutes of is he or isn't he, I force myself to ask, as casually as possible, "Where's Strand today?"

"Haven't seen him," says Krina. "I think he's out sick."

First there is relief, because I can postpone the awkwardness for at least one more day. And then there's an irritating sense of disappointment, because even though I'm too chicken to face Strand, it's still one less day I get to see him. Is he physically sick, or emotionally ill from kissing me? Is he going to avoid me now that I hit on him? The thought of losing him, even as a friend, is too much.

In Strand's absence, it's the perfect time to tell Annie about the kiss, but I decide to postpone the revelation. Tomorrow. Tomorrow is my new deadline. That means I get one more day to keep her as my friend.

"You'll meet us there, right, Vi?" Annie asks me.

"What?" I bend over my pizza, staring at the grease pooling on its surface.

"You'll meet us at the Battle?"

I'm not sure what makes me feel sicker: thinking about seeing Strand again, or thinking about watching other bands take the stage at the Battle.

"I doubt it," I mumble.

"What do you mean you doubt it? You're coming with us, and I don't want to hear another word about it."

"I'm grounded for the rest of eternity, Annie. In case you forgot."

"I already asked your parents' permission."

I freeze, holding my slice of pizza halfway to my mouth. "You *what*?"

"I convinced them to let you out for your birthday."

"How did . . . what? You what?"

Krina pats Annie on the leg. "Never underestimate this woman's powers of persuasion."

Annie grins at me, obviously expecting me to be thrilled about the news. Without the excuse of my parents, I have no real reason to miss going to the Battle.

"So? We're going?" Annie's voice cuts into my thoughts.

"She's going," Krina says for me.

Going to the Battle is this last thing I want to do. I want to say no to them. I should be able to, but my mouth hangs open, unable to form the word. I don't know if it's Annie's innocent smile, my overwhelming guilt, or Krina's decisive tone, but I respond instead with, "Fine. We can go."

Even though it sounds like pure hell.

Chapter Fifty-Three

"BALLAD OF BIG NOTHING"
—ELLIOTT SMITH

That night I decide to call Levi. Well, "decide" is the wrong word. It doesn't feel like a conscious choice. It feels like my body is doing everything on its own—reaching into my pocket to pull out my cell phone, pulling me into my bedroom and shutting the door, dialing the number that I deleted but still have memorized.

It's only when the phone is ringing that I realize I have no idea what I'm going to say to him. I haven't thought the plan out that far in advance. I almost hang up. In the silence before Levi picks up, I'm morbidly curious about how I'm going to handle this.

Moments later I hear a click and it's Levi, crackling through the phone speaker. "Victoria?"

My stomach slams into my throat. I wasn't expecting to react so physically to the sound of his voice.

"Victoria?" he repeats.

I hold the phone away from me, get myself together, then bring it back to my ear. "I'm here. Hi."

"Hi. . . . How are you?"

"I'm great," I lie. "Really great. You?"

"I'm doing okay," he says. The question of why I'm calling lingers in the air.

"How's your new girlfriend?" I blurt out. Apparently, I'm over playing it cool. Well, why should I? I played it cool throughout our entire relationship, and in the end it got me stepped on.

"Oh . . . ," Levi starts. "She's not . . . we're just . . ."

If I weren't so hurt right now, I would enjoy making Levi stumble over his words like this.

"Don't bother explaining," I say. "It's not why I called."

I pray he doesn't ask me why I did, because I have no answer for him. Instead, there's silence, always that silence between us that I tried to ignore.

"I need to know something," I say, finally being the one to break it.

"Okay," he says.

"Did you cheat on me during that band trip? Did you break up with me for her?"

"It wasn't like that, Victoria, I swear. Beth and I have been friends for a long time."

Beth. She has a name.

"It hurt, Levi. We'd been broken up for a week."

"We're not official or anything," he counters.

"You look pretty official to me."

"I mean . . ." I can hear his hesitation over the phone. "I did develop feelings for her, but . . ."

Ouch. It hurts more than I expect. I want to ask if he developed feelings for her while we were still together, but I'm not sure I can stomach the answer.

Instead I ask, a little pathetically, "Did I mean anything to you?"

"Of course you meant something to me. It just . . . it wasn't working."

"Because I'm not like *Beth*?" I say her name like it's acid on my tongue.

"Beth had nothing to do with it."

"I highly doubt that."

"Victoria . . ." I hear him take a breath. "Do you think I liked being your security blanket?"

My body turns cold. "What are you talking about?"

"You can act like our breakup came out of nowhere, but the truth is we were over before we started."

"That might be true for you, but . . ." I trail off, Krina's words echoing in my head. *You both played a part. Even if you won't admit it.*

"I pulled the plug," says Levi, "but you hurt me, too. Do you know how much I liked you?"

I hurt *him*?

"I'm sorry," I reply, dumbfounded. "I didn't know . . . I don't know why we didn't work." I lean my head back and stare at the chipped paint on my ceiling, listening to Levi sigh into the phone.

"Probably because you never looked at me the way you look at Strand," he says finally.

I grip the phone so tightly my knuckles turn white. Levi knows. He knew before I did.

I could deny it right now. Pretend that he's imagining things. But I'm tired of pretending. This is the most honest conversation I've had in a long time.

"I didn't want to like Strand," I say. There's a certain relief in admitting it out loud. "I *don't* want to. It just happened."

"Well . . . there's nothing holding you back now."

There is, I want to say. You. Debaser. Me.

Annie.

"You haven't said anything to him, have you?" I ask.

"Of course not. He hasn't spoken to me since we broke up."

It hits me then that I'm not the only one suffering from our breakup. Levi may have been the dumper, but at least he was honest enough to end things. It takes bravery to admit it when something comfortable isn't working. I certainly wasn't brave enough to do it. As a result, he lost his best friend and his band.

"I'm sorry," I say again, and I mean it. We both messed things up. "I was a crappy girlfriend."

"Well, I got you tights for Valentine's Day, so I'm not winning any awards myself."

I start giggling, a little bit at first. Then I picture myself opening the bag on Valentine's Day, full of hope before pulling out those tights. I double over, laughing so hard that my sides ache. Levi laughs too, making his coughing sound, which, surprisingly, I've missed.

"I actually thought you would like them," he says.

"Levi, they were terrible!"

"It could have been worse."

"I guess. You could have bought me a vacuum cleaner or some shoe polish or something."

"See?"

"And the truth is," I say, pulling open my drawer to inspect the tights I hid in the corner, "I really did need a new pair."

The laughter trickles off, and the ensuing silence doesn't bother me when I realize I'm not responsible for filling it. For the first time in a long time, I'm feeling something close to fine.

"It's weird, right?" Levi says. "That Battle of the Boroughs is tomorrow night and we're not playing?"

"Yeah. It's weird . . . it's sad."

"Have you given any thought to maybe . . . getting the band together again? We could have a shot next year."

If I were still his girlfriend, I might feel annoyed that, as usual, his number-one priority is the band.

I'm not his girlfriend, though. I'm just me. Victoria. It's kind of a beautiful thing to not have to care anymore.

"We'll see what happens," I say.

Chapter Fifty-Four

"DO YOU REALIZE??"
—THE FLAMING LIPS

Cafe Wha?, the club where Battle of the Boroughs is held, is smoke-filled and packed with what looks like the entire population of New York City. It's a legendary venue, once graced by the likes of Bob Dylan, Jimmy Hendrix, and Bruce Springsteen. As soon as I set foot inside, I regret my decision to go. I'm not worthy of this place. I tried to tell Annie it would make me feel worse about the demise of Debaser, but as usual, she wouldn't listen to me. Annie knows best and all.

Even through the wall of bodies blocking the club's entrance, I spot Levi right away. I don't know why I'm surprised to see him here. He's been talking about the Battle since the day we met. Just because we're not performing doesn't mean he would miss it.

His arm is slung around Beth's shoulder and she's looking up at him adoringly. He catches my eye before I can pretend not to have seen him and offers me a wave with the hand that isn't around Beth.

I'm not fully on board the Levi train just yet, but I've stopped harboring a desire to see him killed or horribly maimed, which is an improvement. He was my first kiss, my first date, my first boyfriend, and, for better or worse, none of that can be erased.

I wave back because I think we're supposed to be friendly again, or at least at the point where we acknowledge each other's existence in public.

Past the crowd and right in front of the stage are Annie and Krina. Krina's Mohawk is spiked extra high tonight.

"Levi's here," I tell them in greeting after I squeeze through the crowd.

Annie wrinkles her nose. "Ick. Really? Is he with that tart of his?"

"Tart?" Krina echoes. "Are you sixty years old?"

"'Tart' is a perfectly fitting word to describe her."

Krina rolls her eyes, but she's smiling. "Tarty or not, I think Victoria is being cool about the situation."

I smile wanly. I'm undeserving of such high praise. Krina won't think I'm so cool when she finds out that I kissed Strand. I'm the real tart here. Will I lose Krina's friendship too? Is it possible that one kiss can sever all my ties at Evanston?

"I don't know if I can stay," I say to them. I glance at the exit door, which looks especially warm and inviting right now.

"Come on, Vi, it'll be fun." Annie looks at me with wide, pleading eyes.

"It's depressing. I have to see my ex with his new girlfriend, and then I have to sit through a competition we were supposed to be a part of."

And worst of all, I add silently to myself, *watch you be with the boy I might love.*

The idea of performing here, in an actual venue, never seemed real until now. The lights, the crowd, the high stage . . . this is the venue I've always imagined.

And I blew it. In typical Victoria fashion.

"Let's just stay for a little bit," Annie insists. "If you want to leave after a few songs, we'll leave."

A tap on the microphone interrupts the conversation. Annie pulls me beside her, her fingernails digging into my arm to hold me in place. A long-haired man with tattoos poking out of his shirtsleeves is onstage welcoming us to the sixth annual Battle of the Boroughs. He launches into the history of the show and what the tradition means to the city before listing some of the famous musical acts that the competition has launched.

As he drones on, I think about how nothing worked out the way it was meant to. Our band was supposed to take the stage as one unit tonight, not watch from the audience, scattered in pieces.

The other thought, the one that constantly pokes through even when I try to bury it, is Strand. Where is he? Is he coming tonight? Does he regret the kiss? Does he hate me for leaving the band in the lurch? Did something happen between him and Annie?

Why can't I stop thinking?

The first act is a guy named Dragos wearing a long trench coat even though it's ninety degrees inside the club. One side of his head is shaved, and the other side is a grown-out mane of dyed-black hair. He steps behind a DJ booth and begins to play a variety of squeaky vocal samples and syncopated rhythms. It's . . . not good. The crowd is welcoming though, and they cheer him on. Throughout the piece, Dragos closes his eyes and bounces up and down like a man possessed.

Annie dances around, still clutching my arm. Krina watches Dragos onstage with a bored expression.

I clap politely when the noise ends and can't help but think, *Debaser could have done better.*

A group of middle-aged men take the stage next, all with the same long greasy hair and bushy beards.

"First a Skrillex wannabe, now aging hippies?" Krina groans as the band begins to play. "This lineup sucks."

Not just any aging hippies, I realize as the spotlight washes over the lead singer, who is significantly younger than his bandmates. He radiates calm and croons with a clear, pitch-perfect voice.

"Oh my God, is that—" Krina begins.

"Yes," I finish, staring in disbelief. "It's Greg."

Annie stands on her tiptoes to get a better view. "Who's Greg?"

"He tried out for the band before Vi," Krina says.

I stay quiet, listening. Seeing Greg up there is another twist of the knife. I wonder if I've accidentally fallen into an alternate universe, one where everyone is getting what I was too scared to take for myself. Annie, who has Strand. Greg, who has my spot in Battle of the Boroughs. And here I am, a sad spectator to the life that could have been mine.

"Vi, they're playing Creedence!" Annie cries over the soft acoustic chords. "Remember?"

I try to smile. Years ago, my dad bought a Creedence Clearwater Revival greatest hits album that would become the soundtrack to our summer weekends at the Jersey Shore. Listening to Greg, I remember Dad, straining his voice to hit John Fogerty's notes; iced lemonade and the smell of fried dough emanating from the board-walk; Annie and I kicking up sand as we turned cartwheels on the beach. Matty had a terrible crush on Annie back then. He built her elaborate sand castles and Annie humored him, telling him they could live there as king and queen of New Jersey.

Annie throws her arm around my shoulder and belts the song's chorus. Her hair, worn loose again tonight, tickles my cheek, and my guilt turns unbearable. If I hold it in any longer, I'll self-detonate.

"Annie?" I interrupt. "I have to tell you something . . ."

"Yeah?" She stops singing, but her eyes are glued to the stage.

"It's kind of serious."

That gets her attention. She turns away from the stage to face me. "Oh God. Okay. Tell me."

"I did something . . . bad."

"Bad?" She blinks. "Like cheating on a test bad?"

"It has nothing to do with school. It's . . . worse. A lot worse."

The sound of applause surrounds us as Greg and his band end the song and exit the stage. The crowd around us cheers. This is it. A true test of our friendship. I'm determined to do whatever it takes to fix things. Even if it means cutting Strand out of my life for good. I'm going to tell Annie that I will always choose her.

"Tell me," Annie urges over the thundering noise. "Whatever it is, I can help you fix it."

"Don't." I hang my head. "Don't be nice to me. Not when I'm about to tell you this."

"Tell me what? You're making me nervous . . ."

"On my birthday . . . after school . . ." I take a gulp of air and concentrate on forming the words, ignoring Annie's pitiful, puppy-dog stare. "I kissed him."

"Huh?"

"I kissed him," I say loudly as the applause fades. "I kissed Strand."

It's the strangest thing, because immediately after I say his name, the bald man is calling it out onstage. For a second I think there's an echo in the club, but then I see Strand up there, sitting on a stool, armed with his acoustic guitar and his trademark Pixies shirt.

My entire world comes to a screeching halt. Strand is on the stage. Alone. Without us.

"You kissed him?" Annie asks, and I brace myself for the aftershock.

But something isn't right.

Annie's face. She should be livid, but she's smiling. A toothy, genuine smile.

"I'm impressed!" she says.

Impressed? No. She's supposed to be pissed.

"Why is Strand onstage?" I ask, jarred out of my confession.

He leans into the microphone, and I forget to wonder why Annie's smiling the way she is when she should be flying into a jealous rage.

"I wrote this song for a girl," he says, and the sound of his voice amplified by the mic makes me shiver. The girls in the audience are already losing it, whistling and clapping, and the lights cast a glow around Strand so he looks like a living, breathing angel. "Her name is Victoria."

Strand starts to play his song, and I forget everything I planned to say.

What. Is going. On.

I look at Annie, and her face is marinara red.

"Surprise!" she sings out. I'm too stunned to respond.

With the new guitar accompaniment, his song has taken form. It's real now. Strand's voice is deep and rich and almost flawless, but I hear the way it shakes when he sustains a note. I know him well enough now to realize that, behind his air of confidence, he's nervous. He ends the first verse, breathing heavily into the mic.

Strand's eyes have found us in the crowd and I'm momentarily mute.

"This is all for me?" I ask Annie, not able to look away from him. "You're not mad I kissed him?"

"Mad?" she repeats. "Why would I be mad?"

"Because I thought . . . you guys had that date at Artie's . . ." I trail off.

"You saw us at Artie's?"

"I kinda followed you . . ."

"God, Vi." She nudges her shoulder against mine. "I was helping him with *this*. The music arrangement. Besides, why would I date Strand? It was so obvious you two were into each other."

"No it wasn't . . . ," I start to say, but Annie isn't having it.

"We could all tell," Krina chimes in, leaning across Annie. "I can attest to that."

"And we were getting tired of the Ross-and-Rachel-ness of it all," Annie says.

I have the urge to deny it again, but I realize that I don't have to. I don't have to deny it to Annie or to myself, because I am unanchored. Nothing is holding me back from what I want now.

There is a beautiful boy onstage, playing a song for me, and it's not happening in my daydreams, it's happening in real life. In between the chorus and the second verse, still strumming, Strand presses his face closer to the mic and says, "Everyone please welcome to the stage, Miss Victoria Cruz."

All around me, heads pivot. Murmurs ripple through the crowd as they wonder who could possibly be good enough to merit this introduction. Onstage, Strand is still strumming, still waiting.

"Go get some!" Krina yells. Annie shakes me so hard my teeth chatter.

I could leave. Clam up. Bolt out of here. Spend the night in my room, hidden under the covers. Instead, I zero in on Strand, who's looking at me like I'm the only person in this giant, sweaty room. He's opening up to me by doing something that scares him. I owe it to him, to myself, to do the same. I push my way onto the stage.

It's not my most graceful of moves. I have to throw my leg over the top like I'm mounting a horse and hoist myself onto my knees. I don't care. A smirk-free smile spreads over Strand's face when I stand next to him.

The scariness of this moment fails to register, because everything is happening so quickly. I sing without thinking. Strand is singing it with me, and we're sharing the mic with our faces almost touching. It's not just his song anymore; it belongs to us, to everyone listening.

I look out into the crowd, made up mostly of strangers, but in this moment we're all connected. They're a part of this experience. From the perspective of the stage, I dimly register everything going on around me. I notice some grungy college kids in the middle of the crowd bobbing their heads to the music. I see a teary-eyed girl in the front row smiling up at us. I see Levi quietly exiting the club while Beth hurries after him. I see Annie and Krina kissing.

It doesn't register all at once, only in pieces. Annie and Krina are kissing. Annie and Krina. Together.

My voice carries on as I process what this means. Why Annie was so reluctant to reveal her mystery crush to me. All the time she and Krina spend together, all the inside jokes between them that I didn't quite understand. All along I had spun a story in my head to distance myself from Strand, to invent new barriers between us, instead of seeing the truth. I've been blind this whole time. Missing everything in front of me.

Then there's me. No lipstick, no hairspray, no chicken cutlets. Just me.

Strand has given me the spotlight and I'm soaking it in, letting it fill me until it practically reflects out of my pores. He's not singing anymore, he's pulling away, slinking into the background of the song like he's taken off my training wheels. I feel like I'm soaring, like I'm on the craziest of drugs. I'm putting myself back together again, Humpty Dumpty–style, after being broken these last few weeks. I never want the song to end, but inevitably it does, all too soon.

It's only when I sing the last note that I see my parents, Jorge and Gloria Cruz, standing awkwardly in the back of the room.

Dad came straight from work, still wearing his company polo. Mom is wearing a faux leather coat that I know she carefully chose to match the venue. We lock eyes, and they're clapping hard, both of them crying. For once in my life, I made them cry in a good way. I think.

I swear, as the stage dims and the curtains close, that there is an expression close to pride on each of their faces. I begin to wonder whether anything that took place tonight is real or if I'll be yanked back into normal life by my alarm.

Strand and I are ushered to the side of the stage, where it's dark and hidden away from the crowd chanting for an encore.

I look at him, and he looks back at me. Without the music, I suddenly turn shy.

"Hey," he says. He takes me by the hands and links his fingers through mine.

"Hey." I press my palms into his. I don't care that mine are sweaty, because his are sweaty too. My stomach is full of butterflies on hyperdrive. There's no soft fluttering of wings—they're pinging around in every direction.

He looks at me, the playful smirk returning. "If I kiss you now, do we have to pretend it never happened?"

"No." I crack a smile.

"Are you going to run away?"

"Not likely."

"Are you going to laugh? You have a tendency to do that sometimes."

"Only if it's funny."

He smoothes my hair off my forehead and his hand trails down to my cheek. Then he leans into me so we're nose to nose and I get a close-up view of his midwinter-sky eyes.

"I'm glad you're not secretly dating Annie," I whisper.

"What?" He pauses, his lips close.

"Never mind," I say, not wanting to waste any more time. "Go ahead."

When he kisses me, it's tender and passionate in all the right ways, and nothing about it is funny.

Chapter Fifty-Five

"SEA CALLS ME HOME"
—JULIA HOLTER

Strand and I didn't win the Battle of the Boroughs. Greg did. But three weeks later Strand and I are making out in my room, and it feels almost as good as winning the Battle of the Boroughs.

Matty barges in every ten seconds because he possibly has a bigger crush on Strand than I do.

"Are you guys kissing?" he asks accusingly as we jump apart.

"Yes," says Strand.

"No," I correct him. "We're doing homework. Very important homework."

Matty glares at us. "Strand, you said you were going to teach me a new chord today."

"Tell you what, buddy." Strand sits up, face flushed, hair more disheveled than normal. "Go to your room and count to two hundred. When you're finished, I'll teach you the chord."

"Swear?"

"Swear."

Matty gives a drawn-out sigh and leaves my room, mumbling, "One Mississippi, two Mississippi . . ." on his way out.

I wait for Matty's voice to disappear before launching myself at Strand to resume our session.

"Strand!" Mom calls from the kitchen. Exasperated, I flop down beside him.

"Yes?" Strand calls back.

"Do you want to stay for dinner tonight?"

"Sure. . . . Thanks, Gloria!"

"You're going to get sick of my family," I warn him. This is the third night in a row he's stayed for dinner.

"Or you'll get sick of me," he says, fingering a lock of my hair. I'm wearing it down today, even though it's the size of a small country.

"Not gonna happen."

"Good. Because I'm pretty happy with you."

"Um, pretty happy?" I lay my head against his shoulder. "You should be ecstatic. . . . I'm kind of awesome."

"No arguments here. I wanted to ask you out when I first saw you."

"Liar. I couldn't even speak."

"I can have that effect on a woman."

I pinch his arm and he jerks away, laughing. "Don't be an ass!"

"Sorry," he says, but his eyes glint. "And then when you auditioned in person, and you were so adorably nervous."

"An adorable train wreck, you mean."

"I think the final nail in the coffin for me was when you pulled out your chicken cutlets."

"And you realized I had no boobs?"

"Your boobs are perfect."

"They're small."

"Stop it. You're doing it again."

I feign a syrupy smile. "I mean . . . thank you for the compliment, Strand."

"I meant it."

"Well, I'm happy you like them."

"I love them. I love *you*."

Record scratch.

At first I wonder if he really said it or if I misheard it. It's so soon. I dated Levi for months and it never came close to love. And this is Strand. Strand doesn't fall in love. But when I raise my head to look at him, he has his serious face on.

"I have for a while," he says in my ear.

The beautiful thing about being with Strand is that I never have to wonder what he's thinking or feeling, because he tells me. No games, no overanalysis necessary on my part.

"I love you, too," I say, and he pulls me in for a soft kiss, one that warms my entire body. Strand is absurdly good at this whole kissing thing. Like, he's a better kisser than Annie is a violinist.

"So . . ." The familiar smirk returns to his face and he nods toward my breasts. "Do I get to touch them now?"

I elbow him hard in the ribs. "Pervert."

"Cashew milk," Strand advises my dad at dinner. "It's the best for ice cream."

"Cashew milk," Dad repeats to himself. He takes a slow sip of soda, ruminating on this nugget of wisdom.

"There's a place in the East Village that makes awesome cashew ice cream. You should go, Jorge."

"We can take a family trip," Mom suggests. "That'd be fun. Right, Ria?"

I nod, trying not to laugh at the ridiculous picture of my family strolling among the pierced, tattooed students in the East Village. "Sure."

"How did you find this ice cream place?" Dad asks him.

"My sister's in the neighborhood," Strand replies. "She goes to NYU."

"Good for her," Mom says, smiling.

"Yeah. She loves it. She even invited Victoria to come visit and check out the school."

Strand clearly doesn't get the bomb he just dropped. My parents freeze for a fraction of a second. All of time stands still, except for me, chewing on a spaghetti noodle and staring with interest at the tomato sauce staining my napkin.

Mom gains her composure back first. "I didn't know you were interested in NYU, Victoria."

I try to interpret her tone. It's icy but not completely closed off. An iciness that could maybe, potentially thaw at some point in the distant future.

"I'm not," I say cautiously. "I mean, I don't know much about it. But . . . it doesn't hurt to have options?"

This statement is met with silence. A grim silence that not even Strand tries to puncture. The truth is, NYU is only one of the many schools I'm considering. Annie has been helping me research colleges based on their music programs. So far, the list is made up of schools that my parents would deem "not good enough."

The idea of college doesn't seem so hellish or foreboding when I think about studying something I actually enjoy. It's scary in an exhilarating way. Just like the way auditioning for the band was scary, and singing in the Battle. I'm slowly learning that the scary things in life might be the things worth chasing.

"I guess it's reasonable to have some safety schools," Mom says. She misses the point entirely. She is a hundred miles away from the point.

"I'm going to Harvard," Matty chimes in with his mouth full. Matty is eating the spaghetti tonight without complaints because Strand complimented it. Strand gives him a thumbs-up, and he beams.

"Don't talk with your mouth full," Dad reminds him.

"Gloria, can you please pass the salt?" Strand asks my mom.

It's only when the conversation moves on that I can breathe normally again. The topic rolls around to music, and how much Matty has learned on the guitar. Mom wants to know how long Strand has been playing, and Dad wants to hear him play Creedence.

"Only if Victoria sings along," Strand says.

He really is doing the most tonight. I'm going to kill him.

"I just don't understand why you never sang for us before," Mom says to me. Ever since the Battle, she's held this over my head.

"You never asked," I try to say, but she talks right over me.

"I mean, I only carried you for nine months, birthed you, raised you . . . and then you sing for everyone else but your own *mother*?"

I make a face at Strand, a *See what you started?* face, and he doesn't look at all apologetic. It figures. Why am I to blame for having a decent voice? And why would I sing for them when they weren't the slightest bit supportive about it?

"You know," Mom muses, "it might not be a complete waste of time."

"What?" I ask.

"Singing. That band you were in. Do people pay you to perform?"

"In theory," Strand says.

"Think about it, Victoria," Mom says. "You can put some of that extra money toward Harvard."

Sometimes, right when I think my family is close to getting it, I realize they are still incredibly hopeless.

Dad is uncharacteristically quiet as Mom yammers on about how competitive scholarships are, and how money from our gigs can help pay for Harvard's room and board. His face is blank, and he's twirling his spaghetti around his fork without actually eating anything. Matty interrupts to ask about dessert.

"Here's the thing." Strand puts his fork down and clears his throat. "I think Victoria has something really special. I've never heard a voice like hers before."

I turn into a puddle of embarrassment and pride. No one has ever complimented my singing to my parents. My strong work ethic? Yes. My ability to run a five-and-a-half-minute mile? Sure. Never my voice. When someone else talks about it, the idea of me singing takes a stronger form. It feels real, like something I can touch.

"She has a beautiful voice, Strand," Mom agrees. "But singing is a hobby, not a career."

I know what Strand's doing. He wants me to bring my family into our world, help them understand, but his charm can only go so far. They will never deviate from the plan. They think the key to life is staying in my lane and working hard, and for me to actually pursue a singing career means swerving out of my lane and off a bridge.

When I walk him to the front door to say good night, I tell him this. I tick off the reasons why my family is a lost cause. He doesn't know them as well as I do, they're stubborn, and they'll never embrace what I want no matter how hard he tries to convince them.

"I think they'll come around," he says, so confidently that I would almost believe him if I didn't have sixteen years of evidence to back myself up.

"No, they won't. They're totally closed-minded."

"And what about you?"

I point to my head and say, "Wide open, babe."

"Open as Fort Knox," he replies, and then he kisses me before I can respond, the type of kiss that makes me forget what I had to say.

Later that night I'm in my room putting on my pajamas and I hear a noise outside my room. I look down and I see that Dad has slid his beloved Creedence CD under the door. There's a Post-it note on it that says, *Can you and Strand learn #17?*

Chapter Fifty-Six

"DEBASER"
—THE PIXIES

I think about Strand's words from the night before the quince. I can control the course of my life, even if it means disappointing my family. The fact that they risked everything to come to this country doesn't make my decision any easier. But I have to think that they came here so I would have the freedom to make choices for myself. To find my own happiness, whatever that might be. Maybe I won't get in to NYU. Maybe I'll get in to Harvard and spend the next four years keeping my family sane. Maybe I'll run away with Strand and enroll in the College of Life. The important thing is that I know something that will make me happy now . . . and I can figure out the rest later.

I slip the note into Levi's locker early Friday morning before he gets to school. There's nothing else to do but wait. I go through my morning classes, and at lunch I tell Strand and Krina to meet me in the music room after school.

"You can come too, Annie," I add.

She shakes her head. "Too much homework."

Krina makes a face at me. She and Annie are a full-fledged couple now, although they're not out to their families and everyone at school. I thought it would be strange to see Annie in any kind of relationship, let alone one with Krina. But together, they work. They work so well that it's strange I *didn't* see it. Krina loosens Annie up, and Annie softens Krina's hard edges. I asked Annie when she realized she had feelings for Krina, and for the first time, Annie didn't know the answer to a question. She smiled and said, "Sometime in between Sleater-Kinney and Bikini Kill."

"Does this mean what I think it means?" Strand asks me.

"Yes."

"And you're ready for this?"

"I am so ready."

Annie claps her hands. "Finally! I get to watch my girlfriend bang on the skins!"

"No one calls it that, you big dork," Krina tells her, lightly tugging on the end of Annie's braid.

"And we don't know if Levi's in," I add.

No one, including me, has talked to Levi since Strand publicly declared his feelings for me at the Battle of the Boroughs. It may have permanently put a damper on their friendship and any possibility of the band getting back together. Why would Levi want to share the stage with an ex-girlfriend who's dating his former best friend?

So Strand, Krina, and I wait together in our old practice room down in the Fridman building. In an optimistic mood, they set up their instruments while I sit off to the side, staring at the door.

It's five minutes after I told Levi to meet us here.

"He's probably running late," Krina reasons.

"Levi doesn't run late," Strand says. He paces back and forth across the room, and I can tell, as cool as he tries to play it, that he's nervous about seeing Levi.

Five more minutes pass, and I'm feeling discouraged.

"We can play without him," Strand suggests, but even he sounds unconvinced.

"We need a bass player," I say. "Levi is a fantastic bass player. And he was your best friend."

"You're my best friend. And we'll find a new bass player."

Krina hunches over her drum set. "We won't find someone as good as he is."

We wait for two more minutes, and I'm about to call it a day, when the door to the music room swings open and Levi is there with his bass guitar strapped to his back.

"Sorry I'm late," he says. "Hi, everyone."

I get to my feet awkwardly. "Levi, hey! We're—we're really glad you came."

I don't know whether I should hug him or shake his hand or what. Levi does none of the above. He takes his bass guitar out of its case and starts to tune it. Down to business, as always.

"You're not wearing your glasses," I notice.

"Oh yeah. . . ." He reaches for his eyes, like he's making sure the glasses are really gone. "I finally got contacts."

"You look good, man," Strand says.

Levi gives him a brisk nod. "Thanks."

They're not exactly fast friends again, but it's a start.

"So, Cutlet, what now?" Strand asks, guitar in hand.

Everyone is looking to me like I'm the one in charge. Even Levi, who is usually the one to declare the set list.

I guess I am. I was the one who called the band together. I jump up to take my place in front of the mic stand and say with more authority than I feel, "We'll pick up where we left off."

Krina counts us off, slapping her drumsticks together, and I feel a rumble of excitement in my belly, the way I always feel before the music starts.

Acknowledgments

Victoria would exist solely in my head if not for the help of so many people.

Endless thanks to Jane Dystel and Miriam Goderich at Dystel, Goderich & Bourret LLC. Jane, thank you for your professional guidance and expertise. More important, thank you for believing in me as a writer. Miriam, many thanks for your kindness, your thoughtful input, and for taking a chance on me.

I am truly grateful to my amazing editor, Jen Ung, for seeing the heart of my story and loving the Cruz family as much as I do. Jen, I cannot imagine a better editor for this book. Thank you for your honest, yet somehow always encouraging feedback, and for having my back throughout this process. To Sarah Creech, thank you for the truly badass cover design. The hand-lettering, the images, the colors . . . I drool over it all at least once a day. Also big thanks to the team at Simon Pulse: Mara Anastas, Mary Marotta, Liesa Abrams, Carolyn Swerdloff, Jodie Hockensmith, Christina Pecorale, Chelsea Morgan, Sara Berko, and anyone else who helped turn this story into an actual book.

I owe the biggest debt of gratitude to my parents, Jacqueline and Carlos Milanes, for their unending support. Mom and Dad, none of this would be possible without the sacrifices you've made for us. Thank you for being dream squashers when it was warranted and dream builders when it mattered. Thank you for humoring me when I wrote plays, books, and stories growing up. Thank you for the trips to Barnes & Noble so I could restock on Judy Blume and Baby-Sitters Club books.

Alyssa, my first reader ever, you gave me the confidence to go through with this writing thing. Thanks for putting up with my neediness and slapping some sense into me during my moments of self-doubt. You're the ultimate beta reader and sister. Thanks also to my brother, Nick, for looking over my writing with a keen editor's eye. Your writing skills constantly impress and inspire me. To my bro-in-law, Alex, thanks for the constant reminder of my Cuban roots. *Dale.*

Mima, my Miami marketing agent, you are an inspiration to me and everyone around you. Your positive outlook on life, in stark contrast to my worst-case-scenario attitude, is boundless. I try to be more like you every day.

I am thankful to my New York family—the Mulhalls and the Sanzos—for their support, enthusiasm, and love. And, of course, all of the delicious food. To the BFG and other close friends, I could not have survived the publishing process without you. Our weekend trips, shows, dinners, and game nights have kept me sane. Thank you all for reminding me to close the laptop and get out of the house once in a while like a functional human being.

Finally, to my husband, Dan. Thank you for loving and supporting me always, especially in my lowest of moments. Only you can handle me when I have tears in my eyes and toilet paper stuffed up my nose. Here's to continued writing sessions at Panera, Starbucks, the Coop, Caffé Bene, and whatever spots we try next. For many, writing is a lonely endeavor, but not so for us. Love you.

About the Author

Janelle Milanes is originally from Miami, Florida, and studied English literature at Davidson College. A lifelong YA addict, she moved to New York for her first job in children's publishing before leaving to pursue teaching and writing. *The Victoria in My Head* is her first novel and reflects many of her own experiences growing up as a second-generation Latina in America.

Janelle lives in Brooklyn with her husband and their two cats. Her favorite Disney princess is Belle, since she was also a big book nerd.